Television's Strangest Moments

Television's Strangest Moments

Extraordinary but true tales from the history of television

**Quentin Falk
& Ben Falk**

ROBSON BOOKS

First published in Great Britain in 2005 by Robson Books, The Chrysalis Building, Bramley Road, London W10 6SP

An imprint of **Chrysalis** Books Group plc

The authors have made every reasonable effort to contact all copyright holders. Any errors that may have occurred are inadvertent and anyone who for any reason has not been contacted is invited to write to the publishers so that a full acknowledgement may be made in subsequent editions of this work.

British Library Cataloguing in Publication Data
A catalogue record for this title is available from the British Library.

ISBN 1 86105 874 8

Typeset by SX Composing DTP, Rayleigh, Essex
Printed by Creative Print & Design, Ebbw Vale, Wales

For Little Marlow Cricket Club

Contents

The 1960s

The 2000s

Television's Strangest Moments

INTRODUCTION

This book was published to mark the eightieth anniversary of that history-changing moment in 1925, when the Scots inventor John Logie Baird gave his first public demonstration of television in Selfridges store. Less than three months later, he repeated the eye-boggling experiment for selected guests, scientists and the odd newspaper reporter. The 'box' was born.

Just as that pioneer cinema audience must have gasped disbelievingly at the earliest moving pictures thirty years earlier, arguably no television moment since has been similarly surpassed for sheer Strangeness than by those first flickering small-screen images during the mid-1920s before even talkies began.

Another ten years would go by before the world's first regular, high-definition television service was launched by the BBC at Alexandra Palace, and it took two more decades until telly became not just affordable but also, thanks to the Coronation in 1953, genuinely popular. That was the year when more TV sets than radio sets were manufactured, each costing around £85, a considerable improvement on the immediate postwar years, when you'd get precious little change out of 115 guineas – the same price as a decent small car.

A couple of years after the Coronation, which had been witnessed live by a TV audience of more than 20 million, the BBC finally lost its monopoly. On 22 September 1955, commercial television took to the air at last, despite the Beeb's opening-night 'dirty trick' when it tried to lessen its new rival's impact by broadcasting on radio the tragic death of a much-loved soap character, Grace Archer.

The advent of competing channels – incidentally, ITV celebrates its golden anniversary in 2005 – instigated the notion of a ratings war. It wasn't, however, so much war as audience fury that greeted one of TV's earliest and strangest, albeit more ambitious, stunts conducted by the magician Chan Canasta. He announced one night on his BBC show that he'd invented a 'tube-destroying machine', and that he was going to click his fingers and the screen would go completely black, beginning with the old diminishing white dot. And it happened. Bemused viewers quickly *got up* and *switched over* – remember, this was years before that 'thingamabob' helped create generations of couch potatoes – and ITV proved to be blank too.

Imagine the onset of nationwide panic. However, less than forty seconds later, the picture on both sides was fully restored but not before switchboards were swamped with angry calls. It transpired that the crafty Canasta had taken out a commercial with a warning that the screens would go blank, at exactly the same time as his BBC stunt, so the darkness coincided with spectacular result.

Now we have no fewer than five terrestrial channels competing for our eyeballs alongside, in the English language alone, hundreds of others in every area of 24-hour 'niche' cable, satellite and digital programming. Some would champion this proliferation as the triumph of 'choice', others dismiss it wearily as 'mass dumbing-down'. In a channel-surfing age, television itself must resort to more and more outrageous ploys in order to compete for our ever-diminishing attention span. Which is why, to borrow another salty analogy, we must presently endure that visual tsunami, better known as 'reality TV'.

Shamelessly biased towards American and British pro-gramming – which has, after all, dominated the authors' own small-screen attention for more than fifty years and 25 years, respectively – our survey begins at the dawn of television's popularity. The result is more than 250 stories – some well known, others hopefully more unfamiliar to all but the most die-hard TV buff (who should get out more often) – which span everything from game shows, sitcom and documentary to drama, sport and, yes, reality TV. We have also sometimes stretched the word 'strange' to embrace both 'funny peculiar' and, depending on your sense of humour, 'funny ha-ha'.

Television regularly feeds on itself with programmes ranging from *It'll Be Alright on the Night* and *Auntie's Bloomers* to *The Most Outrageous TV Moments . . . Ever.* Easily digestible, endlessly repeated – 'regurgitated' might be a better word – 'bloopers' and continuity errors have, bizarrely, become almost as familiar as more cherished moments of the unadulterated bigger picture. We hope we have, on occasion, gone beyond merely the bits and the bites to provide not just a sidebar of Strange in almost every televisual form but also a useful companion to sixty years of popular television.

We have especially tried to make it as accessible as possible, so that you don't have to be a telly know-it-all to understand some of the jargon.

Perhaps the only thing to watch out for is the oft-repeated notion of the 'pilot'. A pilot is the first *filmed* episode of a particular show, made primarily to try to predict what will be a hit and what won't. Several pilots of all different genres are made by American television companies every year. Only some of these are subsequently transmitted and even fewer manage to muster an eventual series. Pilots are frequently retooled or recast (*Desperate Housewives* being a current case in point) and so we have used the term 'pilot' to mean either the first episode in a series, or an abortive stab at a show.

Readers may sometimes find the chronology of the Moments a little curious, as most entries are listed under the year the programme/series was first transmitted as opposed to a specific sighting of its Strangeness.

Which is why one of our favourite stories is told here in the Introduction, because we simply couldn't find the actual date. One Christmas Eve, teenager Michael Morpurgo – these days a distinguished author and former Children's Laureate – was watching television with his mother and stepfather (whose name he carries), the only father he'd known since his own had moved away when he was just two. It was the opening episode of a BBC adaptation of *Great Expectations* and that spine-chilling moment in a cemetery when the little boy Pip is suddenly accosted by the fleeing convict Magwitch. At that moment, Morpurgo's mother clutched her son's arm and reportedly cried out, 'Oh my God, Michael, that's your father!'

These stories are often the result of research for other various books as well as print and broadcast journalism. We've also indulged (at times been submerged) in the copious reading of an almost unhealthy number of biographies and memoirs written by or about directors, producers, executives and stars. Those sources can be found in an extensive Bibliography.

Our very special gratitude goes to Abdullai Adejumo, Stephanie Billen, Anwar Brett, Charlie Campbell, James Cellan-Jones, Greg Childs, Mel Crawford, David Crichton, Peter Duffell, Tony Earnshaw, Dick Fiddy, Tony Imi BSC, John Millar, Dave Moreland-Green, Tim and Emily Muffett, Steve Nallon, Oliver Parker, Colin Paterson, Mike Pickwoad, Pat Reid, Ben Robinson, Peter Scott, Will Scott, Mark Shivas, Ian Soutar, Nicky Waltham, Ivan Waterman and Darryl Webber for help (and recall) often above and beyond. Also thanks to many other friends, colleagues and especially websites too numerous to mention.

Finally, we'd like to thank our agent Jane Judd as well as Jeremy Robson, Jennifer Lansbury and the editorial team at Robson Books for seeing this latest Strange collection through to completion.

Little Marlow/Muswell Hill/Los Angeles 2005

THE 1940s & 1950s

BLOWING IN THE WIND
KALEIDOSCOPE (1946–53)

This fortnightly BBC magazine used to go out live from Alexandra Palace on Fridays at 8.30 p.m. As well as regular items such as 'Leslie Welch: Memory Man' and 'Iris Brooke's Collector's Corner', members of the Rank Organisation's Company of Youth, better known as the 'Charm School', would perform a charade in the 'Word Play' slot.

Apparently viewers were often so distracted by the neat plots that they forgot to guess the word. Budding star Christopher Lee, just 24 at the time, hopes that the audience were more than simply distracted when it came to one of his 'Word Play' appearances on *Kaleidoscope*.

He was playing the Commissaire of Police and at a given point had to burst in on his inspector in order to tear a strip off him for being so slow with the investigation of a particular case.

Now, whether it was the sheer power of his intervention or the fact that his fellow actor, Richard Molinas, was like himself incredibly nervous tackling live TV, but their clash unleashed a barrage of farts from Lee's co-star.

Lee recalled, 'We played a ten-minute scene without once looking at each other. And he never stopped farting. It was like fifty rounds rapid. People behind the camera were rolling in agony, but there was nothing they could do to help us.'

AMAZING STORIES
BELIEVE IT OR NOT (1949–50; 1982–86; 2001–)

Dubbed 'The Merchant of Strange' and 'Impresario of the Outlandish', Robert Leroy Ripley first got into the oddity business in 1918 as a sports cartoonist for the *New York Globe*.

Eventually extending his range beyond the sporty into a fascination with weirdness of all kinds – such as the two Ukrainians who slapped each other's face for 36 hours straight, and the man whose name was Ab C Defghi – Ripley eventually parlayed his speciality into a radio series before switching to TV in March 1949.

Ripley would tell viewers amazing stories using exhibits and reconstructions. Less than three months later, Ripley was dead and, after a very brief hiatus, various others took on his mantle for a while.

Its creator may have been gone but he certainly wasn't forgotten for, when the show returned more than thirty years later, it was now titled *Ripley's Believe It or Not*, with the rather sinister-looking Hollywood actor Jack Palance as host. After another long break from the screen, the show returned yet again with TV's *Superman*, Dean Cain, and a British presenter, *Red Dwarf*'s Craig Charles, at the helm.

I AM A CAMERA
THE PLAINCLOTHESMAN (1949–54)

Some shows occasionally turn to gimmicks for ratings: *The Plainclothesman* was one giant gimmick, albeit a pretty successful one.

Airing on the now-defunct DuMont network, this series was one of few in which you never saw the lead character. The camera was subjective, showing the world through the eyes of the unnamed big-city police lieutenant. The camera was the actor. If he got hit in the face, the camera wobbled and fell to the ground, if he ran his fingers through his hair, a hand went up past the picture and the image jiggled.

Other than that, it was a regular police drama, with the lieutenant (played in fact by Ken Lynch) solving crimes with the aid of Sergeant Brady (Jack Orrison). Luckily for Lynch, he did finally get some screen time, three years into the run, in a show that contained various flashbacks.

For those unfamiliar with the DuMont network, it was American television's fourth network from the mid-forties, until 1956, founded by the inventor Dr Allen B DuMont, a.k.a. 'The Father of Television'. After creating various television and electronic equipment, DuMont got into programming, but was hindered by lack of finances and inadequate broadcasting facilities.

Although it featured several innovative shows, as well as serving as an early home for the comedian Jackie Gleason, the DuMont legacy finished on a sorry note. The actress Edie Adams testified to the Library of Congress that a tragic fate befell most of the tapes of DuMont shows in the early seventies. As DuMont was being bought by another company, the lawyers argued as to who would look after the back catalogue.

One of them said that he would take care of it. So, early one morning, a number of lorries pulled up outside the warehouse where the original tapes were kept and loaded them up. Allegedly, they were then taken to a boat, from which, after leaving the dock, were then dumped hundreds of pieces of stock, videotapes and kinescopes. A damp – and, yes, strange – end to a slice of television history.

OUT IN THE COLD
THE ALDRICH FAMILY (1949–53)

No fewer than five different young actors played Henry, the son of the household, and three actresses daughter Mary in this popular sitcom during its four-year run, while just one actor, House Jameson, portrayed their confused dad.

However, when it came to casting wholesome American mom Alice Aldrich, it turned out to be a whole different ball game. They were all set to go with Jean Muir, veteran of thirty films, including *A Midsummer Night's Dream* and *The Constant Nymph*, when politics intervened.

This was the hardening of the Cold War era and, when Muir's name suddenly appeared in a Red-baiting pamphlet shortly before the show was to start on NBC, the network caved into right-wing protests and she was fired. The sponsor and its ad agency also demanded the cancellation of the first episode.

Muir had been given no opportunity to defend herself and later, before a Congressional committee, she denied being or ever having been a communist. The incident would help drive her into alcoholism although she did get a chance to resume her career some years later.

As if having so many different-looking children wasn't tricky enough, the long-suffering Mr Jameson would also have to encounter four versions of his missus following Muir's abrupt axing.

TARTAN BACKLASH
COME DANCING (1950–95)

Who said that being a television presenter was always a glamorous and exciting job? Certainly not the late Peter West, urbane rugby and cricket commentator as well as sometime host on BBC's *Come Dancing*.

Future presenter Terry Wogan remembers a trip to Scotland, where, to his surprise, he discovered that West was still *persona non grata*. After one regional heat, which the Scots just lost, West found himself on the unpleasant end of the perma-tanned, twirling maestros. When the competition finished, the participants decided to blame West for the close defeat.

Rather than being able to unwind after a hard show, the hardy Englishman found himself having to hide in his dressing room, while a crowd of bloodthirsty Scottish terpsichoreans demanded his head. They never forgave him and, as Wogan recalls, West '. . . never had the nerve to go back there again'.

EBONY AND IVORY

AMOS 'N' ANDY (1951–53)

This TV spin-off from one of American radio's most popular and long-running shows had one big, politically correct plus over its audio predecessor.

Unlike the wireless version, in which rather simple-minded Andy and philosophical Amos – both African-Americans – were played by white actors, the small-screen version at least had the decency to cast black actors in the eponymous roles.

It took a while to make the transition – four years, in fact – while CBS searched high and low for the main cast. However, not even casting 'of colour' would silence the protests from civil rights groups such as the NAACP (National Association for the Advancement of Colored People), which argued the show merely helped foster racial stereotypes.

Long after the show ceased airing, the network still claimed to have a healthy interest in overseas sales – notably, if curiously, in African countries such as Kenya and Nigeria.

When Kenya suddenly announced in the early sixties that it would be banning the programme, an old hornets' nest was once again stirred up. And as for ill-advised plans to rerun some of the creaky programmes in the States, that was really the final straw. CBS finally decided to withdraw *Amos 'n' Andy* altogether and bury it.

It would take more than a decade for Britain to achieve a similar kind of sensitivity. *The Black and White Minstrel Show*, in which white performers 'blacked up' for more than twenty years in BBC primetime, finally got the axe in 1978.

AUSSIE RULES

IN MELBOURNE TONIGHT (1951–70)

The Australians have always had their own way of doing things, and that was never more the case than with the legendary Oz TV host Graham Kennedy.

A kind of Antipodean Johnny Carson, Kennedy hosted the nightly talk show *In Melbourne Tonight* on Channel Nine. It was a typical show in the American format, with guests, comedians, dancers and banter between Kennedy and his sidekick, Bert Newton. The former was an idiosyncratic television presence, known for his amateurish delivery and laid-back attitude. It was a persona that became a hit with the viewers.

However, not everyone was enamoured of him, especially the sponsors and advertisers who paid to be associated with the show. These were the days of on-air promotional spots, when the host of a particular programme would often read out a blurb, or actually demonstrate a product live on air. Most simply got on with it. Kennedy, for whatever reason, decided that advertorials were something that should get the Kennedy treatment.

His twist on the spots became legendary. Take, for example, an ad for Pal dog food. He brought his own dog, Rover, onto the set, and the idea was for the pooch to eat the food and look happy.

Instead, he ignored it, before heading off on an impromptu quest around the studio, finishing up by urinating on one of the studio cameras. Suffice it to say, it went down a storm.

Kennedy also seemed to have a particular aversion to Raoul Merton shoes. One time, he simply ended up in a fight with Newton, the pair flinging shoes at each other. In 1960, he attacked Merton again, proclaiming, 'If it weren't for Raoul Merton shoes, my feet would not be in the condition they are now. Truly, it's only because of Raoul Merton that I have ingrown toenails, for instance.

'No, that's a load of rubbish. It's only because Raoul Merton shoes are not expensive, they're only . . . I've forgotten how much they are . . . there's a lady in the front row who knows . . . No, it's not the best, but for the price . . .'

Perhaps the oddest one was for Colvan Potato Chips. Looking at the packet, he appears to take great umbrage to how empty it appears. He looks aggrieved and says, 'Well, it's got nearly a quarter of a potato in it – and they've got the hide to charge twenty cents. Now that's terrible.'

Then he looks as if a bulb had appeared over his head and he tips the crisps out onto the table and crushes them into crumbs, before pouring them back into the bag. As if that weren't enough, he starts folding the bag again and again, until it is about two inches big. Finishing the stunt, he says, 'It's down to there – where the hell's the potato? I'm in the mood to lose them all tonight.' (Perhaps this last comment was directed at his advertisers.)

A people's champion, then, and a unique broadcaster, but it's highly unlikely that he got an invitation to the Colvan Christmas party.

BABY BOOM

I LOVE LUCY (1951–57)

Filmed in front of a live audience – something that didn't become commonplace in the world of TV sitcoms until the 1970s – *I Love*

Lucy was not so much a programme, more an American institution.

Flame-haired Lucille Ball, who'd tried and failed to become a Hollywood star, was approaching forty when she and her Cuban husband Desi Arnaz forked out $5,000 of their own money to pay for a 'pilot' episode of a show that they thought could transform her popularity.

The idea, which was snapped up by CBS, featured Lucy and Desi as a . . . yes, married couple – she a wacky housewife, he a Cuban bandleader – endlessly confronted by life's little domestic problems.

What the network hadn't quite bargained for was the moment when Lucy, now 41 and with the series well established and the ratings heading for stratospheric, fell pregnant.

'How about Lucy Ricardo [her character's surname] having a baby as part of our shows this year?' Desi suggested, helpfully. The reaction was, at first, a horrified negative. The very idea of bodily functions, let alone sex and its by-products, was then anathema to the TV corporate-powers-that-be.

The most piqued was the show's sponsor, the tobacco giants Philip Morris, whose executives mooted that the increasingly *enceinte* Lucy could perhaps be hidden behind chairs. Finally they relented and agreed to 'one or two shows' on the subject. No way, replied co-producer Desi, who ultimatum-ed that there should be at least eight.

When his entreaties fell on deaf ears in New York, Desi decided to write fiercely to Philip Morris's British boss, Alfred Lyons, in London. Less than a fortnight later all the negative comments had ceased and Desi was given *carte blanche*. Later, it became clear that a memo had been swiftly sent by Lyons to certain key employees, It read, 'To whom it may concern: Don't f*** around with the Cuban! A.L.'

The 19th of January 1953 was the projected date for Lucy's real-life Caesarean delivery. But what about the sex of the baby? The real-life couple already had a daughter, and Desi was so anxious to have a son this time round that, in art if not in life, Ricky Jr would be scripted into the show.

Ever the willing trouper, Lucy actually delivered a boy (Desi Arnaz Jr) and a sanitised version of the proceedings became Episode 51 'Lucy Goes to the Hospital'.

The show coincided with the inauguration of General Eisenhower as 34th US president, an event watched by 29 million on TV. The White House press corps were naturally delighted until they read that the Arnazes'/Ricardos' 'little dividend' had been enjoyed by an audience of no fewer than 44 million.

MONKEY BUSINESS

TODAY (1952–)

Now called *The Today Show*, this was NBC's morning magazine pick-me-up.

Hosted by Dave Garroway, Jack Lescoulie and Jim Fleming, the personable, laid-back, news and current affairs show was the precursor of pretty much every morning show since. Except in one respect.

In 1953, the programme makers had a unique idea: introduce an animal co-host. Welcome J Fred Muggs, a cheeky chimpanzee in a nappy, who played around on set and probably annoyed the hosts immensely.

Not exactly top-notch journalism, but a savvy idea. When American children heard that they could see a live chimp on this new-fangled television, they persuaded their parents to buy sets, so sales, as well as ratings, went up.

Muggs lasted until 1957 and was then replaced by another chimp, called Kokomo Jr, who stayed until 1959.

The show went from strength to strength and is now one of the most prestigious – and profitable – programmes on American TV, having made stars out of everyone from Estelle Parsons and Barbara Walters to Matt Lauer and Katie Couric.

THE CURSE OF KAL-EL

THE ADVENTURES OF SUPERMAN (1952–57)

The so-called 'Curse of Superman', which had one of its sadder manifestations in late 2004 with the premature death of the quadriplegic actor Christopher Reeve, is said to have started right here.

George Reeves starred as the small screen's first son of Krypton so successfully that he found it almost impossible to get work outside of the show.

What really fuelled the notion of a curse was Reeves's violent end at the age of 45 in 1959. He was found in his home, killed by a single gunshot wound to the head. While it was deemed a suicide, brought on by depression at his inability to get other acting jobs, rumours abounded that he had actually been murdered.

This theory gained some currency when it was discovered that he had been having a long-term affair with the wife of a top MGM executive, Eddie Mannix. Whatever the real truth, the *Superman* hex was up and running.

ALL IN THE FAMILY

THE ADVENTURES OF OZZIE & HARRIET (1952–66)

Long before the Osbournes were the Nelsons – but there the resemblance entirely ends. We're talking chalk and cheese. And, unlike the stars of its contemporary, *I Love Lucy*, in which a real-life couple was also the basis for a popular sitcom, but 'with the names changed' etc., Ozzie, Harriet and, more importantly, their two young sons, David and Ricky, were a sanitised reality. These gentle 'Adventures' of a typical middle-class family – how typical is Hollywood, though? – had first begun on radio in 1944, when the boys were played by professional actors.

When the Nelsons eventually arrived on TV eight years later with ex-bandleader Ozzie as producer, director and head writer, he and his wife – who'd been the band's vocalist – allowed the sons to play their thinly disguised real-life selves.

Which is how we got to hear the dulcet tones of the teen idol Ricky Nelson, whose fifties and sixties chart-topping pop hits – such as 'Stood Up', 'I Got a Feeling', 'Poor Little Fool', 'Never be Anyone Else But You', 'I Wanna be Loved' and 'Young Emotions' – received their first airing on the family show.

When Ricky and David eventually got married, even their new wives were played by the real thing. Remember, this kind of 'reality TV' was long before *The Truman Show*.

BETTER DEAD THAN RED
LIFE IS WORTH LIVING (1953–57)

Shows about psychics are all the rage now, but that wasn't the case back in 1953 – making Bishop Fulton Sheen's on-screen exploits all the more incredible. Sheen started off in radio, handing out religious instruction and advice, before moving to television in 1952 with this 'inspirational' weekly show.

Broadcasting from a studio-based 'study', the Catholic cleric continued God's work, and, it being the Cold War era, this often meant ranting on about the dangers of communism.

But things took a ghostly turn on one show when he read the burial scene from Shakespeare's play, *Julius Caesar*, giving it a commie twist by replacing the names of Caesar, Cassius, Mark Antony and Brutus with Stalin, Beria, Malenkov and Vishinsky – all major Soviet Union politicians of the day.

Finally, he said, 'Stalin must one day meet his judgement.' It was a live broadcast, and conspiracy theorists blanched when, less than a week later, the monstrous Soviet dictator had a stroke and died. This led to Sheen's being branded Public Enemy Number One by high-level Communist Party members.

Sheen uttered his final 'God Love You' weekly sign-off four years later, but the show gets repeated to this day on some religious cable channels.

UNEARTHLY POWERS

KLEE (1953)

The spooky story goes like this.

Several viewers watching television in Britain during September 1953 suddenly saw a strange test signal come up on their screens, advertising a local US TV station, KLEE of Houston, Texas.

Not only was this fundamentally impossible in the days before satellite, but, what's more, KLEE had been off the air since 1950! This led many people to theorise that radio and television signals never stopped bouncing around and you could indeed accidentally pick them up at random.

However, despite the science, the whole thing was a hoax. KLEE had been bought out and replaced with a new station, KPRC. One day, an international letter came into the office from Britain, saying, 'Enclosed herewith is a photograph . . . of what I believe is your test signal . . . would you be so kind as to confirm or deny by return mail that this is so . . .'

When engineers were unable to prove that the pictures were faked, the myth was confirmed: ghost pictures from three years previously had rebounded around the world and ended up on British television sets.

The reality is somewhat different. In fact, several other stations had received a similar letter, but KPRC was the only one to change its branding, thus making it a particularly peculiar instance. Also, all the pictures were solely of test signals.

KPRC responded to their letter and found out that it was actually a scam by a couple of inventors who were promising a new TV system capable of receiving signals over large distances – impossible at the time. It turned out that they had pulled a similar stunt with stations across Russia and South America.

Their ploy was to project these faked cards onto the screens of their sets and then tell prospective investors to photograph them and send the photos to the stations in their respective countries. They would never have been found out if KLEE hadn't been off the air.

After the fact, there were subtle flaws in their plan. The cards were sometimes slightly different from the actual ones and often foreign test cards were still broadcast in English.

Nonetheless, the story still passed into lore and remains one of the most common strange-but-true stories – probably because no one understands the inherent scientific fallibility of this tall tale.

DRYING UP
CRIME AND PUNISHMENT (1953)

With a running time of two hours and the judicious use of no fewer than twenty sets – and just two weeks of rehearsal – this was to be one of the most complicated live productions ever staged by the BBC.

As the Welsh actor Kenneth Griffith, who was playing Raskolnikov, waited nervously in the slips that Sunday night in November (repeat the following Thursday), he was informed that there'd been a slight technical hitch with a camera crane – 'but don't worry!'

Then it was time for the off and Griffith began to wend his way through the various sets, 'dashing' (as the actor recalled it) from scene to scene until he reached the last lap.

This, taking place in a small white cell, was the climactic confrontation with Sonia (Frances Hyland), who asks Dostoyevsky's tragic character the central question of the whole drama: 'Why did you kill the old woman [a female moneylender]?'

As the camera edged towards Raskolnikov's face, Griffith's mind went completely blank. While a nation waited, Sonia slowly asked the question again. What his character was meant to say was, 'To steal', actually a lie.

Finally gathering his thoughts, Griffith simply bypassed the lie and went straight to the unvarnished – but redemptive – truth, which Sonia eventually elicits from him.

'But what about the disaster?' Griffith asked everyone, including his director John Fernald, after the show had finished. Apart from him and his co-star, no one had spotted it.

Later, after receiving the princely sum of £45 for his acting stint, Griffith wrote to the BBC complaining about this miserly stipend:

> You exist on the poverty of my profession. If my profession were, generally, not so hard pressed and desperate for opportunities to demonstrate and exercise our talents, a few of us would agree to entertain the British nation for such a pittance. I am still poor, but please do not offer me any more work; it would only waste your time – and mine.

As a result of this note, Griffith claims he was 'blacklisted' for starring roles by the BBC for many years.

PASTA MASTER

PANORAMA (1953–)

Cuban missile crises come and go, but the Great Spaghetti Harvest lingers on for ever.

Recalling the BBC's flagship current affairs show's strangest moment – forget that bloke who once took LSD live on the programme – we must turn back to 1957.

In gleaming monochrome, there were these girls in bright national costume climbing ladders as they plucked dangling, damp spaghetti from trees before laying the stuff out in the sun to dry. A guitar played in the background as the three-minute item concluded with presenter Richard Dimbleby's voiceover intoning, 'We have this marvellous festival. The first harvest of the spaghetti.'

Surely television's most stylish April Fool's item actually originated with an idea hatched by the distinguished film cameraman Charles de Jaeger, who recalled a schoolmaster constantly telling him and his fellow pupils, 'You're so stupid, you'd think spaghetti grew on trees.'

It was March and de Jaeger flew to Lugano hoping to find the weather sunny and the flowers out. Instead a mist pervaded the area. There was no blossom or leaves out anywhere. So he and his crew quickly moved on to Castiglione, where, joy of joys, there were tall laurel trees with leaves on.

Back in Lugano, they purchased some home-made spaghetti, put it all on a big wooden platter and returned to the trees. By the time they got back, the pasta, by now dried out, simply wouldn't hang. So they cooked it and tried again, this time to find it was too slippery.

The solution finally came thanks to the chap from the local tourist board, who suggested they put the spaghetti between damp cloths before hanging it.

As some viewers puzzled slightly about the oddly arboreal origins of the world's favourite pasta, the magisterial Dimbleby concluded the week's edition with, 'Now we say goodnight on this first day of April.'

ENTER 007

CLIMAX! (1954–58)

The cinematic bow of James Bond 007 in *Dr No* – instigating filmland's longest-running series – was still eight years away when Ian Fleming's hero, nominally at least, made his debut on the screen.

Introducing crew-cut 'Card Sense Jimmy Bond', as the undercover American CIA agent was billed, *Casino Royale* – which was production thirteen in this long-running CBS drama series – broadcast live on 21 October 1954.

Bond was played by square-jawed Yank Barry Nelson, and the hour-long show co-starred Aussie-born Michael Pate as Bond's British sidekick Clarence Leiter, before the character eventually became American with a change of first name to 'Felix'. Given the honour of starting the tradition of great 'Bond villains' was the Hollywood veteran Peter Lorre, who played the evil cardsharp, Le Chiffre.

There had been talk of spinning Bond off into his own TV series but it seems that the reaction to this inaugural incarnation was less than seismic, so the world had to wait until a new decade before Bond-age became a reality.

INTO ROOM 101

NINETEEN EIGHTY-FOUR (1954)

The first and, arguably, the best ever screen adaptation of George Orwell's grim, prophetic novel (published just six years earlier), caused questions to be asked in the House of Commons.

This followed headlines such as TORTURES ON TV HORRIFY WHOLE NATION and TORTURES ON TV START BIGGEST PROTEST STORM the day after its live transmission on the BBC.

The fuss was over the notorious Room 101 (not to be confused with the amiable chat show half a century later) scene in which our hero (played by Peter Cushing) was confronted with his greatest fear. In his case, rats.

A rodent wrangler had managed to track down a couple of sewer rats for the final rehearsal but, by the time it came for them to leap aggressively at Cushing's throat, the pair had been so sated with kindness, warmth and food that they were happily asleep.

With time running short before the actual broadcast, another pair were snared at the local pet shop – tame ones, which had to be dyed a menacing dark brown from their normal, unthreatening white.

This time round, food was kept well away. But just before going on air, these rats were making so much noise that they had to be removed to a separate studio with a camera and microphone all to themselves. There, with bits of food dangled above their heads, they rose to the occasion, snapping with genuine rodent ferocity.

Meanwhile, in another studio, completely out of sight of this monstrous tandem, Cushing was horrifiedly reacting to their attack. But, for a TV audience viewing the actor's superior thesping (not to mention the ratty gnashing), two and two made five.

For this piece of emoting, Cushing said later, he became known as 'the horror man on the BBC' – and this was well before he would begin his long association with the gory world of Hammer Films.

THE BIG RED BOOK

THIS IS YOUR LIFE (1955–64; 1969–2003)

For years the famous red book proffered by Eamonn Andrews (later Michael Aspel) was a sign that the lucky recipient had been accepted into an exclusive club of celebrity and achievement.

The idea for this popular light entertainment show was imported from America, where its creator Ralph Edwards originated the format of 'doorstepping' the great and the good before reviewing the highlights of their life and career with the aid of old friends and colleagues. But the very first British show nearly came a nasty cropper.

The surprise element for what started out as a live show was vital, so when the *Daily Sketch* revealed that the first life to be celebrated was that of the footballer Stanley Matthews the producers hurriedly had to change tack.

Their replacement was the former world light heavyweight champion Freddie Mills – or at least that was what the host and one-time boxing commentator Eamonn Andrews was led to believe. For, in a neat twist, the producers made Eamonn the subject of the very first show, to his evident shock.

In the years that followed, major figures in show business, sport and public life reacted with admirable stoicism when Andrews, then Aspel, stepped out before them and intoned the words, 'This is your life'.

There were, though, a few exceptions. In 1961, the Tottenham Hotspur captain Danny Blanchflower was so appalled at the thought that he turned down the opportunity point blank, leaving Andrews as the surprised one when the footballer turned on his heel and walked away from the host live on air.

Blanchflower was the first of only three subjects to turn down this TV honour, the author Richard Gordon (who later relented) and Bill Oddie following his example. No surprise to learn that, in order to avoid those embarrassing 'live' no-shows, the programme moved to a prerecorded format.

THE KEY TO MEMORY
DIXON OF DOCK GREEN (1955–76)

Back in the early days of television, every programme went out live because there simply wasn't the technology to record it.

Inevitably, actors would forget their words and, *in extremis*, the prompter would use what was known as the 'cut key' facility, whereby a button would be pressed and the sound would be cut out, enabling the prompter to feed the actor his or her line.

Back home, the viewer would simply bang the TV set, curse the technical hitch and breathe a sigh of relief when the sound came back a moment later.

Peter Byrne, PC Andy Crawford in this classic police series, remembers how he and Jack Warner (Dixon) would try to avoid having to use the cut key. 'Jack was getting on a bit and he had the lead lines every week. I had this agreement with the PA that he would never, ever use the dreaded cut key, because if Jack dried I would get him out of it and vice versa . . .'

What he had not bargained for was a situation where Jack was struggling, an ageing character actress was forgetting her lines as well and their usual PA was on leave. 'We had a young girl who panicked and was pushing the cut key down when they were speaking and lifting it up for when she was giving the cue!'

Suddenly aware of what was going on, Byrne leaped to the rescue: 'I moved away to get the camera off him and did "I know what you're thinking" kind of acting – summarised the whole thing in thirty seconds . . .'

After this disastrous episode, the programme makers wanted to give Byrne most of the lines the following week, but it is a tribute to the actor's sense of honour that he refused to allow them to do this, saying, 'If you do that, you'll destroy him! You've got to let him get back on the bicycle.' They did, and, after a brief dry in the first minute, Warner rose to the challenge.

Jack Warner was to continue as everyone's favourite TV bobby until he was eighty – perhaps just a tad beyond usual retirement age. Evenin' all . . .

FUNNY MONEY

SOUPY SALES (1955–79)

Depending on whom you believe, between 19,000 and 25,000 custard pies were hurled during Sales's quarter-century reign as, arguably, the king of kiddies' TV in the States.

Sales – real name Milton Supman – graduated from local television to the network and finally to nationwide syndication with his brand of sketches, jokes and, most enduringly, pie throwing.

However, being the king can sometimes give you ideas above your station – like the occasion in 1964, which nearly ended his career. Sales jokingly told his young viewers to 'take some of those funny green pieces of paper with pictures of George Washington, Benjamin Franklin, Lincoln and Jefferson on them' from their parents' wallets and send them to him, and he would send them a postcard from Puerto Rico.

There was an immediate outcry from outraged parents and he was suspended from television for a week, but the incident made his show 'cool' and boosted his ratings when he returned to the air.

It transpired that several children did indeed send Sales some money – guesstimated at around $80,000 – of which around only $50 was in real money, the rest in play money and Monopoly notes.

We can't, however, leave Soupy without recounting the time when the tables were turned on him by the studio crew during a live broadcast of one of his shows.

On opening a prop door on his set, he was confronted by a nude dancer, who was gyrating in front of him as a recording of 'The Stripper' was playing over the studio loudspeakers. While the woman was out of camera shot for the television feed, the studio monitors were rigged so Sales could see the nude dancer on them, giving the impression that she was being broadcast live on his children's show.

Convinced that his career was over, yet still laughing with his crew, he asked that they cut to a commercial. Only then was he told that the nude dancer wasn't shown on the live feed. He later joked, 'All I really wanted from her was her autograph.'

TWICE THE MISERY
DOUBLE YOUR MONEY (1955–68)

Chirpy little Londoner Monica Rose proved such a popular contestant on this weekly ITV quiz show that she was invited back as hostess two months later following her sixteenth birthday in 1964.

The British version of American TVs *$64,000 Question*, albeit with far less reward (£1,000 max in the soundproof booth), was hosted by the irrepressible Hughie Green.

Now, the working-class teenager suddenly found herself thrust into the showbiz spotlight, making more money than she could dream of and mingling with the televisual A-list.

Unfortunately for Monica, fame was not all it was cracked up to be. She gave an interview on her seventeenth birthday, saying that she missed all of her old friends. Then, in October 1966, she dared to wear a dress that showed too much skin for most of the conservative viewing public and she received a barrage of complaints.

Poor Monica couldn't handle the anger and ran away, only to return two days later when she heard that her mum wanted to know where she was.

The following March, she decided to give up television and quit the show. A month later she took a drugs overdose. Television bosses obviously felt sorry for her and offered Monica her old job back.

Following the show's cancellation after Associated-Rediffusion lost its franchise, Rose found it difficult to get work and wanted instead to get married. Her boyfriend/manager didn't see it the same way and never took her down the aisle.

Salvation came again in the form of Green, who was hosting a new show called *The Sky's the Limit* and asked Monica to come and be hostess. Needing the money, she ditched the boyfriend and took the job.

Sick of being thought of as a mindless TV hostess, in 1977 she ploughed her savings into a play in a theatre in Morecambe, but lost it when the show went bust shortly afterwards. In 1980, she was back in hospital, suffering from nervous exhaustion.

If you think that was the end of Monica's troubles, think again. She managed to find a nice husband, becoming a born-again Christian and marrying a preacher. Sadly, she didn't have any children and had to have a hysterectomy.

Never fully recovering, sad and working in a supermarket in Leicester, Monica committed suicide, aged 45, on 8 February 1994.

IN A FIX

TWENTY-ONE (1956–58)

As TV quiz shows began to prosper in the postwar years on both sides of the Atlantic, the rewards contrasted vividly between Here and There. In the States, for example, contestants on *The $64,000 Question* really did play for that sum of money.

With such temptation there was bound to be an occasional lapse. Networks had to preserve ratings and keep advertisers happy after all if they were to be able to offer such riches.

The bubble burst in 1957, when a contestant on the ratings smash *Twenty-One* went public with a story that scandalised America.

Returning champion Herb Stemple claimed that he had been told to lose deliberately to the charismatic Ivy Leaguer Charles Van Doren, so that the more polished and telegenic man could continue to bring viewers in.

Stemple's assertion was rebuffed by the network's lawyers, and the show's producers attempted to sue him for libel. But the New York district attorney was taking a keen interest after a trickle of complaints over such shows grew into something stronger.

When the case was put before a grand jury in late summer 1958, the industry suffered a terrible blow as the grim picture emerged of shows that were being routinely rigged, with participants shown questions in advance and being coached with their answers. The *Twenty-One* case that set everything in motion would later become the basis for Robert Redford's 1994 film *Quiz Show*.

BOOM A BANG . . . ON A STRING
EUROVISION SONG CONTEST (1956–)

This warbling bun fight still unaccountably remains one of TV viewing's guilty pleasures – if only to observe the shamelessly partisan way certain countries vote at the annual show's climax. Old loyalties still die hard, even in the new world order.

However, it's privately joked that the last thing you need is actually to win because then you (the successful nation, that is) are stuck with having to stage the actual contest the following year.

So, much as we all thrilled in 1976 to the sight – rather less, the sound – of the British pop group Brotherhood of Man triumphing in Holland with 'Save Your Kisses For Me', there soon dawned the ghastly realisation that the whole circus would be set on home soil twelve months on.

It's now 1977, at the Wembley Conference Centre, and what's going on backstage is considerably more tense than anything confronting a loyal Saturday night audience on BBC1. The first problem has been with those little interval films used to fill the gaps between the various acts. There aren't any.

Apparently, in the days before the live contest, the BBC had taken the various performers to the Cockney Pride Tavern in London's West End in order to film them doing cheery, Cockney-type things for the inserts.

The trouble was, the party spirit got out of hand as the liquor flowed. The mostly unusable film consisted of people lying on floors, across tables, waving legs in the air and being sick in corners. So, instead of using jolly, Cockney-style inserts, they had to cut instead to the Conference Centre audience for reaction shots.

Another glitch was that the BBC's Outside Broadcast crews had been on strike until just hours before the event. This had necessitated the cancellation earlier of the *Song For Europe* programme, featuring all the British entries, which are then voted on by the great British public. It aired instead only on radio and there had been some confusion between the entries by Lynsey de Paul (and Mike Moran) and one-time New Seeker, Lyn Paul.

Meanwhile, a private bet had been taken among some of the BBC backroom boys that sports 'talkback' – the stream of instruction between the studio and backstage via an intercom system – was generally 'ruder' than entertainment 'talkback'.

Unfortunately, the person deputed to ensure a recording of that day's *Grandstand* 'talkback' had forgotten to do so. The resulting, infamous, collection from the Eurovision show would remain a stand-alone treat.

But even the increasingly four-letter tensions in the intemperate director's booth as the programme began to overrun severely were still being matched by other problems in and around the Conference Centre.

For the first time, the BBC had taken on a private security firm to 'police' the building. So, when a man arrived at the door claiming to be the corporation's director-general but failed to produce a suitable identity card, he was given very short shrift by the tough minders. In fact, it *was* the director-general himself, who was due to hand out the big prize at the end of the evening. Eventually, he managed to fight his way in (by which time, most of the audience were probably wanting to fight their way out).

As minutes seemed to turn into hours, the next big time waster was during the interminable, albeit compelling, voting process. This was exacerbated when the Luxembourg jury got into a row with presenter Angela Rippon live on screen.

With the studio urging the director to 'come off air', the show finally limped to its end. As the winning act, the petite French songbird Marie Myriam with her *'L'oiseau et l'enfant'*, did its traditional reprise – but not before some difficulty in actually locating the little mademoiselle somewhere in the building – the director was being screamed at to 'run the roller'. That's the contractual list of credits including all the show's Eurovision production partners.

As the winning song died away, the only credit that finally arrived on our screens was that of the talkative director. And, on that much-circulated talkback tape, the man in question can be clearly heard saying, 'Well, I think that went rather well . . .'

The only consolation was that after the UK finished second with 'Rock Bottom' – which perfectly summed up the evening – at least this dubious extravaganza wouldn't be returning to these shores for a while.

GOING ON HAIR
PRIME-MINISTERIAL BROADCAST (1956)

The Suez Crisis had just erupted and the BBC were summoned to Downing Street to set up for a live broadcast by the prime minister, Sir Anthony Eden.

Eden, who would resign the following year, was clearly not a well man. He looked pale and drawn; even his famous moustache seemed out of sorts. As he moved into the lights preparing to make his well-rehearsed speech to the nation, a makeup girl dabbed furiously at his sweaty face with powder.

A minute before he was due to go on air, Lady Eden yelled out, 'Is this a conspiracy? I've just seen a monitor. The broadcast can't go ahead. The prime minister's moustache is invisible.' With just seconds to go, she took matters into her own hands, grabbed her mascara and quickly darkened her hubby's legendary lip fluff.

COMEDY ON CUE
HANCOCK'S HALF HOUR/HANCOCK (1956–63)

By the turn of the sixties, Tony Hancock was the top comedy star in the British showbiz firmament. For most of the fifties, his radio programme had been the most popular on the airwaves, and his transition to television had maintained this level of success.

But, in spite of his experience, Hancock suffered from stage fright, and in addition found learning his lines an arduous task. This was made all the more difficult when he was involved in a car accident on the way home from a recording. Badly shaken, and with two black eyes, he was otherwise physically unharmed.

Determined to go ahead with the next recording the following week, he was unable to get down to learning his lines for the new episode, scripted as ever by Ray Galton and Alan Simpson, which was entitled 'The Blood Donor'.

Producer Duncan Wood stepped in and devised a new series of camera moves to accommodate the use of a teleprompter (or autocue) for his star. So it was that Hancock, heavily made up to cover the bruising, read much of the show that was widely regarded as the finest of his illustrious career.

If you watch any reruns, note how Hancock looks past 'Nurse' June Whitfield and the rest of the cast as he utters many of his immortal lines.

MIND YOUR LANGUAGE
THE BUCCANEERS (1956–57)

Only old sea dogs will have likely spotted that Cap'n Dan Tempest's vessel *Sultana* bore a remarkable resemblance to Captain Ahab's whaler, *Peaquod*, as portrayed in *Moby Dick*, which was in cinemas at the same time as this salty television adventure series.

The ship – which had also done sea duty back in 1950 as the *Hispaniola* in Disney's *Treasure Island* – was nothing if not versatile. Which is how Robert Shaw, playing the swashbuckling Tempest, also viewed his own acting skills.

Shaw, who boasted – possibly for publicity purposes only – an authentic West Country piratical ancestry, decided to employ a

Cornish accent for his role as the free-spirited eighteenth-century freebooter.

But, on the first day of rehearsals, producer Hannah Weinstein, an old Hollywood hand, decided to put him right. She took him to one side, told him that the series was pre-sold to the States and it might be best if the American public could actually understand what he was saying.

She then added, with some finality, 'See, I know 'cause I'm an American – and I can't get one damn word.' Shaw, who always knew where the bucks were buried, hastily returned to the Queen's English.

COMMERCIAL BREAKS
JIM'S INN (1957–63)

Wilful 'product placement' in films and drama was still just a gleam in the corporate eye when ad mags were one of the more curious staples of independent television.

As if commercials *between* the programmes weren't enough, these were advertising magazines – or 'shopping guides', as they were first termed – disguised as short, starry sitcoms.

Jim's Inn, the most popular of the bunch, took the form of fifteen-minute weekly visits to fictitious Wembleham, where Jimmy (one-time film star of *The Huggetts* and *The Blue Lamp*) 'ran' the village pub with his real-life second wife, Maggie.

Regular characters such as the beauty salon owner Roma (Roma Cresswell) would pop by to discuss love, pain and the whole damn thing in between 'plugging' various household or gardening gadgets.

Cresswell recalled, 'We went out live for the first few years, which was terrifying. There was a huge glass ashtray on the bar under which we sometimes put difficult-to-remember parts of our scripts. We had very little rehearsal and, if I remember correctly, only got the scripts at first run-through.'

Much shorter-lived than *Jim's Inn* were *Slater's Bazaar*, starring long-faced actor John Slater; *Where Shall We Go?*, in which a couple, Peter Butterworth and Janet Brown, concentrated on holiday plans; and *Send for Saunders*, in which the caretaker of a block of flats helped out the residents when they ran short of household goods.

These ad mags, surprisingly popular with viewers, were finally banned in 1963, following a recommendation for their abolition in the Pilkington Report of the previous year.

HIS WISH GRANTED

WAGON TRAIN (1957–65)

The great John 'I make Westerns' Ford had directed more than 120 films – in all kinds of genres – when, in 1960, for a fee of just $3,500, he helmed an hour-long episode of this popular TV 'oater' at the height of big vs small screen enmity.

It all stemmed from a visit he'd made to the set to visit his old friend Ward Bond, a regular member of Ford's stock company of actors. Bond was the star of this particular long-running show, playing wagon master Major Seth Adams in tales of a post-Civil War, east-to-west trek of frontier pioneers.

Ford had always wanted to make a film about Ulysses S Grant and with Bond's blessing, he was able to realise at least part of his dream within the format of the series for an episode entitled, 'The Colter Craven Story'.

To give it his true trademark, Ford was also able to persuade his greatest star, John Wayne, to make a brief 'guest' appearance as Confederate General William Tecumseh Sherman.

Not that anyone but the Duke's most devoted fans might have known about it, for his screen credit was under the pseudonym 'Michael Morris' and, for what proved to be Wayne's only ever TV appearance (other than 'as himself'), he was shown only in long shot.

By the time the episode aired, Bond – who'd originally been derided by Ford for 'prostituting' himself in a weekly television series – was, sadly, dead. *Wagon Train* would, however, run another couple of years when, ironically, with a new wagon master (John McIntire) in the saddle, the show finally got to Number One in the American ratings.

CONNERY IN THE CORNER

REQUIEM FOR A HEAVYWEIGHT (1957)

A week before BBC rehearsals were due to begin on a live performance of Rod Serling's searing play, Jack Palance, had to pull out of the title role because of Hollywood commitments.

He'd already played the tragic boxer Mountain McLintock live on American TV to much acclaim some months earlier and there was huge expectation about this transatlantic switch. Suddenly without a star, director Alvin Rakoff was beginning to get desperate.

He'd already cast a young Scots actor called Sean Connery in one of the minor roles when Rakoff's then girlfriend (later wife) and *Requiem*'s co-star, Jacqueline Hill, suggested a swift promotion for the 26-year-old former bodybuilder.

The director was especially worried about Connery's accent – to his Canadian ears, impenetrable at the best of times. But, despite this and the fact that twentysomething Connery hardly shaped up as a grizzled old 'pug', he gave him the gig (at the princely sum of £35).

As the big night approached, tension mounted, not least because some in the BBC hierarchy were distinctly unconvinced by Connery's suitability. It would prove a star-making role for him – a Hollywood contract quickly followed – but not for the actor who took over the bit part, vacated by Connery, of a new young fighter in the play's final scene. That went to a certain Michael Caine.

ROTTEN TO THE CORE
AMERICAN BANDSTAND (1957–87)

The US's most-cherished, family-oriented music show – yes, their *Top of the Pops* – started on local TV in 1952 before becoming fully networked five years later.

Featuring every act under the sun, lip-synching happily to their latest single, the show was the brainchild of the perennially youthful Dick Clark.

Public Image Ltd (PIL) was a post-punk band fronted by former Sex Pistol Johnny Rotten (a.k.a. John Lydon). Bearing in mind their notorious antecedents on and off screen, it inevitably spelled problems when the group were invited to appear in 1980.

Band member Martin Atkins remembers Clark coming into their dressing room and greeting them. Not knowing who he was, bass player Jah Wobble replied: 'Hey, I'm Jah Wobble, who the f*** are you?'

Meanwhile, Clark knew exactly what he was dealing with. Road manager Larry White recalls being summoned to Clark's office before the taping, where Clark asked him: 'What can I expect from this asshole?'

White placated the legendary presenter, saying that the band were excited about performing. Nothing could be further from the truth. The band were appalled that they were expected to mime and – didn't they show it?

Having stepped out on stage, Lydon and the rest of the band basically stopped pretending to play their instruments, invited audience members up on stage and, in the ultimate act of defiance, invaded Clark's podium – something that no one *ever* did. Atkins remembers one of the guitar players giving his guitar to an audience member and wandering off.

While it appeared to be a washout, the show became one of the most famous of all *American Bandstand* shows. PIL fans argued that it was the perfect subversion of the mainstream by the greatest of all punks. But Clark told *Entertainment Weekly* years later that Lydon 'told me he was going to be rambunctious. I said "be my guest". We were in total control.'

The words of a consummate professional smoothing over an embarrassment or, at 51, a closet punk? As they say, the decision is yours.

ROYAL GREETING

THE QUEEN'S CHRISTMAS MESSAGE (1957–)

Rudyard Kipling wrote the first-ever broadcast Christmas message for George V to deliver live on the wireless from the regal study at Sandringham in 1932.

From 1960, three years after Queen Elizabeth II had finally embraced TV, the message was recorded a few days in advance. It has generally been a mix of her talking directly to camera and some royal footage from the year.

Apart from 1992, when she spoke rather movingly of her '*annus horribilis*' – including two marriage breakdowns, one divorce and a fire at Windsor Castle – the broadcast defines bland.

How much fun it might have been on one particular occasion had they used the first take from some footage shot in the Royal Mews (the stables) where the Queen was filmed handing out presents to royal staff.

Her Maj had made her way down between a line of horses to receive a posy from one of the children before ending up on a mark from which she delivered her lines perfectly from a teleprompter.

While the producer, David Attenborough, was thanking her effusively, the cameraman started tugging at his sleeve, whispering that she must do it all over again. 'Why?' Attenborough asked. 'Tell you later,' said the cameraman, mysteriously. The Queen was persuaded to do another 'take' after which she headed off to greet more of the children.

So what had been the problem? 'As she started to speak,' the cameraman explained, 'the big black horse peering over her left shoulder got that funny tickle of its upper lip that horses often get and started to waggle it. It looked as though he was doing the talking.'

That seemed to be the end of it, but, after the team had finished editing various versions of the broadcast for particular corners of the Empire, the Queen's press secretary rang Attenborough and asked if the his boss could see 'the Khartoum version'.

Attenborough was slightly bemused, unaware that the Sudan was still part of this nation's overseas holdings – until it was explained that 'Khartoum' was the name of the ventriloquising horse. The Queen, he was told, simply wanted to share the joke.

THE JOY OF HEX
BLUE PETER (1958–)

When they talk of 'The Curse of *Blue Peter*', it doesn't mean that elephant dumping massively on air, the poignant deaths of various programme pets or even the shameful vandalising of *BP*'s beautifully maintained garden.

This so-called hex usually refers to presenters who have had various reverses after (some, while) being associated with a show, which started during the Macmillan government with merely a seven-week run in mind.

Who can forget the screaming *Sun* headline BLUE PETER! after it was revealed that boyish Peter Duncan (1980–84) had been spotted in a soft-porn film? What about Anthea Turner's (1992–94) various public and private crises? How else can you explain the bizarre goings-on in the life of John Leslie (1989–94)?

And then there was Richard Bacon (1997–98). Bacon's career with *Blue Peter* came to an abrupt end when his contract was terminated after a report in the press telling the world that he had taken cocaine.

Following his dismissal, the then head of BBC children's programmes, Lorraine Heggessey, actually went on air to explain the situation to bemused CBBC viewers about the perils of snorting something that they probably thought was fizzy and in a bottle.

At the time, Bacon also released a statement, which read, cringingly,

> I fully accept and agree with the decision that has been taken. I regret what I did but it was in my personal time and I therefore hope that it does not reflect on the show. I am very grateful to *Blue Peter* for the opportunity it has given me and am very sorry that I have let everybody down.

Enough of the human stuff. There's at least one animal who'd justly claim the show's curse extended to the natural world.

Peter Purves (1967–78) was filming an insert with the rare American eagle owl, who, from the off, never looked happy to be hanging out at the BBC. What was amazing about this bird is that he wasn't all mean. In fact, he had a very special friend – a sweet little mouse.

Purves was chatting to the owl's owner and asked him to bring out this friend, which then cavorted happily between the bird's claws. 'How amazing,' remarked Purves. 'In the wild, they would be natural enemies.' 'Yes,' replied the proud owner, 'but they've been friends for—' He was halfway through his sentence when the owl barely twitched his head and, before you could say, 'The Curse of . . .', the little rodent was halfway down his friend's feathery throat.

At first, there was silence in the studio and then you could hear a harried director shouting through talkback, 'Quiet, studio. *Blue Peter* eagle owl, take two.' Demonstrating his true professionalism, Purves began the interview again as if nothing had happened.

'An eagle owl is a very unusual pet, isn't it?' smiled Purves.

'And he's got a very unusual friend, too,' joked the owner. 'It's a mouse, but he can't be with us today . . .'

THE BITER BIT

WANTED: DEAD OR ALIVE (1958–61)

It's difficult to imagine Steve McQueen anywhere but on the big screen, but, like so many postwar tough-guy actors, the epitome of cool first paid his dues on television.

Appearing in 117 straight episodes, McQueen played bounty hunter Josh Randall in America's Old West and, at the same time, staked his claim for Hollywood stardom.

Scheduled on Saturday nights after *Perry Mason* and directly opposite established crooner Perry Como, the show, featuring McQueen and his trusty sidekick – a sawn-off carbine nicknamed 'Mare's Leg – soon blitzed the ratings.

However, the less attractive aspects of that mix of perfectionism and insouciance, which would later so endear him to cinema audiences, soon came to the fore. He fired three stuntmen – two because they had the wrong look, a third because he'd apparently teased McQueen about his name – on the very first day of shooting.

The 28-year-old star also had a decidedly ambivalent attitude towards the show's sponsors, Viceroy cigarettes. McQueen's contract required him to appear as Josh from time to time to tout the brand. This he usually did with a lack of enthusiasm bordering on insolence. And it wasn't as though he could plead being a nonsmoker. In fact, to strain relations still further, he'd further infuriate the Viceroy suits by flamboyantly smoking a rival brand.

McQueen wasn't the only ornery character on the show. His jet-black bronco Ringo started out with almost as much attitude as its rider. On one occasion, McQueen was rehearsing with another actor when Ringo first head-butted him and then reared up and stamped on his back.

As McQueen spun round, Ringo prepared to bite him. The actor cocked back his fist, slapped the horse then hurled his script in the air and, as the nag snapped its halter, he ran for his life. After that initial spat, the pair seemed to get on famously.

DEATH ON THE TUBE
UNDERGROUND (1958)

Forgetting your lines or tripping over the scenery weren't the only hazards of live television. In the case of the 33-year-old actor Gareth Jones, it was terminal.

Jones was part of a small cast, including Andrew Cruickshank, Peter Bowles and Donald Houston, in this tense *Armchair Theatre* drama, directed by Ted Kotcheff, about some survivors of an atom-bomb blast on London who take refuge in the Tube.

After rehearsals in London, cast and crew moved to studios in Birmingham, where an elaborate tunnel set had been constructed, complete with masses of rubble.

Jones was playing a character with heart trouble and had to take pills during the course of the unfolding action. Transmission got under way, and some of the actors were gathered talking on camera as they awaited the arrival of Jones's character.

Peter Bowles recalled, 'We could see him coming towards us and he was going to arrive on cue, but we saw him drop . . . We had no idea what had happened, but he certainly wasn't coming our way. We could see people tending to him.

'The actors, including me, started making up lines: "I'm sure if so-and-so were here he would say . . ." Then they stopped the show for the adverts and I always remember Ted Kotcheff coming onto the floor and shouting, "What the hell is going on?"

'We were told that the actor had fallen and hurt himself, whereas in fact they knew he was dead. He had had [like his character was due to do later in the play] a heart attack. It was dreadful.

'He was a very close friend of Donald Houston's and it became quite apparent after the show that, if they had told us he was dead, Donald would not have been able to continue. He was in a terrible state.'

On TV, as with the theatre, the show must go on.

41

CHANGE OF IMAGE
THE THIRD MAN (1959–62)

Voted in 1999, on the fiftieth anniversary of its first release, Greatest British Film of the Century, Carol Reed's peerless movie featured a memorable character called Harry Lime.

As originated and then scripted by Graham Greene, the film saw the charming but murderous Lime stalking the darker corners of postwar occupied Vienna. Among his various scams was a penicillin racket leading to the deaths of the vulnerable children in the city hospital. So fans of the film must have been a bit surprised when the title and the character – who had been shot to death in the Vienna sewers – re-emerged ten years later in a half-hour thriller format, which lasted 77 episodes.

This time round, Lime, played by suave Michael Rennie, was the hero, an art expert, ladies' man and part-time sleuth, still operating – perhaps for old time's sake – out of Vienna. Oh, yes, they also used Anton Karas's famous zither music just to complete the confusion.

TEARS FOR FEARS
FACE TO FACE (1959–62)

Reality TV was perhaps never more real than this head-to-head interrogation of celebrities conducted, generally live on a harshly lit set at the BBC, by stern-faced (although only the back of his head was usually seen in the programme) journalist John (later Lord) Freeman.

In its three years – a Mark II was conducted in the 1990s by Jeremy Isaacs – Freeman grilled some 35 interviewees, ranging from artists, philosophers and actors to the odd King (as in Martin Luther) and Hussein of Jordan.

Oddly, the most memorable has to be with someone who was simply famous for being famous – the unlikeliest TV celeb of his day, Gilbert Harding.

Harding, a former schoolmaster and policeman, shot to fame as a chairman and quizmaster on radio and television game shows such as *Round Britain Quiz, Twenty Questions* and *What's My Line?*, not to mention as a guest artist playing 'Himself' in various British films.

Plump, middle-aged, bespectacled and sporting a fierce moustache, Harding displayed a stock-in-trade that included bad temper and often outright rudeness. To his legion of admirers, however, he was simply 'well 'ard' before we knew the expression.

So imagine a nation's surprise – amazingly more than 4 million regularly tuned in for the programme – when Harding broke down in tears.

'Now,' asked Freeman, 'was your mother, who is still alive—'

'She's not. She's dead,' replied Harding.

Unaware that Harding's mother had died, Freeman persisted with a maternal line of questions. 'I beg your pardon. Was your mother a refuge from stern discipline?' And on he went until, 'Is there any truth in the notion I have in the back of my mind that it is this particularly deep relationship that you obviously had with your mother which has made it impossible so far for you to marry?'

Just eight weeks later, Harding died outside Broadcasting House after recording a radio programme. He was 53.

HAVING A GO

NO HIDING PLACE (1959–67)

While homely PC George Dixon successfully pounded his beat on the BBC, snuff-taking Detective Chief Superintendent Tom Lockhart was ITV's most popular home-grown cop.

Many of the 230 episodes were transmitted live, which meant quite a script-learning load for lead actor Raymond Francis. So, as many other actors in weekly dramas did at the time, he'd hide his lines on various parts of the set.

On one occasion a cameraman spotted one of the cribs in a desk drawer. The 'Super' would inch it open and glance down to a useful reminder. However, while Francis was away in Makeup, the card was removed and replaced with another.

The scene was under way and as Lockhart now looked down he read, 'You will dry now.' Which the normally unflappable lawman duly did.

The treatment once meted out to one of his sergeant sidekicks was altogether more spontaneous. Three policemen – two uniformed and DS Perryman (Mike McStay) – were being filmed chasing a villain on a street by the Embankment.

A passer-by, simply seeing the plainclothesman ahead of the two pursuing uniforms, decided to have go and halted McStay in his tracks with a smart blow of his silver-knobbed cane. Next stop for the DS was Charing Cross Hospital.

Incidentally, *No Hiding Place* was one of the very early examples of people power (see *Cagney & Lacey* on page 169). Taken off in 1965, it was quickly restored to the box for another two years following a public outcry.

THE 1960s

CLOWNING IN THE STREETS
IT'S A SQUARE WORLD (1960–64)

The gently anarchic mastermind behind this inventive BBC comedy series was Anglo-Peruvian Michael Bentine, a founder member of the Goons.

Its diet of weird and wonderful visual gags often took the form of outdoor hoaxes, which, however uproarious to TV viewers, never really seemed to faze the general public.

'The Russian Expedition to climb Woolwich Rubbish Dump' had a band of explorers disembarking from Captain Scott's ship *Discovery*, proceeding, roped together, along the Embankment on skis (with ball-bearings underneath), before crossing the road and disappearing down into the Tube. Without a blink from passers-by, Bentine recalled.

Then there was, 'Sinking the Houses of Parliament with a Chinese war junk', in which, from a full-sized replica of the aforementioned vessel, our venerable seat of government was bombarded with polystyrene cannon balls.

The programme ended with a model of the House of Commons sinking beneath the Thames with the caption, 'You have been watching a party political broadcast on behalf of the British people.' 'Ho-hum' was the reaction of people walking across Westminster and Lambeth bridges at the time.

The following may be apocryphal, but it's said that on the occasion when stocking-masked crooks raided the BBC accounts department at TV Centre before racing off in their stolen Jaguar, the security guards queried, 'When is the programme going to be on, Mr Bentine?'

JURASSIC PUFFS
THE FLINTSTONES (1960–66)

Chances are that a 21st-century cartoon wouldn't allow itself to be associated with cigarettes. But back at the beginning of the more laid-back sixties, when *The Flintstones* first started its run, the world's first 'primetime animated show' was more than happy to take money off Big Tobacco, and the series was initially sponsored by Winston cigarettes.

Since they didn't have cigarettes during prehistoric times, the sponsors had to eschew spots during the actual programme, but that didn't stop them making sure the stars didn't shirk their commercial responsibilities.

Unfortunately for Fred and Barney, they weren't able to say no, which led to the incredible adverts that aired at the end of the show featuring them heading out for a smoke while Wilma and Betty did the housework.

Looking back now, the black-and-white ads were offensive (though probably accurate) on a number of levels, not least because they showed the guys lazily sitting around while the wives vacuumed the cave and then mowed the lawn around the men's feet as they relaxed outside with a Winston.

Remarking on their distinctive filter and proclaiming that 'Winston tastes good, like a cigarette should', the ads subsequently came come in for criticism, since the show was broadcast at 8.30 in the evening, leading many people to believe that the tobacco company was deliberately targeting teen smokers.

By 1964, the US surgeon-general had declared cigarettes bad for your health, and Winston made way for Welch's Grape Juice. This was apparently because Wilma fell pregnant with Pebbles and it would have been *really* inappropriate for a tobacco company to sponsor a show with a baby in it, even if it *was* aimed at an 'adult' audience.

Even so, the Internet still showcases Fred and Barney's fag break and rarely have such lovable cartoon characters seemed so sinister.

48

BEYOND OUR KEN

CORONATION STREET (1960–)

When Tony Warren dreamed up his twice-weekly drama of life in a Northern working-class street he thought of calling it 'Florizel Street', until someone suggested that 'Florizel' sounded like a lavatory cleaning product.

No one could have imagined then that the series would endure for over 45 years; fewer still would have guessed that fresh-faced university graduate Ken Barlow would remain ever present on screen in that time.

William Roache, an improbably well-preserved 72 in real life (seven years older, incidentally, than Ken) has enjoyed a longer association with this one character than many actors enjoy with the profession as a whole. And that has been a little problematic at times, not least when public and critics confuse the actor with the man he plays. This led to a bitter libel action in 1991 that left the actor bankrupt, despite his winning the case.

Roache sued the *Sun* for suggesting he was as boring as his character, together with the more serious charge that he was hated by his colleagues on the programme. The strain of the trial took a physical toll as well as a financial one as Roache suffered a burst ulcer during the long-running case.

But it did demonstrate once and for all the façade of soapland rivalries when Ken Barlow's bitterest foe, Mike Baldwin (a.k.a. Johnny Briggs), took the stand to defend the good name of a man he was proud, in real life, to call a friend.

CARTOON CAPER

TOP CAT (1961–62)

From those prolific animators Hanna-Barbera came this well-loved children's cartoon. Their earlier hit, *The Flintstones*, consciously took an existing live-action TV sitcom success, *The Honeymooners*, as its inspiration.

But, according to Joseph Barbera, any similarities between *TC* and *Sergeant Bilko* were entirely coincidental. And this despite the presence in the voice cast of Maurice Gosfield, who had played the gormless Private Doberman, habitual foil to the sharp-tongued Bilko's scheming.

The shows followed a familiar pattern, though, with the 'indisputable leader of the gang' always looking for a fresh angle for him and his crew to make a few bucks, which frequently meant pulling one over on the hapless Officer Dibble.

However, a generation of British children grew up confused by the jarring disparity between the UK title of the show, *Boss Cat*, and the credit sequence plus theme song that flatly contradicted it.

The reason for this was the strict rules on advertising in place at the time. Top Cat was the brand name of an existing cat food, and any implied endorsement of the product was taboo. So the title was clumsily changed, and children throughout the land were left scratching their heads.

RACE WARS

STRAIGHTAWAY (1961–62)

As titles go, this handle on an American adventure series about a pair of car-racing nuts has to be one of the more bland and uninviting.

But that's just what the programme's sponsors, the Ford Motor Company, craved. Originally it was going to be called . . . yes, *The Racers*, which seemed perfectly to encapsulate the speedy ambitions of designer Scott Ross (Brian Kelly) and mechanic Clipper Hamilton (John Ashley).

That would have suited racing lovers Autolite, the spark plug people, who were originally going to sponsor the show.

However, between committing to the series and the debut on network TV, Autolite were bought out by Ford, who believed safety was the first priority.

Not only did they demand a change of title – Straightaway (yawn!) is the name of Scott and Clipper's garage – but the racing scenes in the ten completed episodes had to be excised before transmission.

FIST OF FURY

THE DICKIE VALENTINE SHOW (1961)

The comedian Bob Monkhouse had just finished his final rehearsal for a six-minute spot on the popular crooner's show and was heading back to his dressing room.

Suddenly, out of the studio corridor shadows, a man leaped forwards and punched Monkhouse in the face. It was the saxophonist husband of vocalist Jill Day, who suspected the comic of having more than just a working relationship with his beautiful wife.

With just forty minutes to go to transmission, Monkhouse's face was pumping blood exacerbated by the fact his left lower canine tooth was stuck through his bottom lip. The studio nurse was hastily summoned and with a mixture of special pink plaster and transparent tubing managed to patch him up enough to allow him to go out before the cameras. With the left side of his face a mess, Monkhouse had to deliver his funny-man routine entirely in profile as he, basically, addressed a wall.

If he'd had to turn the other way, it might have been even more distracting, for he would have been looking directly into the face of Day's angry musician spouse.

BEDSIDE MANNERS
DR KILDARE (1961–66)

A giant star of silent cinema in the twenties before being rediscovered in the fifties after her triumphant turn in *Sunset Boulevard*, Gloria Swanson later bought an old-school sensibility to the world of episodic television.

Take her first day on the set of this medical pot boiler in which she played – no stretch here – a great and self-centred movie star confined to bed at Blair General, where she proceeded to drive everyone mad with her demands.

After her second rehearsal of a scene in which she was very much centre stage with that nice young Dr Kildare (Richard Chamberlain) doing his best bedside manner, she suddenly barked, 'Hilda, Hilda, where's my breakfast?'

At that, her real-life maid rushed onto the set carrying a large tray of morning tucker, which Swanson, oblivious of the conveyor-belt nature of TV, then wolfed down with enormous relish as the rest of the budget-and-schedule-conscious cast and crew stood around blinking. This little tableau was repeated every day.

Finally, it came to the day when her character was due to leave hospital and it required her to drop by a young friend's room only to discover the kid was dying. Cue for huge emotion delivered with huge aplomb as Swanson broke down and wept copiously.

As her makeup was being repaired, the director said to her, 'OK, let's shoot it!' Still recovering, Swanson jerked round, saying, 'What do you mean, "shoot it"? We've just shot it.' Thinking that what had been the final rehearsal was a take, the old girl had given her all.

'OI'LL GIVE IT FOIVE'

THANK YOUR LUCKY STARS (1961–66)

Little could Black Country schoolgirl Janice Nicholls have known that a Saturday visit to Birmingham with her pal Margaret to watch a recording of ITV's high-profile weekly pop show would eventually lead to stardom in her own right.

TYLS trawled in all the big stars of the day to mime to their records. The programme was also planning to introduce a 'Spin-A-Disc' segment (a blatant rip-off of the BBC's *Juke Box Jury*) in which celebs and local teenagers would opine on the latest record releases and give a score out of five.

Janice was sitting in the audience when that week's frontman Brian Matthew asked if any of the youngsters wanted to audition for 'Spin-A-Disc'. When she got home, she wrote in and was, she relates, 'amazed' when she received a telegram inviting her to audition.

The following Sunday, sixteen-year-old Janice went back to ABC's Aston studios, where the kids were called in three at a time and played various records. The first was Brenda Lee's 'Speak To Me Pretty'. Janice recalls, 'I liked it very much and gave it five.' Except the way she said it in her native Brummie, it sounded more like, 'Oi'll give it foive.'

The producer gave her the usual 'thank you, we'll let you know . . .' Two days later, another telegram arrived to tell her she'd been successful in her audition, inviting her to appear on the programme the following week.

This would be the first of the string of appearances over the next three years, at three guineas a time. Not to mention the unwitting launch of an enduring catchphrase that would be remembered long after Janice actually rubbed shoulders with the likes of the Beatles, Gene Pitney, Billy Fury, Mark Wynter, Jimmy Savile and Ketty Lester.

STRIKE IT LUCKY
THE AVENGERS (1961–69)

From the mid- to the late sixties, *The Avengers* was the epitome of deliciously Brit cool and camp as bowler-hatted, umbrella-wielding secret agent John Steed (Patrick Macnee) took on a series of ever more outrageous villains.

But before the kind of trademark action, which marked out the show as, surely, the telefantasy of the decade were altogether more mundane beginnings.

In fact, had it not been for an actors' strike, which delayed the first series in mid-run, we might never have enjoyed the exploits of Steed and his succession of gorgeous, lethal and often provocatively clothed sidekicks. These were, most famously, Cathy Gale, Emma Peel – which you can read as M Appeal ('M' for 'man') – and Tara King (Honor Blackman, Diana Rigg and Linda Thorson).

It all really started way before the sixties began to swing with a 1960 series called, innocuously, *Police Surgeon*, in which Ian Hendry played Dr Geoffrey Brent.

A year later, they decided to give Hendry's character a new name, Dr David Keel, in a new spin-off series, which opened with the young medic out to avenge the death of his girlfriend at the hands of a drugs ring. In desperation he approached British Intelligence for help. Which is how the suave if mysterious Steed first entered the picture.

The Avengers often went out live on Saturday nights, until that first season in 1961 was halted by the strike, at which point Hendry, poised on the cusp of a budding film career, decided to quit the series.

Since Hendry was at least the nominal star, that might have been curtains for the concept. However, with a few unfilmed scripts still about, co-creator/producer Leonard White decided to press on, moved Steed centre stage and, after the odd casting hiccup, then signed up Honor Blackman. Now the avenging could begin in earnest.

YANKEE DOODLE DANDY
THE VIRGINIAN (1962–71)

Written at the turn of the century, Owen Wister's eponymous 'man's gotta do' Western novel had been filmed three times – as a 1914 silent, then with Gary Cooper in 1929, and in 1946, starring Joel McCrea – when telly inevitably came calling.

The producers signed up twentysomething actor James Drury to play the man with no name, casting him, according to *The Complete Directory of Prime Time Network and Cable TV Shows*, 'as a Western dandy replete with shiny hunting boots, skin-tight pants, lace cuffs and a tiny pistol'.

When this pilot episode, made in the late 1950s, failed to sell, they went back to the drawing board and next time round decided to eschew 'the foppish accoutrements'.

The result was, at ninety minutes per episode for nine years, quite literally one of television's longest-running horse operas.

IT'S A KNOCKOUT
THAT WAS THE WEEK THAT WAS (1962–63)

The BBC's trail-blazing late-night live Saturday satire show, hosted by a youthful-looking David Frost, was an instant sensation, blending sketches, song and sacred-cow slaughter.

The most unlikely member of a regular cast of comedians, actors and singers was the diminutive columnist/critic Bernard Levin – he of the corkscrew hairstyle. Perched on a stool, he would deliver some venomous tirade-of-the-week straight to camera.

Levin soon became a popular hate figure and a target for abuse in rival newspapers. It's even said that as he entered the TV studio he'd be spat upon by enraged members of the public.

Perhaps it comes as no great surprise to learn that one night there was even more direct action taken against the man – described unwisely by a tired and emotional Terry-Thomas on the contemporaneous panel show *What's My Line?* as 'a sort of kosher poor man's Billy Graham' – on *TW3*.

Out of the audience one night arose tall, dignified The Hon. Desmond Leslie, ex-RAF pilot, UFO expert and sometime filmmaker. Angered by something Levin had written elsewhere about his actress wife in her one-woman show, Leslie strode onto the set, stated his case and then, unceremoniously, decked the little fella before TV millions.

STRICTLY FOR THE BIRD

ANIMAL MAGIC (1962–83)

'Never work with animals or children' goes the saying. Difficult advice for Johnny Morris to follow as host of this popular teatime wildlife show.

Morris was a legend, broadcasting fascinating reports from Bristol Zoo and doing his own stunts (such as brushing a crocodile's teeth). He became so associated with the zoo that some visitors were dismayed when they found out he didn't actually work there. Often, the zoo workers just told them it was his day off.

One of the problems with making the show at the beginning was that it went out live, with Morris conducting one interview with zookeeper and friend Donald Packham on the ground as they held down a tapir.

Packham recalls the show's producers asking him to bring one of the most temperamental animals in the zoo onto a live show – a rather foul-mouthed (-beaked?) African macaw called Audrey. Although warned against it, the producers insisted and Audrey duly made her way to the BBC studio. There was not a peep out of her until Morris began to sign off, when she suddenly screeched 'Bollocks!'

'She had a very colourful vocabulary,' says Packham. As the show was live, there was nothing they could do about it, other than burst out laughing.

TASTE OF SWEDE

THE SAINT (1962–69)

James Bond 007 had his Aston Martin, while Simon Templar, alias the Saint, roared around in a white two-seater Volvo P1800 coupé with the number plate ST1.

For such an English creation, first dreamed up by the author Leslie Charteris in 1929, it surely seemed a bit odd that he should be driving such a quintessentially Swedish roadster.

It turns out that producers of the TV series, starring Roger Moore, had actually first approached Jaguar Cars about providing an E-Type to 'co-star' as the haloed hero's transport. It would be great free advertising, they insisted.

Unveiled a year before at the Geneva Motor Show, the sleek beast with a top speed of 150 m.p.h. was an overnight sensation. And, no, replied the Jaguar people, we don't need any plugs, free or otherwise.

So *The Saint*'s minders moved on to Volvo, nursing the *second* most eye-catching new sports car. The manufacturers were thrilled and, within a week, an ivory-coloured model was flown in from Stockholm to become Templar's almost constant companion over the next seven years.

HALLS OF SHAME

UNIVERSITY CHALLENGE (1962–87; 1994–)

In what must surely Cambridge's most ignominious moment since the venerable institution was once exposed as a nest of spies, step forward the girls of New Hall College.

In December 1997, Sarah Davies (studying Natural Sciences), Rosie Shaw (Philosophy), Rachel Coleman (Natural Sciences) and Abigail Bradley (Natural Sciences) managed to muster only a measly 35 points against Nottingham University in front of millions of BBC2 viewers. This was a record low for the competition, beating the forty points previously registered by Birkbeck College against Manchester University.

Even getting off the mark was an achievement – at one point wrong answers put New Hall on minus fifteen. Halfway through the thirty-minute show they had clawed their way back to zero. With three minutes to go, New Hall reached thirty, only for five points to be deducted when team captain Sarah Davies answered incorrectly.

With host Jeremy Paxman, a Cambridge graduate, desperately urging them to salvage 'some honour', in the final two minutes, New Hall won cheers and applause from the audience when they reached 35. Paxman tried to console the team – by saying they were perhaps just unlucky.

The team, who beat Nottingham in a warm-up competition, put their massive defeat down to stage fright. Team member Rachel Coleman, who hoped to be an astronaut, insisted that they were all very bright: 'It's not that we didn't know the answers. We were not as well practised and confident as the others. It's not that we're thick, we were just slow.' Just for the record, Nottingham amassed a mighty 335 points.

MARATHON MAN

THE FUGITIVE (1963–67)

During the mid-sixties, walls all over Britain bore the cryptic legend KIMBLE IS INNOCENT. It was part of the extraordinary success of a compelling drama series, which hooked viewers here and in the States.

Starring lugubrious David Janssen as Dr Richard Kimble, falsely accused of murdering his wife, TV's longest-running manhunt began in black and white and ended, in colour, 120 shows later, in autumn 1967, when 16 million British viewers tuned in to discover just who *had* killed the good doctor's missus.

It was inspired by Victor Hugo's *Les Misérables*, and the 'master stroke', according to Canadian actor Barry Morse, who played Kimble's relentless pursuer, Lieutenant Philip Gerard, 'was to create a show that had to have an ending – eventually. So it was always compulsively watchable.'

However, the show, Morse once told one of the authors, was not without its problems. After the pilot episode, for example, it was suddenly realised that the initial setting of Wisconsin was technically incorrect.

'Dr Kimble is on his way to the death cell in that state when he escapes from a train crash. Then someone remembered that Wisconsin no longer carried the death penalty. So the originating story had to be swiftly relocated to a "death" state, Indiana. And, if you carefully watched the opening sequence of each episode, you'll have noticed that the train from which Kimble escapes had "Chemin de Fer" written on the side. They had unfortunately used a French train in a stock shot.'

Four years into the series, it finally came time for the Great Resolution. Was Dr Kimble really innocent of his wife's murder? What had the one-armed man (Bill Raisch) been doing in the vicinity of the house on the night of the killing? And was it more than just duty that had spurred on the dogged lawman, Lieutenant Gerard?

Morse explained, 'We used to have all kinds of joke endings planned. Our favourite was that the camera would pan slowly toward the lighted window of a large house, pass right through and into the bedroom.

'There, it would focus on the face of a woman lying in bed next to David Janssen. She would then turn to him and say, "Darling, do you know, I've just had this most terrible dream . . ."'

THE EXTERMINATORS

DOCTOR WHO (1963–89; TV MOVIE 1996; 2005–)

Generations of children grew up watching TV from behind the sofa as various incarnations of the nation's favourite Time Lord were menaced by the worst kind of aliens the BBC's designers and special-effects department could muster inexpensively.

Most absurd of them all and yet, ironically, most enduringly popular were, of course, the Daleks, dreamed up by scriptwriter Terry Nation.

Blurting 'Ex-ter-min-ate! Ex-ter-min-ate!', these strange, tinny creations – a kind of malevolent ancestor to that nice R2D2 in a much later sci-fi opera – first arrived in Episode Five thanks to the ingenuity of designer Ray Cusick.

Getting them actually to move about and appear menacing was the job of the visual effects designer Jack Kine and his team. Each Dalek – and there were six designed at the outset – had an actor inside, sitting on a stool that had three castors with a little skirt round that hid everything.

Then, as Kine once explained, 'The actor sat wearing plimsolls, and it was like pushing yourself around on a typist's stool. Then, of course, you had the two arms, and there were flashing lights which, would you believe, were really the indicator lights off the old Morris Eight.

'I remember looking at it and thinking, This'll never take off. But, once one of the actors got inside, the things took on a life of their own.'

Briefly furious about the instant success of the Daleks was the show's creator, Sydney Newman, who at the outset had ordered absolutely 'no BEMs' (bug-eyed monsters). Try telling that to the *Doctor Who* fanbase.

IN THE DRINK
DINNER FOR ONE (1963–)

We may have the Queen's Christmas message, but German television viewers wouldn't watch anything but British comedian Freddie Frinton's drunk act every Yuletide.

Starting in the year that President Kennedy was assassinated, an eighteen-minute black-and-white comedy short film called *Dinner for One*, with Frinton and veteran British actress May Warden, has been served up every Christmas on German TV without fail.

Long forgotten here, Frinton – who once co-starred with Thora Hird in a BBC sitcom, *Meet the Wife* – remains a cult figure in Germany for his annual role as James the butler, serving up dinner and mostly drinks (which he then consumes) to his befuddled mistress's long-deceased friends.

Sadly, Frinton isn't still around to enjoy his popularity in the land of the lederhosen. He died in 1968, three weeks before *Dinner for One* was due to be reshot in colour.

THANK YOU FOR THE MUSIC
TOP OF THE POPS (1964–)

For many years *the* place for British youngsters to see their pop heroes perform on television, this showcase for chart hits also enjoyed a few lows in a forty-year span. And that's not counting some very strange miming.

One of the most frequently recalled bloopers had Dexy's Midnight Runners performing their 1982 hit 'Jackie Wilson Said' against a huge backdrop photograph of the rotund darts player Jocky Wilson rather than the svelte soul star quoted in their song. But this has been accounted for as a witty visual pun on the part of the Dexy's lead singer Kevin Rowland.

What was almost christened *The Teen and Twenty Record Club* kicked off with an impressive line-up that included live contributions from the Rolling Stones and Dusty Springfield, with a film of the Beatles' Number One 'I Want To Hold Your Hand'.

Fashions have come and gone; Pan's People have sadly left the stage, replaced but never bettered by Ruby Flipper and Legs & Co.; and the dominance of MTV from the 1980s onwards changed the landscape of music programmes for ever.

But still the ego-driven antics of some guests have made for fun, such as the time Cliff Richard was unexpectedly bombarded with wigs from the BBC's props department courtesy of the Who's entourage; or reported diva-like antics from American actress/singers whose expectations went some way beyond the usual standards of BBC hospitality.

Then there was the time Rod Stewart performed 'Maggie May' less than seriously, kicking a football across the set, with the late DJ John Peel pretending to play the mandolin in the background.

Once the bellwether of musical taste, *TOTP* has also had to contend with risqué lyrics such as those in Frankie Goes To Hollywood's 'Relax', bizarre pop videos and the difficulties posed by bands who were incapable of miming to their own songs.

The ambient-music duo the Orb dealt with this nicely by playing chess for three minutes rather than maintaining the charade of a live performance that was nothing of the sort.

CASTAWAY QUERY

GILLIGAN'S ISLAND (1964–67)

Madonna, Prince, Topol . . . Those are the stars important enough to have only one name. And now you can add Gilligan to the list.

That's Gilligan from this hit American sitcom, starring Bob Denver as the titular member of a hapless group of stereotypes shipwrecked on a desert island.

Ever since the team first got washed up on their tropical prison, debate has raged about Gilligan's full name: is that his first name or surname? After all, the Skipper is called Jonas Grumby, the Professor was Roy Hinkley, and a later episode even revealed that 'Lovey' Howell was actually called Eunice.

But poor old Gilligan, the hero of the show, had but a single moniker. Or did he? In 1992, CBS finally broadcast the lost 'original' pilot episode, as the series had had to reshoot its pilot, because they changed various actors and ideas (thus, in 1964, audiences had actually seen the second show ever produced).

Media speculation stirred up gossip that Gilligan was actually called Willy Gilligan and *TV Guide* even announced that it had found an early press release confirming it. However, it became apparent, in true media fashion, that a number of truths had got mixed up. Being perpetuated on the Internet was that Willy was Gilligan's first name and that you heard it used only once – on the original pilot show during a radio broadcast about the group's island fate. This is, in fact, not true. In the original pilot, some explanation was given as to how such a motley crew came together on the boat that was eventually shipwrecked.

The first regularly broadcast episode, however, on 26 September 1964, started with the group already stuck on the island. And so the programme makers came up with the radio broadcast as a way to give some 'back story' to the characters. We hear that Thurston Howell III was 'one of the world's wealthiest men' and that Ginger (a sexy movie star) 'boarded the boat after a nightclub singing engagement'. But the broadcast also said that the crew 'included a young first mate called Gilligan' – nothing more.

Where the confusion may have arisen is that there *is* knowledge that, during the original brainstorming for the show, its creator Sherwood Schwartz did consider calling him Willy Gilligan and that there is material proving it. But it didn't make it into the show.

Similarly, Schwartz jokes that every time he sees Denver they argue about the true designation of their most famous character. He says that Denver is convinced Gilligan is his first name, while Schwartz propagates the surname theory. 'He doesn't want to discuss it. He insists the name is Gilligan.'

And the answer? Well, it's probably best just to pick a story and stick with it. After all, there is a suggestion that Gilligan was once Willy Gilligan, but, even if you have watched every episode of the series, there is no on-screen proof. And let's face it: if the creator of the character and the man that played him can't make up their minds, what chance do the rest of us have?

FADE TO BLACK
THE LAUNCH OF BBC2 (1964)

The arrival of the UK's first new TV channel for nearly a decade was, rightly, a cause of huge excitement. On 20 April 1964, the final countdown to a night of 'music, comedy and celebratory fireworks' began in earnest.

But, as last-minute rehearsals were drawing to an end, a fire at Battersea Power Station suddenly plunged Television Centre into turmoil. The resulting blackout across much of west London meant that all that was about to glitter became steadfastly dark instead.

Instead of treating new viewers to the fresh face of the presenter Denis Tuohy 'trailing' the delights of *Kiss Me Kate*, due on in half an hour or so, the channel quickly switched to a short news bulletin from Alexandra Palace, still blackout-free in north London.

But the problems persisted, as only lip readers would have understood the news reader Gerald Priestland, who remained resolutely soundless for the first two and a half minutes of his newscast.

As if missing out on a Cole Porter musical weren't bad enough, other postponed treats included 'Arkady Raikin: the Soviet Union's top comedian', those fireworks from Southend pier and, rumour has it, a boxing kangaroo, who was, apparently, trapped in a lift with his increasingly nervous BBC 'minder' when the power went off.

What the viewers actually got was a less-than-riveting evening consisting of test cards reading 'BBC will follow shortly' punctuated with regular apologies.

So what was BBC2's first scheduled programme actually to get aired? At 11 a.m. the following day, *Play School* began what would be a 24-year run in the vanguard of tots' television.

SEXY SETS

HOGAN'S HEROES (1965–71)

You couldn't get much more anodyne than this amiable American sitcom. At least, it was anodyne on screen; off screen, it was a whole different ball game.

The show followed Colonel Hogan (Bob Crane) as he led a motley crew of PoWs in a German camp during World War Two. They got up to all sorts of wacky schemes and tried to avoid the wrath of the bumbling Nazi commandant Colonel Klink (played by Werner – son of Otto – Klemperer).

But while Crane's Hogan was a knockabout, all-American nice guy, his real life was anything but. After meeting technical whiz John Carpenter, Crane set out on a journey of sexual self-discovery, which led to his self-taping hundreds of adulterous sexual encounters.

Celebrity seemed to bring out the dark side in Crane and his shenanigans came to an ignominious end when he was found murdered in a hotel room. Although Carpenter was tried for the murder, he was acquitted. The real killer has never been found.

But Crane's tapes were not the only undercover sexual activity on the set of *Hogan's Heroes*. The tasteless, badly made, but decidedly cult S&M sexploitation flick *Ilsa: She-Wolf of the SS* (in which a sadistic female Nazi officer carried out evil sex experiments and castrations) was actually filmed on the disused sets of the CBS series in nine days, reportedly without the permission of the studio.

Of course, if the studio had known of their star's off-screen proclivities, they might have been more forgiving about a movie in which the film's male lead uses his sexual prowess to trick Ilsa into letting him tie her to a bed so that he can lead an uprising against the SS guards.

THE BIG BANG
THE WAR GAME (1965)

Nowadays, we are positively blasé about seeing violence and terror on our television screens, but in the mid-1960s things were a little different. That was, until a BBC assistant producer turned director, Peter Watkins, decided to turn the documentary format on its head with *The War Game*. A fifty-minute drama-documentary in stark black and white, it charted a typical British city during and after a nuclear attack.

Part interview, part acting, it featured Michael Aspel, then a news anchorman, talking us through the chaos and had a cast of mostly nonprofessional actors (as well as an uncredited Kathy Staff before she became *Last of the Summer Wine*'s Nora Batty) to add authenticity. However, deeming it shocking and brutal, the BBC yanked it from the schedule, saying it was too violent and potentially distressing to broadcast.

Conspiracy theorists suggest that the actual reason for the ban was that it criticised Civil Defence tactics and argued that Britain was not ready for such an attack. Some argued it was forced off the air by the government.

Watkins went on to release it in cinemas and the film won both a BAFTA (for Short Film) and an Oscar (for Documentary Feature). It was finally televised in the UK twenty years later as part of the fortieth anniversary of the Hiroshima bombing.

However, Britain isn't the only one who tackled the nuclear issue. America – and Hollywood – had its say, too, but, unlike the BBC, broadcaster ABC made the American viewing public a little more aware. Broadcast on 20 November 1983, *The Day After* was a feature-length drama that dealt with the annihilation and subsequent aftermath of a typical Midwestern town by a nuclear bomb. It starred an ensemble cast including Jason Robards, JoBeth Williams and Steve Guttenberg (who thought it important enough to be credited as Steven Guttenberg).

It was shot in Lawrence, Kansas, ironically a town that would in theory not be affected by any politically motivated nuclear attack on America, since it was in the exact geographical centre of the United States.

Rather than surprise the public, as Watkins wanted to do, the US government was very concerned with ensuring people not be adversely affected by the programme. Meetings were held in school districts all over the country to decide how to handle the students after they had watched it, and during the broadcast there were freephone numbers set up to deal with frightened viewers.

Rumour has it that President Ronald Reagan even saw an advance copy and sent suggestions for a bunch of re-edits. And, because the government was worried that it might somehow upset the entente (un)cordiale with the Russians, it ensured that ABC agreed to let Secretary of State George P Shultz appear on the network to put forward the pro case for nuclear armament.

As it turned out, despite a mammoth audience of more than 100 million Americans, no one was that adversely affected, and, while it is certainly a moving drama, many critics felt that the destruction was slightly watered down.

This may have been partly due to the fact that the programme makers were unable to get permission to use actual Defense Department footage of mushroom clouds and so had to recreate them by injecting oil into a water tank. Incidentally, this was remarkably similar to the way Steven Spielberg represented clouds being shifted by the alien spaceships in *Close Encounters of the Third Kind*.

Immediately after the show, ABC broadcast a live discussion between the antinuclear thinker Dr Carl Sagan and right-winger William F Buckley. It was during this discussion that Sagan coined the phrase 'nuclear winter'.

A year later, Britain bounced back with yet another glimpse of Armageddon in the shape of *Threads*, which was filmed in Sheffield. The council had actually designated the city a 'nuclear-free zone' but that didn't stop it from being flattened by a one-megaton Soviet bomb for the purposes of this extremely vivid BBC drama-documentary.

ENTENTE CORDIALE
THE MAGIC ROUNDABOUT (1965–77)

Le Manège Enchanté was a hit on French television in the early 1960s, a delightful stop-motion cartoon for children devised by Serge Danot and animated by Ivor Wood and his wife Josiane.

When the BBC were offered the rights they politely declined, deeming it 'charming' but 'difficult to dub into English'. Then someone had the bright idea of asking *Play School* presenter Eric Thompson to have a go at voicing it.

Thompson, father of the actresses Emma and Sophie and husband of Phyllida Law, did more than just that. He rescripted the existing episodes entirely, reimagining the adventures of Pollux the dog, Margot, Amboise and Zebedee into quirky little dramas featuring the distinct personalities of Dougal, Florence, Brian and – well – Zebedee.

Just as it was rumoured the Gallic original had a satirical French political subtext, the scuttlebutt this side of La Manche persisted that there was some kind of drug-related inner meaning to the translated characters and their daily stories.

This is probably as apocryphal as the dubious names often attributed to Captain Pugwash's crew. It only serves to prove the enormous adult audience these ostensibly child-oriented programmes achieved.

DUD AND PETE

NOT ONLY . . . BUT ALSO (1965–66; 1970)

. . . Or *The Dudley Moore Show Starring Not Only Dudley Moore But Also Peter Cook and John Lennon* was how the first programme in one of the BBC's most enduring of all comedy sketch show series was clumsily titled.

Actually, 'enduring' is perhaps not the best word for it because, thanks to a corporate blunder, the videotaped antics of Dud and Pete were mostly wiped. Luckily, some old shows were salvaged with material rescued from the archives of overseas TV companies to which the BBC had sold copies.

After John Lennon's guest appearance on the show – for which the Beatle earned a princely £15, barely covering the cost of a lost contact lens during recording – the title was subsequently amended to its better-known abbreviated version.

The pair seemed to get away with murder, especially when it came to bad language, using generous helpings of 'bloody' and 'bum' that would previously have been unthinkable at the Beeb. Cook was especially delighted when he could manage to sneak in some extra vulgarity. Like the time he was discussing a bottle of Châteauneuf-du-Pape and called it instead, Shat All Over the Carpet.

On one occasion, Moore was actually quite lucky to get away with his life. While shooting a scene on the Thames, the duo were sitting on a large board, suspended by four cables, which had to be lowered into the water. As the board hit the water, the cables went slack and one wrapped itself around Moore's shoulders and neck.

For a moment there was an horrific possibility that once the cable became taut again it could easily slice Moore's head off. In the event, it only gave him a glancing blow.

FOUR-LETTER FELLOW
BBC-3 (1965–66)

A successor to *That Was the Week That Was*, this late-night satire and discussion show would be long forgotten if it weren't for one broadcast-shattering moment on 13 November 1965. That's when the F-word was used for the first time on television – anywhere.

The perpetrator was the writer and critic Kenneth Tynan, who was discussing censorship with American author Mary McCarthy. Host Robert Robinson had asked Tynan whether he would allow a play showing sexual intercourse to be staged at the National Theatre (where he was dramaturge).

To which Tynan then replied, 'Oh I think so, certainly. I doubt if there are very many rational people in this world to whom the word "f***" is particularly diabolical or revolting or totally forbidden.'

Tynan hadn't warned anyone in advance, especially the programme's producer Ned Sherrin, about the use of *that* word. Yet, in response to the question, it seemed not just out of context but positively wilful. Later, Tynan would say that he would have used it in similar conversation with any group of grown-up people.

By that time, all hell had broken loose: the BBC switchboard was jammed, questions were asked in the House of Commons and, most ominous of all, the clean-up-TV campaigner Mary Whitehouse, who'd begun her campaign a year earlier, suggested that Tynan 'needed his bottom smacked'.

IT'S ONLY A PUPPET – NOT!

THUNDERBIRDS (1965–66)

Reality was hardly a prerequisite of this strangely popular futuristic marionette series, which combined brilliant modelwork and thrilling special effects with rather ropy puppetry and comic-strip dialogue. That seemingly irresistible blend, however, resulted in a cult following that continues nearly forty years after it ended production.

Creating special effects was difficult enough with models but for an episode vividly titled 'Attack of the Alligators' something more than just cleverly recycled bits of wood and plastic was clearly required.

Inspired by an old Bob Hope comedy-thriller set in a remote house up an alligator-infested river, the tale concerned giant reptiles attacking a group of scientists who'd developed a growth serum. Under the watchful gaze of their handler and an RSPCA minder, some alligators were duly trucked into the production company's studio on an industrial estate just off the A4 in Slough. Although these particular alligators weren't full-sized, they would certainly look suitably monstrous seen in scale on the puppet sets and effects stages.

Unfortunately, when they arrived in the studio, all they actually wanted to do was bask peacefully under the heat of the lights, which sometimes touched 130 degrees. However, when they actually decided to move around, they were not, unlike models, exactly predictable – as effects wizard Derek Meddings would nearly discover to his cost.

He once recalled, 'We were rehearsing a particular scene, and I was standing in a tank with one of the alligators on a short rope ready to pull it into shot, when it slipped its leash. My crew never saw me move as fast as I did to get out of the tank when I pulled the rope and realised the creature was free . . .'

OH GOD, IT'S FRIDAY!

MISSION: IMPOSSIBLE (1966–73; 1988–90)

The lighted fuse, the throbbing Lalo Schifrin-composed theme and then . . . 'Good morning, Mr Phelps. Your mission, should you decide to accept it, is [followed by specific details]. As always, should you or any member of your IM Force be caught or killed, the secretary will disavow any knowledge of your actions. This tape will self-destruct in five seconds.'

'Mr Phelps' was, of course, Jim Phelps, played by the silver-haired actor Peter Graves, who each week would then sort through various photographs (often friends of the producers) before settling on his usual team of nerveless operatives. They were played, principally, by Martin Landau, Barbara Bain, Greg Morris and Leonard Nimoy (after he'd finished with *Star Trek*'s Mr Spock).

But, before bland-faced Graves came to the party in 1967, the message would begin, 'Good Morning, Mr Briggs . . .' For the pilot episode and the first series, the Force's fearless leader was called Dan Briggs and played by intense actor Steven Hill, born Solomon Karansky.

The show's creator, Bruce Geller, had fought for and finally signed Hill, an Orthodox Jew who ate only kosher food and wore specially lined clothing. His contract stipulated that he wouldn't work on Jewish holidays and that he leave the set before sunset on Fridays.

Hill's religiosity caused minimum waves during filming of the pilot, but, once the series got under way in earnest, it became an increasing hindrance, especially as Fridays were the last workday for TV production, and most companies would shoot late to complete the schedule.

But a contract was a contract. Even his shoes and socks had to be kosher and were shipped in specially from the Big Apple. However, Hill's requirements and his general inflexibility finally proved too much even for the once-supportive Geller.

First his leading role began to get cut back and then he was the last to hear – via a paragraph in the trade paper, *Daily Variety* – that he was being replaced for the next series by Graves.

After being fired, Hill, a founder member of the Actors' Studio, quit showbiz to spend more time devoted to religion, writing and selling real estate. But the lure was too much and he came back to become one of Hollywood's most in-demand character actors in films such as *The Firm* and *Billy Bathgate*.

He also signed up for another long-running TV series, *Law & Order*, in which he played District Attorney Adam Schiff for ten years until 2000.

FACING REALITY

CATHY COME HOME (1966)

Television has the power to shock – often for the wrong reasons – but it too rarely manages to provide an effective 'wake-up call' to the authorities.

However, that was the worthwhile legacy of probably the best known of all dramas in the BBC's *Wednesday Play* slot. The aftermath (such as the founding of Shelter) of this fulminating story about contemporary homelessness was almost as dramatic as its subject matter.

No scene will be recalled more the final, terrible climax, in which Cathy (Carol White) and her two children (one played by the actress's own son, Stephen) were cruelly separated by social workers on Liverpool Street station.

If it seemed realistic for TV viewers, then it was even more so for passers-by at the time, who observed this domestic turmoil with mounting horror as director Ken Loach filmed it at the busy terminus starting at a discreet distance. The children's cries were for real, as were White's, whose hysteria, she'd admit, was authentic.

Forty years later, cinematographer Tony Imi, armed that afternoon with a handheld camera, told us, 'Being with her own child made it more harrowing for Carol, and, while we were shooting, one woman dived out of the crowd and started freaking out, which made Carol start to do the same.'

Loach has since explained that his pursuit of realism caused only temporary upset: 'The frame of the shot was only ten yards wide. OK, they [the children] were taken, but they stopped twelve yards away and were then allowed back to their mother. It wasn't as if they were taken off.'

KUNG-FU FIGHTING

BATMAN (1966–68)

Despite being criticised by hardcore comic fans for its comic slant and camp imagery, the Batman television series was a successful and lucrative show during its two years on the air on ABC.

Played here by Adam West as the Caped Crusader and Burt Ward as his sidekick Robin, the fictional pair began a tradition that would continue when the franchise hit the big screen – that of the big-name cameo performance.

Every star under the sun wanted a guest slot on the show and so it was when the stars of *The Green Hornet* (see *Kung Fu* on page 109), the other hit sixties superhero show, came to the set. Van Williams played the Hornet with Bruce Lee as his trusty sidekick, Kato.

Lee was well known for his physical trickery on set, kidding around, doing stunt kicks on members of the crew, even – as Adam West recalls – kicking cigarettes out of people's mouths as they stood in front of him. When Lee came to the *Batman* set, however, he was a different man – quiet and glowering.

West asked Williams whether this was normal. Williams replied nervously that it was the first time he had seen Lee like this. Even more scared was Burt Ward, who was scheduled to fight with Kato. Coincidentally, Ward knew Lee mildly as a laid-back sparring partner, but it was a different martial artist facing him, today and Ward didn't like it. As anyone who has watched Lee in action knows, once he gets going, it is difficult to stop him.

Ward asked Lee if he was OK, but Lee refused to reply and West recalls that Ward looked rather ill, and wondered whether he had done something to upset him. The director called them to the scene and the two actors faced up. Lee began to make motions around Ward's body, a look of pure hatred on his face. As he did so, he began to make frightening kung-fu noises.

Ward looked petrified and prepared for a kicking. Reaching a pinnacle of anger, Lee suddenly jumped back, stuck his tongue out, burst out laughing and shouted, 'Robin's a chicken!' As Robin himself might have said, 'Holy Thank God I'm Not Going To Get My Head Smashed In!'

TITLE FIGHT

HAWK (1966)

Burt Reynolds always prided himself on doing his own stunts and, as Iroquois Indian Lieutenant John Hawk of the NYPD working the night beat in the Big Apple, he had plenty of scope.

The problem was that they were beginning to run out of local stuntmen to match the star and his daredevil prowess. 'Bring me some guys who really know how to fight,' pleaded Reynolds.

Various contenders were paraded before him for inspection, including one whom he vaguely recognised. 'He's a hairdresser,' Reynolds was told, 'but he's a great fighter.'

The star laughed, dismissively, until he suddenly realised that the man was the former world welterweight boxing champion, Emile Griffith, and he'd actually been present at that infamous title bout four years earlier when Griffith's opponent, Benny Paret, took such a hammering that he later died.

Reynolds recalls, 'We did a few gags [stunts] together and he was a terrific fighter, but he taught me a great lesson: you never fight a professional fighter. If he sees an opening, he *will* hit you. It's instinct: too many years to unlearn.'

AURAL SEX APPEAL

STAR TREK (1966–69)

So familiar are Mr Spock's pointed ears and quizzical eyebrows that it is easy to forget just how strange a character he is. In fact this half-Vulcan, half-human character with his green blood and unemotional take on life could easily have turned out even odder.

Star Trek writer Samuel A Peeples recalls that Spock was originally conceived as 'a red-skinned creature with fiery eyes, who had a plate in the middle of his stomach. He didn't eat or drink, but he fed upon any form of energy that struck this plate in his stomach.'

The creator of the hit sci-fi series, Gene Roddenberry, confirms that Spock went through several evolutionary changes. 'I wanted Spock to look different and be different and to make a statement about being an outsider looking in.' As a result he considered casting a black man in the role or a dwarf, but finally chose Leonard Nimoy for his attractiveness.

Roddenberry's problems were not over at this point, though. Nimoy tried to get out of wearing the ears: 'The crew began chuckling and calling him "jackrabbit" and so on, and he finally started to get a little upset.'

Long after he had been persuaded to wear them, they still bothered him, not least because they were so painful to unglue after filming. Producer Robert Justman relates, 'He wanted less pain and so he came to me and said, "Bob, can we do something about those ears?" I thought for a bit and I said, "I know how. I know what we can do. I've got a surgeon friend who can operate and make your ears pointy and you'll have that for the length of a series, and at the end of that season we can go to the surgeon again, he can take your ears and put them back the way they were originally." And Leonard wanted this to happen so badly that he believed me – for a few seconds.'

There was just one consolation for the long-suffering actor. One day, a beautiful actress visited the set. 'I was in costume with all the makeup on when we were introduced,' remembers Nimoy. She said, "Oh, God, can I touch your ears?" That was the first indication I had that women might be attracted to this character.'

Unlikely as it might seem, the hard-to-cast, Satanic-looking alien had become an overnight sex sensation.

EYE OF THE TIGER
SEXTON BLAKE (1967–71)

In a long, winding cave that was a TV studio set, the daring twenties detective was being menaced by a full-grown Bengal tiger. The idea was that as Blake made his escape, a portcullis dropped down between him and the beast, effectively halting the big cat in its tracks.

The clapper boy was standing well back to mark the scene but, as he smacked the board down, the noise must have sounded like a rifle shot to the tiger, which was immediately spooked. It quite literally took off. With its forward path barred by the portcullis, it leaped straight over the camera and all the accompanying paraphernalia, including the hapless cameraman.

Not only did the tiger clear it all, but it also took with it its minder from Chipperfield's circus, who was holding onto the tiger by means of a concealed chain. As the minder clung on for dear life, he was dragged around the floor of the studio on his stomach.

Normally, the rest of the crew sit around reading newspapers or drinking tea. On this occasion, within seconds some thirty or forty technicians seemed to have found their way up on to an overhead gantry.

OUTBACK OUTRAGE
SKIPPY, THE BUSH KANGAROO (1967–69)

Before Paul Hogan, the biggest Australian star in the world was this lovable marsupial. Star of his own series, Skippy spent each week doing a Lassie and helping out his ranger 'dad' (Ed Devereaux), as well as his best pals Sonny (Garry Pankhurst) and Clancy (a young Liza Goddard, later the star of *Take Three Girls* and *The Brothers*).

But, after the series ended, darkness was to hit Skippy's world. Having retired to a kangaroo enclosure in Waratah National Park, Skippy occasionally ventured out for personal appearances. Then, one April night, an horrific event rocked the compound. Thirteen of the kangaroos were attacked and killed by an unknown intruder.

People were in shock. Was their beloved Skippy one of the deceased? Apparently not, said the local rangers, as Skippy lived a life of luxury in a separate VIP area. Still rumour persisted that it was a gigantic cover-up: the theory was that Skippy had been the victim of a Shergar-style assassination attempt that had boiled over into a full-blown massacre.

Also, because most kangaroos look pretty similar to the untrained eye, no one could be sure whether Skippy had indeed survived. Park bosses insisted that he had, and that he had been moved to a high-security enclosure for protection.

So what is the real story? Kidnap plot, serial kangaroo killer? The most likely answer is peckish wild dogs – but, then, that's not the kind of problem that Skippy should have to deal with. As someone once said, 'Between the truth and the legend, print the legend.'

If Skippy could talk, as opposed to just being able to make his distinctive 'tut tut', he would probably say the same thing.

MUCH ADO ABOUT NOTHING
THE PRISONER (1967–68)

Any series that can spawn a literary part-work nearly thirty years after it was originally aired has surely to be the stuff of serious cult. When that series, which lasted just seventeen episodes, was also the stuff of Strange, then . . .

With the hard-boiled if conventional international secret agent series, *Danger Man*, Patrick McGoohan was already a major TV 'face' on both sides of the Atlantic when he first mooted the idea of *The Prisoner*.

What that idea exactly was at the outset, nobody quite knew, but McGoohan managed to persuade independent TV mogul Lew Grade to back it on the strength of just one meeting. Grade, in his turn, 'sold' the series to CBS in the States.

It seems that co-creator, George Markstein, who'd worked with McGoohan on *Danger Man*, favoured a concept based on a project devised during World War Two, whereby burned-out Special Operations operatives were held in beautiful sur-roundings in an attempt to pry out their secrets. McGoohan, desperate to get away from sub-007 heroics, clearly favoured something rather more highfalutin. Using the picturesque North Wales seaside town of Portmeirion as its eye-catching base, the resulting series proved to be an often impenetrable, Kafkaesque mix of both.

Grade later told of how he was visited by one of the CBS's top executives, who, after viewing the first few episodes, complained, 'I really can't understand what it's all about.' Grade suggested he fix up a meeting with McGoohan – '. . . he'll explain everything to you.'

The executive returned saying that he still didn't understand the series and, furthermore, 'I really don't understand how you can get on with Patrick.' To this Grade retorted, 'I have no problems with him. He's very easy to get along with. I just agree to all his requests.'

BOSIE THE BARD

NEWS AT TEN (1967– 2004)

ITN's *News At Ten* was originally fronted by Alastair Burnet and Andrew Gardner. But it was Reginald Bosanquet, with his slurred voice and sarcastic twinkle in his eye, who really caught the public's imagination. Naturally enough, in his autobiography, *Let's Get Through Wednesday: My 25 Years with ITN*, he seized the chance to lay to rest a few myths.

Yes, he had a tendency to 'pause and sidle up to' difficult words giving some viewers the impression that he had had 'slightly too much lubrication before going on the air'. Yes, he liked a drink and wouldn't mind being counted among the 'gin and tonic brigade'. In response to a newspaper article claiming that he had been on the champagne at 10 a.m., boozy Bosie argued simply, 'But apart from at weddings, when else does one drink champagne except at breakfast?'

Reggie was happy to confirm that he did indeed wear a toupee, not out of vanity but because of a 'recurring inflammation of the scalp', for which the only treatment was to shave off the hair in the affected parts. 'It would not be a very good image for me to appear on screen with a different part of my hair missing each time. So I wear a hairpiece.'

What viewers really wanted to know, however, was what his relationship was with his glamorous colleague, Anna Ford. Nothing doing, Reggie declared, except, that is, for their kinky habit of exchanging comic poems in the ad break. Here, at last, was the reason for those cheeky glances! Indeed Ford is to be congratulated on keeping a straight face at all on being handed such cryptic odes as:

To Anna aged -?5

Query five
Still alive.
(No sex-drive)

Quite attractive
– Almost active –
Poses questions
Makes suggestions
Demands ballads
And fruit salads
Should be cherished
And embellished.
Hardish task –
But one can ask.

Or

Woe

I prayed – I vowed – that I'd be good
(And many people thought I would)
But then I got my just reward
Eighteen nights with Anna Ford!

'We are very fond of each other as friends,' he concluded primly. 'I adore her, not least because she calls me "Old Bean".'

BOLT FROM THE BLUE

THE GOLDEN SHOT (1967–75)

'Heinz, the bolt!' Doesn't exactly trip off the tongue. But when this ITV game show – in which viewers and live contestants guided a blindfolded crossbow operator towards money and prizewinning targets – first started, it was still rather bogged down in its dour Teutonic origins.

That would all change when Bob Monkhouse took over as presenter on the Sunday afternoon series. He knew that there was nothing like a good catchphrase to capture an audience's imagination. Preferably something alliterative.

Heinz, the show's first crossbowman, had long gone to be replaced by a mild-mannered chap called Derek Young. Monkhouse suggested to him that, for the purposes of the show, he could be called 'Bertie' or 'Beauregard'. 'Why not Derek?' came the disgruntled reply.

Two days later, Young sidled up to Monkhouse in the studio canteen and whispered, 'Bernie' – apparently a name suggested by his wife. Within a year, the nation would be chanting along with: 'Bernie! The Bolt! Please! Thank you!'

THE FILTH AND THE FURY
TODAY (1968–77)

In these days when the F-word is heard so often on our screens, it is hard to believe that a few foul-mouthed punk rockers should have made such a stir on an admittedly pre-watershed programme back in 1976.

Bill Grundy, veteran, laid-back presenter of the London current-affairs show, had no idea what he was letting himself in for when he invited a group of teens to talk about the newest craze – punk rock. The Sex Pistols arrived drunk, however, and the live show rapidly deteriorated after Johnny Rotten mumbled the word 'shit' and Grundy egged him on to repeat the word.

With what was, in hindsight, appallingly bad judgement, Grundy invited the youths to 'say something outrageous', prompting guitarist Steve Jones to oblige with, 'You dirty bastard, you dirty f***er!'

The next day, the newspapers gleefully counted the swear words and the *Daily Mirror* ran a front-page story entitled THE FILTH AND THE FURY, reporting that a lorry driver viewer had put his boot through the screen when his son had heard the swearing. 'It exploded and I was blown backwards!' he alleged.

For the Sex Pistols, about to start a nationwide tour, the broadcast proved disastrous. Though they had achieved national notoriety, almost all their venues cancelled. As for Grundy, his career never recovered. Accused of having been drinking himself before going on air, he was suspended by Thames, then reinstated, but his contract was not renewed in 1977.

The Pistols' Glen Matlock claims he saw Grundy one more time while driving past Thames TV studios some six months after leaving the band. Grundy was laden with papers and looked as if he had just cleared his desk, ready to leave for good.

When Matlock stopped to jeer; 'Oi, Bill, remember me?' Grundy carefully put down his briefcases and documents, looked all around him and then looked back at the punk. Says Matlock, 'He just went wallop, giving us two fingers with each hand. At last he had been able to tell the Pistols to f*** off!'

PAPER WEIGHT

ORIGAMI (1968)

A distinctly low-tech approach to kids' TV was the order of the day in this ITV series, presented by paper-folding expert and magician Robert Harbin.

Amazingly he managed to sustain interest over 32 episodes, each of 25 minutes, spanning three years, with only a ten-inch-square piece of paper for company.

FERRETING ABOUT

CALENDAR (1968–)

It is a peculiarity of local TV news that the presenters are household names within their own region yet virtually unknown elsewhere. But, even before Richard Whiteley became an authentic small-screen star as the avuncular frontman of C4's

Countdown from 1982, some earlier Yorkshire Television antics had given him nationwide notoriety. Whiteley, a reporter on the very first instalment of this teatime regional news magazine (then fronted by one Jonathan Aitken, who would also acquire a national reputation) had graduated to presenter by 1977.

It was a *Calendar Tuesday* edition and Whiteley's main guest on the six o'clock show was modish ventriloquist Roger de Courcey with Nookie the bear. It was generally felt that the odd couple couldn't sustain a whole live programme, so a 'starter' was quickly sorted.

Local author Brian Plummer had just published *Ferrets and Ferreting*, so he and some of his furry friends were summoned to the studio. Stroking one of Plummer's chums, Whiteley had just asked, 'Are they easy to look after?' when he suddenly felt a stinging pain in his index finger.

Nookie may have been lippy, but this fellow was decidedly toothy and, the more Whiteley tried to disengage, the more it clung on by two very sharp gnashers. Plummer's 'keep still, it won't hurt you' cut no ice as the intrepid presenter endured a full twenty seconds (to him it seemed like half an hour) of agony before the pair were finally prized apart. After being given a tetanus shot, Whiteley resumed with his less dangerous guests who, as he later revealed, seemed decidedly miffed about being upstaged by *ferae naturae*.

Whiteley's parochial embarrassment would soon become the stuff of endlessly repeated TV legend. 'When it was happening it was like a car crash,' he has said, 'but it's made me about five thousand pounds over the years.'

GHOSTWRITER

FROST ON SUNDAY (1968)

Ronnie Barker took a while before he plucked up the courage to become a writer on the show he was working on. The difference was that no one else knew that he was the one coming up with their best lines.

Part of the cast of this topical news show with comedy sketches and monologues – which also co-starred his future partner Ronnie Corbett – Barker finished recording one week and decided that the material was simply not up to scratch.

Convinced he could do better, he went home and started writing a few sketches. Because he didn't like having his name on the credits too many times, and because he was concerned that people would treat the sketches differently if they knew he was the person behind them, he came up with a pseudonym – Gerald Wiley.

He told his agent, who came in on the deception, even concocting a story that Wiley was a recluse, just in case anyone asked to meet him. The Wiley scripts were sent to *Frost on Sunday* and the programme makers were impressed. Over the next few weeks, several Wiley scripts made their way onto the show, in among those of the other writers.

In the meantime, it was becoming increasingly strange for Ronnie to keep Wiley a secret. When one sketch bombed, he criticised Wiley, only for Corbett to defend him. Comedian Frank Muir wanted to meet Wiley, so Barker got his agent to arrange a meeting and then call to cancel.

It got *really* difficult when Corbett asked about buying some of Wiley's sketches to use in his stand-up routine. Barker's agent told him about the enquiry and Barker told him to tell Corbett that he could have the sketch for £250. Corbett confided in Barker that Wiley was charging him a lot of money and Barker told him to refuse. Then he instructed his agent to send Corbett the sketch free of charge as a Christmas present.

Shortly afterwards, a set of crystal glasses arrived at the agent's office with 'GW' engraved on them.

Soon, people began to suspect that Wiley didn't exist, but they didn't know who he was. Some suggested it was the alter ego of another writer trying to get more stuff on TV and soon there were wagers flying about as to the writer's real identity. Candidates mooted included were Willis Hall, Tom Stoppard and even Noël Coward.

Choosing to put an end to the speculation, Barker wrote a letter, on Wiley stationery, inviting the cast and crew to lunch at a Chinese restaurant. Everyone turned up to find out who the mysterious Wiley really was. When Frank Muir arrived late, everyone applauded, assuming that he was the one.

Only then did Barker own up to his deception, although he admitted to biographer Bob McCabe that he wished he had kept it a secret. Nonetheless, Gerald Wiley lived on through other series of Barker's, most notably *The Two Ronnies*. And he wasn't the only one: Dave Huggett, Larry Keith, Jonathan Cobbold – they were all pseudonyms of the multitalented Ronnie Barker.

SWISS CONSPIRACY

NBC AMERICAN FOOTBALL (1968)

Sports fans can be an irate lot – and they certainly don't like it when a mountain girl in pigtails spoils their fun. Unless, of course, she is wearing a miniskirt and cheerleading.

One of the greatest games in American football has gone down in infamy because no one saw the best part. It was the year of Love & Peace and the match was between the Oakland Raiders and New York Jets.

With 65 seconds left on the clock, the Jets went ahead 32–29. When the Raiders made only a short gain after kick-off, the game's broadcaster NBC went to a commercial break – and never returned.

Instead, they continued with their scheduled programming, showing the children's film, *Heidi*, starring Julie Andrews's stepdaughter, Jennifer Edwards, as the little Swiss miss.

Problem was, the game wasn't over. Back in the stadium, the Raiders immediately scored a long-range touchdown, going ahead with 42 seconds to go. Then, following the kick-off, the

Jets lost the ball and the Raiders scored another massive touchdown to win one of the most dramatic last-gasp victories in history: 43–32. In fact, the game is often voted the most memorable game in NFL history.

The fans went nuts and NBC was forced to eat humble pie. The story made the front page of the *New York Times*. Network president Julian Goodman made a statement saying, 'It was a forgivable error committed by humans who were concerned about children expecting to see *Heidi* at 7 p.m.'

Plans had been made beforehand that, regardless of whether the game was finished, the network would go to *Heidi*. The supervisor at the time had heard nothing, so followed the plan. The only problem was, no one was able to get through to him because the switchboard had gone down.

Thousands of viewers were calling NBC, either to check that *Heidi* was still on, or to make sure that they would be able to see the end of the game. The phone system couldn't take it and melted. As a result, no one could get through to *anyone* to make a decision.

The aftermath? As a result of what became known as 'The Heidi Game', NFL television contracts require matches to be televised in their entirety.

GOING FOR OLD

DAD'S ARMY (1968–77)

The Fighting Tigers based in Brightsea-on-sea? That was an early blueprint for this hit sitcom, eventually set in fictitious Walmington-on-sea, some of whose ensemble cast made *Last of the Summer Wine* seem positively adolescent.

When it first aired, Arthur Lowe (Captain Mainwaring) was 53, John Le Mesurier (Sergeant Wilson) 56, John Laurie (Private Frazer) 71 and Arnold Ridley (Private Godfrey) 72. Clive Dunn, playing the Great War veteran, Lance Corporal

Jones, the unit's most ancient wrinkly, was, in fact, a comparatively youthful 48.

That the series ended after a run of nine years was as much to do with the collective age of this marvellous cast, who – with the exception of James Beck's (Private Frazer) death at the tragically young age of 44 – remained ever present throughout.

This posed a problem or two for a production team ever conscious of their star performers' frailties. John Laurie and Arnold Ridley were, after all, authentic veterans of the Somme in 1916 and both invalided away from the front as a result.

Laurie contracted bronchial problems and spent the rest of the war in London (and was an authentic member of the Home Guard), but Ridley's wounds were more severe. He suffered for the rest of his life from the blackouts brought about by blows to the head from a rifle butt.

Legend has it that these two venerable old timers would compete on set for the most aches, pains and age-related problems. The show, like both *M*A*S*H* and *'Allo 'Allo*, lasted a lot longer than the wars they were portraying.

The show's oldies all died within four years of each other – between 1980 and 1984; Ridley was 88, Laurie, 80, Le Mesurier, 71, and Lowe, 66. Clive Dunn is alive, well, aged 85 and living in Portugal. His character, according to the show's back story, was born in 1870 – which would make him 135.

DOGGY HEROICS

SCOOBY-DOO, WHERE ARE YOU! (1969–72)

For a start, the show was never supposed to be called *Scooby-Doo* in the first place. *Who's Scared?* and *Mysteries Five* were the original options, but, when the pilot show was deemed too dark, it was given a comedy makeover and its final title.

The original incarnation put Scoob in a similar role to that of 'Timmy' in Enid Blyton's Famous Five stories – merely a canine sidekick to the humans. Called 'Too Much', he was a bongo-playing hippy.

That all changed while CBS children's programming head Fred Silverman was listening to the radio. He heard Frank Sinatra singing 'Strangers in the Night' and was particularly enamoured of the way Sinatra scatted in the middle of the record. The phrase 'scooby-dooby-doo' stuck in his mind and suddenly 'Too Much' had a new moniker.

Not only that, but he was promoted from supporting cast to the show's lead character and a reluctant hero was born.

JIMI'LL FIX IT

LULU (1969)

The archetypal wild man of rock who wasn't averse to playing the guitar with his teeth or setting fire to the instrument on stage, Jimi Hendrix showed he could also be a bit of a joker when he guested on the Scots pop star's show. He performed 'Voodoo Chile' first, and then closed the show with 'Hey Joe'.

But midway through the number Hendrix announced, 'We're going to stop playing this rubbish and dedicate this to the Cream . . .' upon which he and his band, the Experience (Noel Redding and Mitch Mitchell), started playing 'Sunshine Of Your Love'.

Less than a year later he was dead at 27, having choked to death on his own vomit.

TALKING OF REPTILES

MONTY PYTHON'S FLYING CIRCUS (1969–74)

Would 'Arthur Megapode's Cheap Show', 'Vaseline Parade' or 'Gwen Dibley' have had quite the same ring? What about 'Owl

Stretching Time' (briefly, the hottest favourite), 'A Horse, a Spoon and a Basin', or 'The Toad Elevating Moment'?

In retrospect, it's difficult to imagine anything but the final version for, arguably, the most influential British TV comedy series of all time. But actually finalising the juxtaposition of all those bizarre title elements proved to be an extremely tortuous business.

The 'Flying Circus' bit was, curiously, one of the easier decisions, and, for a breath or two, 'Baron Von Took's Flying Circus' (after Barry Took, then a BBC comedy guru, who helped assemble the team) had some currency. According to Michael Palin's diary at the time, 'Bunn, Wackett, Buzzard Stubble and Boot' then slipped into poll position after the first day of filming on 8 July 1969. It seems likely that John Cleese offered up, albeit separately at first, both 'Python' – because he had a thing about animals – and 'Monty', since it reminded him of a sleazy agent.

Two were finally blended together with the 'Flying Circus'. Palin recalled, 'The BBC's reaction was, "Well, we don't know what it means, but I think you'll find that in years to come it'll be remembered as 'The Flying Circus'." '

THE 1970s

DATE WITH A LEGEND
NIGHT GALLERY (1970–73)

All kinds of stories are told about the geeky young film buff who used to spend his summer holidays as a teenager hanging around Universal Studios. What's absolutely true is that, at the age of 22, a year before he was due to graduate from college, Steven Spielberg was offered a seven-year directing contract by Universal starting at $275 a week. As Spielberg once described it, with some slight exaggeration, 'I went from Cal State at Long Beach to Stage 15 at Universal – where Joan Crawford met me at the door.' With just one, acclaimed, student short 'in the can', the movie brat with long hair and acne had been signed up to direct an episode called 'Eyes' in this new supernatural anthology from Rod Serling, the creator of *The Twilight Zone*.

First choice for the role of a wealthy blind woman who comes up with a diabolical plan to have her sight, at least temporarily, restored, was Bette Davis – but she balked at the notion of being directed by such a young man. Joan Crawford, Davis's erstwhile co-star, clearly had no such qualms. When asked about her new director's age, the 65-year-old joked, 'They told me when I signed to do this he was twenty-three!'

When Spielberg walked onto the set on the first day of shooting, it seemed that almost everyone apart from La Crawford thought it was a joke, a publicity stunt even. The beardless Spielberg later recalled, 'I couldn't really get anyone to take me seriously for two days [of a seven-day shoot]. I set up . . . a real gimmicky shot – and I remember seeing people titter and say, "He doesn't have long to go." '

At the end of Day Four, there was another, potentially terminal, crisis. Crawford, who'd taken a sickie for a day when she contracted an ear infection, had, on her return, requested

Spielberg's close counsel on how to tackle one of the show's biggest scenes – the removal of eye bandages.

The director, preoccupied with finishing off some scenes so that the set could be 'struck' for use the next day on another of the studio's productions, had forgotten all about Crawford's plea when he was summoned urgently to the presence.

He found the old girl blubbing in her dressing room. She said she felt let down by him. With the sort of finesse befitting a filmmaker who would later become, arguably, the most successful director in the history of Hollywood, Spielberg placated his Oscar-winning star so successfully that they eventually became firm friends.

DOG ON A HOT (NON-TIN) ROOF

EYELESS IN GAZA (1971)

There's plenty of strange imagery in Aldous Huxley's tenth novel, published in 1936, but perhaps nothing stranger than . . .

As James Cellan-Jones, director of this BBC dramatisation, explained, 'We had to shoot a sequence where Ian Richardson and Lynn Farleigh were making love on a rooftop when a passing plane dropped a dog out, which landed on the roof beside them covering them all in blood.

'We found the only suitable biplane in Portugal, pointed the camera at a revolving mirror, telling the pilot by radio where to fly for the best shot. We had a quarter-inch model of the fox terrier, which we put on to the mirror and revolved it so it looked as though it were falling through the sky. We had two prop men standing by with fake blood, and John Baker, the cameraman, swung a woolly toy past the lens so that it looked like a blur.'

Finally, the prop men threw the blood onto the actors and the director cut to a canine corpse of fake fur with plastic ribs sticking out. The noise of flies was dubbed on later. It was,

94

said Cellan-Jones (a self-confessed 'sentimental dog lover'), extremely 'effective'.

DISAPPEARING ACT
NICHOLS (1971–72)

Shows are frequently retooled on the fly and unsuccessful characters mysteriously, or violently, disappear. But the case of *Nichols*, later renamed *James Garner As Nichols*, is still a unique one.

It was set in 1914, and Nichols was a laid-back ex-army man who ended up as sheriff in a small western town. Despite his military background, he hated violence, preferring to spend his time coming up with get-rich-quick ideas.

However, viewers didn't take to the show and producers concluded that they didn't respond to a nonviolent lawman (Nichols didn't carry a weapon). With stunning ingenuity, they came up with the following: Nichols was gunned down and killed before the opening credits – replaced by his twin brother (also played by Garner), who was a more traditional, gun-toting Old West hero, who came to town to avenge his sibling's death.

Ironically, this was done during the final episode of the first series. The producers assumed that, with this fresh twist, the show would be renewed and the new character would carry on where he left off. Unfortunately, the network didn't agree and, by the time the episode aired, the show had been cancelled.

WILD ABOUT LARRY
THE GENERATION GAME (1971–82; 1990–2002)

When Bruce Forsyth decided to quit this durable all-family game show after a six-year reign (having also gained his second wife, the show's hostess Anthea Redfern, in the process), the BBC signed up authentically camp comedian Larry Grayson as his replacement.

Apart from his trademark mince-and-pout, mildly risqué tales of 'friends' like 'Everard' and 'Slack Alice', not to mention the odd catchphrase such as 'Shut that door!', 'Oh, what a gay day!', and 'He seems like a nice boy!', Grayson was positively one-dimensional by comparison with Brucie.

And, unlike his predecessor, Grayson wasn't exactly a dab hand at thinking on his feet – especially when it came to surprises and ad-libs. In fact, the job of assistants was often to make sure that information was regularly posted on large cue cards for the nervously sweaty presenter – including catchphrases, ad-libs and, perhaps most important of all, the name(s) of the next contestant(s).

Because 'doors' (as in, 'Shut that door!') were part of his *shtick*, the producers introduced a pair of them as part of the regular set. From one would emerge the show's contestants; from the other, 'the mystery door', would occasionally loom a celebrity guest.

The idea was that Grayson, let alone the hyped-up audience, used never to know which star was lurking unseen until the door opened and he, and they, would then go into extra paroxysms of excitement.

With so much already on his mind, Grayson usually panicked even more when the door opened because although he probably could vaguely recognise the guest – even before a flunky had written 'Lionel Blair' in big letters – he'd still usually be stuck for the actual name. Luckily, the instant applause of the crowd diverted attention from his visible alarm.

On one occasion, the ageing Hollywood star Lilian Gish was in town and the producers thought that, as Grayson was a huge fan of silent movies, it would be great to have the old girl on the show.

The door opened and the elegant octogenarian stepped through. It was clear that Grayson recognised her instantly. He

96

clutched his chest with pleasure and was . . . speechless. However, on this particular occasion, the fail-safe audience simply didn't have a clue as to the identity of this guest whose heyday was fifty years earlier.

Dreaded silence ensued until the producer, realising that Grayson was still quite overcome and couldn't say a word, grabbed a card and quickly penned Gish's name in big letters. Cue wild, if somewhat belated, applause.

Grayson remained at the helm for four years before the show was cancelled. The nation breathed a sigh of relief when Brucie was back in charge on the show's resumption in 1990.

SHOT IN THE DARK

ALIAS SMITH AND JONES (1971–73)

Sadly, the sound of gunfire wasn't confined to the set of this deservedly popular comedy Western series, which originally rode in on the coat-tails of *Butch Cassidy and the Sundance Kid*.

Just a few episodes into the droll frontier tales of Joshua Smith (a.k.a. Hannibal Heyes) and Thaddeus Jones (a.k.a. Kid Curry), amiable Pete Duel, who played Smith, was found shot dead in his Hollywood Hills apartment. The verdict was suicide.

However, the formula was too good to drop, so ABC drafted in Roger Davis, who had been supplying the show's witty narration, to take over as Hannibal. Davis, first of four husbands to *Charlie's Angels* star Jaclyn Smith, simply redid some scenes already filmed by Duel and carried on the role without so much as a blink for the rest of the two-year run.

THE HONOURABLE MEMBER
CASANOVA (1971)

Dennis Potter's typically juicy six-parter about the life and loves of the great Italian rake, which so scandalised clean-up-TV campaigner Mary Whitehouse before she'd even seen it, contained scenes that, recalls producer Mark Shivas, 'made the very calm, sensible and supportive head of plays, Gerald Savory, a little nervous.

'Prior to production we went through the six episodes of script together identifying "potential problems", following which he understandably sent me a memo for his own protection. It contained the following gem: "You assured me that the naked nun in Episode Three would be shot with circumspection."

'The opening scenes of the first episode see Casanova praying as a naked, laughing girl – played by Christine Noonan – waits for him in bed, sitting up, her splendid breasts to the fore. Casanova – Frank Finlay – had then to throw off his robe before jumping on her.

'At that moment, on the first take, her laughter doubled. Unseen by the camera, Frank had tied a large ribbon to his penis!

'Thirty-three years later, these same scenes were part of a compilation shown at BAFTA in Piccadilly and I introduced them, telling the audience how Frank had tied a pink bow to his member.

'After the screening, a lady who I didn't recognise, presumably from the costume department, came up to me and said, reprovingly, "The bow wasn't pink you know. It was yellow."

'Such a memory for detail.'

GIVEN THE BIRD
PARKINSON (1971–82; 1998–)

When they come to write Parky's epitaph, he'd probably wish to be remembered for classic chat-show interviews with the likes Muhammad Ali, George Best, David Niven, Billy Connolly, Elton John and even Kenneth Williams (who once described mine host as a 'North country nit' before eventually becoming a *Parkinson* regular).

But all these great and good are but dust when it comes to the *most* enduring – and Parky's *most* ignominious – encounter of them all. No, we're not talking about one of those embarrassing non-chats with boringly reticent film stars such as Meg Ryan.

Naturally, we're referring to the night of 7 April 1977 when the laid-back presenter was physically laid out by his feathery guest Emu, with, quite literally, a helping hand from the big bird's 'minder', Rod Hull.

The best thing about it – apart from the sight of an elegantly-coiffured Parky floored by an outsized glove puppet – was that he was genuinely rattled by this close encounter and let his usual Tyke composure drop for his millions of viewers to relish.

Was it some kind of awful belated payback when, nearly 22 years later, Hull died after falling off the roof of his house while trying to fix the TV aerial? And where was Emu at the time?

COOLING THE ARDOUR
COUSIN BETTE (1971)

Dame Helen Mirren has been taking her 'kit' off on screen for more than 35 years – some suggest, mischievously, it's her signature – from the sixties to, most recently, the film *Calendar Girls*, when she was 58.

She was, however, still in her voluptuous prime, not to mention her first major dramatic role for TV, when, as Valérie in this five-part BBC adaptation of Balzac's classic, she prepared to skinny up for the small screen.

While this was, potentially, a cause of considerable pleasure to her growing legion of admirers, it was of altogether more concern to Mirren's red-blooded young co-star, Colin Baker.

Playing the weak-willed artist Steinbock, Baker (who would later become the sixth Doctor in *Doctor Who*) was, quite crudely, scared of the consequences of clambering into bed with her.

But, according to Mirren's biographer, Ivan Waterman, a wardrobe girl saved his blushes on the day of the big love scene, providing him with flesh-coloured knickers to cover his private parts.

Said Baker, 'Being a bloke and things being as they are, I thought it best in case. I needed to hide my embarrassment, so to speak. Bless my heart, on the day, she [Mirren] turned up, dropped her gown, and was completely starkers. She looked absolutely knockout. She had an incredible figure. But she wasn't at all self-conscious, which helped me a great deal.

'We didn't actually have to be seen on camera doing anything; it was like the morning after. But I kept looking straight into her eyes to avert glancing down, thereby avoiding any biological accident. Boys will be boys. If you think Helen is beautiful today, you should have seen her then. I had to keep a grip on myself in every sense!'

THE ODD COUPLE

THE SONNY AND CHER COMEDY HOUR (1971–74)

After several chart-topping hits in the mid-sixties, the careers of pop duo (later married couple) Sonny and Cher were decidedly on the wane when they were spotted doing an inspired singing-and-bickering stage act in a Los Angeles supper club.

This led to an invitation to guest-host TV's popular *The Merv Griffin Show*, and as a result of their double-act – he bumbling and apologetic, she witty and acerbic – they were offered their own primetime variety show, and a way back to the top.

Their careers – especially Cher's as a solo singer and clothes horse – quickly revived in stark contrast to their private life, which began to disintegrate often in full view of their adoring TV public. Those in the know knew that Sonny had been the brains behind the pair but for the purposes of the show, and to his national detriment, he played up the role of buffoon and joke singer. Behind the following – typical – exchange on television was an increasingly turbulent domestic scenario.

With Cher glaring at him after he's jokily taken credit for their opening number, Sonny says, 'Look, folks, now don't worry about Cher's smarting off. 'Cause when she gets out of hand, I, like, give her a few belts when she gets home. In fact [turning to Cher], I'm surprised you're still popping off. Didn't you get enough last night?' To which she replies, deadpan, 'I didn't get any last night.' Now stumbling over his words, Sonny retorts, 'Cher, you know, I thought our marriage was getting better all the time.' 'Don't you think it's time your mother got a bed of her own?' Cher replies, witheringly.

The truth seemed to be that Sonny was a control freak – who also had to endure accusations of wife beating – while Cher, nine years his junior, became completely worn down by his smothering. Just a year into their show, the couple were, effectively, separated. And yet the ratings remained high.

Nine days after taping their 25th and last show – which concluded, ironically, with their trademark number, 'I Got You, Babe' – Cher sued Sonny for divorce, charging him that he'd been holding her in 'involuntary servitude'.

ALL AT SEA

THE ONEDIN LINE (1971–80)

It's curious to view much-loved classics from the past, massive ratings hits that drew great critical acclaim, and realise the circumstances in which they were made.

The BBC, in particular, has produced a great deal of hits on whatever-the-next-thing-down-from-a-shoestring-budget-is – shows such as *The Onedin Line*, which recounted the adventures of James Onedin, a would-be shipping magnate in nineteenth-century Liverpool.

The star of the piece, Peter Gilmore, got a hint of the chaos that would characterise production of the show. 'Everybody else had turned it down, I suppose,' he said. 'But I think they saw so many people that they got the names a bit muddled up, and I was in the middle of filming something else when I went to the audition at the BBC. I wanted to know if I'd got the part, and one of the producers put his arm round me and said, "As far as we are concerned you've got the part, Graham." '

It was a slow-burning success, and audiences responded to the dramatic storylines and the exotic locations, which were not always as they seemed. 'There was an enormous amount of acting skill required to make the audience believe we were actually somewhere exotic,' adds Gilmore. 'Even now it stretches the bounds of imagination.'

His co-star, and his wife in real life, Anne Stallybrass, continues, 'We were meant to be in the Southern States of America during the Civil War and it was actually Devon in October. They found a house that looked like a Southern house.'

Another trick employed by the ingenious crew was to get the maximum screen time out of the ships. 'They used to paint one side of it white and the other side of it black and pretend it was two different ships. They were very good at that. Peter Graham Scott, the producer, could make two pounds look like five.'

WHAT'S UP, MAC?

COLUMBO (1971–77; 1989–93)

With his filthy raincoat, cheroot, straggly black hair and permanent squint, Peter Falk created an iconic cop in the person of Los Angeles detective Lieutenant Columbo, who always got his man (or woman) after a tortuous cat-and-mouse investigation.

Apparently inspired by Dostoyevsky's dogged police inspector, Petrovitch, in *Crime and Punishment*, Volvo-driving Columbo – we never did discover his first name – was a real one-off.

Actually, he wasn't. Eleven years earlier, on Sunday night's *Chevy Mystery Hour*, barrel-chested Bronx-born actor Bert Freed played Lieutenant Columbo in an episode called 'Enough Rope'.

That might well have proved an authentic one-off until, a decade later, it was decided to revive the character in a series format. Peter Falk wasn't, however, first choice for Columbo even then. That honour went to pipe-smoking crooner Bing Crosby, who quickly decided that a recurring TV role would interfere with his golf game and turned it down.

CASTLE IN THE AIR

RECORD BREAKERS (1972– 2001)

A thinly disguised 'product placement' for its equally popular inspiration, *The Guinness Book of Records*, this BBC teatime show was a fixture of children's TV for nearly thirty years.

But for all its more recent incarnations, whose presenters included hyperactive ex-athletes such as Kriss Akabusi and Linford Christie, an erstwhile pop singer (Cheryl Baker) and even a former US president's son (Ron Reagan Jr), the 'Daddy' was Roy Castle. Amiable Castle – tap dancer, singer, trumpeter and *Carry On* star – was the show's main frontman from the beginning until his untimely death (from lung cancer due, allegedly, to the effects of passive smoking) in 1994.

As if his professional showbiz versatility weren't enough, Castle famously parlayed that many-sidedness into becoming a regular record breaker in his own right – whether it was for tap dancing, parascending or perching precariously atop a motorcycle human pyramid.

And so to the August Bank Holiday weekend in 1990 when Castle, just short of his 58th birthday and still seemingly very fit, found himself suitably harnessed on the wing of a biplane preparing to take off from Gatwick airport.

This 'wing walk' – for which Castle, clad in a star-studded leather suit and flying helmet, didn't technically have to walk at all but merely endure bravely for a little over 200 miles – was from West Sussex to Paris's Orly Airport. Even to this day, no one quite understands why the stunt was mounted from one of Britain's busiest airports on one of the busiest weekends of the year.

Nevertheless, there on the runway, taking its place amid the hectic queue of normal holiday flights, was Castle's biplane – mounted with little 'gun' cameras – followed by a small, single-wing 'pursuit' aircraft, stuffed with a large cameraman, a fairly hefty director and an only marginally smaller assistant sound recordist. The rest of the plan was for the show's producer, Greg Childs, and co-presenter, the aforementioned toothy Ms Baker of Bucks Fizz fame, to grab a scheduled flight to Paris and be at Orly in good time to welcome the intrepid Castle's eventual arrival, France-side.

As the pair sat inside their Air France jet and quaffed champagne, it quickly became clear there was some kind of delay – perhaps not surprising on this particular day, when stacking on the ground probably equalled stacking in the air. Then there was a message over the loudspeaker inviting Childs, 'to please come to the captain's cabin'. A little fearfully, he put on a headset through which he heard his director explain that there'd been an 'incident . . . no one was hurt . . . I need your authority to hire another pursuit plane.'

As their jet taxied down the runway, Childs and Baker could now, to their horror, clearly see the pursuit plane being bulldozed away. As a result, flight delays were up to about an hour long. The 'incident' had effectively closed Gatwick down.

What had apparently happened was this. The biplane eventually took off, Castle strapped on, 'gun' cameras blazing away. As the pursuit plane followed it down the runway, its female pilot suddenly realised that her craft, thanks to 'excess baggage' from the BBC, wasn't going to get off the ground. In fact, the undercarriage gave way altogether and shuddered to a halt.

Castle, who was now up, up and away, then heard from his pilot about the 'incident' on the ground. Should they abort? Absolutely not, Castle replied gamely. By this time, Childs and co. were en route to Paris, and landed at Charles de Gaulle airport before jumping into a cab and making it to Orly with thirty seconds to spare before Castle touched down.

Thanks to clever manoeuvring by Castle's pilot, great pictures had already been captured of the White Cliffs and shipping in the Channel. And, when the substitute pursuit plane caught up near Paris, they got great shots of Castle wing-walking past the Eiffel Tower.

According to Childs, Castle didn't want to appear at all traumatised by the events and even came in to land singing 'There's No Business Like Show Business'. In reality, he was completely exhausted after being in the air for three record-breaking hours.

In fact, Castle was 'miked' for sound throughout the trip but his commentary – including some obvious stress – proved to be virtually inaudible. 'In the end, we had to redub the whole thing,' Childs recalled. 'We had to get Roy to tell what he said then rewrite it as a script. He then dubbed it and we distorted it all to sound like it was coming out of his mouth at the time.'

By the time the programme went out a month later as the new series' opener, some details had already emerged about the 'incident', which only added to the buzz. Meanwhile, Gatwick tried to sue the BBC for £1 million. Unsuccessfully.

CRIMES & MISDEMEANOURS
THE STREETS OF SAN FRANCISCO (1972–77)

This popular cop show paired Hollywood veteran Karl Malden with 'Kirk's boy' Michael Douglas, who generally did the chauffeuring as the crime-fighting duo sped Bullitt-like round the hilly city.

Once Malden got used to his partner's daredevil driving, usually bracing one leg against the dashboard as Douglas frequently sent the car airborne over the famous bumps, they became firm friends.

But the older man suddenly got another perspective on his co-star's driving style in an episode in which they had to use a police computer to run someone's licence number to see if they had any convictions.

Once the scene was safely in the can, Malden asked to try it for real. He put in his own number and came up with a single parking ticket, which was more than ten years old. Then he put Douglas's number in and stood back in a mixture of horror and astonishment as the computer threw up pages and pages of violations.

What Malden probably didn't realise at the time was that his junior co-star was somewhat preoccupied with matters other than police procedural.

As a producer, he was helping 'package' all the elements for one of the seventies' most successful films, *One Flew Over the Cuckoo's Nest*, which in 1975 would earn him an Academy Award for Best Film, long before his own award-winning big-screen acting career would take off in earnest.

BLOODY SUNDAY
WEEKEND WORLD (1972–88)

You first have to imagine the context. The IRA mainland bombing campaign was in full cry with bloody outrages already perpetrated at Aldershot, Woolwich and Guildford.

Suddenly right there, over Sunday lunch, David O'Connell, an IRA spokesman, was on ITV (in conversation with Mary Holland) threatening that the campaign would continue unless Britain released Republican prisoners. He also demanded that Britain should declare its intention to withdraw from Northern Ireland and also help sponsor reunification.

It's not difficult to imagine how many of the great, good Disgusteds of Tunbridge Wells and even everyday folk must have considered the programme's content and timing not just Strange but also deeply insensitive.

The calls of protest flooded in and when, four days later, the Birmingham pub bombings took place, furious questions were asked in the House. Lord Hailsham even suggested that, during the TV interview, it might have been likely O'Connell had issued an encoded bombing order to a mainland IRA cell.

BYE BYE BABY
MAUDE (1972–78)

Right from the off, this was a unique sitcom. Starring future Golden Girl Bea Arthur, it was spun off from the successful *All in the Family* (based on our *Till Death Us Do Part*), after Arthur had appeared on the show as a cousin.

The appearance was so successful that she came back and CBS finally asked producer Norman Lear to create her own 'vehicle'. A fierce liberal, Maude had an African-American maid and was on her fourth marriage – pretty revolutionary stuff for 1972. But nothing could prepare the audience for the two-part 'hurricane', which hit television screens in an episode entitled 'Maude's Dilemma'.

The storyline featured Maude, in her mid-forties, finding out she was pregnant and opting to have an abortion. Bear in mind that this was a full year before the landmark Supreme Court decision in *Roe v. Wade*, which protected legalised abortion.

When the episode first aired, it received 7,000 complaints. A number of CBS affiliates refused to run it. It was rerun in the summer of 1973 and got 65 million viewers, a 41-per-cent share of the audience. When the time came for the rerun, pro-life campaigners put pressure on various affiliates throughout the country not to show it. To CBS's credit, it didn't back down, despite reports that Lear had been sent pictures of aborted babies.

When it aired for the second time, a staggering 17,000 complaints were received by the network. But they stood firm – and 'Maude's Dilemma' remains an important juncture in televisual history.

SPIKE IN THE OINTMENT
FOLLIES OF THE WISE (1972)

Spike Milligan's erratic genius and reputation for difficult behaviour travelled before him, raising doubts of a trouble-free shoot on this comedy travelogue about some of the bizarre monuments of Britain.

This was demonstrated by his lack of cooperation at a radio interview in Edinburgh after the very first day of filming north of the border. Talking to journalist/broadcaster Renton Laidlaw, he proceeded to slag off the Scottish capital's finest thoroughfare, Princes Street, naming all the stores that ruined it. This was, of course, against the advertising code of the day and so necessitated a restart of the interview each time.

He ended by saying that, far from being the 'Athens of the North', Edinburgh was much more like 'the backside of the South'.

Later during filming they were in the West Country, where Spike suddenly took against a new development in Exeter. To the crew's bemusement, he then walked around the city calling everything 'cardboard', the Cathedral included. Here today, Goon tomorrow.

KICK IN THE TEETH

KUNG FU (1972–75; 1992–96)

Just before (and, even more weirdly, after) his untimely (and generally unexplained) death in 1973 aged 33, San Francisco-born Bruce Lee was, briefly, the biggest star on the planet thanks to his pioneering martial-arts skills.

Lee's strength and athleticism in Hong Kong-produced chop-socky films, such as *The Big Boss*, *Fists of Fury* and *Way of the Dragon*, cemented his burgeoning reputation, which had begun when he won endless tournaments and instructed some of Hollywood's finest.

But his cult following actually started even before this, when he played (for a measly $400 per episode) Kato, inscrutable sidekick to the eponymous comic-book hero in *The Green Hornet*, which lasted just thirty episodes during the mid-sixties.

So when, at almost the height of Lee's popularity, ABC TV was contemplating this series – which Lee himself had helped dream up – you might have thought he'd be the perfect choice for the lead role.

This was the Buddhist monk Kwai Chang Caine, who had to swap the Shaolin temple – a re-dressed standing set from the 1967 film musical *Camelot* – of his China upbringing for the nineteenth-century American West when he became a fugitive.

Certainly Lee fancied his chances, and was justifiably devastated when ABC-TV company president Fred Silverman decreed that an Asian lead would not be accepted by mainstream American audiences.

During the first season of *Kung Fu*, starring David Carradine as the fortune-cookie-spouting, high-kicking hero, Lee's last completed film, *Enter the Dragon*, hit the cinemas and turned a cult into an authentic box office phenomenon. Sadly, TV's loss and cinema's gain would prove to be posthumous.

CHAIR OF FEAR

MASTERMIND (1972–97; 2003–)

Almost as soon as it debuted in 1972 the quiz show *Mastermind* became an unexpected ratings hit on BBC1. And this was after TV bosses had expressed concerns that it was too 'highbrow'.

But it was a test of nerve as much as general knowledge as the tension would mount as soon as the theme tune, appropriately entitled 'Approaching Menace', struck up.

One man who knew exactly what the contestants were going through was producer Bill Wright, who devised the long-running quiz show, basing the format on his experience of being interrogated as a prisoner of war.

Wright unwittingly created a national institution with the famous black chair set in a spotlight, and the three questions about the contestants' name, occupation and specialist subject closely echoed the name, rank and serial number that a PoW was obliged to divulge when captured.

WAR STORIES

M*A*S*H (1972–83)

Although Robert Altman's 1970 film was popular and critically acclaimed, no one could have ever imagined that both would apply to the eleven-year-run of this award-laden spin-off, in which only Gary Burghoff, as Radar, reprised throughout his role from the original movie.

It was based on author Richard Hooker's experiences as a medic in the Korean War, but the timing of the film adaptation meant it was clearly intended as an anti-Vietnam War black comedy.

The Vietnam War was still raging by the time the TV sitcom started its transmission. But by the time the last instalment was aired in 1983 – boasting, at 125 million, the largest ever audience for a single programme (beating the *Roots* finale in 1977 and *Dallas*'s 'Who Shot JR?' episode in 1980) – the war had actually been over for eight years. The Korean War had, of course, lasted three years.

And yet the continuing unpopularity of the conflict in its aftermath meant that the programme's dark satire continued to resonate, with audiences revelling in the antics of 4077th Mobile Army Surgical Hospital.

STARS AND BARS

PORRIDGE (1974–77)

A favourite among viewers on the outside and, especially, the inside, this breezy BBC sitcom, starring Ronnie Barker as old lag Norman Fletcher seemed an unlikely candidate for Home Office scrutiny. Yet, thanks to recent files released under the thirty-year rule, we can now see that the programme was the subject of some debate back then.

This followed a request by the BBC to film 'one or two sequences against an authentic prison backdrop'. The producers wanted three scenes: an actor sweeping the yard; two or three actors exercising with prison buildings in the background; and an actor being marched from one part of the prison to the other.

At first, the prison department appeared sympathetic. One official reported that *Porridge* presented 'a fairly authentic and wholesome image of prison life' and argued there was 'some merit in being seen to be helpful to the series'.

However, this final ruling was handed down by one M J D Jones. In a sentence of no fewer than 48 words, he pontificated:

> *Porridge* has been promoted quite successfully without the facilities required and we cannot see what gain there will be to the producers, the Prison Service or the Home Office looking intensively through the system for some 'secluded area' where a day's filming could be allowed with minimum disruption.

He then added, without irony, that governors were already under pressure from high prison numbers.

Intriguingly, when they came to make a feature-film version of *Porridge* in 1979, permission was granted to shoot in HMP Chelmsford while it was being refurbished following a fire.

SPINNING OFF

HAPPY DAYS (1974–84)

It's a sure sign of a show's popularity that it can spawn sitcom spin-offs – this one, a sort of small-screen *American Graffiti*, hatched no fewer than three.

The stars of *Laverne & Shirley* were brewery workers Laverne De Fazio (Penny Marshall) and Shirley Feeney (Cindy Williams), who appeared in three episodes of *Happy Days* before their own seven-year run. *Joanie Loves Chachi* expanded, less successfully, on the teenage romance between Joanie Cunningham (Erin Moran) and Chachi Arcola (Scott Baio).

But the most influential, if oddest, of all was *Mork & Mindy*, spun off from just one memorable episode in February 1978, when – and, yes, it was quite a stretch – an alien from the planet Ork tried to kidnap *Happy Days'* main young man, Richie Cunningham (Ron Howard).

First choice for the alien was John Byner, already well known on TV for the soap spoof, *Soap* – from which another great comedic talent, Billy Crystal, would emerge – but he turned it down. So, instead, the *Happy Days* producers finally settled on 26-year-old stand-up comic Robin Williams, who, following a sensational response to his *Happy Days* one-off, quickly became a household name when his ad-libbing extraterrestrial then ruled the ratings for four years.

As for *Happy Days* – itself a spin-off from an episode called 'Love and the Happy Days' in the turn-of-the-seventies TV comedy anthology, *Love, American Style* – its cheerfully nostalgic take on small-city (Milwaukee, Wisconsin) suburban life also proved to be a remarkable launching pad for some of Hollywood's more serious future talents.

Just for starters, creator Garry Marshall and co-star Ron Howard (but still called 'Ronny' in those TV days) would become two of Hollywood's most successful directors – with, between them, credits such as *Pretty Woman*, *Beaches*, *The Princess Diaries*, *Splash*, *Apollo 13* and *A Beautiful Mind*.

Then, of course, there was cool biker Arthur 'The Fonz' Fonzarelli – probably the show's most memorable character – which led actor Henry Winkler into a productive producer-director career. Even some of the bit players found stardom, most notably, Noriyuki 'Pat' Morita, who, after playing fast-food joint owner Arnold, went on to portray inscrutable martial artist-philosopher, Mr Miyagi, in four *Karate Kid* films.

CRISIS MANAGEMENT
THE PALLISERS (1974)

Churchgoing in Britain was disrupted when *The Forsyte Saga* was screened on Sunday evenings in 1967. Seven years after the BBC triumphed with Galsworthy in black and white, it came hurtling back down to earth with Trollope's all-colour Victorian saga. Why?

Like the earlier, sprawling, series, this was conceived as another mighty 26-parter and even had the reassuring presence of Susan Hampshire – who'd captured a nation's heart as Fleur Forsyte – in the central role here of flighty Lady Glencora.

But perhaps the big difference between then and now was not so much a nation's heart but its very state in the early 1970s.

The country was in the middle of an energy crisis prompted by rising oil prices and strike action by train drivers, power engineers and miners. The government had ordered a three-day week, petrol-ration coupons and, most dramatic of all, a ban on any broadcasting beyond 10.30 p.m.

Schedules were slashed, with BBC2 being so badly hit that some nights the channel opened for only three hours before closing again. *The Pallisers* had been slated to run every Wednesday night from January to July. It appeared on cue, but to muted acclaim and virtually no publicity.

Filming of the final episodes was then disrupted by more industrial action, this time inside the BBC, meaning that transmission had to be put on hold.

The whole enterprise eventually ground to a close in November, nearly eleven months after it had first started screening, and only after the BBC had been forced to repeat five earlier episodes in order to keep the audience in the loop. It was generally felt not to have been worth the effort.

114

FINDING THE TRUTH

THE SIX MILLION DOLLAR MAN (1974–78)

Everyone loved the special effects as hunky Lee Majors convinced the world – well, at least a generation of children who revelled in his slo-mo antics – that former astronaut Steve Austin really was bionic.

But trickery went out of the window on the set of the episode called 'Carnival of Spies' in 1976, when the production inadvertently stumbled on a very American legend.

They were filming in a funhouse in Long Beach, California, and the director wasn't happy with the shot. It seems that there was a dummy hanging off a rope and he thought it didn't look right, so asked a crew member to move it. When the technician grabbed it, the wax that he thought it was made of came off in his hands. Sticking out of the wax arm was a real skeleton.

Forensics experts were called to the scene and it was discovered that the skeleton was the body of famous Old West outlaw Elmer McCurdy. McCurdy was a cowboy who had been killed in a gunfight following a botched robbery. His body was taken to Oklahoma, but wasn't claimed so, apparently, the undertaker charged people to see the body of the celebrated gunslinger.

Five years later, two men arrived saying that they were there to take the body away, but they were actually conmen and they covered it in wax and put it in a circus.

Eventually, poor old Elmer ended up hanging in a Californian carnival. There was a happy ending: after the body had been officially named, it was given a proper burial. Several of the crew members took time out from the set of *The Six Million Dollar Man* to see McCurdy off to his final resting place.

PIE MAN UNMASKED

TISWAS (1974–82)

Was there ever a time when Jim Davidson was actually funny? Only if you believe the story that the bluish comedian was actually 'The Phantom Flan Flinger' on this iconoclastic Saturday morning kids' show.

The Phantom was one of the highlights of a totally enjoyable and utterly anarchic programme. Clad in a black mask and cape, he occasionally leaped onto the set to thrust a custard pie into the face of an unsuspecting guest.

In fact, gunge and water being thrown on people became the thrust of the show. And the Phantom was the king, kersplatting everyone from presenters Chris Tarrant and Lenny Henry, to guests such as cricketer David Gower and comedian Bernard Manning.

Rumours abounded for years that Davidson was actually behind the mask. It was a myth that Davidson only intensified, replying to a letter in the *Daily Mail* that posed the question of the Flinger's identity. He admitted that it was him, but went on to write,

> As I became more involved in the show, it was decided I couldn't play the Phantom any more. My girlfriend at the time, Jane Beaumont, was asked to play the part.
>
> After the show, we were walking to the dressing room, with Jane in her costume with the hood off. A passing *Tiswas* fan remarked 'my, The Phantom Flan Flinger's a girl!'

Not everyone believed Jim's story, though, and reporter Rob Davies believed he finally cracked the story in a local West Midlands newspaper, the *Express & Star*. He eventually tracked down Benny Mills, a cab driver in his late sixties living in Solihull, who revealed that it was him doing all the flanning. Before that other suspects had included news presenter Helen Piddock and minder Tony 'Banger' Walsh.

But it seems that Davies did actually get his man. During the interview, Mills brought out an old suitcase containing his Flinger costume, relegated to the attic since the end of the show.

LET IT ALL HANG OUT
WINNING STREAK (1974–)

Is it just the occasion, or does the fact that television cameras are minutely trained on the event spur (mostly) young people to disrobe in public?

Aussie accountant Michael O'Brien got the ball rolling – if you'll pardon the expression – when he startled not just the crowd at the England–France rugby match at Twickenham but also millions of viewers of this Five Nations encounter. His modesty – and it was pretty modest, joked a police officer – was eventually covered by a bobby's helmet.

Streaking was officially launched that cold day in April 1974. But, as if to underline the diehard sexist nature of the press, the phenomenon didn't get proper front-page coverage until the day after bouncy Erika Roe bounded onto our screens for a half-time cavort during the England–Australia match at Twickers in January 1982. Since then, televised tennis, cricket, golf, snooker and even indoor bowls have enjoyed their fair share of exposure by – and commentator John Arlott mispronounced it rather appropriately on one occasion – 'freakers'.

BURNING RUBBER
THE SWEENEY (1975–82)

'Yer nicked!' and squealing car tyres were the twin trademarks of this no-nonsense British cop series, which finally shook off the old Dixon image for ever.

Though the two stars, John Thaw and Dennis Waterman (as, respectively, Inspector Regan and Sergeant Carter), didn't actually do the driving – the Flying Squad employed the equivalent of chauffeurs – they'd regularly be in the back for some of the hairier chases.

But even they'd be replaced by stuntmen now and then. Which was just as well on one occasion when their car crashed and the passenger side was stove in.

However, the pair were very much in the frame when, as per the script, the call came for them to race out of the office and into their Ford Granada for some squealing-tyre action.

But nothing happened – not even the dramatic ticking over of an engine. It turned out that the supposedly daredevil driver hired for the hot seat not only couldn't drive but didn't even have a licence. So Thaw's stand-in took over and remained at the wheel for the rest of the series.

A RIPPING TUNE

SATURDAY NIGHT LIVE (1975–)

It was supposed to be a musical performance just like any other week. *Saturday Night Live*, the legendary weekly comedy show on NBC, was renowned for its talent (Dan Akyroyd, John Belushi, Bill Murray, Eddie Murphy etc.), but it had also become known for its hip musical acts.

In September 1992, Sinead O'Connor was the most talked-about pop star on the planet and, for her debut performance on the programme, she wanted to do something special that would accentuate the fact that the show genuinely is *live*.

Backstage at the show, O'Connor and her manager agreed with the crew that her second song would be an *a cappella* version of 'War', by Bob Marley, and, since it was a protest song about child abuse, she was going to hold up a picture of a child. Everyone agreed, including executive producer Lorne Michaels.

In rehearsal, O'Connor sang the song and then held up a child's picture. The director, Dave Wilson, zoomed in for a close-up and everyone decided that it was a very poignant moment.

The show began and, after being introduced for a second time by guest host Tim Robbins, O'Connor began her performance. Wilson started getting nervous, but only because she appeared to be singing it more slowly than in rehearsal and he was afraid that they were going to overrun. Eventually, the song came to an end and he went in for the planned close-up.

Unfortunately, unbeknown to anyone, the controversial star had cooked up another plan. She brought out a picture, not of a starving child, but of the Pope (the late John Paul II), which she proceeded to rip in half, live on air.

Unsurprisingly for a country where you are not even allowed to swear on late-night network television, this 'blasphemous' protest caused uproar. However, at first, all there was was a stunned silence. Normally, the applause sign was cued after the performance, but the director shouted to keep it off.

A disgruntled audience member tried to rush the stage and had to be taken away by security. And, as you would imagine, the rest of the show didn't bring many laughs.

Ironically, the show's backroom staff were far more focused that week on the plans of the host, Robbins, notorious for his polemical outbursts, who wanted to make a protest about the business ethics of NBC's owner, General Electric. When he stood on stage at the end of the show with a General Electric T-shirt with a line through it, no one even noticed.

At first, everyone was worried how O'Connor's actions would affect the show and, unsurprisingly, the religiously sensitive press was outraged. When O'Connor performed at a Bob Dylan concert the following week, she was booed – essentially ending her musical career in America.

But NBC executive Warren Littlefield remembers telling Michaels that, when *Saturday Night Live* goes too long without controversy, they must be doing something wrong. Thanks to Sinead O'Connor, the cutting-edge show kept its anarchic reputation for the foreseeable future.

SKETCHING BASIL
FAWLTY TOWERS (1975; 1979)

As every fan knows – and moans about – there were only twelve episodes of this legendary sitcom ever made. Or were there?

Some have argued that Basil first appeared some years earlier in *Doctor at Large*, the 1971 spin-off to London Weekend Television's *Doctor in the House*.

Writer/performer John Cleese famously based his character on a real-life Torquay hotel manager he once met while filming with the Pythons. Cleese (and fellow Python Graham Chapman) contributed scripts for *Doctor at Large*, which led to a rude hotelier popping up on an episode called 'No Ill Feelings'.

The storyline of the show is similar to *Fawlty Towers* in several ways, including a moment where the lead character pours food on a guest's head, and a know-it-all wife. However, as interpreted by actor Timothy Bateson, 'Mr Clifford' was far less angry than Basil, and was played as an altogether more submissive character.

It gave Cleese all the foundation he needed, however. Legend has it that after the show was filmed, producer Humphrey Barclay went up to him and told him that the character was strong enough as the basis for an entire programme. A couple of years later, Cleese (along with his then wife Connie Booth) had written *Fawlty Towers* and treated Barclay to a slap-up meal. Sadly for Bateson, he was not asked to reprise his role and Basil's magnificent rudeness became synonymous with John Cleese for ever.

IN THE LINE OF FIRE
BARETTA (1975–78)

In a career spanning more than sixty years – ever since he started aged six as a member of MGM's *Our Gang* comedies – Robert

Blake has constantly tangled with the law.

Either side of his award-winning role as colourful undercover California cop Tony Baretta – more of which in a moment – the diminutive Blake often played very convincing psychotic killers.

In 1967, he was one of a pair of Kansas drifters who slaughtered a family in a startling adaptation of Truman Capote's documentary novel, *In Cold Blood*. In 1993, he portrayed another real-life killer, John List (in *Judgment Day*), who murdered his wife and children before going on the run for years.

Meanwhile, back at *Baretta*, Blake's increasingly self-destructive real-life character would eventually help drive his once top-rated show towards cancellation. His first marriage to Sondra, who was a frequent guest star, ended soon after.

Cut to more than twenty years on, and Blake, after well-publicised bouts with drink and drugs, was, at 68, now married to bit-part actress Bonny Lee Bakley. Then, less than six months into their union, on 4 May 2001, Bonny was fatally shot outside an Italian restaurant in the San Fernando Valley.

It didn't take long for fans of *Baretta* to recall that the pilot episode of their favourite show way back in 1975 centred on the brutal killing of Tony's new wife – yes, outside an Italian restaurant.

Blake, aged 71, went on trial in California for the murder of Bonny Lee Bakley, mother of their four-year-old daughter, Rose, but was finally acquitted by the jury in March 2005. He was said to be anxious to get back to work.

MONEY MATTERS

WHEEL OF FORTUNE (1975–91)

There are countless stories of film folk incurring huge credit card debt in order to try to finance their projects.

For Jim Taylor, one half (with Alexander Payne) of an award-winning screenwriting team (*Sideways, About Schmidt, Election*), attempting to win big on the popular American game show *Wheel of Fortune* was an intriguing twist.

At a time when he was still an aspiring scribe, Taylor had become increasingly frustrated with, among other things, menial jobs and the inability to afford his own apartment. So, with the help of his pal Payne, with whom he was sharing accommodation, he started training for the show and the prospect of 'a chunk of money'. As he prepared, he felt that, in case he was unsuccessful, he should perhaps at least try to get something other than money out of the exercise.

And that is how he came up with the idea for a short film based on, explained Taylor, 'a third-grade teacher who is engaged to be married and loses on the *Wheel of Fortune*. After the show, not only does his fiancée leave him but his students also make fun of him for being such a dope'.

Before he started taping the show, he approached host Pat Sajack and told him that he wasn't actually a writer as previously mentioned but a 'third-grade teacher'. As he was being introduced, Taylor also slipped in that he was 'engaged to be married to my lovely fiancée Beth'.

What then happened was that Taylor actually ended up winning one show before losing the next (which meant he had suitable 'loser' footage). After winning a boat, and with the show's credits rolling, Taylor raced up to his new vessel and overacted horribly for the cameras.

Sajack was clearly not amused. Bemusement was more the reaction of Taylor's extended family when they saw him announce his engagement to the fictitious Beth on this prime-time slot.

Taylor still has a tape of the show, but as for his film, it never went any further.

PUNCH-DRUNK LUVVIE
ROGUE MALE (1976)

Geoffrey Household's thriller novel – about an Englishman who tries to shoot Hitler and is then pursued back to England – required a sequence with a chase and an electrocution on the London Underground. To film in the Tube requires official sight of the script and discussion before permission can be given. The authorities also made the producers aware that, whenever there's a scene on television in which someone dies on the track, the incidence of suicide on the Underground goes up.

The night before this sequence, they realised that it was too elaborate to be contained within the one Sunday that the Aldwych station and the period tube train were available to them. So, after Saturday filming in Lincoln's Inn Fields was completed, the director, two assistant directors and the producer, Mark Shivas, repaired to a nearby pub to cut the script and rewrite the schedule.

A burly drunk was watching them and asked what they were doing with all the paperwork. They told him, but that only made him more aggressive and he hovered over them, shouting how television people were all 'a bunch of poofs' and didn't know what hard work was.

'Considering that it was ten o'clock on a Saturday night and that we'd been working since dawn, this was truly annoying,' Shivas recalled. 'On he went. We all sat there pretending he wasn't there until I snapped, stood up and told him to go away and leave us alone. For which I got a punch in the mouth and no help from anyone else. My mouth streamed blood and two of my front teeth were loosened.

'The following morning this incident was known to the whole crew and my foolish valour endeared me to our star Peter O'Toole, who, for the rest of the shoot, addressed me as "Knuckles Shivas".'

As for the drunk, he may, of course, have been auditioning for the title role.

ANYONE FOR DENNIS?

BRIMSTONE AND TREACLE (1976)/SCUM (1977)

A week after Dennis Potter's play – about a kind of suburban Satan – had been recorded at BBC Television Centre, and just three weeks before it was due to be transmitted, Alasdair Milne, director of programmes for television, was asked to view a tape of the controversial programme.

Milne, recalling the incident in his autobiography *The Memoirs of a British Broadcaster*, found *Brimstone and Treacle* 'repugnant' and thought it would cause 'outrage' among viewers. Not least of Milne's concerns was a scene in which the cheerfully diabolical Martin (Michael Kitchen) appears to cure a catatonic young woman by raping her. Apparently, this made the sensitive Milne, who would later become the BBC's tenth director-general, feel 'almost physically sick'.

Without any consultation with Potter, Milne decided single-handedly to ban the play (part of a Potter trilogy along with *Double Dare* and *Where Adam Stood*), and it was withdrawn from the imminent schedule.

In a press handout, the BBC explained that 'the rape by the devil . . . of a girl physically and mentally crippled . . . [was] likely to outrage viewers to a degree that its importance as a play does not support'. Kenith Trodd, the producer, had, meanwhile, secretly shown the play to TV critics, who generally rallied round Potter's creation.

Potter used his own *New Statesman* column to rip into Milne and the banning of a work that he noted 'may be the best play I have written'. He invited his readers to ring up Milne c/o the BBC and ask for 'the Ghost of Lord Reith'.

The play would finally be transmitted eleven years later, in 1987, as the concluding work in a Potter retrospective. Intriguingly, one of the critics wrote then, 'I find it less easy to defend now than eleven years ago . . . I don't think the use of rape is clear in [Potter's] mind.'

In between, Potter did at least have the satisfaction (for what it was worth – which wasn't much considering generally poor reviews and precious little box office) of writing a film version of the play, with Sting as Young Nick.

The film version of *Brimstone and Treacle* is mostly long forgotten, unlike the movie of *Scum*, which has become one of British cinema's cult classics. This one followed just two years after the BBC banned Roy Minton's original play, which (like the film) was directed by another *enfant terrible*, the late Alan Clarke.

This harrowing and undeniably raw tale of Borstal boy rivalries was shot in a former old people's home in Redhill with a youthful cast of newcomers including Phil Daniels, Ray Burdis, David Threlfall, and twenty-year-old sometime boxer Ray ('I'm the Daddy now!') Winstone.

The story's suicides, violence and male rape necessitated what was known at the BBC as an 'Early Warning Synopsis', which was relayed in bald terms to management by *Play for Today* producer Margaret Matheson. There appeared to be no concerned reaction as a result.

But *after* production and *before* scheduled transmission, Bill Cotton (son of the old 'wakey, wakey!' bandleader), who had in the interim taken over as Controller of BBC1, wanted a postponement of the broadcast. Then Matheson was told that certain cuts would be required. No suggestions were forthcoming. With, now, the backing of Alasdair Milne (yes, him, again), *Scum* finally became what was wittily dubbed 'The Billy Cotton Banned Show'.

The BBC version was eventually transmitted for the first time in 1991, a year after Alan Clarke's death.

MINE'S A TRIPLE

CHRISTMAS ICE SPECTACULAR (1976)

John Curry, Britain's first-ever figure-skating Olympic gold-medal winner, was still basking in the glow of his Innsbruck

Winter Games triumph when he was invited by London Weekend TV to be the climactic act for its glittering ice spectacular the following Christmas.

Filming took place at a suitably redecorated Streatham Ice Rink, where the elegant Curry was required to repeat his gold-winning performance topped off with an eye-boggling triple salchow (a spectacular rotating jump).

The trouble was, in the less competitive atmosphere of south London, Curry was having enormous difficulty recreating his Austrian magic. Every time he attempted the triple, he fell over.

After more than thirty takes, it was clear that the increasingly distraught Curry, feet now bloodied, had some kind of mental blockage. With Take 40 about to be attempted, the director decided on a more personal approach. He inched carefully across the ice and whispered something in the skater's ear.

Cue music, and this time Curry soared successfully into and, more importantly, out of his triple, landing perfectly on the ice. So what had been the magic piece of advice proffered by the desperate director?

'Listen, son, either you do it this time or you can f***ing well go home!' was the helmsman's admirably concise counsel. And it clearly worked.

STARTING AT THE BOTTOM

THE COLLECTION (1976)

What became known infamously as the 'Bog Wars' started when the prestige cast of Laurence Olivier, Alan Bates, Helen Mirren and Malcolm McDowell gathered at Granada's studios in Manchester to record a new ITV version of Harold Pinter's play.

Apparently, the management were so thrilled to have snared Olivier and co. that they assembled new luxury dressing rooms and toilets for the ensemble.

But, perhaps worried that Larry and his fellow thesps might become tainted, personnel from Granada's other onsite productions – notably *Coronation Street* – were banned from using the facilities.

The *Corrie* residents were especially incensed and formed a deputation to protest to drama executives. The usually affable Bryan Mosley, who played Councillor Alf Roberts, was heard shouting, 'If we can't wipe our arses on the best soft loo paper paid for by you, I, for one, will bring my own in.'

True to his word, he arrived the following day carrying a bumper packet of twelve rolls, which he distributed in the greenroom, where the cast would relax. Another *Corrie* regular, Lynn Perrie (Ivy Tilsley), brought in a plunger, which she kept by her side.

Meanwhile, the Pinter cast – carefully kept clear of the 'soap mob' – remained blissfully unaware of the storm caused by this lavatorial apartheid.

Two years later, the late Michael Elphick, a one-time *Corrie* actor, was working at Granada on the series *Holding On* when he heard about the two-tier loo system (which was still in existence). He sneaked into the security office and announced over the Tannoy that 'with immediate effect, through a change in policy, the special bathroom facilities are now open and available to everyone.'

Guess who was first in the queue for the posh loo. The *Corrie* gang, of course. Elphick later remarked, 'It was the Day of the Great Unwashed. Of course, all hell broke out when the suits got word of what was happening. But the point was made. Granada was not a place fit for snobbery. In fact, there was no place for that kind of stuff in British television – apart from the BBC!'

CHUCK-A-MENTAL
THE GONG SHOW (1976–80)

Can you imagine Anne Robinson jetting off after a recording of *The Weakest Link* to assassinate an al-Qaeda terrorist? Probably not, but that's a modern equivalent of the incredible story of Chuck Barris.

To many, Barris is a televisual genius, revolutionising popular television with his game shows *The Dating Game* (the forerunner of every modern dating show under the sun) and, more importantly, *The Gong Show* – a wacky talent contest cum comedy variety programme. The influence of the latter can be seen today in shows such as *Pop Idol* and *The X Factor*.

To everyone else, he was a nut – a producer lowering the standards of television and championing idiots. What they didn't call him was a stone-cold killer.

This changed following the publication of his autobiography *Confessions of a Dangerous Mind* (since adapted as a movie, directed by George Clooney) in 1984. In it, Barris suggested that he combined his production career with a sideline as a covert agent for the CIA. That's right, the CIA, travelling round the world, murdering people to protect the American way of life.

So is it really true? Well, most people say no, referring to the fact that Barris is a known prankster and because the book is subtitled *An Unauthorised Autobiography* and thereby a work of fiction. At the same time, the beginning of the book talks about Barris heading out of the house and talking to a cabbie, who then tells him he is off to New York to 'kill a wop named Moretti'.

He continues by talking about being recruited, about his CIA boss, Jim Byrd, and about run-ins with the KGB and other Secret Service operatives.

The more romantic (or perhaps the sicker) among us would like to believe that there's something to the story. Certainly, Barris used to accompany his *Dating Game* contestants on their dream date abroad as a chaperone – the reason being, he says, so that he could either plan a hit or carry one out. And staff members on his production team do remember his being away for periods of time with little explanation.

Whether Chuck Barris is a government-sanctioned killer or simply a televisual entrepreneur and storyteller, he certainly does have a Dangerous Mind.

TWO OF A KIND
THE PROFESSIONALS (1977–83)

The Bullshitters, as a glorious 1982 *Comic Strip* short spoofed the show, were Bodie (meathead Lewis Collins) and Doyle (afro-haired Martin Shaw, who should have known better and often wished he had), a pair of absurdly macho British secret agents for covert CI5.

The show was undeniably popular, though whether you were laughing *with* them or *at* them as they blended violently OTT action with cartoon-bubble dialogue is hard to say. In fact, the final episode of the first series, called 'Klansman' (about inner-city racism), was banned from transmission altogether for being too violent.

Shaw, a more peaceful lawman these days playing P D James's doomy detective Adam Dalgleish or self-righteous Judge John Deed, claims he hated every moment of his *Pro*-bondage – especially his haircut ('Lewis used to call me the Bionic Golliwog').

A bit precious about his more serious thesping, for many years Shaw blocked repeat TV showings of the series. Although he gave his reason as not being able to negotiate fees for TV repeats with the programme makers London Weekend Television, it was also alleged he wanted not to be typecast with the 'hard man' image the show portrayed. He only eventually consented to repeat showings in the mid-1990s, when it was discreetly pointed out to him that the widow of another cast member could do with the income generated by repeat fees.

PICTURE THIS

TAKE HART (1977–83)

What connects cravat-wearing Tony Hart and the Vietnam War? Was the silver-haired artist really once a 'black' operative who parachuted regularly into Saigon on secret missions? Or did all the children whose pictures never made it into the Gallery resort to a water-pistol version of Russian roulette?

Strange as it might seem, the latter is not so far from the truth. Perhaps the best part of the educational-but-always-entertainment art show was the aforementioned Gallery, a segment where we saw doodlings sent in by kids.

The height of cool was to have the BBC cameraman pick out your handiwork, stuck haphazardly to a wall, and broadcast it to a grateful nation.

And what ditty did they use to accompany this kid-friendly slot? None other than the theme from one of the most depressing and decidedly adult antiwar movies ever made. As little Johnny's rice collage of 'my house' crept onto the screen, you could hear the crescendo of Stanley Myers's 'Cavatina', better known as the theme to *The Deer Hunter*.

Kids, thankfully, were blissfully unaware. But film-literate parents must have been secretly astonished. Was this a quietly subversive ploy by a witty television producer, or just coincidence?

The answer remains a mystery, but. when Christopher Walken blows his brains out in *The Deer Hunter*, there are probably adults of a certain age who see through the horror and visualise a beautiful, crimson still life.

NAILING CHRIST

JESUS OF NAZARETH (1977)

Long before 'Mel Gibson's *The Passion of the Christ*', there was 'Lew Grade Presents *Jesus of Nazareth*'.

Britain's favourite Charleston-dancing showbiz entrepreneur was having an audience at the Vatican with Pope Paul VI to celebrate the transmission of *Moses The Lawgiver*, Grade's co-production with Italy's main TV channel, RAI. At the end of their get-together, the pontiff said, 'I hope one day you will do the story of Jesus' – and cigar-sucking Grade promised he would.

Not that he claimed to have any recall of this pledge – his wife, relieved he'd kept his word, would remind him of it later – when a fortnight later he was having dinner with the head of RAI, who asked Grade what they should next make together. 'Jesus of Nazareth,' he replied without hesitation.

With Franco Zeffirelli directing the six-hour marathon, the idea was to have a name in every frame: Olivier, Ustinov, Ralph Richardson, Anne Bancroft, Christopher Plummer, Rod Steiger, and so on. Except for the actor playing Jesus, who should, effectively, be an unknown and therefore with no distracting baggage.

Grade's wife alerted him to Robert Powell, a young British actor in a BBC adaptation of Hardy's *Jude The Obscure*, remarking on 'his wonderful blue eyes'. After he'd been signed up, the only problem was the reaction to Powell's casting in some of the tabloids because it turned out he was living 'in sin' with his girlfriend, raunchy Pan's People dancer, Babs Lord. When Grade saw some of the headlines, he is said to have remarked, quite guilelessly, 'What are they trying to do? Crucify the boy?' Powell and Lord married soon before shooting started.

In a 1999 list of what became dubbed 'The Pope's Oscars', a rundown of 45 films that were seemed to be 'suitable viewing for the faithful', *Jesus Of Nazareth* was the only TV production, sandwiched in at Number Five between Chaplin's *Modern Times* and *Ben-Hur*.

A Jew, born in Russia, Grade could hardly have been described as one of the 'faithful'. He did, however, claim that there was some serendipity in his choice of the subject matter, for he was born on 25 December.

BEST OF THE BREAST

PENNIES FROM HEAVEN (1978)

While working on Dennis Potter's landmark series, the lovely Gemma Craven became the centre of some unwelcome attention.

The offbeat adventures of song-sheet pedlar Arthur Parker (played by Bob Hoskins) and his affair with a beautiful young teacher Eileen (Cheryl Campbell) was already creating a stir at the Beeb's west London studios.

Then word leaked out from the production that Craven, who was playing Hoskins's screen wife, was having particular problems coming to terms with a disturbing love scene in which she had to rouge her nipples to excite Arthur.

Best known to that point for her role as sweet Cinderella in *The Slipper and the Rose*, Craven, a strict churchgoing Roman Catholic who had attended a nuns-supervised Catholic high school in Leigh-on-Sea, Essex, tried to find various ways to cover herself for the scene. She pleaded with producer Kenith Trodd and director Piers Haggard to make 'alterations'. This, following discussions with Potter, they decided they could not do.

On the day in question Craven, close to tears and trembling, appeared on the 'closed set' with Hoskins. But lurking in the shadows were six BBC executives, unconnected with the production, who had crept in and had positioned themselves behind props to get (or sneak) a good view of Craven disrobing and jiggling her naughty bits in front of Hoskins.

Unfortunately for them, their giggling and shuffling alerted the protective Hoskins, who stepped forwards past the cameras and headed in their direction. On realising that the gaggle of suits had nothing to do with the production, Hoskins, a 'bit of a nutter from Finsbury Park' (his own words), tore into the Oxbridge set, dispersing them in many directions – all out of the studio.

He later said, 'Bastards, bastards . . . you'd think they would have given the girl a break.' They continued with the scene, which to this day still leaves Craven blushing. Hoskins said, 'I'm a gent, I am,' echoing Pygmalion. 'Got to protect a girl's honour, 'aven't you.'

REQUIEM FOR A DREAM

DALLAS (1978–91)

The bounds of reality were tested more than once by *Dallas*, a homage to 1980s excess, hairstyles and family feuds. A rollicking tale of the oil-rich Ewing family, the series introduced an almost operatic quality to the weekly adventures of a curiously photogenic but utterly dysfunctional clan.

It made an iconic antihero of J R Ewing, too, the bad boys' bad boy. The fact that he was played by Larry Hagman, a perennial nice guy in series such as *I Dream of Jeannie* until then, only underlined the programme's twisted values.

JR was certainly a more interesting character than his goody-two-shoes younger brother Bobby, played by Patrick Duffy, yet it seems that the appeal of the characters rested on their opposing personalities coming into conflict. So it seemed when Duffy left the series in 1985, his character dying in a car accident, never to return.

A dip in ratings was enough for producers to insist that death should have no dominion over their clean-cut hero. Hagman personally persuaded Duffy to return, and he was reintroduced a season later.

As Bobby emerges from the shower to face his understandably baffled wife Pam (Victoria Principal), his absence was dismissed as merely 'her dream'. Even in the rarefied world of Texan oil barons, this strained credulity.

Confusingly, Gary Ewing, who appeared in the spin-off series *Knot's Landing*, had a call informing him of Bobby's death, suggesting that Pam's frenzied imagination had dreamed up whole chunks of that show's plot, too.

GREEN FOR DANGER

THE INCREDIBLE HULK (1978–82)

'You wouldn't like me when I'm angry.' Who can forget scurrying behind the sofa every time Dr David Banner (Bill Bixby) uttered those words? And who can possibly forget the muscled, green-skinned, strangely coiffured monster (Lou Ferrigno) that emerged from his transformation?

But for Ferrigno, a renowned bodybuilder and mate of Arnold Schwarzenegger, it almost never was. That's because the producers first decided to cast another man-mountain, Richard Kiel, best known as Jaws in the 007 films.

Kiel was hired by executive producer (and director) Kenneth Johnson to play the role because he felt that Kiel was a better actor than Ferrigno and they wanted someone who could pull off the pathos and drama needed for the Hulk.

Unfortunately, they realised that Kiel simply wasn't *big* enough to play the role and so he was replaced. However, although all his scenes were reshot, Kiel does remain in the pilot episode. One high-angle shot from a tree, looking down on the Hulk as he rescues a little girl from the lake is, in fact, the metal-toothed monster.

Rumour has it that Kiel wasn't too fussed anyway – the green contact lenses were apparently irritating his eyes.

SCHOOL FOR SCANDAL

GRANGE HILL (1978–)

This deceptively simple saga of students at a London comprehensive is one of the longest-running children's programmes in history. But it's also a show that tends to provoke the reaction, 'Well, it's not nearly as good as it was in *my* day.'

People who say that are generally those who joined the fanbase around 1982, when the top dog at Grange Hill was Zammo Maguire (Lee MacDonald).

Zammo caused a furore when he became addicted to heroin. There was a national debate between those in favour, who said it was bringing a serious problem to attention, and those against, who said the show was polluting kids' minds.

For those who actually watched it, it was a touching, well-executed and gritty storyline. But it generated something that genuinely *did* pollute kids' minds. And it was called 'Just Say No'.

'Just Say No' was a terrible song with a positive message, encouraging youngsters to stay away from toxic substances. It even got to Number Five in the charts and spawned a spin-off album. Unfortunately, it was sung very badly by the cast, with Zammo centre stage.

So 'good' was its message, however, that the Grange Hillers were invited to visit the then American first lady, Nancy Reagan.

A good thing done for a good cause by good people, then? Well, apparently not, because Erkan Mustafa (who played resident fatty Roland) shocked everyone subsequently by revealing that several of the cast were actually high on drugs while they were shooting the 'Just Say No' video.

135

STAR CRAZY

THE STAR WARS HOLIDAY SPECIAL (1978)

A TV special spin-off to (then) the biggest movie of all time sounds like a no-brainer. And that must have been the thinking at CBS on 17 November 1978, when they launched this fiasco on an unsuspecting public.

Unfortunately for the viewers, who were looking forward to two hours of space battles, one-liners from Han Solo and an extra glimpse into the mind of George Lucas, what they got was something altogether more surreal.

In fact, Lucas doesn't seem to have had much to do with it, and so disappointed was he with the final product that he tried to buy up all the master tapes to ensure that it was never seen again. He wasn't able to do that, but it has never been repeated on television and is impossible to buy commercially.

However, bootlegged copies have circled for years, leading Lucas once to remark at an Australian sci-fi convention, 'If I had the time and a sledgehammer, I would track down every bootleg copy of that programme and smash it.'

So why was Lucas so dismayed? Surely a follow-up to the greatest of all sci-fi fantasy flicks couldn't have been that bad, could it? Think again. Co-written by Pat Proft (one of the men behind *Airplane!*), it must have appeared to the viewer as one giant spoof – but it's not, and the show is a litany of disaster.

The spine of the 'story' is simple: Chewbacca is trying to get back to his home planet to celebrate the Wookiee festival, Life Day, with his wife Mala, son Lumpy and grandfather Itchy. Unfortunately, the Empire (minus Darth Vader) are on the tail of the Rebel forces. Since Wookiees don't speak any English, they are helped by a local human trader and Rebel sympathiser, played by Art Carney.

Obviously deciding that the doglike Chewie was the most fuzzy (and probably most available) cast member from the film, we get a glimpse of Wookiee family life, as well as catching up with all the stars of the movie. However, nothing really connects with anything, but it doesn't matter, because everything can be seen on the viewing screens, or inside Lumpy's holographic units. Argued like that, it doesn't seem so bad – slightly misjudged, perhaps a touch embarrassing and sentimental.

It's much worse. For example, the show opens with an unsubtitled sequence of Chewbacca's family at home. This lasts for ten minutes, as they potter about their tree house and make growling noises.

To lighten the boredom now shared by cast and audience alike, they switch on their hologram unit, unleashing a parade of miniature gymnasts, who proceed to perform a Lilliputian dance montage.

Mark Hamill shows up with R2-D2 on a monitor to wish them a 'Happy Life Day' and looks as if he is on the brink of laughter throughout his scene.

To introduce Art Carney, we see him in his workshop, while an Imperial Guard browses for goodies. The scene ends with the guard walking off with a personal groomer (a.k.a. nose-hair trimmer).

Mala prepares a meal by watching a drag-queen cooking show.

There are shots of starfights from *Star Wars*, with specially shot footage of Han and Chewie in the cockpit. Harrison Ford does his very best to lend some credibility to the proceedings, but even he finds it difficult when he has to say such lines as, 'I feel the same way about you, pal – and your family.' And then remark about little Lumpy, 'I think his voice is changing.'

There's a ten-minute, rather sexually charged kaleidoscope effects sequence, in which white-feather-hat-wearing singer Diahann Carroll tells a Wookiee repeatedly that she finds him adorable, before launching into a love ballad.

Boba Fett makes his first appearance (remember, this came out before *The Empire Strikes Back*) in a cartoon in which Luke and the druids go to rescue Chewie and Han from an evil Imperial talisman. Fett initially pretends he's their friend, before being caught chatting to Darth Vader and making his escape.

Bea Arthur from *The Golden Girls* shows up as a sassy bartender in the Tatooine cantina from the movie. First she is chatted up by a besotted customer, then she leads the bar clientele in a song about the Empire's decision to shut down her establishment, accompanied by the band from the film.

The special culminates with everyone important from the movie (except Alec Guinness and Vader) standing at the Tree of Life, while the Wookiees – dressed in gospel-choir crimson cassocks – celebrate Life Day. After a stirring speech about coming together to defeat evil, Princess Leia (Carrie Fisher) dazzles the crowd with an epic tune about happiness, to the melody of the movie's title music.

Now why would George Lucas want to make sure that no one saw that?

CLOSE ENCOUNTERS

BBC NEWS (1978)

On New Year's Eve, after *My Fair Lady* . . .

In the late hours of 30 December, an Argosy freight plane left Wellington, New Zealand. On board with the aircrew was an Australian TV unit from Channel 10 Network hoping to capture a UFO on film.

For some weeks UFOs had been sighted over Cook Strait. When the aircraft was flying over the Pacific Ocean, to the northeast of South Island, the pilots observed a strange object in the sky; they endeavoured to verify their sighting with radar confirmation at Wellington air-traffic control.

Reporter Quentin Fogarty stated that he saw a row of five bright lights that were pulsating and grew from the size of a pinpoint to that of a large balloon. The whole sequence was then repeated, the lights now appearing over the town of Kaikoura, between the aircraft and the ground. This object pulsated from a pinpoint to the size of a large balloon.

At this stage, cameraman David Crockett was wearing the headphones and was warned by Wellington control that an unknown object was following the Argosy – the pilot immediately turned the plane 360 degrees in order to ascertain what had been behind them.

The people aboard the aircraft saw nothing but yet once more Wellington control warned them, 'Sierra Alpha Eagle, you have a target in formation with you . . . target has increased in size.'

At this, the crew and passengers saw lights outside the aircraft but were unable to film them because of interference by the plane's navigation lights. When the navigation lights were turned off, however, everyone aboard the aircraft saw a big, bright light which Crockett was able to capture on his hand-held camera.

In order to do this, Crockett had to exchange seats with the copilot, causing the resultant filming to suffer from the effects of camera shake. However, he managed to obtain thirty seconds of decent footage.

Another radar confirmed an object filmed from the aircraft. The pilot then turned the plane completely around once more and the object was not visible, but Wellington control maintained that its echo was still evident on radar.

As the Argosy approached Christchurch, the fuel gauge went haywire but apparently this was not necessarily something unusual and they tuned in on the UFO off Banks Peninsular. Wellington control now had the object on radar while the aircraft landed at Christchurch

At 2.15 a.m., on 31 December, the aircraft set off on a return flight and very quickly two strange objects came into view. Crockett observed one of the objects through his camera and described a spinning sphere with lateral lines around it, and one of the objects appeared on the aircraft's radar for four minutes.

As the aircraft approached the end of its flight, two pulsating lights were observed – one suddenly falling for about a thousand feet before eventually stopping in a series of jerky movements.

The resultant film taken during these two flights was shown all over the world – the BBC giving it priority on the main evening news programme.

Despite the fact that the filmed events were also evident on ground-based radar, sceptics were driven to extreme and strange lengths to explain the filmed evidence, including the lights from shrimp boats, top-secret US remote-controlled planes, etc.

It should be noted that the Royal New Zealand Air Force was so concerned about the event that Skyhawk jet fighters had been put on full alert in order to intercept the UFOs.

Following the broadcasting of the film by the BBC and the subsequent investigation, the *Daily Telegraph* remarked, 'The scientist who suggested that all [on the aircraft] were seeing Venus on a particularly bright night can be safely consigned to Bedlam!'

The presence of this object was confirmed by Wellington air-traffic control. As for the broadcast, it remains in the minds of all who saw it.

STAYING IN CHARACTER

TAXI (1978–83)

Who the hell is Tony Clifton? That's the question everyone was asking when the corpulent, disruptive, arrogant, mustachioed and mysterious lounge singer immediately started causing chaos after arriving on the set of the US sitcom.

Clifton was the creation of Andy Kaufman, the eccentric, some-say-genius comedian/performance artist best known for his role as Latka Gravas on *Taxi*. Kaufman was a character comic and, for him, Clifton – an alcoholic, abusive, sexually depraved, talentless Vegas lounge singer – was perhaps his finest creation.

It was a few weeks into the first series of *Taxi* and Kaufman was bored. Hardly a stickler for routine and despite smash reviews for his portrayal of the naïve immigrant, he found it all too mundane, a far cry from the adversarial characters he preferred to play.

He had already been the scourge of *Saturday Night Live* and had wrestled women live on TV, but that wasn't enough. So he sent his manager George Shapiro to the producers of *Taxi* to tell them that they had to write a role for Tony Clifton in an upcoming episode.

Knowledgeable of Kaufman's wacky ways, but with a hit on their hands and keen to keep him happy, they agreed. Little did they know what they were letting themselves in for.

A special show was written, originally entitled *Brother Rat*, in which Tony would play the brother of Louie De Palma (series regular Danny de Vito). When the rest of the cast read it, they sat around asking who Clifton was, and casting director Rhonda Young, who was in on the joke, told them that he was an abrasive, caustic character, perfect for the role.

Afterwards, she went up to Kaufman, who had remained silent. When she asked him how she had done, keeping the secret, he told her that he was going away for three weeks and that the *real* Tony Clifton would be there to play the part.

However, one of the supporting actors remembers the show's creator, Ed Weinberger, quietly taking everyone aside and telling them that someone who looked a bit like Kaufman, but wasn't Kaufman, would be on set and that Latka wouldn't take part in the episode.

Soon, everyone – nervous about the inevitable difficulties but excited about the deception – waited in earnest to start preparing for and then shooting the show. Andy and his best friend Bob Zmuda employed the skills of a makeup artist, who designed Clifton's unpleasant visage – double chin, booze-ravaged nose, thick muttonchops, deliberately bad wig and luxurious moustache. Each morning, Kaufman went to the artist's house to spend two hours having the makeup applied.

Add to that a cheap tux, fat suit and naff shirt and the monster that is Tony Clifton was ready to be unveiled. The makeup artist, Ken Chase, remembers that, once the face had been put on, Andy Kaufman ceased to be – he just *became* Clifton.

An episode of *Taxi* took a week to make, starting with a table read of the script on Monday and finishing with the live recording on Friday. Clifton arrived early on Monday and relaxed in his Winnebago (because he was Tony and not Andy, he refused to use the same dressing room) and chatted with two shapely blondes who had been procured for his pleasure (many thought that they were prostitutes).

It must have been an amazing sight – everyone sitting around the table, not knowing what to think, as Clifton swigged whisky and chain-smoked (Andy was a nonsmoking teetotaller), stank of BO and tried it on with every woman in the room, something that Andy would never do.

After a disastrous run-through on Tuesday, in which Clifton barked his lines and failed to gel with the rest of the cast, Weinberger nervously realised that he was going to have to fire him. The show was still in its infancy and, anarchic as this was, it was still too risky.

Of course, he was worried that, by sacking Clifton, he would offend Andy. So he called Clifton's trailer and asked whether Andy would be able to come up and see him at his own convenience. When Kaufman (as Andy) showed up, Weinberger, staying in character, explained that Clifton was simply too big for the show, that he took over the episode and that he was going to have to get rid of him.

Much to his relief, Kaufman agreed, but asked that he wait until the following day, when Clifton would come in late and be unprofessional and give Weinberger an excuse to fire him properly, in front of the entire cast and crew.

The next day, presents of a little toy dog were handed out to the cast from Tony, with a card attached, saying, 'It's a pleasure working with you. I'm proud to be a member of the cast of *Taxi*.' However, there seemed to be stirrings of a scene, as fellow cast member Tony Danza had brought along a video camera and manager George Shapiro had his little tape recorder.

Finally, Clifton arrived, swigging whisky, announcing that he had rewritten the show, but being nice to everyone. Weinberger came down to the set, aware of what he had to do, and pretended to be angry, saying Clifton was late, that he had hired someone else to play his part and that he had to get off the set.

Of course, Andy/Tony had other plans. Rather than live up to their gentlemen's agreement, Clifton went mad, shouting

'Getcha hands off me!' even though no one had touched him, and threatening to call the police.

Another cast member, Jeff Conaway, who was renowned for disapproving of Kaufman's eccentricities, moved in to hit him and had to be held back by the director James Burrows. It was left to the more tranquil Judd Hirsch, the nominal star of the show, to smooth the waters. But Clifton continued to cause a ruckus and, whether it was acting or not, Hirsch flipped, grabbed him and, along with some security guards, bundled him out of the studio.

Clifton was banned from the Paramount lot for life and, later on, Kaufman excitedly called Weinberger and Shapiro and thanked them for playing their part in the charade.

Although slightly bemused by the whole incident, the cast returned to normal and even gathered to watch Danza's footage that he had shot during the debacle. As the movie played, Andy walked into the room and stood watching, while everyone else looked at their feet. Danza remembers the movie finishing and an ominous silence, before Kaufman cleared his throat and said, 'Gee, who was that asshole?'

Of course, Andy Kaufman being Andy Kaufman, *Taxi* wasn't the only time he stirred up television. Perhaps his most infamous performance came when he was guest host of *Fridays* (1980), a *Saturday Night Live* knock-off on ABC.

His sketch was supposed to be simple – a group of people sitting in a restaurant, taking turns to go out back and smoke marijuana. Each would come back in turn and act stoned. Very simple, very eighties.

This wasn't enough for Kaufman. He called a meeting with the producers and said that he wanted to break character halfway through the sketch, ruining it, and then make everyone angry by refusing to do it. (Kaufman loved to deliberately sabotage a comedy bit. His manager George Shapiro called it his 'bombing routine'.)

There are conflicting stories as to how many of the other sketch participants were let in on the joke. Michael Richards (later to find fame as Kramer in *Seinfeld*) certainly was, but many think that Maryedith Burrell and Melanie Chartoff weren't.

Halfway through the sketch, in front of a live studio audience, Kaufman wanders back from the 'bathroom' and starts complaining that he can't carry on and that he feels idiotic trying to act stoned. Everyone else, including the audience, sat there nervously, not sure what to do.

Richards, looking angry, stormed off the set, picked up the cue cards and threw them down in front of Andy. Burrell sat, embarrassingly cackling, as Kaufman threw a glass of water in Richards's face. Then Chartoff started to push a bread roll onto Andy's head and the producer sprinted onto the set and shouted at the director to cut to the advertisements. And – like most of Andy's stunts – it all ended in an on-set fight.

Of course, the audience in the studio were all watching with wide-eyed awe, while the viewers at home jammed the ABC switchboards. Did they think they were watching a real fight, or were they aware that they were just another 'character' in the Andy Kaufman pantomime of life?

SHORT FUSE

DANGER UXB (1979)

One of the features of this excellent ITV series, which dealt with the Bomb Disposal Unit during World War Two, was its sense of authenticity. Perhaps it was just a bit *too* authentic.

The art director used to keep all his prop bits and pieces in the back of his small station wagon, which had Northern Ireland number plates. One day he asked for the afternoon off because his wife had managed to get two last-minute matinée tickets for *Evita*, which was showing in the West End. He drove to the theatre and managed to park the car round the corner in Soho.

When the couple emerged around teatime, they found the street cordoned off, full of policemen and bomb-disposal experts, all eyeing his car with caution, for inside they could see suspicious-looking canisters and a large aerial bomb . . .

ELECTION FEVER

NOT THE NINE O'CLOCK NEWS (1979–82)

The first major revival of political satire on the BBC since the golden days of *TW3*, this often painfully funny, and highly quotable, current-events spoof made stars of Rowan Atkinson, Mel Smith, Griff Rhys-Jones and Pamela Stephenson.

But, had it not been for the 1979 general election, we might never have seen at least three of those faces in their various *NTNOCN* guises.

Only the rubber-faced Atkinson and Chris Langham (who would appear in just the first series) were among the line-up in the first-ever episode of the show.

The other co-stars were ex-Scaffold singer John Gorman, Christopher Godwin, Jonathan Hyde and outsize fiftysomething Willoughby Goddard (best known as the greedily evil Austrian governor, Gessler, in ITV's *The Adventures of William Tell* two decades earlier).

They filmed a series of sketches, but then an election was called and, because of a rule about political content on TV during a campaign, this pilot episode had to be shelved – for ever.

CAUGHT ON THE CHEAP

SHERLOCK HOLMES AND DR WATSON (1979)

The great Baker Street detective and his faithful sidekick have been a staple of series television dating back more than half a century to 1951, when Alan Wheatley (later the Sheriff of Nottingham in TV's *Robin Hood*) partnered Raymond Francis in six 35-minute stories for the BBC.

Three years later, Ronald (son of Leslie) Howard linked up with Howard Marion-Crawford for 39 American-financed, half-hour episodes, which were supervised by maverick producer Sheldon Reynolds – in a studio in Paris. A week's location shooting had been allocated for England to try to get some authentic-looking footage for the whole series, but it apparently rained so much that most of the material was unusable.

Since then, the BBC cast Douglas Wilmer, then Peter Cushing, opposite Nigel Stock in the mid-sixties; and then we saw Granada's stylish Jeremy Brett–David Burke (later Edward Hardwicke) tandem in the eighties and nineties. And that's not even counting serials and one-off TV films that have dotted the decades.

But the strangest English-language version must surely be this late-seventies offering, which has never actually made it onto British television. It co-starred a deerstalkered Geoffrey Whitehead, with Donald Pickering as the good doctor, and perhaps its least Strange aspect was that it had been packaged by the aforementioned Mr Reynolds, who simply recycled the scripts from many of his old monochrome fifties episodes – but now in living colour.

Ever one to try to snare a good deal, Reynolds, this time round, came up with the oddest location yet for Victorian London's 221B Baker Street – Poland. To be precise, the state-run Poltel Studios in Warsaw. Remember, these were still, ostensibly, the dark days of Soviet domination long before almost the whole of Eastern Europe would become open season for Western producers seeking cheap deals in dollar-hungry, newly market-force-led states.

According to Val Guest, who directed nine of the 24 episodes, one of the producers told him that it was 'a matter of foreign currency. They [the Poles] need foreign currency desperately and this is one way they can get it.'

In his memoirs, Guest professed himself suitably gobsmacked by the sheer size of the Baker Street set at Poltel, not to mention the huge numbers employed by the production. 'This, I was informed gently, was communism. No one was allowed to be out of work, so they were drafted into any going operation. The fact that most of them slipped away to sleep in the fields or hidden doorways meant nothing to the studio. They were not out of work and that justified the system.'

Another of the series' directors, Roy Ward Baker, recalled hearing that, towards the end of shooting, the head of the studio, who'd sanctioned the show, had been arrested for corruption. And it also seems that not even the normally Teflon-coated Reynolds was immune from disaster.

Caught up in a currency-changing fracas with the Polish authorities, Reynolds was forced to hand over all the film negatives of the series, leaving him only with the so-called 'cutting copy' to sell around the world. Which perhaps explains why this version of the famous sleuth remains the lowest-profile of them all.

FLY-ING TONIGHT

AN AUDIENCE WITH JASPER CARROTT (1979)

The ITV stand-up comedy show that launched Carrott almost caught him with his trousers down – literally! During the 'live' stage show the Brummie funny-man had cracked a gag about his trouser zip breaking.

The audiences were in stitches, and so were the stage and TV crews. But he wasn't joking! The zip had come apart. When Jasper (real name Robert Davis) called over to the wings that he would need new trousers during the first commercial break, they thought it was part of the act.

When the penny finally dropped, it was a last-minute rush to get a new set of trousers and the comic was standing in the wings in his Y-fronts squeezing into another pair of trousers just as the adverts finished.

COLOUR COORDINATION
SAPPHIRE AND STEEL (1979–82)

Don't confuse the ravaged, coke-snorting old slapper that's Patsy Stone in *Absolutely Fabulous* with svelte action girl Sapphire, who could see through time in this mildly inventive adventure series a decade earlier.

Of course, both were the creations of Joanna Lumley, who'd first honed her heroic high-kicking skills as bob-haired Purdey in *The New Avengers*.

You knew when Sapphire was going all psychic because her blue eyes would start glowing vividly. This was achieved by an electronic colour process known as 'chromakey'.

From a close-up of Lumley, the vision mixer used an invisible mask to select her eyes and then keyed on a colour to make them shine blue. During the various series, the exact shade of her peepers was taken from the colour of her dresses and makeup.

Strange to think that, originally, Sapphire's psychic powers were to have been evidenced by a vein throbbing in her head. Apparently a makeup girl had created this using a rubber patch, which, according to producer-director Shaun O'Riordan, 'looked grotesque, like a huge growth on her [Lumley's] head'. Shades of Patsy?

CAR TROUBLES
THE DUKES OF HAZZARD (1979–85)

'Just the good ol' boys/Never meanin' no harm/Beats all you've ever saw/Been in trouble with the law since the day they was born.'

So began each episode of everyone's number-one mindless car-driving-round-a-lot-and-doing-stunts, Southern-fried favourite.

John Schneider and Tom Wopat played Luke and Bo Duke, who spent their time burning rubber in their souped-up motor, nicknamed *General Lee*, easily evading the not-so-evil clutches of Boss Hogg and his dim-witted lieutenant, Roscoe P Coltrane.

But, after four seasons of high ratings, Schneider and Wopat decided it was time to play bad ol' boys. Feeling that they were being exploited, they attempted to renegotiate their contracts for higher salaries as well as a share of the show's merchandising rights.

Unfortunately, CBS didn't see it the same way and dumped Luke and Bo. Instead, they held a national search to find their replacements and did so in the shape of Byron Cherry and Christopher Mayer, who were chosen from more than two thousand hopefuls.

When the fifth season began in autumn 1982, the episode was called 'The New Dukes' – introducing the original Dukes' cousins, Coy and Vance. The plot explained that Luke and Bo had gone to fulfil their dream of racing on the NASCAR circuit, but luckily their cousins had returned to Hazzard County after a six-year absence to help Uncle Jesse on the farm.

Viewers didn't really buy into the new characters and audience figures fell, not helped by the fact that Schneider and Wopat's feud was fairly public.

After only eighteen episodes, an agreement was reached with the original pair and they returned to the show. Turns out that, although they had a great NASCAR season, they were missing home. And wouldn't you know it? Coy and Vance had to go and look after a sick relative – somewhere else. For ever. The show ended up running until 1985.

A quirky sidebar to the story goes like this. When the contract feud was in full flow, a Saturday morning cartoon version of the show was being developed. When it was first shown, it featured Coy and Vance. When Wopat and Schneider returned to the main show, the faces of Coy and Vance were replaced with those of Luke and Bo. However, the animated show was cancelled soon afterwards.

THE 1980s

PAXMAN COMETH

NEWSNIGHT (1980–)

BBC2's nightly current-affairs programme has enjoyed its fair share of controversy down the years, much of it fuelled by the often combative – 'robust' if you prefer – way some of the presenters have tackled topical subject matter.

The show's most notorious human Rottweiler has to be Jeremy Paxman, who was, unsurprisingly, at the centre of perhaps the *Newsnight*'s oddest exchange to date.

It was during the final run-up to the 1997 general election and under the 'Paxo' cosh was the then home secretary, Michael Howard. He'd been accused of overruling Derek Lewis, the head of the prison service, in relation to the sacking of a governor.

Paxman asked him about it on the programme and Howard was evasive. So Paxman asked again:

Paxman: Did you threaten to overrule him?

Howard: I was not entitled to instruct Derek Lewis and I did not instruct him. And the truth is—

Paxman: Did you *threaten* to overrule him?

Howard: I did not overrule Derek Lewis.

Paxman: Did you *threaten* to overrule him?

In the end, Paxman asked the same question no fewer than twelve times and never got an answer. Apart from sheer bloody-mindedness, did something else lie behind this relentless inquisition?

According to a report in the *Guardian* three years later, Paxman said he persevered because his producer said the programme's next taped report wasn't ready.

There was surely a sense of *déjà vu* when eight years later, 'Paxo' had PM Tony Blair in the hot seat during the run-up to the

153

2005 general election. In *The Paxman Interviews*, he urged Blair twenty times to name the number of illegal asylum seekers in the UK.

These somewhat repetitive telecasts were certainly strange for viewers, but, as far as Paxman himself is concerned, nothing matches the programme's live outside broadcast on the night of German reunification in 1990.

For a start, it was completely inaudible as fireworks went off in the background, drowning out the best efforts of the presenter and his guests. It ended with veteran reporter Charles Wheeler turning to Paxman and saying, 'Jeremy, this is pure Monty Python.' Paxman has described it as 'the worst outside broadcast, ever, in the history of the BBC'.

HOT WHEELS

B.A.D. CATS (1980)

Not even the alluring presence of Michelle Pfeiffer as Officer 'Sunshine' Samantha Jensen could do much for this short-lived cop show about the LAPD's Burglary Auto Detail, Commercial Auto Thefts squad.

More a series of eye-catching car chases – the two main male cops were former racing drivers turned lawmen – it lasted just five episodes.

In a refreshing bout of *mea culpa*, the leading producer, Everett Chambers was quoted thus: 'It was an ill-conceived and ineptly executed series. The network [ABC] was responsible for some of it and I'm responsible for some of it.

'We bought $40,000 worth of cars to smash up, and we never got a chance to smash them up. I think that's kind of immoral. $40,000 worth of cars to smash up when people are starving in India. I'm not putting this on my credits.'

These days, the A-list Ms Pfeiffer tends to give it a miss on her CV, too.

GRACE UNDER PRESSURE
THE SULLIVANS (1980)

Grace Sullivan died on 18 February 1940 in an air raid, while visiting her recuperating soldier son in London. And fans of one of the most popular characters in Aussie TV history never saw it coming. That's probably because they were tricked, cleverly duped by a television network that hated to see a stalwart behind one of its top-rated programmes leaving.

Actress Lorraine Bayly was, without doubt, *the* star of *The Sullivans*. At the time she was Australia's highest-paid female television star and the matriarch of the show – a soapy drama about a typical Aussie family living through World War Two.

Phenomenally popular from the moment the show first aired on Channel Nine in 1976, Grace stood astride the family as the perfect mum. Unfortunately, by 1979, Bayly wanted to leave the show. Permanently.

Which is where the subterfuge began, as the programme makers realised that, if audiences thought they were killing off the lovely Grace, they might turn on the show. The plan they cooked up was worthy of its own soap opera.

Bayly actually left the show in early 1979 and, at the same time in the show, Grace travelled to London to see if her son John, a soldier who had been missing in action, was there. However, after filming an emotional farewell to her family before heading overseas, Bayly also filmed a series of inserts set in London featuring her own death.

Nowadays, it's almost inconceivable that anyone would be able to keep a showbiz secret like that, but in 1979 the producers were able to suggest that they didn't know whether she was going to come back – even though she had already been filmed getting killed. She went on extended sabbatical, explained away by the fact that she was trying to locate John.

Six months later, it was time to see what Grace had got up to in London (the scenes, of course, had already been filmed). Incredibly, in an article in *TV Week* two days before her death, there is not a suggestion of the carnage to follow. Another article said that even the cast didn't know what was actually going to happen.

The episode itself is ultimately fairly low-key. Grace has found her son John, who is wounded, and is preparing to fly back to Australia with him. There is documentary footage telling us of the beginning of the Blitz on London and then Grace appears, framed in a window, writing an entry in her diary. There is the sound of a doodlebug and we see footage of a bomb dropping. It cuts back to Grace and John hand in hand, and suddenly the room explodes. The window blows out and rubble falls onto them. And that's it. The end of the 'nation's favourite mother'.

Naturally, this caused a ruckus Down Under, as viewers bombarded Channel Nine – and Bayly herself – with letters demanding to know why she had been killed off, especially since there had been no build-up to her death. Grace's passing has become a pivotal moment in Antipodean television history and the strange thing is she had actually died six months earlier.

DEAD HAIRY

MAGNUM P.I. (1980–88)

Who'd have thought that a show like *Magnum P.I.* would have its conspiracy theorists? But according to legend, in the final eighth series, starring Tom Selleck as a Hawaii-based private dick, the mustachioed one is not all he should be. In fact, despite still running around in those impossibly small shorts solving crimes, he is, actually, dead.

Rewind to the end of the seventh series of the popular show, which was beginning to lose the interest of the viewers, and so the show's creators began to feel that they should finish the season with a bang.

Literally, as it turned out, because, in the episode 'Limbo', Thomas Sullivan Magnum was shot and went into a coma. He spends the episode (which was co-written by Selleck himself) walking among his friends as a ghost in between life and death and the original plan was to have him die at the end.

However, CBS saw fit to grant the show a reprieve and the producers were faced with another batch of episodes. The eighth series began with 'Infinity and Jelly Doughnuts', in which Magnum's friends and family try to pull him out of the coma, while he experiences an out-of-body experience in heaven, guided by supporting character Mac.

Finally, at the end of the episode, he comes out of the coma and back to real life, and it was explained that he had only dreamed of going to heaven in his delirious state.

So Magnum survives – or does he? According to the show's conspiracy theorists, Magnum doesn't survive his gunshot wounds and there is evidence that he never came back to life at all.

For starters, he is still seeing Mac's ghost in the second show after he had supposedly recovered. They point to the final ever episode, in which Magnum appears to change instantly into his navy uniform and has a different haircut (à la *The Sixth Sense*). And he is also seen with a young girl who might be his dead daughter.

There is also a revelation as to who might be the unseen benefactor of the series, Robin Masters. The finale suggests that it is actually Higgins, Magnum's trusted British lieutenant. But that contradicts evidence from earlier in the series. However, there are enough loose ends to interpret the show in a number of different ways.

Some even go so far as to suggest that Magnum finally dies for real in the final episode, and that it takes place in heaven. Whatever you believe, you could probably do with a good PI to help you uncover the truth.

FERRY UNINTERESTING
TRIANGLE (1981–83)

While American TV had *The Love Boat,* which charted romance and adventure on a luxury cruise ship in the tropics, we were subjected to chilly tales of a ferry plying its trade between Felixstowe, Gothenburg and Rotterdam.

Like *El Dorado* but without the sun, this biweekly series of spellbinding awfulness desperately tried to achieve some glamour in the person of sultry Kate O'Mara – later, Caress in *Dynasty* – as the new chief purser.

In the very first episode, one erotically charged scene (as much as it could be for the early-evening audience) set the tone. It featured O'Mara's character topless sunbathing (face down) on the deck of the ship, a stunt that would have surely demanded danger money in the chilly, choppy waters of the North Sea. No wonder she jumped ship – metaphorically, of course – before they finally scuttled the series, which deservedly sank without trace.

Everything was shot on cutting-edge, lightweight equipment, which meant greater realism and flexibility, enabling cast and crew to work on location on a real ferry, the *Tor Scandinavia.*

However, the roughness of the sea presumably meant the makeup budget for a bilious cast and crew ate up any savings in the new camera technology. And the difficulty of getting decent light levels in the cabins meant that the curtains had to be permanently drawn, so it might as well have been shot in a studio anyway.

DUNNE AND DUSTED
HILL STREET BLUES (1981–87)

It's rare that the life story of a cast member on a cop show is as unpleasant as their on-screen character. Unfortunately for

Dominique Dunne, who arrived on the set of this quirky copy show in 1982 to play a domestic-abuse victim, she really *was* her character.

Dunne was the daughter of novelist Dominick and sister of actor/director Griffin, who had an austere upbringing in New York and Beverly Hills. After going to college to study acting, she journeyed to Hollywood and within three weeks she was on screen. Although she was probably best known for her role in *Poltergeist*, it was Dunne's off-screen existence that was truly ghoulish. She met chef John Thomas Sweeney at a party and soon began a relationship. It was an abusive one, with Sweeney prone to uncontrollable rages.

She was hired to play the character of Cindy in *Hill Street* – a mother who had been beaten by her boyfriend. On the day of her shoot, the makeup artists were all ready with their pots and brushes to turn her into a bruised and battered woman. There was no need. She turned up to the set sporting numerous marks and abrasions, given to her by Sweeney. All the bruises in the final show were her own.

There is a sad end to the story. On 30 October 1982, Dunne decided enough was enough and ended the relationship. Later on the same night, she was busy rehearsing a scene from her new project, *V*, when Sweeney showed up, dragged her outside and strangled her, leaving her brain dead. She died five days later.

The *Hill Street* episode aired two weeks after her death and was dedicated to her memory.

BEYOND THE SEE

THE BORGIAS (1981)

Aiming to do for one of Italy's most notorious historical families what *I, Claudius* had, in 1976, done for an earlier vintage of Roman excess, this absurd ten-parter couldn't hold a candle to the award-winning adaptation of Robert Graves's classic.

As if the sex, violence, garish sets and terrible scripts weren't bad enough, there was the central performance of Sicily-born Adolfo Celi to set the seal on this fiasco.

Many years before, Celi, a great Italian actor in his own tongue, had created one of the best Bond villains (Emilio Largo) in *Thunderball* with a little help from dubbing artist Robert 'Voice of Them All' Rietty.

Sadly, there was no Rietty to help Celi out this time, and his naturally fractured English simply piled on the agony for viewers, who might just have thought they were witnessing a colourful spoof – but without any intentional laughs.

When the series was screened in Italy, the Vatican issued a formal censure. Perhaps the Holy See was furious that, according to the Beeb, it appeared popes in the fifteenth century had all the fun . . .

LOSING FACE

DYNASTY (1981–89)

Forget the fact that Joan Collins was only eleven years older than one of her screen sons or that, unprecedentedly for a 'soap', a former US president and secretary of state agreed (unwisely) to appear as 'themselves'.

No, the strangest thing about this lush, lip-glossed, Colorado-set, oil-rich melodrama – which somehow epitomised 1980s excess – was that not just one but two of the main characters underwent complete facial transformations during the series' eight-year run.

Step forward Steven Daniel Carrington, gay (OK, possibly bi-sexual) son of blue-haired patriarch Blake Carrington. A year into the run, Steven (played by Al Corley) left for Indonesia, where, we learned, he was hideously injured in an explosion.

Then, next series, it was 'welcome home, Steven' swathed in bandages, which, once unpeeled, revealed not just a new-look

Carrington sprog but also an entirely different actor – Jack Coleman – but at least demonstrating the same sexual proclivities.

But, just to make matters even more confusing, when they came to make a telemovie sequel to the series in 1991 called *Dynasty – The Reunion*, Steven was now played by . . . you've guessed it, Al Corley.

Connecticut-born, five-foot-eight Pamela Sue Martin did four years at the oil face as flirtatious Fallon, another Carrington offspring, before she was replaced without even the excuse of a serious accident. Six years her junior and four inches shorter, Londoner Emma Samms stepped into Fallon's high heels without so much as a second glance – and she even got to retain the juicy role for the sequel.

Talking of faces, you would, incidentally, have not spotted Joan Collins's when her man-eating character, Alexis Carrington, was first introduced at the climax to the first season in which her ex-husband Blake was on trial for murdering Steven's male lover.

The character hadn't actually been cast yet, with names like Sophia Loren, Elizabeth Taylor and Raquel Welch variously under consideration. So, for the cliffhanger episode, they used a stand-in actress, reportedly a friend of the producers, camouflaging her in a white suit, a hat and a veil.

Collins, who you could say had been in training playing her sister Jackie's creation, *The Bitch*, on the big screen, finally got the nod during the break between Series One and Two.

DEADLY REHEARSAL

THE LATE, LATE BREAKFAST SHOW (1982–86)

Very few television presenters are really worthy of the tag 'Mr Saturday Night', but, during the eighties and nineties, very few presenters were so synonymous with weekend television than Noel Edmonds.

Having made his name on the radio and on Saturday morning TV, Edmonds had carved a niche for himself as the people's presenter, regularly involving his viewing public in his shows. And it was this involvement that almost spelled his downfall.

The Late, Late Breakfast Show, broadcast on early Saturday nights on BBC1, had got off to a rocky start thanks to the palpably poor chemistry between Noel and his co-hosts. They were soon binned and Mike 'Smitty' Smith was brought in as the go-getting OB man who zoomed around the country interacting with the audience.

The most famous segment that he did was the Whirly Wheel Challenge, a recurring item in which members of the public were invited to train for and then complete an audacious stunt. Edmonds himself once said, 'You wouldn't catch me doing half the things we get our Whirly Wheelers to have a go at.'

Despite its amateur participants, the slot had suffered relatively little mishap, with only Barbara Sleeman in 1983 suffering a broken shoulder after she was shot from a cannon. That was all to change on 13 November 1986.

Unfortunately, the episode in which Michael Lush died has acquired a kind of mythical status, whereby everyone swears they saw him plummet to his death on live television.

In fact, Lush was rehearsing his stunt, in which he was to fall from an exploding crate on a bungee rope, when it went wrong and he fell to his death.

The show was pulled immediately and Edmonds took it as a personal tragedy, even though the subsequent inquest showed that it was death by misadventure and confirmed that the BBC hadn't covered some safety issues.

Edmonds's career briefly hit the rocks, although it wasn't long before he was back with a similar show. However, the catastrophe was felt higher up the corporate food chain, as the BBC director-general Alasdair Milne was sacked by the Board of Governors.

KIDDIE POWER
SILVER SPOONS (1982–86)

Little Ricky Schroder became a Hollywood darling overnight when aged nine he cried effortlessly opposite Jon Voight in Franco Zeffirelli's schmaltzy *The Champ*.

Three years later, and with his tear ducts still awesomely on autopilot, he was starring in this popular sitcom as the very self-possessed twelve-year-old son of a very immature 35-year-old millionaire father (Joel Higgins), whom he hadn't seen since his parents' divorce.

With Schroder came the stretch limo and the entourage including mom, pop, sister, business manager, lawyer and agent. And, when the show proved a big hit, along came the excessive star demands, too.

He wanted his co-star Jason Bateman, a year his senior, fired because apparently the lad was getting more laughs than he was; his fourteen-year-old sister hired to play a role; and, most crucially, an agreement to direct at least six episodes in the next series. Remember, Schroder was *only* twelve.

According to Michael Grade, who was then heading the production company, Embassy, he eventually managed to persuade the boy and his 'people' to retain Bateman as well as allow Ricky's sibling only the odd appearance. But 'I forgot to give Ricky any directing,' Grade added.

Now, some twenty years later, and with his first name shortened to 'Rick', father-of-four Schroder has recently directed his first film, *Black Cloud*. Whether he can still cry on cue no one will confirm.

DREAM OF A PAY-OFF
NEWHART (1982–90)

The dream plot device is a good old standby, especially in cheesy soap operas (see *Dallas* on page 133), but perhaps it has never been so strangely used than in this sitcom.

The show featured comedian Bob Newhart as writer Dick Loudon, who decides to leave New York with his wife Joanna (Mary Frann) and open an old-fashioned inn in Norwich, Vermont.

The show ran successfully on CBS until 1990, until the classic – and wacky – final episode. The storyline had a Japanese businessman buying up Norwich, all except Dick's inn, which our hero refuses to sell. Five years later – and the inn has become a Japanese hotel on the fourteenth hole of a golf course. All of the old townsfolk come back to visit Dick and decide to return to Norwich. In the midst of this, Dick goes out of his front door and is hit by a golf ball.

Next thing you know, Dick is waking up in bed. He turns to his wife but, instead of seeing Joanna, viewers were flabbergasted to see Suzanne Pleshette – who played Newhart's wife on his previous sitcom, *The Bob Newhart Show*, which ran from 1972 to 1978!

The explanation? Bob Hartley (Newhart's character from his previous show), tells Pleshette that he has just had the strangest dream about running an inn in Vermont . . .

Bobby Ewing, eat your heart out: Bob Newhart just dreamed an *entire* series.

DEADLY TIMES THREE

SIN ON SATURDAY (1982)

It seemed a good idea at the time. At least that's what co-editor Sean Hardie thought of this infamous TV disaster, one those 'dinner party ideas' that unexpectedly got the green light.

Debuting on 7 September 1982, this was considered an ideal filler during Michael Parkinson's hiatus from the screens, an eight-part series of live discussions on the theme of sin. These would be illustrated through music, comedy and discussion, chaired by the amiable broadcast journalist Bernard Falk.

His irreverent take on each topic was made clear in pre-publicity that promised 'eight discussions interspersed with music and comedy that is thoroughly sinful'. Falk, who played up to the theme by stressing that he himself was 'incredibly pleased with myself and incurably slothful', was a genial though inexperienced host.

The first show boldly tackled 'Lust', and invited guests as diverse as Linda Lovelace, a former nun, a gaggle of beauty queens and Oliver Reed to discuss it. Things did not go well, stranded deep in the no-man's-land of tasteless TV.

Any attempt at serious analysis was stranded by the cheesy setup, while attempts at comedy also floundered. The flaws in this series ran deep and it quickly became clear that the second show on the theme of 'Covetousness' (guests included disgraced MP John Stonehouse) was no better. BBC1 controller Alan Hart was not alone in his opinion that the series had committed the worst sin of all in television terms, 'being both boring and banal'.

Episode Three, 'Envy', duly followed but the days for this inglorious series were numbered and the axe fell before Falk and co. could gorge themselves on the subject of 'Gluttony'.

BOSTON DRINKS PARTY

CHEERS (1982–93)

For a start, Ted Danson, as owner/bartender Sam Malone, wasn't even supposed to be in it. The role was originally given to *Hunter* star Fred Dryer and he was to be a retired football player. When Danson took over the part, he was changed to a baseball player more to match the new actor's physique.

Norm's wife, Vera, was never seen on screen (much like Nile's wife Maris in the spin-off, *Frasier*), although her voice was provided by the Norm actor George Wendt's real-life wife. She finally appeared on a Thanksgiving Day episode, but was hit in the face by a pie thrown by Diane (Shelley Long), before the audience could actually see her face.

There was an episode filmed that never aired, called 'Uncle Sam Malone'. In it, the guys at the bar try to convince Diane that US savings bonds were a good investment. This was a special episode produced for the US Treasury to be used during savings bonds drives.

One of the most popular characters, postman Cliff Clavin, wasn't in the original script. Actor John Ratzenberger came in to audition for the part of Norm, but the producers didn't think he was right for it.

Convinced the audition hadn't gone well, Ratzenberger started ranting to himself in front of them, and they loved it so much that they decided to create the character of idiotic Cliff just for him.

CLEANING UP HIS ACT

MOONLIGHTING (1982–85)

Their template was the dialogue-crackling Cary Grant 'screwball' comedies of the 1930s and 1940s updated to the 1980s, co-starring, preferably, a suave Grant for these times. But the vision that first confronted Glen Gordon Caron, the writer/creator of arguably the decade's biggest hit, was far removed from the elegant Hollywood star of yore.

The 26-year-old Bruce Willis rolled in late for his audition, wearing earrings, battle fatigues and dirty trainers. His hair was close-cropped, almost shaven in fact, with, Caron recalled, 'those bits that stood up like angry cockatoo feathers'.

Caron and his team had already been on the road for ages visiting ten cities and checking out three thousand possibles for the role of David Addison, wise-cracking private detective sidekick to the show's star, Cybill Shepherd.

'Where are all the men in this town?' Caron would moan. 'They've all gone soft. They're wimps. They sit around drinking white wine and are wiped out if they meet a real woman. I want a guy who is sharp, glint-eyed and isn't afraid to be sexist.'

On what was likely to be the last day of interviews and decision time, Willis read his lines and, with an '*adios*', headed off. The casting team weren't unhappy to see him go: to a person, they were convinced that he wasn't remotely right for the role. But for Caron, Willis was instantaneously the real thing – 'edgy . . . scary . . . the sarcastic, arrogant New York wise-guy I always had in mind'.

His colleagues thought him mad, while Caron knew he'd still have real problems getting Willis past the conservative-minded ABC network executives who preferred traditional, chiselled-featured leading men.

With a final threat that if he couldn't have Willis he'd pull out of the project taking his script with him, ABC decided to humour him and Willis was invited to screen-test in Los Angeles. This time round, the punk look had gone, replaced by normal-length hair, a smart suit and shiny shoes.

Naturally, Willis got the role, stardom and, ironically, the chance to renew that old look, stubble, dirty vest, close-cropped hair and all, in perhaps his most famous – and certainly best-paid – role of all, that of Detective John McClane in the subsequent block-busting *Die Hard* film series.

BEGORRAH HORROR
REMINGTON STEELE (1982–87)

Magnum P.I. is often remembered as the show that meant its contracted star, Tom Selleck, couldn't take up an offer to play Indiana Jones on the big screen. So it was that Pierce Brosnan, in this eponymous role, was similarly stymied in an earlier bid to become James Bond before eventually becoming the secret agent eight years later.

The odd thing is that *Steele* was actually on the slide and probably due for the chop when it first became known and, more importantly, globally publicised that Brosnan was being scouted for Bond-age. This was enough to persuade the series' producers to hang onto their infuriated star so they could get more mileage out of the character on the back of his 007 'heat'.

Never quite repeating its early American success on this side of the Atlantic, the show – in which Brosnan, as a suave sleuth, might have been auditioning for Bond – was nevertheless very popular in the actor's native Ireland.

So there was naturally huge excitement when cast and crew decamped from Hollywood and arrived in Dublin to shoot an episode. But delight later turned to fury when the episode was shown in the Emerald Isle. This was over a scene in which Steele walked into a pub one morning and found the colourful locals quaffing their first ale of the day. The programme was angrily accused of reinforcing Irish stereotypes.

Embarrassingly, Brosnan then had to go on record to assert that the programme was 'not a true description of Ireland', before adding that he hadn't actually seen that particular episode.

AUDIENCE BACKLASH
CAGNEY & LACEY (1982–88)

This trailblazing 'feminist' cop show was (eventually) a triumph of American audience power. All three networks first turned down the idea of a series featuring 'buddette–buddette' policewomen Chris Cagney and Mary-Beth Lacey.

But, when the ratings for a telemovie version went sky-high, CBS decided haltingly to commit to a limited run. The trouble was that Loretta Swit – best known as 'Hotlips' Houlihan in *M*A*S*H*. – was now unavailable to carry on as Cagney opposite Tyne Daly's Lacey.

So they cast instead icy-eyed Meg Foster. And the ratings plummeted. The network's thinking was that the audience now perceived the pair as too – well, manly (or, whisper it, a bit Sapphic) for primetime tastes. This, despite the fact that the character of Lacey was happily married with a child.

Ms Foster proved to be the scapegoat for such dim thinking and she was replaced by the altogether fluffier and warmer Sharon Gless – much to the fury of various gay groups who had championed the show. The ratings, however, remained poor and the series was cancelled.

This was the cue for an almost unprecedented viewer backlash with a flood of letters and telephone calls to CBS. When *Cagney & Lacey* then won a belated Emmy, the network relented and recommissioned the series, using the ad line, 'You Want Them! You've Got Them!'

Over the next four years, the show copped almost a dozen Emmy awards including Best Actress on more than one occasion to both Gless and Daly. The character of Cagney remained single. In reality, Gless married the producer of the show, Barney Rosenzweig, in 1991. A year earlier, Rosenzweig had divorced his wife of eleven years, Barbara Corday, who was . . . the creator/writer of *Cagney & Lacey*.

169

MONSOON WARNING

THE COMIC STRIP PRESENTS
(1982–88; 1988–93; 1998–2000)

You may be surprised to know that Jennifer Saunders was not the first in her family to play a character called Eddie Monsoon.

In fact, her husband Adrian Edmondson played one ten years earlier in an episode of this ground-breaking comedy. Only difference is, Ade's first attempt never made it onto the screen.

After the *Comic Strip*'s trailblazing film, *Five Go Mad In Dorset*, was shown to acclaim on the first night of Channel 4, their innovative, albeit near-the-knuckle, humour was altogether *too* close to the bone with an episode to be called 'Back to Normal with Eddie Monsoon'.

Edmondson played the title role, a vile chat-show host with a fondness for bigoted topics. He sang a song about capital punishment in schools, discussed how to pick a fight at pub closing time and wondered what homosexuals' favourite hobbies were. Channel 4 found it all a bit too disturbing and the show remained in script form, never being produced.

However, Edmondson managed to resurrect the character during the second *Comic Strip* series in the mockumentary, *Eddie Monsoon: A Life?*. In it, he played the same bed-ridden, drug-addicted presenter, while a documentary crew sensationally combed through his controversy-packed career.

When his off-screen wife (and *Comic Strip* co-star) Jennifer Saunders got her own show, *Absolutely Fabulous*, she resurrected darling Eddie (short for Edina) Monsoon with just a nifty change of gender. You see, nothing's ever wasted in comedy.

A CRYING SHAME
SHOGUN (1982)

For a man who claimed he was never too keen on horses, the great Japanese actor Toshiro Mifune seemed to spend much of his screen career astride various mighty steeds.

Surely celluloid's finest samurai, Mifune, at the age of 62, was back in sword-wielding period character once again as Lord Toranaga for this six-part miniseries version of James Clavell's epic seventeenth-century novel set in Japan.

For the climactic scene, a huge army was mustered for the moment when Toranaga would come galloping in, leap off his horse and stride purposefully towards various warlords assembled on a dais.

Everyone was in place but there was still no sign of Mifune. Then, with a rumble like thunder, he rode in at mighty speed, stopped his horse precisely on the mark, quickly dismounted and joined the throng. Inch perfect.

Perfunctorily congratulated by the American director – the Americans and Japanese endured an uneasy collaboration throughout filming – Mifune was then asked to do another take. In fact, not just one more but a further five takes of this decidedly hazardous manoeuvre.

On the seventh take, Mifune's horse had had enough. It shied and threw the actor to the ground. While one suspects that he might have had just cause for berating the filmmakers for their excess, Mifune's immediate reaction was rather different.

As he sat on the ground, he wept with shame, saying that he felt he'd let everyone down. As if this weren't enough, he then sent flowers and notes of apology to the director and the producers.

Sadly, Mifune's accident was too late for a rather belated priestly blessing (using a sacred snake) on the production to ensure smooth filming.

BIG IN KOREA

JOANIE LOVES CHACHI (1982–83)

This ill-fated sitcom spin-off (see *Happy Days* on page 112) boasts the highest-rated premiere in Korean television history. Truth or myth? According to creator Garry Marshall and co-star Scott Baio, their show, which lasted a dismal seventeen episodes, rated big in Korea for one reason.

Why? Because, they declared, 'Chachi' is the Korean word for 'penis' and Koreans just couldn't get over the hilarity of a sitcom called *Joanie Love Penis* and so watched in their millions. This story turns out to be slightly apocryphal. The Korean word for penis is actually 'jaw-jee', so, when you say 'Chachi', it could just about be misconstrued.

In fact, the show was broadcast only on the Armed Forces Korean Network. In English. Which suggests that the series were never actually aired before the real Korean audience, which makes the ratings claim pure hogwash.

Of course, anyone who ever saw the show might well agree that Chachi's Korean moniker was the perfect fit for a character who was, after all, a bit of a dick.

GOING FOR A BURTON

WAGNER (1983)

Tony Palmer's nine-hour film (albeit better known in its six-hour TV version), about the turbulent life and times of dyspeptic composer Richard Wagner, was an epic in every sense. 'A long film about a guy who wrote long operas,' carped one critic, however.

Starring Richard Burton, it filmed for seven months on two hundred locations in six countries. The cast was pretty remarkable, too, and also reunited Britain's top triumvirate of theatrical knights – Olivier, Gielgud and Richardson – on screen for the first time since *Richard III* in 1955.

Sadly, the best scene, involving the trio together with Burton, was never actually filmed. In fact, it wasn't even in the script.

This was at a party hosted at Vienna's swanky Palais Schwarzenberg by Burton for the three knights – after all of them had separately held their own bashes with varying degrees of success.

Burton, a legendary drinker, had been off the booze for a while. Instead, he'd nurse a glass of wine, which remained untouched while another glass, with water, would be constantly refilled. However, this was one party too far and as Burton warmed to his old anecdotes so he grabbed and then quickly drained the handy vessel of vino.

According to *Rich*, Melvyn Bragg's biography of the actor, 'about five minutes later a transformation had taken place. It was, so it is utterly reliably reported, quite extraordinary: Jekyll to Hyde.'

Before the increasingly embarrassed guests, first he ripped viciously into Olivier, then Gielgud and, finally, Richardson. Maybe Burton resented the fact he'd never been given a 'K'. As Palmer walked him to his car, Olivier said, 'I know now why you chose Richard to play Wagner . . .'

CRACKING THE SYSTEM

PRESS YOUR LUCK (1983–86)

Like all good game shows, *Press Your Luck* was very simple. Answer a question and then gamble your winnings by stopping a flashing light on a large prize board.

Whatever square you landed on when you pressed your button, that was what you got, whether it was money, or a washing machine. On the downside, if you landed on a Whammy, you lost everything you had accrued during that round. Whenever you felt your luck running out, you passed on your turn to the next contestant.

The board was supposed to hit the various squares at random, but unemployed Ohio ice cream truck driver Paul Michael Larson knew better. An avid watcher of the show, he began videotaping it to see if the Whammies really did have a pattern. After all, it was all controlled by a computer, and computer programs often have patterns.

Sitting down to research, he realised that the board did indeed work in a certain way, using only six different sequences. He memorised them and set about applying to appear on the show.

He finally made it in 1984 and quickly put his plan into practice. After answering a question, he played for an unprecedented 35 turns, bagging a total of $110, 237. The largest win in single game-show history at that point, Larson's run was split over two episodes of the show. As he continued to win and win, the programme-makers realised that they had been played. However, he wasn't doing anything illegal and, as long as he didn't pass, there was nothing they could do.

Eventually he did relinquish his turn and walked away with his money. While programme makers publicly congratulated him (and capitalised on the publicity), the board was quickly repro-grammed to being genuinely random and the upper win limit was capped at $75,000.

It was a masterful display by Larson that put him in the record books and into television history. However, his winning streak didn't last long. After the show, he spent most of his money in less than two years and ended up as an assistant shop manager.

Nearly twenty years later he was able at least to relive his glory days when, in 2003, the Game Show Network broadcast a documentary called *Big Bucks: The Press Your Luck Scandal.*

BETTE ON THE BOX
HOTEL (1983–88)

At 75, with two Oscars and four unhappy marriages behind her, Bette Davis excitedly signed up to do seven episodes a year (at $100,000 a time) for this portmanteau drama series – her first-ever extended TV stint – set in a swanky San Francisco hostelry.

After filming the pilot and one episode, Davis, who was playing the hotel owner, went for a doctor's checkup after noticing a lump in her left breast while showering. The diagnosis was a malignant tumour and she urgently underwent a radical mastectomy.

Nine days after being assured that the cancer was successfully arrested, Davis then had a minor stroke followed by three embolisms in rapid succession, which left the right side of her face twisted and her speech slurred.

As a result, Davis was seen only in the premiere show before the rest of the staff – and an enthusiastic TV audience – were informed that her character had gone on an 'extended trip'.

Despite these various drastic health reverses, the doughty Davis survived to live another six years and appear in five more films.

LESS IS MORE
BLACKADDER (1983–89)

Such is the unremitting comic brilliance of Series Two through Four, it's odd to recall that this belatedly inspired BBC sitcom nearly didn't survive beyond Series One.

With scripts by Richard Curtis, even though still ten years away from the beginning of his extraordinary run of British film success, and a generous budget, which allowed location filming in and around Alnwick Castle, *The Black Adder* (as it was first titled) should have been a palpable hit.

With a silly pudding-basin haircut and a deeply annoying streak that suggested a kind of medieval Mr Bean, Rowan Atkinson's Edmund was still a long way off the deliciously devious character we grew to love in later adventures, which spanned the Elizabethan age to the end of World War One.

To Michael Grade, then director of programmes as well as controller of BBC1, it was 'expensive, unfunny and self-indulgent'. Frankly, a view shared by all right-thinking viewers.

So, when a second series was proposed, Grade laid down the law. Either cancel the series or else convert it into a studio production in front of an audience.

Intriguingly, in view of his later fame and fortune earned with sole credit on films such as *Four Weddings and a Funeral*, *Notting Hill* and *Love Actually*, Curtis was required to take on a co-writer, Ben Elton, in order to 'sex' it up a bit.

The result was almost instantaneous. Wearing its new poverty like a badge of merit, *Blackadder*, as the title now became, suddenly moved from forgettable to instant classic.

MAJOR RODENT AHEAD

GOOD MORNING, BRITAIN (1983–92)

A month after the BBC had launched its own *Breakfast Time* programme, the much-vaunted ITV version finally made its own delayed way onto our early-morning screens.

With its 'Famous Five' presenters – Robert Kee, Angela Rippon, David Frost, Michael Parkinson and Anna Ford – *Good Morning Britain* was at least expected to give the Beeb a good run for its money. In fact, the well-scrubbed quintet, with their rather smug 'mission to explain', proved to be more of a turn-off for still bleary-eyed viewers.

For a while, as advertising revenue began to dip alarmingly and chief executive Peter Jay fell on his sword followed by a couple of his high-profile troupe (Rippon and Ford), it looked as if TV-am might prove extremely short-lived.

But they'd reckoned without a puppet called Roland ('Yeeeahhh, number one Rat Fan') Rat – the brainchild of eccentric puppeteer David Claridge. Roland, who appeared in an 8 a.m. slot just as children were leaving for school, was beginning to get a bit of a cult following.

Newly appointed Greg Dyke, brought in from LWT as editor-in-chief to try to turn things round, decided to check out the rat's ratings and was impressed. Years later, Dyke would record the following observation about Claridge in his memoirs: 'A miserable, rather dull man who only came alive when he put his hand up this puppet's rear end.'

Much to the consternation of his more serious-minded new colleagues, Dyke ordered they move loud-mouthed Roland to the key 9–9.30 slot, and the ratings not only followed but also began to soar.

It was, as some wag would coin for posterity, perhaps the only recorded case of a rat that saved a sinking ship.

BOMBER IN THE BLACKOUT

AUF WIEDERSEHEN, PET (1983–2004)

At six foot five and built like a brick khazi, Birmingham-born Pat Roach became a household name, thanks to his role as genially gigantic labourer Brian 'Bomber' Busbridge in this popular comedy-drama. Its four series were spread across twenty years and various locations ranging from Middlesbrough and Arizona to Germany, Spain and Cuba.

However, Roach had another life before, and often during, the filming of *Aufpet*. He was a successful professional wrestler with the nickname 'Bomber' and also a bit-part movie actor specialising in 'heavies'.

In *Raiders of the Lost Ark*, as a German officer, he'd memorably grappled with Harrison Ford before being mangled by an aeroplane propeller. When Spielberg was back at Elstree studios a couple of years on to shoot *Indiana Jones and the Temple of Doom*, he naturally sent again for 'Big' Pat. This time, Roach was required to play an Indian guard who gets dispatched in a rock crusher after tangling with Indy.

Aufpet was at Elstree, too, filming its first series, so there seemed no big problem with Roach briefly 'moonlighting' for Spielberg. Having got permission from director Roger Bamford, who told him he had to be back by six o'clock that evening for a crucial scene in which the builders' hut is burned down, Roach headed for *Indiana*.

His scene was set on a conveyor belt and the normally carrot-topped Roach, now sporting a big black beard, had continually to be 'blacked down' because the makeup kept rubbing off.

As his final 'cut' was called shortly before 6 p.m., Roach now realised he didn't have time for a shower and raced back to the nearby *Aufpet* set. Arriving breathless, he was told that it was a supper break so a relieved Roach headed swiftly for the showers, where he spent some happy minutes scrubbing off all his makeup.

Back at the set, he now got his orders for the evening: 'Pat, you need to go to makeup and be blacked down.' It turned out that they needed the cast covered in soot for the fire scene.

Roach, who'd earlier auditioned unsuccessfully for Darth Vader, later got a chance to complete a unique *Indy* treble, when he appeared in *The Last Crusade*.

A member of the original seven-man *Aufpet* team, Roach at least managed – along with five others (Jimmy Nail, Tim Healy, Kevin Whately, Chris Fairbank and Timothy Spall) – to complete all four series before dying of cancer in 2004 aged 67.

Not so lucky was Gary 'Wayne' Holton, who at 32 died of drink- and drug-related problems while Series Two was still being completed. With so much material already 'in the can' and some crafty rewrites, only once did a double have to be used as Wayne 'lived' for *Aufpet 2*.

However, when it was decided to revive the programme six years later (in 2002), the 'Wayne' question was clearly an issue. 'We could,' explained writers Dick Clement and Ian La Frenais, 'have said, "Wayne's emigrated. He's gone to Australia." But we decided to deal with it directly and give it a slight poignancy. All of us wanted to be respectful to Gary's memory.'

Their eventual solution was to replace Wayne with his son Wyman (Noel Clarke), whose reason for joining the group would be that they knew his dad, while he never had.

DIE ANOTHER DAY

TAGGART (1983–)

Imagine *Ironside* without Raymond Burr, *Magnum P.I.* without Tom Selleck, or *Parkinson* without Parky (don't tempt us!). In other words, when you tune in to these titular shows, you rather expect to see what's on the tin.

But scour the credits of this ever-popular Scottish cop series and you won't actually find any mention of the eponymous Mr T. That's because the character ceased to be in 1994.

This followed the death at 59 of granite-faced actor Mark McManus, who created DCI Jim Taggart, hard man of Glasgow Maryhill CID, a decade earlier.

By the time of his untimely demise, McManus and his nuggety character had made such an impression on viewers, the producers decided to retain the name partly as homage and partly because the concept was simply too good to kill off.

More than ten years on, the show still commands primetime on ITV. By implication, noted one commentator, Taggart still seems to be there, 'back at the station in Northern Division glumly issuing orders and pronouncements'.

TURKEY TURMOIL
SPITTING IMAGE (1984–94; 1996)

Rubber foam and latex were the usual materials for *Spitting Image*'s wicked range of puppets depicting the celebrities of the day. Just occasionally, other ideas came into play, as when a wobbly Neil Kinnock was created out of raspberry jelly, a substance that collapsed spectacularly under the heat of the workshop lights.

Steve Nallon, impressionist, puppeteer and, most famously, the voice of Margaret Thatcher, also remembers a disastrous occasion when it was decided to introduce frozen poultry onto the set for a Christmas special involving ten singing turkeys.

'It was in the days when television had enormous demarcation and there were a lot of regulations about what could and couldn't be done in a television studio and who could or could not touch certain objects,' he says. 'We, as puppeteers, were expected to operate these turkeys – waggling them about on our hands – but it was then decided that they weren't puppets: they were props, because they had been brought in by the prop men.'

As the prop men and the puppeteers disputed, the turkeys started defrosting under the lights. 'Blood went everywhere and eventually the prop men just looked at them and said, "Well, I think we should let the puppeteers do it . . . We've decided they're not props, they are operable turkeys." '

The puppeteers' victory was hollow. 'We ended up covered in blood. It was just gross!'

THE ITALIAN JOB
THE FAR PAVILIONS (1984)

On screen, former matinée idol Rossano Brazzi has had a habit of opening his mouth and sounding like someone else. In the film musical, *South Pacific*, for example, it was the glorious tones of Giorgio Tozzi that streamed forth as Brazzi serenaded Mitzi Gaynor with 'Some Enchanted Evening'. However, when it came to the role of Kaka-Ji, elder statesman of the Kingdom of Gulkote, surely Brazzi's own powerful Italian voice would be perfectly in sync for this wily old Indian politician. Durrr! When director Peter Duffell heard that the 'money' behind this lavish, three-part adaptation of M M Kaye's nineteenth-century epic of the Raj demanded an 'Italian element' he was furious. He fought for and got Christopher Lee for the role. Yet Brazzi had somehow to remain in the mix so he was cast instead as . . . another Indian, naturally, this time the villainous Rana of Blithor.

Perhaps recalling his past glories when he'd wooed Katharine Hepburn in *Summertime* and Ava Gardner in *The Barefoot Contessa*, the one-time heartthrob, now approaching seventy, was a bit demanding. He was adamant, for example, that he would not be made up with a beard and moustache, which, of course, an Indian rajah would most certainly have had.

Duffell was summoned to the makeup department, where he met Brazzi in his costume, 'looking rather like a doorman at a provincial curry restaurant. I asked him politely what the problem was: he wanted to be recognised as Brazzi, he announced, not heavily disguised.' The director finally coaxed to him to don the facial hair.

However, Duffell was unable ever to completely reassure the actor when it came to dealing with elephants. 'Getting up and down from the *howdah* on his regal elephant for the wedding filled him with terror. And, when he was carried to his funeral pyre, he would not put on his costume. Under the coverings, he was still garbed in a sports jacket and Gucci shoes, hoping perhaps for a quick getaway after the shot,' recalled the filmmaker.

And, to add insult to potential injury, when the large Channel 4 audience finally saw Brazzi on TV, it wasn't even his familiar Bolognese voice they heard issuing from within the luxuriant face fungus.

Instead, to turn a 'very Italian delivery into passable English', said Duffell, they had signed up the South African-born David de Keyser to dub him. Clearly, it was a pavilion too far for Brazzi.

SHOW MUST GO ON
THE PRICE IS RIGHT (1984–88)

Leslie Crowther glowed with satisfaction as the packed audience at Central Television's £25 million TV centre in Nottingham thundered its applause.

The star had completed an hour of music and comedy – none of which had been rehearsed. In fact the act that Crowther had staged hadn't been what the audience had come to see. Instead the host was supposed to have presented the biggest game show to be produced in the UK – *The Price Is Right*.

But an electricians' dispute meant that the recording had to be cancelled at the last minute. And, instead of turning away the three hundred members of the public who had turned up to see the TV show being made, Crowther offered to put on an impromptu entertainment. And for a full hour he had the studio audience in the palm of his hand as he went through a mixture of comic gags and musical interludes.

Once the union dispute was resolved, *The Price Is Right* went on to become the top game show on ITV.

FAT OF THE LAND
JENNY'S WAR (1985)

This telemovie, about a courageous mother's search behind enemy lines for her missing son in Germany during World War Two, was actually filmed in Yorkshire. Every day, extras who were required to play PoWs in a German camp had to be bussed out to the location near Leeds.

Filming happened to coincide with the height of the miners' strike and every day, without fail, the bus would be stopped by police, convinced it was packed with flying pickets. 'We're prisoners of war,' they'd protest before being allowed to proceed.

Towards the end of shooting, some of the extras were recruited for close-up work and, as the first assistant director made his way down the line of hopefuls, he finally arrived at Jackie Hamilton, a well-known Liverpool comic.

To his surprise, the Scouser was told that he simply wasn't suitable. Why, he asked. The AD said, 'To be honest, you're supposed to be all skinny and haggard from months without decent food. Look at you! You're fat, red-faced and you've got a boozer's nose.' To which Hamilton apparently quipped, 'I know, but I only got captured yesterday!'

UP THE POLE

THE LAST PLACE ON EARTH (1985)

Scott's curse struck the makers of this dramatised series about the adventures of Polar explorer Captain Scott. When he heard that a TV drama was to be made about his father, naturalist Sir Peter Scott had wished bad luck to the production team. And that's just what happened as the series, which starred Martin Shaw as Scott of the Antarctic (and Hugh Grant, long before fame beckoned, as the splendidly named Apsley Cherry-Garrard), suffered a bunch of mishaps.

The original director quit the production, actors narrowly escaped serious injury after a car crash in Norway and a frightened horse kicked an actor, who needed urgent hospital treatment.

As if that weren't bad enough, while also on location, a pack of huskies ran away, never to be seen again, and a unit driver broke his neck after an accident at a hotel while filming in Scotland.

ARMED AND DANGEROUS
SATURDAY LIVE (1985–87)

Back then, when 'alternative comedy' was at its height and comedy clubs were springing up all over the place, it seemed a great idea to bring some of this action into our living rooms.

Channel 4's new show, produced by Paul Jackson, aimed to recreate some of the raw excitement of America's long-standing sketch and stand-up show, *Saturday Night Live*. But, while the word 'danger' may have been bandied about at meetings, nobody expected quite the level of peril that the Dangerous Brothers (alias Rik Mayall and Adrian Edmondson) managed to inflict on the show.

Inspired by the anarchy of punk bands such as the Damned, whose drummer once set himself on fire, the two young comics had created an act that consisted of little more than cartoon violence against each other.

Ritchie (Mayall) liked nothing better than tormenting Sir Adrian (Edmondson) by throwing him off a building, shooting him out of a cannon, putting his hand in a blender or whatever else occurred to him. Edmondson explained, 'We love doing stunts – we're both quite agile, and not particularly afraid of hurting ourselves.'

Although the show was mostly live, the sections featuring this dastardly duo were prerecorded, which was just as well in view of what happened on one occasion.

Mayall was supposed to be setting Edmondson alight but what nobody realised at the time was that Sir Adrian's convincingly pained expression was because the flames had started burning through his protective clothing. 'We had to stop the tape and start again – I burned my eyebrows off,' recalls Edmondson.

Needless to say, this rather too incendiary sketch has become a particular favourite among Dangerous Brothers' fans ever since.

DOUBLE YOUR MONEY
HOME TO ROOST (1985–90)/YOU AGAIN? (1986–87)

Can you be in two places at the same time? Try asking British actress Elizabeth Bennett, who somehow managed it in a pair of sitcoms linked by similar scripts yet separated by six thousand miles.

In *Home to Roost*, she was housekeeper Enid Thompson to gruff divorcé Henry Willows (played to the manor born by John Thaw), who has to readjust his selfish lifestyle when teenage son Matthew (Reece Dinsdale) comes to live with him.

A year after the show began its five-year run on ITV, an American version called *You Again?* began on NBC with Jack Klugman and John Stamos recreating Willows *père et fils*.

In a TV first, the only British cast member plucked from our *Roost* was the lucky Ms Bennett, who was required to reprise her good-hearted domestic with just a change of surname, to 'Tompkins'. As if a double payday weren't reward enough, she must have chalked up a few Frequent Flier miles with her transatlantic commuting.

WHAT A DIFFERENCE A GAY MAKES
BLIND DATE (1985–2003)

There are some TV shows that are so identified with a particular presenter that it's difficult to imagine anyone else in charge. Step forward Miss Cilla Black, everyone's favourite aunt. Classless, sexless . . .

But Cilla actually wasn't at the forefront of London Weekend Television's mind when it first bought a game show format from Australia called *Perfect Match*. Transmitted Down Under at 5 p.m., it was both explicit and raunchy – in other words, entirely unsuited to a similar slot here because of Independent Broadcasting Authority guidelines.

It would, ITV's then controller, John Birt, later recalled, have to be 'sanitised for the UK'. The programme's first producer, Alan Boyd, was convinced he could allay any IBA fears that the show could be seen as a 'passport to sex' by casting a 'camp' presenter to run the show.

According to Birt, the lucky chap, 'a young comedian in the Frankie Howerd mould', was signed up for the pilot. It proved, said Birt, 'a disastrous miscalculation. The presenter's improvised stream of gay innuendo not only put sex centre stage but also got in the way of the strong central message of *Blind Date* – heterosexual attraction.'

Birt was committed to showing the pilot to the IBA, where it was made clear that as early-evening fodder this was entirely unsuitable. Step forward Cilla. And just who was the comic on the cutting room floor?

CULTURE SHOCK

NEIGHBOURS (1985–)

Across twenty years of this peerless (according to Falk, Q – *Ed.*) soap, there has been love, death, pain and the whole damn thing. Not to mention the likes of one-time cast members Kylie Minogue, Jason Donovan, Russell Crowe, Radha Mitchell, Delta Goodrem and Natalie Imbruglia, who've all since graduated with honours.

And yet the longest-running drama in Australian broadcasting history barely survived its first six months. Cancelled by one network so it could be replaced by a news programme (audience apathy didn't help either), it was sold to another. The rest is, well . . .

However, the tumultuous happenings over two decades in fictitious Erinsborough scarcely begin to compare to the original fallout from the show 13,000 miles away in Northern Ireland.

When the BBC first bought the programme in 1986, it was scheduled to air twice a day – at 10 a.m. and 1.30 p.m. Then the network's controller, Michael Grade, had the cracking wheeze of switching the 10 a.m. transmission to early evening, thus trawling in a massive teatime audience.

For years, Northern Ireland had enjoyed a regional cultural programme in that slot, so, when that was unceremoniously dumped in favour of *Neighbours*, there was uproar in some highbrow quarters. There were, according to Grade, accusations of 'cultural vandalism . . . of replacing high Irish culture with Australian schlock'.

In his memoirs, he reports that the Northern Ireland governor raised the issue in London, though 'the Ulster Unionists were pleased about the change because they had suspected all along that Irish cultural programmes were crypto-IRA propaganda'.

A couple of months later, there was a newspaper rumour that *Neighbours* was to be discontinued in favour of a 'return to pukka Irish broadcasting complete with leprechauns and Irish harpists'. This, noted Grade, 'almost led to rioting in the streets of Belfast'.

CHEWING THE FAT
DESIGNING WOMEN (1986–93)

There's only so much People Power can do. When CBS decided after just a year to cancel this sitcom about four smart Southern women running an interior-decorating business in Atlanta, a public outcry saved it from the axe.

But there was no such reprieve when, five years into its run, actress Delta Burke, one of the original quartet, was given her marching orders. Ms Burke, a former Miss Florida, played thrice-married Suzanne Sugarbaker, a former beauty show contestant, who was the sexiest and flirtiest of the women.

The problem was that time and possibly the good life had begun to take their toll and, at 41, Ms Burke had piled on the weight. This, the producers felt, was beginning severely to belie her sexy image. Ms Burke was given an ultimatum and the subsequent row between her and the producers was played out in the glare of the tabloids. She lost – not the weight, but the role.

Soon after this blow, and having set up her own company suitably named Perseverance, Ms Burke starred in the eponymously titled *Delta*. With this much shorter-lived sitcom about an aspiring country singer, she tried to exploit her more ample shape, but it seems that US television was interested only in the old-look Delta.

Now came perhaps the strangest turn in this saga. Four years after being fired from *Designing Women*, Ms Burke was reunited with her old producers as she reprised the role of Suzanne, recently widowed after her fifth husband, in *Women of the House*, a Washington-set sitcom.

Sadly, the old magic had gone, but Delta Burke probably had the last laugh, setting up a New York clothes design business, which thrives to this day.

MATTER OF PRINCIPAL

THE LATE SHOW (1986–88)

Abrasive comedienne Joan Rivers has never exactly shied away from trouble, and, when she hosted the new Fox network's inaugural series, it was no different.

A fairly straightforward chat 'vehicle' – on almost exactly the same lines as Johnny Carson's show on a rival network, for which Rivers had been a regular guest presenter – it was given its edge by the fact that the hostess spent most of her time offending her guests. Not so great when your 'booker' is trying to line up future celebrity fodder.

She went a step too far, however, when they had tried to get Victoria Principal on the programme. After failing to contact her by phone live on the show, an irate Rivers then blurted out the actress's ex-directory number on air.

Was Victoria happy? Er, no – she filed a lawsuit. Suffice it to say, the show didn't last very long.

GAME FOR A DISASTER
IT'S A ROYAL KNOCKOUT (1987)

Until a cold June day in 1987, the closest the TV public had ever really come to our First Family was the Coronation coverage in 1953 (and subsequent royal weddings), those annual Christmas broadcasts by the Queen and Richard Cawston's dignified but rather delightful documentary, *The Royal Family*, in 1969.

There was absolutely nothing dignified or delightful about *It's a Royal Knockout*, which predated the Queen's own self-styled '*annus horribilis*' in 1993 and the various TV probes into Charles and Diana's marriage breakdown.

Some even suggest that the Fall of the House of Windsor began at Alton Towers. Prince Edward – late of the marines and new to the theatre (later television) – was the driving force behind this royal twist on the BBC's long-running, intertown slapstick contest, which had wisely gone into retirement five years earlier.

Ostensibly to raise funds for charity, Prince Edward's idea seemed to be that, by mounting a special edition of this garish hoopla, it might also help humanise the royals. So, together with showbiz and sporting pals, he, Princess Anne, Prince Andrew and the Duchess of York ('Fergie') stepped into the full glare of primetime television as respective team captains.

In his 1996 biography, *Elizabeth II, The Queen*, author Ben Pimlott recorded:

'It was a terrible mistake,' says one of the Monarch's friends. 'She was against it. But one of her faults is that she can't say no.' 'There was not a single courtier,' one recalls, 'who did not think it was a mistake.' Their advice was confounded by youthful enthusiasm and the Queen's maternal indulgence.

The programme was excruciating – 'Give us a B . . .' bellowed the Duchess of York – and made the public stunningly aware that a sense of decorum was not an automatic quality in the Royal Family, and even that some members might be more deserving of their Civil List incomes than others.

Journalist and royal biographer Andrew Morton was standing alongside *Daily Mirror* royal watcher James Whittaker at the time. There was, he recalled, 'one moment on this bitterly cold June day, where we saw the Duchess of York running round this muddy field, shouting her head off looking like a sixth-form schoolgirl. We just simultaneously turned to each other and said, "Well, this spells the end of her and the House of Windsor," because it was a joke. They were just making themselves into figures of fun and this is where television during the 1980s did the royal family no favours at all.'

As if the contest – presided over by giggling, idiotic Stuart Hall – weren't embarrassing enough, the aftermath merely compounded the felony. Conducting a press conference – more an autopsy – Prince Edward unwisely asked the throng, 'What did you think of it?'

The hacks mumbled something like, 'Well, nothing very much,' at which the fresh-faced but clearly overwrought Prince Edward stormed out in full view of the cameras like, noted Andrew Morton, 'a ballerina with a ladder in his tights.'

END OF TERM
HARDWICKE HOUSE (1987)

This mildly titled ITV production has the dubious distinction of being probably the least successful sitcom to be transmitted on British television.

The first series of the programme was originally supposed to include seven episodes. There was such a flood of complaints after transmission of the first two episodes, however, that the remaining five were promptly cancelled (together with the planned second series) and the programme was pulled from the schedules.

The programme, co-starring Kevin Allen, Pam Ferris, Roy Kinnear and Liz Fraser, chronicled the day-to-day misadventures of a bunch of rather odd and unpleasant teachers at a third-rate school.

TRIGGER HAPPY
BUD DWYER LIVE (1987)

The infamous case of Bud Dwyer remains one of the most shocking and horrifying television moments ever.

R Bud Dwyer was a Pennsylvania state treasurer, who found himself caught up in a bribery-and-corruption scandal in the mid-eighties. In 1987, Dwyer was convicted of receiving kickbacks and found himself facing a maximum of 55 years in prison, as well as a hefty fine. Naturally, he was also expected to resign.

On 22 January 1987, Dwyer called a live press conference at his office in Harrisburg, PA. About thirty members of the press and television cameras crowded the room, waiting for the announcement of his resignation.

Broadcasting live on TV, Dwyer read a prepared statement, gradually getting more and more nervous and sweaty. Several of the cameramen began to pack away their equipment, but Dwyer warned them that they might not want to leave yet.

On the verge of tears, Dwyer now started handing out sealed envelopes to his staff and then proceeded to pull out a .357 magnum. The room went silent and several reporters pleaded with him not to do anything rash. He then asked anyone who might be offended to leave the room, cocked the gun, put it in his mouth and pulled the trigger, blowing his brains out live on television.

Congressman Dwyer is not the only one who decided to end it all in such a spectacular – and public – fashion. Years earlier, on 15 July 1974, Christine Chubbock, a 29-year-old anchorwoman on Miami's WXLT-TV's *Sun Coast Digest Show*, had just finished reading the news bulletin when she chose a more horrific sign-off.

Looking down the camera lens, she said, 'In keeping with Channel 40's policy of bringing you the latest in blood and guts, you're going to see a first: an attempted suicide.'

To the horror of everyone around her and the viewing public, she pulled out a revolver and shot herself in the head. Pictures showed her slumping forward onto her desk before the screen went blank.

Sadly, she died fourteen hours later. Obviously, she just couldn't take it any more.

GRASS IS GREENER

21 JUMP STREET (1987–90)

You can understand why Johnny Depp had a certain reluctance to head the cast of this police drama about a bunch of young cops who go undercover in schools to 'grass up' recalcitrant pupils. After all, the sometime rock guitarist had, by the age of 23 when he began filming the series, led a somewhat chequered existence himself.

Depp had dropped out of school, dabbled in drugs, undergone the odd police 'bust' and even been married to, and divorced from, a woman five years his senior. With feature aspirations, he also didn't like the idea of being tied to a TV series.

So he turned down the role of Officer Tom Hanson, which went instead to one Jeff Yeagher. After shooting the pilot and part of the first episode, the network felt they might just have a hit on their hands – but not with poor Yeagher, who was fired. Depp was approached again, and this time, with the promise of big money – he'd had, to that point, small roles in just a couple of films – he opted for security and joined up.

Depp who, twenty years later, would be an authentic superstar regularly voted 'the sexiest man alive', got a first taste of all that in the late 1980s, when *21 Jump Street* quickly became a monster hit.

The fan magazines ate him up, revelling in his pouty defiance of the role that was making him famous: 'Hanson is not someone I'd want to have pizza with. I don't believe in having undercover cops in schools – it's spying.' (The series was inspired by a real-life initiative in Los Angeles during the 1970s.)

One of the gimmicks of the series was that, at the end of each episode, a cast member would do a sort of helpful public-service announcement about the issue of the week. Depp proved to be pretty much an issue of the week in his own right as he regularly defied authority on and off the set, mostly in the hope that he might get fired from what he was beginning to feel was a kind of jail sentence.

In fact, the series lasted three years with, in Depp's case, no time off for bad behaviour. He probably wished he'd had the fate meted out to Frederic Forrest, playing the eccentric cop in charge of the squad. After seven episodes, he was killed by a drunk hit-and-run driver.

GOOD GOLLY, IT'S OLLIE

AFTER DARK (1987–91)

Before programmes like *World's Wildest Police Videos* were common TV currency, the closest we came to observing street fights or traffic accidents was watching Oliver Reed live.

Perfectly aware of his, shall we say, erratic behaviour, producers would shamelessly line up Reed as a kind of performing seal to add a little danger to chat shows or serious discussion programmes.

When, on *Aspel & Co.* in 1986, he performed the Troggs' 'Wild Thing', shirt half open, lurching about the stage, clutching a large jug of what was thought to be gin and orange, it apparently turned out to be a prank (which badly misfired). A year later, he stopped just short of producing his manhood on *Des O'Connor Tonight*.

Four years after that, as a guest on Channel 4's late-night show, Reed was invited to be on an eight-strong panel to discuss, 'Do men have to be violent?' Reed had every right to be in good spirits because he'd just won a substantial libel settlement (and costs) from the *Sun*, which had accused him of beating up his wife, Josephine.

The programme's dimly lit set included a bar, to which Reed would make regular visits. As the earnest discussion got under way, odd Reed comments off camera could be heard, such as, 'I've had more fights in pubs than you've had hot dinners, girl' and 'A woman's role in society depends on whether she wants to get shafted'.

That was enough to get the outraged calls started. Then, it seems C4's chief executive, Michael Grade, rang in demanding to know why the show was being allowed to continue.

Deciding to try to verify whether this call was genuine, the director pulled the plug on *After Dark*, and a black-and-white documentary called *The Importance of British Coal Mining in the*

Fifties was shown instead. Twenty minutes later, however, having decided the call was a hoax, the director ordered live discussion to recommence.

Reed was now working himself up to full throttle, abusing guests generally, staggering to and from the loo, and finally plonking himself down next to the American feminist, Kate Millett. To her horror and a cry of, 'Do I have to put up with this? It's obnoxious and offensive', Reed kissed her sloppily on the cheek.

With a retort of, 'Do you want me to go?' Reed finally got up and left the studio. Whether he was actually drunk – as he also appeared to be on *The Word* – or, according to him, just play-acting what was expected, is not absolutely clear.

One hopes he felt no pain, however, when, aged 61 and with scenes still to complete on the historical epic *Gladiator*, he died of a heart attack in a Malta bar after, reputedly, downing three bottles of rum and beating five sailors at arm-wrestling.

TALKING TRASH
GERALDO (1987–98)

Geraldo Rivera is often credited – if that's the correct term – with inventing the modern style of 'trash' talk show. Brash and confrontational, Rivera frequently took on adversarial topics and goaded his guests. Rather than focus on conventional issues, he tended to concentrate on emotional topics that were guaranteed to cause a stir – and preferably a full-scale riot.

The 3rd of November 1988 was both the high point and, arguably, the low point of his show. Entitled 'Young Hate Mongers', this particular show garnered an audience of around 13 million viewers. Unfortunately, it was not all celebration.

The guests were an array of racial activists: Roy Innis from the Congress of Racial Equality, John Metzger of the Aryan Youth Movement, Robert Heick of the National Front and Rabbi

A Bruce Goldman. The audience was packed with white supremacists, as well as ordinary people who said that they had been victims of racists.

From the off, it was pretty clear that Rivera was spoiling for a rumble. The white supremacists were taunted and verbally attacked. Meanwhile, they accused Innis (a black man) of being an 'Uncle Tom'. They also used insulting terms for Jews. Finally, it seems that everyone had just had enough. Innis walked over to Metzger, grabbed him by the throat and, before long, the studio had turned into virtual carnage.

All good, apparently, for Rivera, who stood back and admired his handiwork. That is until a chair went flying across the room and smashed him in the face. Blood pouring from a broken nose, the crew tried to break up the confrontation and the brawl was lambasted in the papers.

The controversial host admitted that he had let things get out of hand and promised to tone down the show. But not everyone was unhappy to see him wearing a bandage across his face . . .

HURRICANE FISH

BBC WEATHER (1987)

On 11 January 1954, a 32-year-old Yorkshireman called George Cowling was the first person to present a weather forecast on British television. A little over 33 years later, in October 1987, Michael Fish, a meteorological man from Sussex, turned weather forecasting into headline news. The balding Fish, at thirty, had first startled the nation in January 1974 with his patterned jackets, kipper ties, strange hair and unfortunate moustache.

But it was another thirteen years before Fish became truly a household name – for all the wrong reasons. 'Earlier on today,' he smilingly told his BBC1 audience, 'apparently a lady rang the BBC and said she had heard that there was a hurricane on the way. Well, don't worry if you're watching, there isn't.'

A few hours later Britain was in the grip of one of the greatest and most destructive storms of the twentieth century.

Fish, who retired in 2004 at the mandatory age of sixty, seems unrepentant. 'I was actually referring to Florida at the time,' he told the *Independent on Sunday*, 'and it was completely taken out of context. I blame the media. It was very frustrating.'

Then, with an admirable blast of pragmatism, Britain's longest-serving weather forecaster added, 'I hope after all this time at long last I might be able to cash in on it . . .'

THE SPY GAME

SECRET SOCIETY (1987)

The brainchild of freelance journalist Duncan Campbell, this BBC2 documentary series was to consist of six half-hour programmes, 'each illuminating a hidden truth of major public concern'. Campbell would detail a particular aspect of national security that had previously been, if not deliberately then certainly conveniently, hushed up.

Nothing more was heard or discussed about the project until April 1986, when a request arrived from BBC Scotland to bug a private detective who claimed he could access a Criminal Records Office computer. After due legal consultations, Director-General Alasdair Milne agreed and work on the series continued.

It was only several months later at the press launch for BBC2's autumn season that the gravity of *Secret Society* became clear: Campbell promised revelations, among other things, about government plans in time of nuclear war. Now stuff began to hit the fan at the BBC with fiercely worded warnings from Whitehall.

Threats followed from BBC governors, but *Secret Society* didn't become a full-scale crisis until it emerged that one episode was to disclose the existence of a secret spy satellite codenamed Zircon.

Panic now reigned among the Corporation brass, which led to the Ministry of Defence's D Notice committee getting involved. The Zircon episode was pulled from transmission, and a furious Campbell set up private screenings of the programme in Parliament.

In the midst of all this, Milne was sacked, and the assistant DG, Alan Protheroe, had to take out a legal injunction against Campbell to stop him showing the tapes to anyone else.

The uproar climaxed with the police's staging of a well-publicised raid of BBC Scotland's offices in a bungled attempt to find leaked Zircon documents and bring a prosecution against the Corporation for breaking the Official Secrets Act.

Protheroe even ended up in jail for a short period for refusing to cooperate with the search. This dramatic chain of events proved fuel to the fire of those, including new DG Michael Checkland and his deputy John Birt, who believed the Beeb's news and current-affairs operations were out of control.

Protheroe quit the BBC shortly afterwards, but the Zircon episode of *Secret Society* had to wait four years and for the intervention of another channel before receiving an official broadcast as part of C4's 1991 *Banned* season.

QUEEN OF TEARS

THE BARBARA WALTERS SPECIAL (1988)

An American television legend, the lisping doyenne of the small screen has been interviewing the great and the good for more than forty years.

But not even her up-close-and-personals with world leaders have managed to generate quite the same kind headlines as when, in 1988, she had *Dirty Dancing* star Patrick Swayze in her doe-eyed gaze.

On this occasion, she gradually cajoled him into talking about his dead father. Suddenly, Swayze started crying his eyes out. 'I made it my passion that I was going to make that man proud of me until I died,' bawled the Swayze, as the network saw huge viewing figures flashing before them.

And that began a trend whereby people started revealing their innermost angst to Walters and sometimes got a bit misty-eyed in the process.

As Walters told *Entertainment Weekly*, 'It wasn't just a sniff-sniff, he really broke down. That led to years of people saying to me "please don't make me cry." '

CHECKPOINT CHARLIES

WALL OF TYRANNY (1988)

The textile city of Bradford has long been proud of the classical architecture that graces part of the city known as 'Little Germany' – a collection of streets and alleys once populated by affluent immigrant German Jews who came to Yorkshire in the later years of the nineteenth century and set up shop as wool merchants.

The Germanic look of the buildings made them a perfect if rather unlikely backdrop for *Wall of Tyranny*, a.k.a. *Freedom Fighter*, an ambitious American-financed TV movie set around the construction of the Berlin Wall in 1961 and starring Tony Danza, David McCallum and Sid Caesar.

Location filming took place largely within Little Germany, where a plastic Berlin Wall, replete with barbed wire made of string, was erected across one of the main streets.

Enthusiastic local reservists from the Territorial Army were hired as extras to play gun-toting East German border guards, while fir trees and hedges were strategically placed across the ends of streets that looked out onto the city to hide the giveaway shapes of modern vehicles and double-decker buses.

It made for a curiously atmospheric and authentic location, and one that occasionally spilled over into the day-to-day lives of

Bradfordians as traffic was halted while scenes were shot involving jackbooted troops and downtrodden civilians in drab 1960s garb.

Curious Yorkshire folk turned out in droves to catch a glimpse of former *Man From U.N.C.L.E.* star McCallum as an East German officer, patrolling the checkpoint by the Wall.

Tony Danza, better known as a popular sitcom actor in shows such as *Taxi*, found himself on the receiving end of some blunt Tyke banter as he was taunted by a crowd of deeply unimpressed local lads from a nearby pub.

Sid Caesar, meanwhile, sat quietly in his chair with growing amusement as Danza became increasingly flustered. 'Hey, I'm the star of this show!' he would wail vainly to anyone close enough to hear.

CRIMEWATCH USA

AMERICA'S MOST WANTED (1988–)

Four years after *Crimewatch UK* started giving us nightmares, despite the reassuring late-night words of smiling co-presenter Nick Ross, came this much grimmer catalogue of misdeeds and misdoers from the US of A.

Billed as a 'weekly nationwide criminal manhunt', and featuring the usual mix of re-creations, interviews and pleas, it had the added cachet of a presenter who knew exactly what he was talking about.

Sometime actor, author and one of *People* magazine's 'Fifty Most Beautiful People in the World', John Walsh had endured the kidnap and murder of his six-year-old son Adam in 1981.

Frustratingly, no one was ever officially charged with the crime, although Walsh was convinced that serial killer Ottis Toole, who died in 1996, was responsible.

That contrasts with perhaps the show's most spectacular success, when, just a week after it had aired the details of a twenty-year-old crime, the murderer was finally apprehended after two decades on the run.

So successful has the show been that, when the Fox network cancelled it after eight years, it was quickly reinstated due to an outcry from viewers, politicians and law-enforcement agencies. Another early candidate for the role of *AMW* presenter was actress Theresa Saldana, who, like Walsh, had also once been at the sharp edge of a crime. In her case, quite literally.

Following her role in *Raging Bull* as Jake la Motta's abused first wife, she was attacked by a deranged knife-wielding fan and badly injured. She recovered to resume her acting career and present *Confessions of Crime* in 1991, which would, unlike Walsh's warhorse, last just thirteen episodes.

GOING AWOL

THIS MORNING (1988–)

A myriad things can go wrong on live television – even when presented by that normally fail-safe tandem of Richard Madeley and Judy Finnigan. One of those times was where viewers of the ITV show assumed that they had died.

To explain . . .

It was the last fifteen minutes of the show and the pair were getting ready to introduce their fun final item of the day, a dynamic trapeze artist. The idea was simple: Fred would do his weather report, giving time for Richard and Judy to drive out to the nearby dockside to the site of the gymnastics; they were to get there in time to introduce the guy and then wait while he performed before doing a brief interview.

Unfortunately, the show had a new floor manager and, unfamiliar with the layout of the studios, she sent the car containing R & J to completely the wrong place. Fred finished jumping around his weather map, the director cut to the trapeze artist, but our beloved couple were nowhere to be seen. What was worse was that the car had gone AWOL and no one knew where it was.

The crew at the dock motioned the acrobat to start his act, which he did, while the audience at home were able to see various panicked crew members waving their arms around and trying to locate Richard and Judy. He finished and, with the pair still unsighted, he was told to start all over again.

Then one of the sound technicians had the bright idea of fading up the presenters' microphones, in a bid to locate them. All well and good, but he decided to do it live on air and, suddenly, viewers were able to hear the duo shouting; 'It's over here!' and 'No it's not, it's over there!'

And that was the way the show ended, with the trapeze artist embarrassedly swinging round and round, while the credits rolled and a random car careered around Liverpool Docks. Unsurprisingly, the phone lines lit up, as viewers mistakenly assumed something awful had happened, because they had not seen them for more than ten minutes. But no, it wasn't Richard having a heart attack, or their car plummeting into the river – it was simply a case of bad map-reading.

As for the floor manager, she was totally mortified, but, since she was new, Richard and Judy forgave her and she managed to hold on to her job.

SHAME ABOUT THE NAME
ANNIE MCGUIRE (1988)

What a difference a decade (or three) makes! For five years, from 1961 to 1966, Mary Tyler Moore played America's favourite sitcom wife, Laura Petrie, in *The Dick Van Dyke Show*.

Four years later, she went on to even greater fame and a considerable fortune during the seven-year run of *The Mary Tyler Moore Show*, as the adorable, single career woman Mary Richards.

But not even the success of those mega-hits could do much for *Mary* in 1978. This Tyler Moore-fronted mixture of comedy sketches and music lasted just three telecasts. The following year saw her return as Mary McKinnon in *The Mary Tyler Moore Hour*, a somewhat bizarre mixture of variety and sitcom. A three-month run was all it could muster despite surrounding the star with household names.

When, a few years later, she arrived on a fictionalised Chicago tabloid as Mary Brenner – fortysomething divorcee and news-paper columnist – for another show called *Mary*, this time a sitcom, the curse persisted and the series failed to survive its first season.

Could a change of name finally spell a change of fortune for the plucky little lady? This time round, Mary became Annie, a mature newlywed working in New York. Sadly, not even this reinvention could help and Annie McGuire completely ran out of steam after two months.

Fast-forward to the mid-nineties as Mary tried yet again, not in sitcom this time but straight drama, as hard-nosed Louise Felcott in *New York News*, set on a Big Apple tabloid.

She was, however, reportedly unhappy with her tough, unsym-pathetic role and, as if to pre-empt the inevitable, asked to be written out of the production. Before the writers could do their worst, the series was cancelled. This was her fifth consecutive TV failure.

To date, *New York News* remains Tyler Moore's last venture into episodic TV. However, the actress, now nudging seventy, has recently had a chance to relive some past glories – in telemovie reunions for both *The Dick Van Dyke Show* and *The Mary Tyler Moore Show*. Full circle, indeed.

FLY ON THE WALL
DINNER AT NOON (1988)

The idea, as originally dreamed up by writer Alan Bennett, was to make a fly-on-the-wall documentary set amid the plush environs of the Crown Hotel, Harrogate. According to his biographer Alexander Games, Bennett wanted, via discreet camerawork, to capture snapshots of the lives of staff and guests. The idea was that they should speak for themselves, but as filming got under way it quickly became apparent that much of what was being recorded was too stilted or banal to be used at any length.

With only ten days allotted for the whole shoot, a solution had to be found and it came in the form of a Bennett commentary dovetailed with the sights and just some of the sounds of the Harrogate hostelry.

While the critics revelled in Bennett's acute observation, some of those present at a screening in the Crown itself felt that the people portrayed – possibly betrayed – in the short film had been, said the local newspaper, 'sent up to a certain degree'.

As for a former mayor of Harrogate, who'd made a fleeting appearance in the production, he railed that Bennett had been 'a bit cruel at times' with his insights.

HOSTS WITHOUT THE MOST
BRIT AWARDS (1989–)

The Brits – the annual UK pop music awards – have frequently come under scrutiny for their uncontroversial nominations, but not even the presence of Annie Lennox and Eric Clapton could help when the supposedly cutting-edge awards show was relaunched for television in 1989. Because what followed was one of the worst debacles in awards show history.

First off was the strange decision to choose lanky drummer Mick Fleetwood and pint-sized ex-Page Three girl Samantha Fox as co-hosts. Not known for their witty repartee, the pink-haired Fox and long-haired rocker found it difficult even to read the autocue. They consistently fluffed their lines and, when they did get them right, they were sometimes in the wrong order. One of the stranger moments was when the duo introduced the Four Tops, only for Boy George to walk out onto the stage. Looking embarrassed, he mumbled: 'I'm afraid I'm just the One Top.'

Not only was the script wrong, but guests turned up late and a video message from Michael Jackson was dropped, only for the BBC show to underrun. A Bros video was hastily added onto the end to fill the time. Fox has said of the experience, 'It wasn't my fault – all I had to do was learn my lines.'

'We've had a great time. Hope you have too. We love ya,' Fox said optimistically at the show's end – more in hope than any genuine expectation considering the palpable derision from the live audience.

Meanwhile, Fleetwood subsequently explained to *Classic Rock* magazine,

It was definitely a fiasco. It was the first time they'd opened it up to the general public and they put three hundred fans of some boy band [Bros] at the front. Consequently, you couldn't hear anything on stage. I was left floundering because they couldn't communicate. They did at least take out an advert trying to explain that it was not our fault, but by then it was too late . . . Such is life.

Michael Jackson played a slightly more important part in the Brits' second major moment of Strangeness. In 1996, he was due to play 'Earth Song' live on stage and was introduced by Bob Geldof, who brought him on saying, a bit scarily, 'When he sings, it is with the voice of angels. When his feet move, you can see God dancing.'

Jacko seemed to take that a little bit literally and came out in a white costume and proceeded to astonish the crowd by singing the song surrounded by kids, standing in various Christ-like poses and appearing to bless his supporting cast by touching their heads.

One man who took offence to all this was Pulp frontman Jarvis Cocker, who was so incensed that he leaped onstage and wiggled his bottom about in front of Jackson, much to the amusement of the viewing audience. He was quickly grabbed by Jackson's minders and later was accused of causing injury to the child dancers, some of whom were apparently hurt in the ensuing chaos.

However, Jackson never sued and Cocker, who had been a fairly anonymous member of the indie music fraternity up to that point, became a national star, while his record sales soared.

HOMER & TONY
THE SIMPSONS (1989–)

If *The Simpsons* is to be believed (and many do believe it), then Britain is being run by Mr Bean. At least, that's who Homer thinks Tony Blair is when the prime minister made his landmark appearance as himself in an episode of the seminal show, called 'The Regina Monologues' (shown in Britain in January 2004).

Blair is the first world leader to lend his voice to the show while still in power. All living former presidents have been asked, as well as George W Bush, but have refused to take part, apart from Bill Clinton (that hasn't stopped them from appearing in the show, though, with impersonators doing the voices).

Because the show was recorded in the midst of the war with Iraq, some felt it was inappropriate for Blair to participate. But, after eight months of negotiations between the programme makers and Number Ten's then director of communications Alastair Campbell, it was felt that it would be churlish to pull out.

Blair – a big fan of the show – used it as a chance to promote tourism in Britain, since the episode sees the Simpsons visiting London. On arriving at the airport, they are greeted by the PM, who urges them to see the sights. Drawn with a cheesy grin and Prince Charles ears, Blair finishes his exchange by igniting his personal jetpack and shooting off into the stratosphere, with Homer calling after him, 'Goodbye, Mr Bean!'

It was recorded by executive producer Al Jean, and, although Blair was at the top of the cameo list, the makers were never sure it would happen. Fortuitously, Jean was in London to promote the show when he received a call telling him that, if he could go to Downing Street as soon as possible, the prime minister would be available.

'He was great with his lines,' Jean told the *Daily Telegraph*. 'And I think that if someone doesn't mind being called Mr Bean, it shows they've got a good sense of humour.'

One thing the government didn't have a sense of humour about was a moment in the script when Blair presented the Simpsons with a corgi dog as a welcome present. Because Blair was berated at the time in the tabloids for being America's poodle, his people decided that it was too risky, so the scene was dropped.

Despite meeting hundreds of celebrities who have contributed to the show, Jean was very anxious about meeting the PM. 'I was so nervous, it was ridiculous,' he says. 'But Mr Blair was very charismatic. He was genuinely interested in the show and asked me loads of questions about it.'

BLOWING HIS HORN

THE ARSENIO HALL SHOW (1989–)

Talk shows are all about the guests – and, for a topical American nightly chat show, a presidential candidate is right at the top of the pile. Ever since the invention of the television, politicians have had to fight an on-screen campaign, and no one knew that more than Bill Clinton.

Many thought that his surprise 1992 visit to Hall's show while he was Democratic candidate for the presidency swung the election in his favour. Until then, papers had focused on his alleged womanising. That didn't seem to matter, however, when he put on a pair of dark glasses, pulled out his saxophone and blasted out a (pretty good) version of 'Heartbreak Hotel'.

As he sat down for an interview with his wife Hillary, the audience went wild, young voters were hooked and Hall joked, 'It's good to see a Democrat blowing something other than the election.'

WARPED TIME TWIST

QUANTUM LEAP (1989–93)

Dr Sam Beckett was a scientist who had invented a time machine, which made him 'leap' into the bodies of various people throughout history and help them out with a problem. Starring Scott Bakula, as Sam, and Dean Stockwell as Al, his hologram pal that only Sam could hear and see, the show was successful for four years, before coming to a close in May 1993.

And it was that final episode that left everyone going, 'Huh?' At the time, it wasn't known whether it was the climax or merely the end-of-season cliffhanger. After it was shot, the programme makers found out that the show had been cancelled and re-edited it into a final hurrah.

That still doesn't explain quite how weird it is. Sam leaps into a bar in Pennsylvania on his birthday at the exact time that he was born. He looks in the mirror and sees his own reflection (usually he sees the person he leaps into).

He starts talking to the barman, who is called Al (played by Bruce McGill, who also appeared in the premiere). Incredulous, Sam begins to think that the bar is some kind of alternate universe. It doesn't help that the bar is populated by actors who appeared in previous series of the show playing different characters.

Sam has been wanting to go home since Day One, but something keeps sending him through time. He even begins to believe that it is the bartender who is controlling his destiny – that he is God. And nothing that Al the bartender says does anything to put this theory to rest. Rarely has there been a more cryptic character on network television.

If you think that's pretty dense so far, it does get even more confusing.

Sam sees someone else surrounded by the familiar blue electrical energy and leaping. He saves some miners caught underground. And, in a strange religious twist, he realises that he is some kind of latter-day saint, controlled by God to save people throughout history.

His final mission sees him leap into Al's home, where his wife thinks that Al has been killed in combat during the Vietnam War. Sam tells her that he has merely been captured and will return home.

Rather than remarry, she maintains hope in Al and the final image we see is a photo of Al surrounded by blue flames, followed by black and the words, 'As a result of Sam's revelation, Beth never remarried. She and Al have four daughters and would have celebrated their 39th wedding anniversary in June. Dr Sam Beckett never returned home . . .'

The final episode (like many series finales) was a divisive issue among fans, many of whom wanted more resolution to the story. Instead, it posed a lot more questions than it answered. Some were happy that Sam was still out there helping people, but others thought he should have got home and that it was a very downbeat finale.

However, ever since it went off the air, rumours have flown around that there will be a reunion TV movie. Scott Bakula has said in interviews that he, creator Donald Bellisario and co-star Dean Stockwell are all raring to go, but the network isn't keen.

Nonetheless, don't be surprised if Sam leaps again, if only to de-muddle millions of Leapee brains . . .

LIFE'S A BEACH

BAYWATCH (1989–2000)

With its irresistible mixture of bikinis and, er, more bikinis, this may once have been the most popular show on the planet, but it didn't always manage to spot the biggest potential talent.

David Hasselhoff, nominal star of *Baywatch*, admitted recently that among the crop of hot young actors who auditioned for beachfront duty was aspiring heartthrob Leonardo DiCaprio.

But Hasselhoff obviously had premonitions of *Titanic* when Leo failed to stay afloat and sank to a watery grave. Yes, he wasn't hired. In an interview with *TeenHollywood.com*, Hasselhoff said, 'He was going to be one of the young lifeguards, but we didn't hire him. Because of that he probably went on to become a huge movie star.'

DiCaprio was jokingly reminded by Hasselhoff of his teenage failure at the 2005 Golden Globes, when he picked up Best Actor for *The Aviator*.

THE 1990s

KRAMER VS. KRAMER
SEINFELD (1990–98)

When Larry David and Jerry Seinfeld were coming up with the cast of characters for their legendary sitcom, David had the clever idea that, as well as basing Jerry's best friend George Costanza on himself, he wanted to include another real-life person.

While struggling to make a living as a writer in a Hell's Kitchen apartment, David lived next door to an eccentric entrepreneur called Kenny Kramer and David wanted to put him on screen, albeit with an actor playing him.

He asked Kramer if it was OK to use his name and Kramer replied that, if he wanted to call a character Kramer, then Kenny should be allowed to play him.

Knowing that NBC would never agree, David changed the character's name initially to 'Kessler' for the pilot episode, but gradually Jerry found himself so attached to Kramer that they made a settlement with the real-life odd neighbour to use his name.

But the eccentricity doesn't end there. When the show became a hit, Kenny Kramer realised that there was mileage in exploiting his role as the basis for the acclaimed character.

So he decided to start the 'Kenny Kramer Reality Tour', an officially recognised New York City tour, during which he takes paying tourists around various sights featured in the sitcom and his day-to-day life. You can see the real Monk's restaurant, where the characters meet regularly on the show; you can meet the real Soup Nazi. And all while the real Kramer talks you through where David got his real-life inspirations for the show and how the show came about.

When the writers of the show heard about Kenny Kramer's idea, the storyline was too good to pass up. In the 1997 season of

213

the show, Cosmo Kramer sells his memoirs to catalogue king J Peterman, so that Peterman can pass them off as his own and use them in his autobiography.

After having second thoughts, Cosmo starts up a 'Peterman Reality Tour', during which he drives around New York, pointing out the real-life locations of his stolen memories. Sounds familiar.

YOU WON'T BELIEVE IT!

ONE FOOT IN THE GRAVE (1990–97; 2000)

Being crucified repeatedly can make a chap really angry. Yes, it was the expression of repressed rage on Richard Wilson's face as he was being hoisted up on the cross for the umpteenth time that convinced scriptwriter David Renwick that the Scots actor would be perfect for the role of Victor Meldrew.

At the time – four years before *OFITG* was up and running – Wilson was playing the beleaguered foreign secretary, Nigel Lipman, in a feature-film version of Renwick's TV show, *Whoops Apocalypse*.

The scene in this spoof comedy about World War Three was being shot at QPR's Loftus Road stadium and Wilson's deeply uncomfortable stunt required no fewer than twenty takes in order to get the sun setting in just the right place behind his head. No wonder he was so 'fashed'.

Perhaps it was the memory of this indignity – scripted by Renwick and Andrew Marshall – that gave Wilson more than just pause for thought when he took receipt of three 'taster' scripts for the proposed *OFITG*.

According to his biographer, James Roose-Evans, Wilson said, 'I didn't fancy it at all. I thought Victor Meldrew was rubbish. I felt he was too angry for too long. I couldn't imagine the audience would believe in him.' So he sent a polite note to Renwick saying he wasn't interested.

Wilson's agent then quickly heard from the BBC that not only had the role been written with the actor specifically in mind but that Renwick wouldn't go ahead with any other actor. After viewing another three scripts, Wilson was eventually convinced and so anger mismanagement quickly became the order of the day.

HOME OF THE STRANGE

TWIN PEAKS (1990–91)

Arguably the very definition of Strange television, David Lynch's surreal, dreamlike soap opera was, as one commentator wryly noted, 'one of the most talked-about but least-watched TV experiments of the early nineties.'

Set in the Pacific Northwest, the thirty-episode (including pilot) tale was triggered by the murder of local high school beauty Laura Palmer (Sheryl Lee). But that was just an excuse for much studied weirdness as the investigation progressed haltingly in lumber country under the direction of FBI Agent Cooper (Kyle MacLachlan), a mystical-minded loner.

The oddness of it all was perhaps summed up by the way at least one piece of crucial casting was achieved – that of the real/unreal character 'Killer Bob', who remains the scary spectre at this unfolding feast of (mostly) enjoyable if self-indulgent tosh.

Prop man Frank Silva was shifting scenery about the set when Lynch spotted his seemingly sinister reflection and it sparked some thoughts. Lynch asked him if he was an actor and, when Silva said yes, he was asked if he'd like to be in the show. 'What am I gonna do?' Silva then asked. 'I don't know, but you're in this movie,' Lynch replied. Yes, it was that kind of programme.

By the end of the decade, the appeal of Lynch's kind of strangeness seems to have worn off – as far as TV commissioners were concerned.

ABC wanted Lynch to come up with a new *Twin Peaks*, liked his idea of a starlet arriving in Hollywood and, in 1999, let him shoot an $8 million pilot. Then they decided that what he did was just too odd and passed on it. With another $7 million from the French producers, Studio Canal, Lynch was able to resurrect his *oeuvre* and shoot new scenes in order to resolve the open ending he'd left for the TV film (anticipating a series).

The result, *Mulholland Drive*, won awards around the world and earned Lynch an Oscar nomination for Best Director.

WHERE THE ART ISN'T

ART IS DEAD, LONG LIVE TV (1991)

A sculptor who fashioned rotting flesh, human faeces and vomit, a film director with a fridge's-eye view of New York, a conceptualist artist designing biodegradable houses in the forests of Bavaria, and a radical Scots author claiming to have 'redefined the novel' . . .

This was the quartet of 'talents' who comprised four of a five-part C4 series. In the fifth programme, they met up together with presenter Muriel Gray for a final overview. As the discussion became extremely heated, the sculptor turned on Ms Gray and threw a glass of red wine over her.

When the programme ended, it turned out that the series – which had originally been titled *Emperor's New Clothes* (bit of a giveaway) – was an entire hoax.

The so-called artists were, respectively, a computer salesman, an architect, an antiques dealer and a beautician.

It seems Gray had set up the whole series 'to show that, whether it's real or not, as soon as it's on the telly it's elevated. TV programmes falsify truth and information all the time. To me, art is so important that, without it, we would cop it. I don't like to see it undervalued or devalued by the duplicity of programme makers.'

Even when some of the newspapers then proceeded to round on Gray for perpetrating the spoof, she took much satisfaction in the fact that, in the course of the series, various critics had taken the programmes very seriously – some even claiming to have heard of the artists in the spotlight.

FATAL CONFESSION
JENNY JONES (1991–2003)

When you're playing with people's lives on a daily basis, it's only a matter of time before you come across someone who can't take it. So was the case with Jenny Jones on 6 March 1995.

Jenny Jones – born in Bethlehem, so possibly harbouring ideas above her station – was the host of the eponymous talk show that, with a crowded marketplace and in the struggle to maintain ratings, had begun to tackle more and more risky subjects.

They were particularly fond of the 'twist' shows, in which someone came on thinking they were there for one reason, when in fact it was something completely different.

For an ill-fated item called 'Secret Crushes', 26-year-old waiter Jonathan Schmitz came to the show excited to be told that someone had a secret crush on him. Unfortunately for him, the person opening their heart was not a beautiful young woman, but an openly gay army veteran from Detroit called Scott Amedure.

When Amedure revealed his secret, Schmitz seemed to take it in his stride, saying that he was flattered, but that he was heterosexual.

Supposedly, that was that, but, unfortunately, that wasn't the end of the saga. Three days after appearing on the show, Schmitz turned up at Amedure's house with a pump-action shotgun and shot him twice at point-blank range. Amedure was killed instantly.

The media went crazy, blaming Jones for the death and berating talk shows in general for screwing with people's lives for ratings. Jones said that neither she nor her staff were responsible, pointing out that Schmitz had been told his crush could potentially be a man.

As a waiter, she argued, Schmitz was used to having men try to chat him up. Since the two of them knew each other, she continued, eventually Amedure might have revealed his feelings and the same thing would have happened.

Amedure's family didn't agree and sued the show for $25 million. Schmitz went to court, where it emerged that he was already fighting alcoholism and depression. He was convicted of second-degree murder and sentenced to 25 to fifty years in prison.

The show continued nonetheless, despite subsequently being shrouded in controversy, before being cancelled after twelve seasons.

NEIGHBOURHOOD WATCH
HOME IMPROVEMENT (1991–99)

This successful sitcom, starred Tim Allen as a handyman with his own television show, *Tool Time*, and a bawdy family that got into endless scrapes.

As well as launching pneumatic Pamela Anderson in her first proper television role, it also featured an unusual sidekick for Allen's lead character Tim Taylor. Wilson Wilson (played by Earl Hindman) was the Taylor's next-door neighbour and was always on hand to dispense wisdom and advice. But you never saw his face.

Well, that's not strictly true: you never saw his *whole* face, whose bottom half was obscured week in week out by the garden fence separating the two houses. Why? Who knows? Suffice to say that it was a running gag.

Although it was easy at first, Wilson soon became a more prevalent character in the show, moving out of his house and into the real world. So fan clubs sprang up debating how the programme makers were going to hide his face next – some of the ways they did it include a wine rack, sand castle, clown costume and surgical mask.

Even during the curtain calls for the show, Hindman would bring out a miniature picket fence to hold up in front of his face so that the studio audience wouldn't be able to see it.

Ultimately, during the series finale, the audience finally got to see Wilson in all his glory after eight years on the air. Sadly, it was Hindman's last major role – he died of lung cancer in 2003.

MIND MY GHOULIES

GHOSTWATCH (1992)

Audiences watching BBC1 on 31 October 1992 – All Souls' Eve, or Hallowe'en – were shocked when popular presenters Michael Parkinson and Sarah Greene appeared to be communing with the spirits on a primetime television show.

Ghostwatch had Parky, Greene, her husband Mike Smith and comic Craig Charles seeking to uncover the secrets behind the most haunted house in Britain, expecting perhaps the odd fright and a probable hoax.

The next ninety minutes turned into one of the most terrifying programmes ever shown on TV, as real ghosts showed themselves on screen, made frightening noises and scared the poor presenters half to death.

There was just one little problem – it *was* all make-believe. Viewers were tricked into thinking it was a real investigation, but was, in fact, the Hallowe'en idea of writer Stephen Volk, who created the scenario and pitched it as a live event. Instead, it featured actors, camera tricks and special effects. As a result, it remains many people's scariest television moment.

There was a helpline that stated at the beginning, 'this is not real', but then people were able to leave messages of their own experiences. And the writer even wanted to put a high-pitched sound over the transmission of the show that would be inaudible to humans, but would send the audience's pets crazy.

It is still unofficially banned in Britain and, although initially nominated for a BAFTA, the BBC withdrew it after all the complaints they received about the show.

The makers of *The Blair Witch Project* are rumoured to have watched it before they made their movie.

BOB A JOB

AFRICAN SKIES (1992–94)

Robert Mitchum at least went one better than John Forsythe, the regular unseen presence in *Charlie's Angels*: he was actually featured on screen.

In this mild adventure series for the Family Channel, Mitchum played the tycoon grandfather of an American youngster who lived in the bush with his mother in post-apartheid South Africa.

However, unlike the rest of the stars who got to film among the wildlife in the new Rainbow Nation, Mitchum – a last-minute replacement for ailing Glenn Ford – didn't. Instead, he was usually seen quite literally 'phoning in' his performance as bluff billionaire Sam Dutton in a weekly cameo from his office at the giant Arcano Corporation somewhere in the States.

BLOOD-STAINED SOAP

OF BODY AND SOUL (1992)

They often joke about the outrageous excesses of Brazilian soap opera, but the tragic true-life case of Daniela Perez, glamorous sex symbol Yasmin in *Of Body and Soul* (*De corpo e alma*) probably outstrips anything the writers could dream up. Even when the show's creator was her mother, Gloria Perez.

After her husband reported her missing, 22-year-old Daniela's body was soon discovered on deserted wasteland near Rio. She'd been stabbed fifteen times. Within 48 hours, Guillaume de Padua, her co-star in the show, had confessed to the murder and later his wife also confessed, though later retracted her statement.

De Padua claimed it was a crime of passion, that Daniela was in love with him and when they argued about it she threatened to kill his wife. As, he alleged, she tried to attack him with a pair of scissors, she got stabbed to death in the ensuing struggle.

After her daughter's funeral, Perez wrote de Padua's part out of the soap, but, as there remained a great deal of as yet unscreened footage of Daniela, Yasmin remained – creepily – in regular flashbacks on the show.

ONE HUMP OR TWO?

A DANGEROUS MAN: LAWRENCE AFTER ARABIA (1992)

Thirty years earlier, David Lean had a limitless budget, eighteen months and locations such as Saudi Arabia, Jordan, Spain, Morocco and London to recreate the exotic world of soldier/ adventurer T E Lawrence.

For this Emmy-award-winning two-hour TV drama – a sort of 'sequel' starring Ralph Fiennes – they had the equivalent of small change and a just a day in a quarry off the M25 in Kent to do the desert stuff.

Producer Colin Vaines takes up the story. 'We'd originally set the film up as a three-million-pound French–British co-production, to be shot in Paris and London. Then the French money fell apart, and we had to reconceive it as a relatively low-budget piece.

'So we ended up shooting the whole thing more or less at Sands Film Studios in Rotherhithe, where we built sets for interior rooms at Versailles, the Crillon Hotel, the War Office et cetera. We then went on days out to places like the Bluebell line to shoot period trains and train stations in UK and France.

'But our triumph was to recreate the footage Lowell Thomas had shot of Lawrence in the desert, which was shown at the Royal Albert Hall as *With Lawrence in Arabia* – the sequence which opens the film, with an unkempt TE watching from the back of the auditorium.

'We hired camels from Chipperfield's circus, which, needless to say, were impossible to control; we ended doing half the shots with Ralph sitting on a stepladder, pretending he was riding along.

'Then we found this quarry off the M25 that had previously been used for *Doctor Who* episodes. With Ralph and Siddig el Fadil [Alexander Siddig, as he now is post-*Deep Space Nine*] who played Feisal, and half a dozen extras, we shot black-and-white footage on an authentic period hand-cranked camera.

'I was so pleased with the result that I made the mistake of telling a journalist how clever we'd been. What a schmuck! They ran a double-page spread in *Daily Mirror* with the headline, LAWRENCE OF SEVENOAKS!'

CRIMEAN WARS

SHARPE (1993–97)

Just three days into filming his starring role as Richard Sharpe, the English army hero of Bernard Cornwell's stirring Napoleonic novels, Paul McGann was enjoying a kickabout on Black Sea beach in the Crimea.

Thanks to the oddities of international financing, this corner of the Ukraine was doubling for the Iberian Peninsular in the first of what would be, it was hoped, many screen adventures for one of contemporary literature's more popular period heroes.

Sadly, McGann didn't have much time to relish either the role or the location for he suddenly twisted his knee and, although he – pardon the expression – soldiered on for a while, it was clear that he wouldn't be able properly to fulfil the demands of such a demanding all-action role.

So, after six years of preparation and several million pounds spent, cast and crew headed back to the UK. Within a week, Sean Bean was cast as the hero. Together with a new director and leading lady (Assumpta Serna replacing Diana Penalver as the fiery Spanish guerrilla and love interest, Comandante Teresa Moreno), they returned, a month later, to the Ukraine to start the whole of *Sharpe's Rifles* again from scratch.

This time round, they ran into an old Soviet winter, with temperatures apt to fall to between 20 and 30 degrees below, the only heat being provided by Russian army vehicles.

But that was probably less hazardous than in one of the later series, when the unit encountered a severe drought, which meant a chronic water shortage. Cholera began to sweep the region and the area of filming was designated a quarantine zone. Bean and company had to make to do with two buckets of water each a day to flush the lavatory.

Despite all these rigours, Bean and Daragh O'Malley, who played Sharpe's loyal sidekick Harper, were probably the only two regulars never to fall ill in the Crimea. However, when, to everyone's huge relief, the production base moved to Turkey for the last two series, there just had to be a downside.

Pity poor O'Malley, who was accidentally kicked in the face during a fight scene shot late at night. He suffered seven broken bones in his face and his infraorbital nerve was severed on the left side. With a smashed sinus he couldn't fly back to England because of the pressurised cabin so he had to be operated on, and recuperate, in Turkey.

Perhaps the Crimean cramps might have been preferable.

ARE YOU POSITIVE?

THE RICKI LAKE SHOW (1993–)

As you can imagine, much unpleasantness has occurred over the years on the talk show hosted by the actress Ricki Lake.

But it would take something pretty special to beat the tale of guest Gwen, a thirtysomething, who came onto the show to talk about AIDS.

After revealing to the audience that she was HIV-positive, Gwen was then asked by Ricki what impact it had had on her life. As the audience jeered and booed, Gwen said that she was planning to have unprotected sex with as many men as possible. She said that, when she died, she wanted her gravestone to say, 'She took ten thousand men with her when she died.'

Unsurprisingly, this caused shock and outrage in the studio, but Gwen wasn't finishing there. She told gaping viewers that she had slept with half of the vice squad in New Orleans, which is where she lived. 'One half of the New Orleans Police Department is going to die,' she said.

When pressed as to why she wanted to do this, Gwen replied, 'I want people to remember me for what I did. When I get together with men, I say, "Do you want a condom?" They say "no" and I smile and think, You're going to die.'

Incredibly, this story has a sort of happy ending. Two days after she appeared on Ricki's show, the Associated Press ran a story that read, 'Gwendolyn Marreo, who claimed to have infected half the New Orleans Police Department, does not have AIDS.'

Yes, incredibly, the seemingly vengeful Gwen had made the whole thing up because she wanted to get on national television and she felt that the best way of doing that was by creating the most sensational story she could.

Don't think she made it onto Ricki's Christmas card list . . .

TEE AND SYMPATHY
BAD GOLF MADE EASIER (1993)

You won't actually find a programme of this title in any TV reference book. It's actually the first in a series of videos – followed by *Bad Golf My Way* and *The Stupid Little Golf Video* – 'starring' silver-haired Leslie Nielsen, who, after a career in straight-faced Hollywood roles, suddenly became a funny-man at the age of sixty.

His golfing prowess – if you can call it that – actually began in the world of TV programmes such as *Pro-Celebrity Golf* and *Around with Alliss*. In these shows, a professional would, as it says on the tin, pair up with a celebrity for a bit of a golf, perhaps a little showbiz gossip and the odd wisecrack as they weaved their way round some eye-catching course.

Most rounds went smoothly enough, with the celebs, despite being amateurs, acquitting themselves adequately. In Sean Connery's case, more than.

That was until the arrival of Nielsen. It was the early seventies and the show's producers needed a Hollywood name. And remember, this was before *Airplane!* and *The Naked Gun*. One day, while scouting for talent at the Bel-Air Country Club (which houses a famous golf course), a producer spotted Nielsen relaxing on the patio.

He was invited to travel to Gleneagles in Scotland, along with a companion of his choosing, to play a round of golf with a celebrity and enjoy the facilities. Somewhat taken aback, Nielsen accepted.

When time came to record the show, Nielsen wandered merrily to the first tee, having enjoyed the hospitality of Gleneagles and its environs. He was paired with the American Tom Weiskopf.

Teeing up, Nielsen was full of good humour. He swung – and missed. So he swung again – and missed. He wound up taking 32 strokes to complete the first hole. As the camera trained on him at the second tee, he swung – and this time the ball flew beautifully down the fairway. Convinced that the first hole had all been about nerves, everyone, including Weiskopf, now relaxed.

When he hit his second shot, Nielsen narrowly missed killing his partner as the ball flew off to the right. Smiling widely, he called to Weiskopf, 'What do I do now?' A livid Weiskopf marched off the course.

Of course, Nielsen had never played golf before in his life. He had been sitting having a quiet drink at a posh venue that happened to have a golf course and someone had come and offered him a first-class holiday to Scotland. Why would he turn it down?

He spent the rest of the week thoroughly enjoying himself, even venturing onto the putting green for a bit of practice. Years later, he'd cash in on both his new comic fame and golfing incompetence with those videos.

QUICK ON THE DREW

THE LATE SHOW WITH DAVID LETTERMAN
(1993–)

There are many perks about being one of the top television presenters in America, not least that you get to meet some of the world's most beautiful women.

David Letterman has never been a great one for self-publicity, rarely giving out details of his personal life. But that wasn't going to stop Drew Barrymore when she appeared on his birthday show in 1995.

As Letterman looked on in shock, Drew reverted to her wild child ways by clambering onto his desk and doing an impromptu sexy dance as a birthday treat.

The finale saw her turn to face the host and lift up her sweater, revealing all to the flabbergasted if grateful Letterman. With red cheeks, he stuttered, 'I can't thank you enough for that.'

Since the flash, Drew has revealed her secret feelings about the presenter, most noticeably in a magazine interview in which she said, 'I've always had a crush on him . . . Dave has intellect and humour.' The 57-year-old funny-man would presumably be very pleased to hear that.

A FAIR COP

HOMICIDE: LIFE ON THE STREET (1993–99)

Always well respected for being an honest look at the Baltimore police force, this show featured one story that took the realism a little too far.

The cast and crew were filming the show when someone ran onto the set. It turned out to be a real-life criminal, who was trying to evade justice. Seeing police cars and uniforms, he decided to give himself up – to actors dressed as cops.

The writers couldn't resist the opportunity to use the incident in the show and wrote a spoof. In a later episode, the *Homicide* detectives chased a suspect onto the set of a fictional television show, where they met the director Barry Levinson (one of the creators of *Homicide*) and some of the 'actors' on the show.

In a programme that strove to be as gritty and truthful as possible, it was a perfect case of art imitating life.

FOLLOW THAT BRONCO

O J SIMPSON – LIVE! (1994)

As with President Kennedy's assassination or the moon landing, ask pretty much any American what they were doing when O J Simpson was driving down the highway on 17 June 1994, and they will be able to tell you.

Viewers and networks alike couldn't believe what they were seeing when pictures began coming in of a white Ford Bronco driving down a Southern California freeway. News choppers followed the carnival, as O J Simpson, who was implicated in the deaths of his former wife Nicole Brown-Simpson and her friend Ronald Goldman, tried pathetically to evade justice.

More than 90 million people tuned in, while others nearer by who had heard about the event on the TV and radio got as close to the action as possible, cheering and jeering as if at a football match.

'The chase left us at a loss,' CNN's Jim Moret told *Entertainment Weekly*. 'All we could do was recount the streets that he was taking and the neighbourhoods he was travelling in. It was like a surreal traffic report.'

The SUV was being driven by Simpson's friend Al Cowling, who was ordered to stop but instead slowed down to a rather boring 40 miles per hour. At the same time, he called the police on his mobile phone to tell them that Simpson was suicidal and had a gun to his head.

The chase went on so long that one helicopter had to land and refuel. With dozens of law-enforcement vehicles in pursuit, Cowling asked permission to drive straight to Simpson's home, which was agreed and so the Bronco got the most comprehensive police escort in history.

When the former footballer-turned film star, a.k.a. The Juice, arrived home, a small army of cops was there to take him into custody – all captured on television.

SUNK BY THE JUICE

DAVID HASSELHOFF & HIS BAYWATCH FRIENDS
(1994)

Former *Knight Rider* star Hasselhoff was at the height of his fame. He was starring in the world's biggest TV show, *Baywatch*, which at that point was showing on every continent except Antarctica.

But hunky Dave still harboured singing ambitions and had a pretty lucrative warbling reputation in Germany. However, he craved musical success in his native US and so decided to mount his own live (from Atlantic City) pay-per-view TV concert event.

He put loads of time and effort into it, but, once the show began, he hit a major snag. At exactly the same time, OJ (see *O J Simpson – Live!* above) started his freeway crawl.

With all the viewing millions for the car chase, there's wasn't much interest for Hasselhoff's pop-star extravaganza. The event was a disaster.

OUT AND ABOUT

ELLEN (1994–98)

To the conservative world of American network television, it was like a seismic shock when one of the country's favourite sitcom stars officially came out of the closet.

For three years, former stand-up comic Ellen DeGeneres, playing the eponymous LA bookstore manager in this ensemble, thirtysomething comedy, had kept her sexuality strictly under wraps on and off screen.

But that all changed on 30 April 1997, when, in a programme titled 'The Puppy Episode', DeGeneres's character, Ellen Morgan, fell for producer Susan (Laura Dern). Simultaneously, the star appeared on the cover of *Time* magazine, announcing, 'Yep, I'm gay.'

The effect was instantaneous. One of ABC's Deep South affiliates refused to air the episode while some of the show's sponsors withdrew their commercials. Less than a year later, *Ellen* was cancelled.

DeGeneres angrily claimed she was fired because she was gay. According to a top ABC executive, it was all about ratings: 'As the show became more politicised and issue-oriented, it became less funny and the audience noticed.'

One of his colleagues went further. 'She had a great opportunity,' he said, 'and she knew it. To some extent, she tried to take advantage of it too much and the result was failure.' Her axing arose, he added, tersely, 'primarily because of sameness, not gayness'.

The fact remains that *Ellen* was the first openly gay leading character on broadcast series TV in the US.

Although the network was criticised for finishing it because of the gay content, the fact that other gay-themed shows began so soon afterwards (such as *Will & Grace*) rather supported the theory that it was the quality and not the storylines that ended *Ellen*'s run.

For the next five years, DeGeneres seemed to be TV poison with all the headlines concentrating on her colourful lesbian lifestyle as lovers – such as Anne Heche – came and went.

Now, she's finally back on the box, this time as host of an award-winning daytime TV chat show.

DEAD MAN WALKING

WITHOUT WALLS (1994)

Dennis Potter, television's pre-eminent playwright, had just been given three months to live when he agreed to a kind of upmarket auto-obit in this Channel 4 documentary 'strand'.

The idea was that, in exchange for a reputed fee of £20,000 (to go to the Potter estate), he'd be interviewed about his imminently ending life and times by Melvyn Bragg.

It needed to take place in the early morning – Potter's 'best time' – and would, Bragg then suggested, be best conducted in a bare TV studio without a set or even punctuating clips to 'illustrate' the subject.

With lights filtered as much as possible to keep the London Weekend studio reasonably cool, Potter, with champagne, black coffee, an ashtray for his ever-present cigarettes and a handy flask of liquid morphine by his side, started his stuff.

The resulting interview was broadcast three weeks later and viewers saw a fascinating hour of Potter in irrepressible form. He was asked, for example, whom he'd like to kill and Potter replied, unequivocally, 'Rupert Murdoch', after whom he'd mischievously nicknamed his pancreatic cancer.

Equally unscripted – and certainly a big and rather expensive surprise to the powers-that-be at the BBC and C4 – was his reply when quizzed about what he was still writing.

Potter told Bragg about a pair of connected plays, *Karaoke* and *Cold Lazarus*. The first dealt with the last days of a terminally ill screenwriter who discovers scenes from his boozy life and fiction beginning inexorably to merge in hallucinatory melodrama. In the futuristic sequel, the writer's cryogenically frozen head and brain would spur flashbacks from his past. So far, so fine.

Then Potter announced, on air, in view of the fact that his life had 'not been insignificant in television', he'd like *Karaoke* to be shown first by the BBC then repeated the same week on C4; with vice-versa treatment for *Cold Lazarus*.

It was, Rick McCallum, one of Potter's collaborators, later proclaimed, 'Perfect Dennis. The final great f***ing performance – and at the same time, "How am I going to make some money out of this?"'

Two months after the programme and a couple of weeks after his 59th birthday, Potter died. Almost exactly two years later, in 1996, *Karaoke* and *Cold Lazarus* were broadcast exactly the way Potter had 'willed' on TV.

DOCTORS AND NURSES
ER (1994–)

Michael Crichton was still a student doctor when, in 1970, he published a nonfiction book called *Five Patients*. Four years later, during which time he had switched from medicine to filmmaking, Crichton turned his experiences at Massachusetts General Hospital into a screenplay, *EW,* short for 'Emergency Ward'.

It would take another twenty years – during which time Crichton had collaborated spectacularly with his long-time chum, the director Steven Spielberg, on *Jurassic Park* – for *EW* to become *ER*, also under their joint stewardship.

Medical dramas had once been all the rage on American TV, but, by the turn of the nineties, they'd been superseded by gritty, realistic cop shows such as *NYPD Blue* and *Homicide – Life on the Street.*

Despite its obvious credentials, everything still hinged on *ER*'s two-hour pilot episode, which, from the outset, would try to establish the freewheeling style, the plethora of regular characters in interweaving action and the unapologetically dense 'medical' references that would characterise the long-running series.

It seemed to be love at first sight between audiences and womanising Dr Ross (George Clooney), pressured Dr Greene (Anthony Edwards), callow Dr Carter (Noah Wyle), gruff Dr Benton (Eriq La Salle), level-headed Dr Lewis (Sherry Stringfield) and rocklike head nurse Carol Hathaway (Julianna Margulies).

But – shock, horror! – at the end of the pilot, the tireless Hathaway appeared to have committed suicide by taking an overdose of pills. When the first episode of *ER* went on air three days after the critically acclaimed pilot, Hathaway was missing – until an overdose victim was wheeled in and it turned out to be, yes, Hathaway.

It seems that her almost miraculous recovery was due to a crucial intervention by co-star George Clooney, who felt that the

Ross–Hathaway relationship had more mileage. In fact, he felt so strongly that Margulies should be a regular on the show, he decided to raise the matter with NBC's network chiefs in New York. 'It's too bad Julianna dies,' he told them, only to hear back, 'She's not necessarily dead.' Executive producer John Wells would admit later that she was meant to die in the pilot.

Thanks to Clooney, Hathaway survived and in fact even got to utter the second episode's memorable opening line, 'I'm here to unload that new shipment of barbiturates.' Clooney himself called Margulies after his NBC meeting to tell her she was still alive and just about well.

'He called me just in time,' recalls the dark, long-curly-haired actress. 'I was just about to cut my hair, dye it red and straighten it for a different job.'

ALL AT SEA

ROUGHNECKS (1994–95)

They were shooting the final episode 'cliffhanger' – in which a helicopter ditches during a terrible storm – for the first series of this macho BBC drama about workers on a North Sea oil rig.

A chopper had been turned upside down beside a seaside quay and fire tenders were standing by to provide heavy rain. Bobbing about in freezing water but wearing wet suits, dry suits and life vests were actors Ricky Tomlinson, Clive Russell and Theresa Banham.

After a yell of 'Cut!' the doughty thesps were dragged from the water and given a chance to warm up – until someone noticed that the helicopter had become exposed as the tide receded. It needed to be dragged to deeper water, which also meant the actors had to go back into the briny.

Now, on his own admission, Tomlinson panicked and they had to send a rescue launch to fish him out of the water. In his memoirs, he writes, 'The rest of the cast were taken back to shore.

Filming was over. I felt terrible. I had cost them the scene. Tens of thousands of pounds had been wasted.'

However, he notes, 'I needn't have worried. The next day, as they sat down to look at the rushes, they discovered that water had leaked into the cameras and not a single frame could be salvaged.'

The scene had to be reshot – this time in the tank at Pinewood studios. And, Tomlinson recalls, 'you couldn't tell the difference in the finished show.'

CLICKETY-CLINKER

THE WEEKEND SHOW (1995)

When Dale Winton thinks that your show is badly made, you know you are in trouble. It's even worse when he is actually presenting it.

The Weekend Show was, briefly, a primetime BBC show, made by the company behind *The Big Breakfast*, Planet 24. In his autobiography, Winton recalls a typical moment, which summed up the rather amateurish nature of the production.

The show was based in a glorified Portakabin in Bow, but crucial to the set-up was a live studio audience. One day, Winton turned up ready to record, looked around and asked one of the team, 'Where's the audience? Shouldn't they be here, seated by now?'

So shambolic was the show's organisation that they had actually forgotten to book an audience. In an absolute panic, someone was sent to a nearby bingo hall in East London to persuade the participants to come and be the studio throng.

However, the only way they could persuade the locals to turn up was by promising them a round of bingo and a £100 raffle, which they would have to accommodate during one of the breaks in recording 'as live'.

In the end, even the prize draw went wrong. When Winton pulled the winning ticket from the hat, two people jumped up and shouted that they had won. Since someone had erroneously given two people the same number, Winton said that they would each get a hundred pounds. One of the cheapskate producers apparently whispered, 'Tell them we'll split it and give them fifty pounds each.'

In the end, both got the full ton.

DON'T MESS WITH THE MAHATMA
NIKKI TONIGHT (1995)

Rupert Murdoch may be one of the most powerful men on the planet, but even he is nobody compared with Mahatma Gandhi.

At least that's what the viewers of STAR TV's *Nikki Tonight* decided following an incident on the chat show.

Hosted by the half-Indian, half-English actress/presenter Nikki Bedi, *Nikki Tonight* was a big-money attempt by Murdoch's huge Hong Kong-based Asian satellite network to woo the potentially massive Indian audience.

In May 1995, Bedi was interviewing a controversial and outspoken gay rights activist called Ashok Row-Kavi, when he said that he had once lost a job for calling Gandhi a 'bastard'.

The furore that this remark caused was sensational. People called for STAR TV to be banned in India and *Nikki Tonight* was immediately pulled off the air. They issued an apology, but debate still raged about the influx into the country of foreign media.

The famous leader's great-grandson sued Rupert Murdoch for defamation, although the warrant couldn't be served because Murdoch wasn't in the country.

Bedi faced the full force of the scandal, despite being blameless. 'I was accused of all kinds of things and never got the chance to defend myself,' she remembers, although she harbours no resentment about the incident.

She returned to England and the radio, hosting a show on the BBC Asian Network.

RABBITING ON

BUNNY BULLETIN (1995–)

Flick around your digital TV channels and you could find yourself transfixed by the extraordinary sight of the news being presented with the help of a giant rabbit, making hand signals behind the newsreader or popping up embarrassingly on outside broadcasts.

This remarkable creature belongs to L!VE TV, the once defunct cable channel, now revived as SKY channel 274.

The News Bunny, as he is known, was first unveiled in 1995 in the days when L!VE TV was run by Kelvin MacKenzie, a man determined to make his mark. This was the station that caused a stir with Topless Darts, Britain's Bounciest Weather, read by a trampolining dwarf, and, when that lost its magic, the weather read in Norwegian by a Nordic beauty in a bikini.

Initially conceived as a glove puppet, the famous bunny grew into a human-sized mascot for the channel, whereupon somebody on the newsdesk unwisely suggested that it might appear on screen behind the newsreader during bulletins. An enthusiastic MacKenzie instantly latched onto the idea, advocating that the bunny should look sad or happy according to the news being read.

Needless to say, the correct tone was difficult to achieve and, when the man in the bunny suit wiped away an imaginary tear during the story of a teenage accident victim, MacKenzie condemned his reaction as insincere. Sometimes, as during the Dunblane tragedy, it seemed safer to do away with the bunny altogether, but it was never long before MacKenzie was storming round the office yelling, 'Where's my f***ing bunny?'

The News Bunny was undoubtedly happiest when involved in silly stunts ranging from ambushing Tony Blair – then leader of the opposition – to finding a female Newsy Bunny mate or being kidnapped by an alternative comedian from Channel 4.

In the most notorious stunt, however, reporter Ashley Hames, now star of *Sin Cities* on Bravo, actually agreed to change his name by deed-poll to News Bunny so that he could stand in a Parliamentary by-election.

Not only did he have to suffer the inconvenience of having News Bunny stamped all over his private papers, but the hapless hack eventually found himself collared by the police and arrested for obstruction while doling out carrots!

WANNABE
THE MICHAEL ESSANY SHOW (1996)

If you want something enough, *make it happen*. Which explains why Michael Essany decided to make a celebrity talk show in his lounge.

Fourteen-year-old Essany was living in Valparaiso, Indiana, and, like millions of other Americans, was a fan of the late-night talk shows hosted by Jay Leno and David Letterman. But, rather than just watch and enjoy them, Essany, who calls himself a 'student of late-night', wanted to be them.

Realising that it was unlikely a major network would let a teenager host a late-night talk show, he and his doting parents, Ernie and Tina, constructed a set in the living room of their home and Michael sent out two hundred interview requests to celebrities. And they were all rejected. So he sent out three hundred more and three of them – former *Tonight Show* sidekick Ed McMahon, showbiz presenter Leeza Gibbons and 007 star Timothy Dalton – said yes.

And so it was that a fourteen-year-old high school geek donned a suit and began making a chat show for his local cable access channel. He managed to get celebrities, either intrigued by this strange young wannabe, or perhaps simply bored, to come to Indiana. And he followed the traditional late-night format – beginning with a monologue that he wrote himself, followed by a celebrity interview, sketches featuring members of his family and even a sidekick, best friend Mike Randazzo.

Other guests, such as Kevin Bacon and Heidi Klum, followed and soon local buzz turned the show into a low-budget sensation. Michael found himself appearing on the real *Tonight Show*, where he was able to tell Jay Leno in person that he wanted to take over the show from him.

And as if this all weren't postmodern enough, E! Entertainment Television decided to make a reality show about Michael making his show.

It was shot like a kind of real-life *Larry Sanders Show*, as cameras followed Michael, now a nineteen-year-old student of Valparaiso University, as he put together his programme and entertained his guests. Which meant we saw him go shopping with supermodel Frederique, cruising for chicks with actor Jerry O'Connell, learning to cook with chef Nigella Lawson and eating pizza with Destiny's Child singer Kelly Rowland.

In breaks in the recording of their interview, the guests also get up close and personal with Michael's parents in the greenroom (a.k.a. the kitchen), where they eat food prepared by Tina, having been picked up at the airport by Ernie.

All in all, a very freaky experience, not helped by Michael's rather mannered and overzealous gurning for the camera, oddly lacquered hairdo and his palpable discomfort around most of the guests, especially the women.

Will Michael ever reach his goal and *The Tonight Show*? Well, first he's got to make it out of his parents' house in Valparaiso.

DON'T AD UP

THE DANA CARVEY SHOW (1996)

Dana Carvey is probably better known this side of the Atlantic as gentle Garth Algar, one half of the overage-teenager tandem in *Wayne's World.*

But, as yet another *Saturday Night Live* alumnus, Carvey has been ploughing a comic trough for years in various other guises, including, very briefly, as the host of his own network sketch series on ABC.

The plan was that each week a different sponsor would 'present' the show, beginning with the Tex-Mex fast-food eatery chain, Taco Bell.

But after a series of risqué sketches – ranging from dubious drolleries about the president (then Bill Clinton) and his first lady to the actual sponsor itself – Taco Bell cancelled all its future advertising. It probably didn't help that the show had opened with a chorus of Taco Bell flunkeys singing the following refrain: 'We paid him [Carvey] a fortune to use our name, 'cause he's a shameless whore . . .'

When Pizza Hut followed suit, it was clear that Carvey's latest creation was on the skids. Less than two months later, with audiences slipping too, the show was cancelled.

THE KIDS AREN'T ALL RIGHT

BRASS EYE (1997)

When Chris Morris – the genius frontman behind *On the Hour* and *The Day Today* – decided to make a new satirical news programme, savvy audiences expected uproar. What they didn't count on was that *Brass Eye* would become the second most complained-about television show in British history (the first being a screening of *The Last Temptation of Christ* – see *Jerry Springer – The Opera* on page 296).

Strangely, this only happened second time around. When the series was first broadcast on Channel 4, it made waves, but it wasn't until it was repeated in 2001 that it really hit the fan. And this was all because of an extra programme, made especially for the repeated run, dubbed 'The Paedophile Special'.

Setting out to lampoon the way the media sensationalised anything to do with child abuse, Morris felt the wrath of the conservative media, as well as some of his celebrity participants, whom he duped into appearing to illustrate his spoof campaign.

Radio DJ Neil 'Dr' Fox was seen hammering a nail into a crab, saying that paedophiles have more in common with crustaceans that humans. Comedian Richard Blackwood sniffed a computer keyboard, saying that abusers could make them emit toxic fumes that would make children more susceptible. Meanwhile, Morris himself posed as a rapper called JLB8, who boasted of having sex with kids.

Perhaps the most trouble was caused by Morris's made-up child-support group Nonce Sense ('Nonce' is a slang word for a paedophile), which he persuaded Phil Collins and Gary Lineker to promote. Collins took legal advice after the show was broadcast, saying, 'I think the presenters of this programme have serious taste problems.'

Morris refused to answer his critics, but Channel 4 defended him, pointing the finger at the media, who exploit child-abuse issues to sell newspapers. Nevertheless, the *Daily Mail* labelled it 'sick' and Tory MP Gerald Howarth, who was tricked into appearing, said that Channel 4 was guilty of 'dereliction of duty'.

However, while there were more than 1,500 callers complaining about the show, there were also more than 750 supporting it. There was an ITC investigation, which concluded in favour of Morris and Channel 4.

Ironically, the reaction to the programme demonstrated the overzealousness that it set out to satirise.

'The Paedophile Special' was not the first time *Brass Eye* had caused trouble. In its show about drugs, Morris talked about how a new, highly addictive drug called CAKE (which doesn't actually exist) had entered Britain unhindered. One MP appearing on the show felt so strongly about it that he posed a question about the proliferation of CAKE to Parliament.

THE KILLING FIELDS
MIDSOMER MURDERS (1997–)

While there's no denying the popularity of this oddly timeless, picture-postcard murder series, especially among our colonial cousins in the US and Australia, a couple of big questions must remain.

Judging by the ongoing slaughter gleefully depicted in various rural English backwaters, how come anybody would still want to live in the country – *and* still be able to command extortionate property prices in these killing fields?

Also, after failing to prevent so much violent death, especially *after* he and his team are on the actual case, why would rustic Detective Chief Inspector Barnaby (John Nettles), the Baron of Bodycount, still be allowed to ply his inept trade? Anyone else would have been busted by now to traffic duties.

As if that were not all strange enough, then cut to a national newspaper article, which appeared some years into the show's run. This reported a rather desperate-sounding *MM* producer, Brian True-May, allegedly urging viewers to write in to him and suggest new ways of killing people because, frankly, they were beginning to run out of ideas.

Well, anyone could have told you that the second part of that was absolutely true. However, it seems that the story was either a shameful exaggeration or, more likely, a complete fabrication.

However, that didn't stop a few folk from ringing in or dropping him a line about inventive ways to die in our picturesque Home Counties.

What's certain is that, despite severely dwindled populations in the quaint villages of Badger's Drift, Midsomer Mallow and Morton Fendle, the killing continues unabated.

SILLY MOOS

COWS (1997)

Comedian Eddie Izzard is notorious for refusing to do television – and, if his brief foray into TV sitcom is anything to go by, you'll know why.

Cows was a comedy about . . . well, cows. The hour-long pilot introduced the Johnsons, a family of moo makers who are shocked when their son Rex (Jonathan Cake) brings home a human girlfriend, played by Sally Phillips.

But this was no *Babe*-a-like. What really confused everyone was that the cows were played by human actors in full animal bodysuits, including Pam Ferris (then best known to television audiences as the jolly, fat Ma Larkin in *The Darling Buds of May*) as matriarch Boo. The cows stood on their hind legs and acted just like real people.

Izzard, who often dealt with the humanising of animals in his stand-up comedy, wrote the script, but critics, executives and viewers alike just couldn't get over the bizarre premise. Izzard himself described the show's reception as being like 'a long-lost relative who turns up at the wrong house with an overdue Christmas card'.

Six years in development, it never got further than a Channel 4 pilot, although there was a series planned. In fact, a later episode was due to feature one of the cows trying to become a Conservative Member of Parliament.

But, although Izzard once envisaged great things for the programme that was supposed to be '*Planet of the Apes* with a *Simpsons* sensibility', no one else agreed and it passed into bad television legend.

BENN IN DA HOUSE

THE 11 O'CLOCK SHOW (1998–2000)

If you don't count white Essex boy Richard Madeley's (of *Richard & Judy*) embarrassingly misguided morning-TV attempt to impersonate Ali G, then some of the spoof character's own encounters with the real-life great and good surely surpass that for strangeness.

Self-styled king of the 'West London Massiv', Ali G – a name designed to lend 'the whiff of Islam' as well as the attitude of Afro-Caribbean gangsta – was the inspired comic creation of Jewish ex-public schoolboy Sacha Baron Cohen for the 'Voice of Youth' slot on this late-night C4 satire show.

Personalities from all walks of life were happy to submit to Ali/Sacha's series of deliberately stupid, often misogynistic, and frequently confusing racial questions in order, it seems, to be seen as 'cool'.

Only one, Tony Benn, has been prepared to admit he was completely taken in by the character. The one-time peer and Labour cabinet minister said he thought the comedian was 'genuine'.

'Even after I left the studio I thought it was genuine, although I was a bit suspicious when he said Margaret Thatcher was a communist.'

RATINGS LOCKS

FELICITY (1998–2002)

Who'd have thought that the fortunes of a show could turn on something as minor as a haircut? Of course, *Felicity* was a show for teenagers, which might help explain why the coiffure of the leading lady became such a big deal for the actress playing her, the programme makers and the network executives.

A romantic comedy-drama series, *Felicity* was about a girl played by Keri Russell who followed her secret crush to college in New York, with the intention of trying to woo him. Instead, she got caught up in university life and what followed was an entertaining, if lightweight, show that brought some modest success to the WB network, which broadcast it.

Until, that is, Keri cut off her trademark long curly hair, a lustrous mane-like 'do' that had become the talk of teen magazines and many a beauty article.

In the summer hiatus following the first season, Russell played a joke on the producers of the show by sending them a picture of herself wearing a short wig, telling them that she had decided to hack off her locks.

After initially going crazy (a lot of television actors sign contracts not to change their looks in any way while they are performing on a show), they decided that, with Felicity going into her second year of college, a new haircut would be a good idea.

What they didn't realise was the storm it would cause. Magazine articles, newspaper columns, television segments, Russell and her bosses never knew how central to the show the lead actress's hair appeared to be. And the viewers felt the same way, as the audience turned away from the show in droves when it returned for the sophomore series.

Those connected to the show argued that it was the lack of compelling storylines, as well as a move to another time slot, that precipitated the drop in figures. The network wasn't so sure. Talking to the *Pittsburgh Post-Gazette* during a press junket, WB Entertainment president Susanne Daniels said, 'Keri Russell as Felicity was becoming an icon in television culture and part of the icon was her hair. When they cut the hair off . . . you diluted the icon.

'What they do with their hair is very much what the audience looks to in our shows. It's not just the storylines.'

There were even thoughts about making Russell wear a long wig to make her look like her old self, but the actress refused. As for star actors' hair in the future? Says Daniels, 'I think it's going to be given more thought at the network than it previously would have.'

Long or short – it's the perfect dilemma for a teen drama.

A CODE AND A COUGH

WHO WANTS TO BE A MILLIONAIRE? (1998–)

Major Charles and Diana Ingram should be millionaires. After all, Charles answered fifteen questions in a row correctly – using all his lifelines – which usually means that you walk away from host Chris Tarrant with a cheque for a million pounds.

Unfortunately, someone was coughing in the audience during Charles's turn in the spotlight. College lecturer Tecwen Whittock, to be precise. And a subsequent complaint by production company Celador and a trial proved that Charlie was a cheat, with Whittock helping him provide the correct answers from the audience using a coded coughing system.

Well, it wasn't really coded, which was the problem.

In September 2001, Charles, an army officer who had served with distinction in Bosnia, made it into the hot seat. Amazingly, his wife Diana had already appeared on the show and won £32,000.

Charles, easily got to £1,000, then started to struggle, using two of his lifelines to get up to £4,000. As he was about to answer the next question, coughs were heard when he mentioned the correct answer out loud. There were no more coughs until the £64,000 question, when there were two coughs as he said the correct answer 'cricket'. There were coughs on the next two questions when he spoke the right answer. Then, on the £500,000 question, another cough was heard when he suggested a wrong answer, which the prosecution later claimed was someone saying 'no' under their breath.

Finally, as he decided whether to answer 'googol' for the one-million-pound prize, there was another cough when he said it out loud. Chris Tarrant announced that he had won.

Sadly for Ingram, it didn't end happily ever after. Cynics have suggested that the prosecution's case was inherently flawed, a desperate push for publicity by a company keen to drum up headlines for their waning show. And the evidence could certainly be interpreted either way.

It is suggested that Ingram didn't seem confident about answering all the questions correctly, but, then, who is, under the television lights? It is claimed that he used up his lifelines too quickly. But look at most big-money winners: it is the pop and cultural trivia questions that make up most of the first few questions that generally stump them.

Other experts say that quiz studio audiences often suffer from 'responsive coughing', whereby they put themselves in the contestant's place and coughing is like a nervous tic.

All this is no matter. The Ingramses and Whittock were taken to court by Celador and found guilty of deception. They received eighteen-month jail sentences, which were suspended because they have children.

As a result, the Ingrams became tabloid hate figures, reduced to hawking their story to whoever would have it. Playing on their notoriety, they appeared on *Celebrity Wife Swap*, while Charles featured on Channel 4's *The Games* (after the *Millionaire* trial, he was found guilty of insurance fraud following a burglary, forcing him to resign his commission). They now reside firmly on the Z-list.

Meanwhile, *Who Wants to Be a Millionaire?* continues apace – the company made a documentary about the incident and there's a screenplay in the works.

So were the Ingrams and Whittock on the end of some rough justice? Or was it simply a badly executed money-making scheme? Better phone a friend.

DOG DAY AFTERNOON

RICKY MARTIN'S CANDID CAMERA (1999)

A powerful urban myth surrounds sexy pop star Ricky Martin, after his supposed appearance on a famous Brazilian television show. One of the segments of the programme is a *Candid Camera*-style element, in which a famous celebrity catches a fan unawares in their daily life. Ricky's story goes like this.

Everyone was very excited because a young female fan was going to receive a visit from the 'Livin' La Vida Loca' singer. Hidden cameras were put in place in this teenager's bedroom and the plan was for Martin to hide in her closet and wait until she came back from school and went up to her room, and then he would jump out and surprise her.

Martin secreted himself in the wardrobe and, before long, the young girl returned home and went upstairs to her bedroom. Then things went slightly awry.

According to the legend (obviously, this footage has never been officially seen), the girl got on her bed, took off her clothes and covered herself in dog food. She then beckoned the family dog into the room and got it to start licking it off.

All this time, the hapless Ricky was stuck inside the closet and, after the requisite amount of time, he jumped out to find the family dog indecently assaulting the girl. One imagines he – not to say she *and* the pooch – got quite a shock.

SEND IN THE CLONE

PAYNE (1999)

Fawlty Towers has much to answer for, judging by American television's various dismal attempts to try to create a copycat sitcom.

This feeble 'clone', starring lanky John Larroquette as – wait for it – Royal Payne, was foisted on an apathetic public fully twenty years after Cleese & co.'s West Country establishment finally closed for business.

Payne and his gossipy wife Connie (JoBeth Williams) ran Whispering Pines, situated on the Californian coast equivalent of Torquay. Polly the maid became Breeze O'Rourke, while Manuel mutated into a dusky if rather indeterminate foreigner called Mohammed.

There were even new personas for *FT*'s two resident old ladies, Miss Tibbs and Miss Gatsby. Now they were marijuana-taking senior citizens, Flo and Ethel.

Commenting on the first two episodes in a very short-lived series, the chap from the *Albuquerque Alibi* noted perceptively,

Basil Fawlty was more than just a penny-pinching bastard with a dilapidated hotel and a carping wife. Under John Cleese's deft comic hand, Fawlty became a model for wounded pride – a modern prig who fancied himself an English gentleman and was *always* defeated in his plans to improve his hellish lot in life. I suppose it's easier in England to create that sense of pompous dignity.

At least *Payne* acknowledged its roots, unlike *Amanda's* sixteen years earlier. In this turkey, Bea Arthur, before she headed for ratings heaven with *The Golden Girls*, ran Amanda's By the Sea, a small Pacific-side establishment, which included an excitable chef and a much put-upon waiter called Aldo.

I CAN SEE DEAD PEOPLE . . . SERIOUSLY!

CROSSING OVER WITH JOHN EDWARD (1999–)

If you can't discover strange stories on a show whose host claims he talks to the dead, where *can* you find them?

This is just one of the myriad cult shows in which a studio audience join a medium to see if they can make contact any dead friends and/or relatives. Whether you believe it or not is another matter, but Edward has built up a considerable cult following for his show on America's Sci-Fi Network.

The format of the show is simple. An audience sits like a normal studio audience and Edward performs what is called a 'gallery reading' – which means he gets in touch with his spirit guides (helpers from beyond the grave), who in turn pass on messages from loved ones of the assembled spectators. In this way, he is *drawn* to parts of the studio, to certain people, and receives certain names and information, which he asks to be understood.

Normally, his hit rate is pretty good, but it looked as if he made a cock-up when one day he was drawn to the back row of his audience. Alighting on a group of women, Edward couldn't understand why they weren't aware of a man who had been killed in a car crash, who was mentioning the names Richard, Tony or Timmy, a connection to a teacher, the number sixteen, as well as a falls somewhere. As there was no one behind this particular group in the studio, he decided to move on to the rest of the other spirits demanding his attention.

When the show had finished, one of the producers told Edward that they thought they had figured out why he hadn't been able to validate his message. One of the team brought out a man wearing a parking attendant's jacket and it transpired that his name was Basil and he worked in the car park adjacent to the studio. Edward was utterly confused until Basil told him that he had a brother who died aged sixteen in a car crash when Basil was a teacher in Jamaica.

The audience were shocked and one of the production assistants told Edward that, when he had pointed to the back row and found nothing, the assistant felt compelled to go looking slightly *further* back and this led him into the car park. This was where he found Basil. Edward then asked Basil whether the name Tony or Timmy made sense to him. Basil replied that his other brother's name was Tonto. Close enough. And pretty good proof that you can be psychic through walls. It gives you chills.

LIVING DOLL
PASSIONS (1999–)

In the wacky world of American soap operas, you don't get much stranger than this NBC saga. Set in the picturesque town of Harmony, *Passions* is a web of deceit, sex and magic.

That's right, magic. Perhaps the show's most popular character is Tabitha, a 300-year-old witch played by Britain's very own Juliet Mills. Tabby is intent on ruining the lives of her foes in Harmony, but misses the doll, which she once turned into a living boy, called Timmy (played by little actor Josh Ryan Evans). He, in turn, was later killed trying to save the girl he had a crush on. Timmy is able to revert to doll form at will, and his favourite pastime (other than avoiding cats) was making his favourite drink, the Martimmy.

In a spooky twist, Evans (who suffered from a form of dwarfism and was plagued by health problems throughout his life) died on the same day his character left the show.

The episode had been taped weeks beforehand and he was due to be resurrected – a plotline that was rewritten and left with Timmy dying heroically.

As well as a living doll and centuries-old witches, the show has also featured a talking tree and axe-wielding psychos – way out by even daytime soap standards.

REANIMATED
FAMILY GUY (1999; 2005–)

This surreal animated sitcom, about the dysfunctional Griffin clan, is among a handful of series to have been cancelled and then restarted years later by the same network.

First aired on the Fox network in 1999, it gained a cult following but never really hit the mainstream primarily because many dismissed it as a *Simpsons* knock-off. It got thrown all over the schedules and finally broadcast its last original episode in early 2002.

But its untapped potential really came to the fore after Fox had dumped it. Reruns of the show scored record ratings on the Cartoon Network and more than two million DVDs of the series were sold. Elsewhere, more than 110,000 people signed a petition to Fox, begging for it to come back on air.

Their wishes were granted when, in 2004, Fox decided to bring back the show. The network committed to at least 22 new episodes of the show, which premiered in May 2005.

THE 2000s

CHEGGERS GOES NUDE
NAKED JUNGLE (2000)

Many people predicted that Britain's Channel Five would go off the air after broadcasting *The Naked Jungle*. Not because of any great number of complaints – simply because it seemed to foster rubbish TV. This show, in particular, caused politicians to question the quality of British popular culture and its host Keith Chegwin simply lived down to his media reputation.

Shown as part of Naturism Week, *The Naked Jungle* was an adventure-style game show, in which a naked Cheggers – once a darling of children's television – led ten nude men and women through a series of challenges to win a prize.

None of them were particular credits to the naked body as they ran and swung through a studio set wearing helmets and safety harnesses that often made them look as if they were riding up into areas the contestants would rather not mention.

With the studio temperature set at more than 30°C, Chegwin was told he could participate without stripping, but he chose to join in the fun (much to the chagrin of the viewing public).

Aiming more for comedy than for titillation, the show received only one complaint and ended up being Five's most-watched entertainment show of the year, with more than two million tuning in, a 20 per cent share.

A pith-helmet-wearing Cheggers said, 'I enjoyed doing it; it was a bit of a giggle.' Not everyone was as happy about the aftermath of the programme.

Aspiring Liberal Democrat councillor Helen Swain – a self-confessed naturist – appeared on the show. Subsequently, leaflets showing her naked and standing beside Chegwin were used as part of a dirty-tricks campaign to stop her from winning a seat in

Mirfield, West Yorkshire. The photos were posted through letterboxes and she ended up coming third.

Swain told the *Daily Mail*, 'Just because I was photographed naked doesn't mean I'd be a bad councillor.'

THE UNGRATEFUL DEAD

GOD, THE DEVIL AND BOB (2000)

By the time NBC's animated series reached screens, it had already caused controversy.

Christian America was up in arms that the network cartoon was blasphemous – and they hadn't even seen it.

What they had seen was the promotional material showing the three main characters: God (voiced by James Garner), the Devil (Scots actor Alan Cumming) and Bob (French Stewart). And God looked like the late Jerry Garcia, frontman of the Grateful Dead.

Yes, the irreverent comedy portrayed the Almighty as a long-haired, chilled-out hippie, and the resemblance to Garcia, who died in 1995, was striking. Believers didn't like it. They didn't like the fact that Bob met God in a bar. They didn't like God's attitude.

People wrote into religious websites, proclaiming, 'God is a dead ringer for the degenerate, Grateful Dead leader Jerry Garcia. [Garcia] died after destroying his body with drugs.

'I wonder what that implies about God modelled after a dead drug addict?' the critic continues. They also complained about the fact that the Grateful Dead had written a song called 'A Friend of the Devil'.

NBC announced that it didn't mean to annoy anybody, but several affiliates across the country refused to run the show. Whatever the motivation behind the programme, it didn't fare well with viewers and was cancelled after a few episodes.

SHACKED UP

BIG BROTHER (2000–)

It consisted of a table covered in sheets, duvets, pillows and cushions – shielding its interior from the outside world. Introducing the *Big Brother* Love Shack.

Five series into Britain's biggest reality show – in which a group of strangers live together during the summer in a prefab house and are filmed 24/7 – producers were getting concerned.

Despite relationships, fights, even marriage, the 'money shot' still eluded them – no one had had sex live on the show. They had in other countries on the Continent, where the show was also broadcast. But things perked up in *Big Brother V* with the arrival of Michelle, a brash Geordie, who soon set her sights on laid-back pretty boy Stuart.

Immediately coupling up with her, Stuart soon found himself in a 'serious' relationship, as Michelle bitched at the other female contestants, who even looked at him and demanded to know where he was at all times. Branded *Fatal Attraction*-possessive in the newspapers, the aspiring glamour model didn't care. She had one thing on her mind.

But even she was too proud to do it in the open, so proceeded to craft a comfort-lined indoor den before dragging Stuart inside in the early hours of Tuesday, 20 July 2004. With cameras desperately trained on the action, all you could see were two entangled pairs of feet and hear some rather odd whimpering. Around an hour later, the lovebirds emerged.

Strangely, they never openly admitted what everyone knew they had done. Michelle merely said to another housemate that her 'immune system' had been 'boosted'. But insiders at the show's network, Channel 4, revealed the truth and the bookmakers were convinced enough to pay out to those who had gambled on whether Stu and Michelle would follow through.

The Love Shack soon came down and the show continued. Neither participant won, but, six months after the end of the programme, they were still an off-screen couple. Getting filmed can obviously add a *frisson* to a relationship.

A PERFECT ALIBI
CURB YOUR ENTHUSIASM (2000–)

What would Larry David think? The curmudgeonly comic, who fronts his own semiautobiographical, improvised sitcom, did more than just annoy people in 2003, thanks to the amazing case of Juan Catalan.

In May of that year, 26-year-old Los Angeleno Catalan was arrested for the murder of a teenage girl, allegedly because she had testified against his brother.

He protested innocence, claiming that he and his young daughter had been watching the Los Angeles Dodgers baseball team on the night in question, minutes before the victim had been killed some twenty minutes from the stadium. It was physically impossible, he said, for him to have got from the stadium in time to murder her.

The police argued that they had a witness placing him at the scene and he says they refused his request for a lie detector test.

Catalan's defence lawyer Todd Melnick watched Dodgervision (the in-house television system) and Fox Network's coverage of the game to see if he could prove his client was telling the truth. Unfortunately, Catalan could not be spotted on the tapes.

Then Catalan had an idea: he remembered that HBO had filmed at the stadium on the same evening.

The lawyer called HBO and was informed that, yes, *Curb Your Enthusiasm* (which is on HBO) was filming at the ground that night. They invited Melnick to look at the footage.

Melnick went to HBO and watched the show in question, but still couldn't see Catalan. Then he started watching the rushes – and there he was! Catalan and his daughter, sitting watching the game behind Larry David's shoulder.

As the tapes were time-coded, Melnick was able to show exactly when Catalan was at the stadium. He demonstrated to the judge that it would have been impossible for his client to change clothes, get out of the car park and then go to kill the victim in the time span.

The case against Catalan – who was facing the death penalty – was dismissed.

Catalan had never watched *Curb Your Enthusiasm*, but he owed his life to the programme. After the incident, David released a jokey statement, saying, 'I'm quitting the show to devote the rest of my life to freeing those unjustly incarcerated.'

PUBIC EXPOSURE

TIM'S AREA OF CONTROL (2000–)

Broadcast on Michigan-based public-access channel 25, this homely-sounding offering is described in its official blurb as a 'half hour show that combines modern day music with video varieties – mainly with a comedic slant towards life in general'.

However, it doesn't say, 'may include male genitalia'. It was the absence of this particular caveat that got Tim Huffman and his wife Sally – the couple behind the show – into big trouble.

While channel-surfing late one night, an East Grand Rapids resident happened across Tim and Sally's programme and was shocked to see a skit featuring a close-up of a man's genitals with a face drawn on them. A narrator was telling dirty jokes such as, 'I was in the Army . . . I didn't do much . . . I just hung around.'

By the time the woman complained, it had already been broadcast six times without incident. Nonetheless, Huffman was charged with indecent exposure (he escaped an obscenity charge because the sketch was not sexually titillating).

After he went to trial two years later, a six-person jury took thirty minutes to convict Huffman, and he was fined and sentenced to a year's probation. Assistant prosecutor Monica

Gall told the jurors just before they went off to consider their verdict, 'He wanted public exposure and he's getting it.'

Prosecutor William Forsyth said, 'Mr Huffman has the right to say on his show what he said, even if I might disagree with him or think it just wasn't very good, but you can't stand naked spouting off and claim all of your behaviour is protected by the First Amendment.'

But that's exactly what Huffman thinks, and what started off as a silly late-night joke has turned into a battle over constitutional rights. He is planning to appeal the verdict.

Because it appeared on cable television, some commentators have argued that, if the courts are prepared to go after Huffman, why shouldn't they go after shows on stations such as HBO, which regularly feature nudity. At the same time, anticensorship advocacy groups rushed to Huffman's defence. Huffman's lawyer Stephen Savickas even suggested that it was a 'rigged case'.

Whatever the outcome, Tim and Sally will still think twice about nude comedy again.

LOW-FLYING J.LO

THE EUROPEAN MUSIC AWARDS (2000)

For an event like this MTV-sponsored shindig, broadcast to millions of homes around the world, you want everything to go absolutely right. For starters, you've got dozens of demanding divas backstage, all haggling over the size of their dressing rooms.

One of the highlights of the show, which is held in Stockholm, Sweden, was a live performance by Jennifer Lopez, singing her latest single 'Love Don't Cost a Thing'.

The stage concept was equally grand. J.Lo was to fly onto the platform in a genuine plane (made out of wood), before screeching her way through the record.

Unfortunately, grand designs often have even grander design flaws and no one knew quite what to do when the plane wouldn't swoop as they intended, leaving the singer perched in midair.

Thanks to some quick thinking by the technical crew, the mishap was barely noticeable on the broadcast, spotted only by insiders working at the event.

The rest of the song went off without a hitch, but, as she trudged off to her dressing room backstage, Ms Lopez came face to face with a broken elevator.

After her hazardous aerial antics, you could perhaps excuse J.Lo when she was heard to exclaim, grandly, 'I don't do stairs!'

MATCH MADE IN HELL

WHO WANTS TO MARRY A MULTI-MILLIONAIRE?
(2000)

As depth-plumbing 'reality TV' goes, this stinker from Fox takes some beating.

Broadcast in February 2000, it was a dating show in which fifty single women competed for the right to marry loaded property developer (and former stand-up comedian) Rick Rockwell.

Filmed at the Las Vegas Hilton, the show featured the 42-year-old bachelor putting the women through their paces. They were asked if they were just after his money and also had to parade around in swimsuits.

After a two-hour special, Rockwell chose 34-year-old nurse Darva Conger and they were married in a lavish civil ceremony in front of a TV audience that peaked at 22 million. They then jetted off on their honeymoon to Barbados.

So a match made in TV heaven? Apparently not. The American media denounced the show as 'televised prostitution' and a 'new low' in broadcasting.

But Fox faced worse controversy than scathing reviews, when it emerged that, despite their extensive background checks on the participants, they had failed to uncover a restraining order taken out on Rockwell by a former fiancée. It turns out that the publicity mad hubby was accused of assault and being threatening, although he denied the accusations.

With egg on its face, Fox cancelled a repeat of the admittedly successful show and stopped developing any further episodes.

Conger then proceeded to go on the television talk shows and explain that she wanted to annul the marriage, that it had been an 'error in judgement'. Having won $100,000 worth of prizes while taking part in the show, she gave back her $35,000 diamond engagement ring.

She revealed that they had not consummated their union and had never been alone during the honeymoon. In her annulment papers to the court, she said, 'Neither the contestants nor the show's producers seriously contemplated creating a proper marriage.'

Luckily, the couple had signed a contract saying they could annul the marriage if things didn't work out, as well as a prenuptial agreement stopping Conger from taking half Rockwell's wealth if it ended in divorce.

Rockwell, to his credit, took the break-up with good grace: 'I still wish her well. And, if she takes the time to get to know me, she'll find me to be a kind and considerate person.' He has since written a book called *What Was I Thinking?*.

BEYOND THE GRAVE

ANDROMEDA (2000–)

How often has someone 'created' a show, nine years after their death? Gene Roddenberry, the man responsible for creating *Star Trek*, died in 1991 – but when has that every stopped Tinseltown from getting their man?

At the time of his death, Roddenberry had notebooks filled with ideas for other shows, and this space saga, starring Kevin

Sorbo, was one to come out of those various creative jottings. The project was taken on by writer/producer Robert Hewitt Wolfe (who had worked on the *Star Trek* spin-off, *Deep Space Nine*), and he merged his ideas with those handed over by the Roddenberry estate and created the new show.

Most of Roddenberry's ideas for a show about a sentient spaceship had been sketched out by him in the seventies, so the technology was updated, Sorbo was cast and, just like that, the Sci-Fi Channel had a Gene Roddenberry programme. He would be very proud.

BLOOD MONEY

CSI: CRIME SCENE INVESTIGATION (2000–)

Unfortunately for actors George Eads and Jorja Fox – a.k.a. Nick Stokes and Sara Sidle – the bosses of the Las Vegas-based forensic thriller series weren't quite as flexible as they hoped.

Rumour has it the younger element of the procedural show's ensemble were seeking more money. However, CBS were less than keen.

According to the *Hollywood Reporter*, they sent letters to the actors seeing if they would be coming to work. But by the time shooting began on the fifth season of the show, Fox had already been fired for not replying to her letter, while Eads showed up late for his call time apparently to show his commitment to more cash.

'There comes a point when we all have to look out for the future of the network television business,' said CBS chief Leslie Moonves, cryptically.

Entertainment sites went nuts for the story, saying that Fox was 'mystified' by her firing. Apparently, she thought that the letter saying she was happy to continue had been sent back.

As for Eads? It seems he 'overslept'. He told the press, 'I woke up three and a half hours after I was supposed to be on set.' He added that he had 'apologised nine ways to Sunday'.

Luckily for the two stars, there's a happy ending. After scolding the two actors, the network reinstated them in the cast, though apparently not with the extra money.

Perhaps next time, they should try 'the dog ate my homework'.

LIFE LESS ORDINARY

TITUS (2000–02)

Could anyone's life be this disagreeably dysfunctional, even in sitcom land?

For one of those 'blurring reality'-type American comedies in which the star uses his own name in various domestic scenarios, the members of Christopher Titus's real-life family had to sign release forms since the show was apparently too close for comfort.

According to the scripts, co-written by Titus, his father was a much-divorced alcoholic adulterer while his mother had been driven into a mental institution. Later she became a killer and then committed suicide. Laugh-a-minute stuff.

Perhaps in keeping with the supposedly surreal nature of the humour, Chris's mom was played by no fewer than three different actresses (Christine Estabrook, Frances Fisher and Connie Stevens) during the show's two-year run.

INJURY TIME

24 (2001–)

Fans of the high-octane American spy thriller *24*, each series of which is set in real time across a 24-hour period, have become used to its heroes and heroines enduring all kinds of injury and – mostly – emerging intact.

That said, Season 2 put its hero Jack Bauer through more than ever. Within a twelve-hour period he survives a plane crash, parachutes from another aircraft and watches an uncomfortably nearby nuclear explosion before being tortured by baddies who administer so many electric shocks that he actually dies before being hastily resuscitated with a view to more torturing.

Needless to say, the show's star Kiefer Sutherland and his fellow actors proved far less resilient in real life. Indeed such was the incidence of minor injuries among the cast that Season 2 could almost be said to have been jinxed.

Action man Sutherland managed to injure his leg while simply leaving his trailer. Hence the writers' hasty decision to show Bauer extracting a piece of wood from his leg after his plane crash, giving him an excuse to limp thereafter.

Carlos Bernard, who played agent Tony Almeida, suffered a similar misfortune, dislocating his ankle while playing basketball during a break in the filming. His character had been earmarked for an elaborate fight with Bauer, but after the accident the scene was rewritten.

'The fight with Jack was actually going to be a cool scene,' Bernard said later. 'They'd written it with us falling down the stairs, just a knock-down, drag-out fight. Of course, two weeks before, I dislocated my ankle, so we turned it into, basically, he sneezes and I fall down.'

As if that weren't enough, Elisha Cuthbert, who played Jack's daughter Kim, was bitten by a cougar during a scene in which the animal was menacing her in the mountains. She told the Calgary *Sun*, 'My stunt double was there and the cougar was nibbling on her hand and I thought, "Oh, it's like a pet." And I put my hand out and he totally attacked me. It was pretty freaky, but I got to go to the hospital.' Despite some scary blood, she had no stitches but did receive a tetanus shot.

Reiko Aylesworth, who played agent Michelle Dessler, must have counted herself pretty lucky to have survived Season 2 unscathed, but in April 2003 she too suffered an off-stage disaster, slipping on some spilled drinks at the production's wrap party and hitting her head. Kiefer Sutherland took her to hospital, where it was found she had bruised both sides of her brain.

This last dramatic accident did at least have a happy ending. You've guessed it: tender-hearted Sutherland looked after the invalid Aylesworth so well that rumours abounded that the pair had found true love ...

TITLE BOUT

UP CLOSE (2001)

Not since Emu versus Parky (see *Parkinson* on page 99) or erstwhile Bond girl Grace Jones versus Giggleswick's very own Russell Harty – apparently he had studiously ignored her on his eponymous chat show in the 1980s – had there been an extra-ring scrap quite like it.

The arena was the studio of ESPN (Entertainment and Sports Programming Network), where host Gary Miller was conducting an encounter between soft-spoken ex-heavyweight world champion Lennox Lewis and Hasim Rahman, the man who'd disposed of the giant Brit in five rounds four months earlier.

The tension was already palpable when Rahman suddenly accused Lewis of acting in a 'gay' manner. That was too much for the ex-champ who, after squaring up, then gave Rahman a little push. This was the signal for the two to lock arms.

As they wrestled to the floor, smashing a table beneath them, one commentator suggested it was reminiscent of Alan Bates versus Oliver Reed in *Women in Love*. Except that there was no blazing log fire and the latter-day chaps somehow managed to keep all their clothes on.

Our own Lennox had the last laugh when, three months later, he regained his boxing crown by knocking Rahman out in the fourth round. *In* the ring.

NAME IN THE FRAME
STAR TREK: ENTERPRISE (2001–)

If there's one thing that Trekkies enjoy, it's trivia. The latest *Star Trek* franchise focuses on the crew of the original *Enterprise* decades before Kirk and Spock strapped on their tricorders. Scott Bakula plays the heroic leader, Captain Jonathan Archer. A good sturdy courageous name if ever there was one.

But it was not the creators' first choice. When news first broke of the series and information went out to casting agents, the cap'n was known as Jackson Archer. So why the change?

Apparently, they checked American citizen records and found that there was only one Jackson Archer in the country. So, to ensure that the real Mr Archer didn't ever feel the need to sue if his on-screen counterpart did something he thought defamed his reputation, they looked for something a bit more common. Thankfully, there were plenty of Jonathans and the name was changed.

However, it appears that Jackson wasn't even number one on the list. Rumour has it he was originally known as Jeffrey. Fine from a US point of view but luckily there were some Brits who quickly pointed out that, in the UK, the name 'Jeffrey Archer', far from being suitable for a square-jawed leading man, actually conjured up mediocrity and sleaze.

A CHRONICLE FORETOLD
THE LONE GUNMEN (2001)

For a show about government conspiracies, the co-incidences in the pilot episode of this *X-Files* spin-off are strangely chilling.

The appearances in *The X-Files* of Byers, Langly and Frohike – three wise-cracking anarchists who provided Fox Mulder

(David Duchovny) with secret information – were so successful, that Fox Television decided to give them their own series.

Broadcast in March, the premiere episode followed the trio as they came face to face with an event that would end up being rather too close to home.

After trying to reveal the shady truth behind a new microchip, they uncover a plan by the US government to crash a plane via remote control into the World Trade Center in New York, in a bid to heighten fear around the world and increase arms sales.

Luckily, in the actual episode, the Lone Gunmen are able to avoid the disaster by hacking into the computer program. Little did the makers of the show realise that just six months later, on 11 September, fiction would become a horrifying reality.

The show lasted only one season, before being cancelled.

GRIM FAIRY TALE

HANS CHRISTIAN ANDERSEN (2001)

For this lavish Hallmark production about the nineteenth-century Danish storyteller, they had, as part of a Copenhagen garden set, to build a classical pavilion in the stand-in lakeside location outside Berlin.

From the start of construction, there had to be 24-hour security to ensure that it wasn't damaged by vandals, or that the public didn't injure themselves.

There was a team of security guards, one of whom was an extrovert local woman who took great delight sitting in the pavilion, telling all and sundry that she would like to have it in her own garden after filming.

She'd also announce to passers-by that she was the princess of the castle in the grounds of which filming was taking place and asked who was going to rescue her.

On the morning of the shoot, there was a torrential downpour as the designer was rung by one of the assistant directors to find out if he'd asked for a dummy to be left on the set.

As he made his way to the set to check this out and inspect for rain damage, he discovered the pavilion surrounded by blue-and-white police incident tape.

A police car and ambulance were parked nearby and a policewoman was standing guard over what looked like a body lying on the pavilion floor covered by a blanket with the feet sticking out.

It turned out that the female security guard, known to have had an acute heart condition, had suddenly died in the night. Sadly, unrescued.

THE MAGIC NUMBER

ALIAS (2001–)

Does the number 47 hold the key to the universe? The writers of *Alias* certainly seem to think so. The sassy spy show is littered with cryptic and other more obvious references to that magic number and, like many of the plots of the show itself, the question is why?

The story actually begins at Pomona College in California, where there is a light-hearted collective called the 47 Society, whose binding principle is that the number 47 occurs more frequently than any other number in nature. Apparently, in a maths proof written in 1964, Professor Donald Bentley proved that all numbers are equal to it.

So how did the theory make it to Hollywood? Well, Joe Menorsky, a writer on *Star Trek: The Next Generation*, graduated from Pomona in 1979 and took his tongue-in-cheek belief to the show. Look closely and you'll find 47 mentioned endlessly in *Next Generation*, as well as its spin-offs, *Deep Space Nine* and *Voyager*.

Alias's creator J J Abrams must be a *Star Trek* fan, because *Alias* has subsequently taken on the mantle. One of the central conceits of the show – the search for the da Vinci-esque inventor/

creator/philosopher Rambaldi – has the ancient genius obsessed with the number. Page 47 of any of his texts is always particularly significant and there are 47 parts to his magnum opus.

But that's not all: when heroine Sydney (Jennifer Garner) is dreaming to try to dredge up forgotten memories, masked men take her into a room marked 47; gadget expert Marshall says that he wants to improve his lipstick camera so that it can take 47 photos; journalist Will unlocks a door in Sydney's spy head-quarters with the pass code 4747 . . . It never stops.

So is 47 the most used number in the universe? It depends on how many series of *Alias* there are.

SECRETS AND LIES

POP IDOL (2001–)

Terence Surin saw it as a 'little white lie' – merely subscribing to the ethos behind *Pop Idol* that anyone, if they really want to, can make it. Unfortunately for Terence, his plan fell flat and made for a painful evening's viewing.

As the twenty-first century's spin on the talent show, *Pop Idol* is a ridiculously simply idea: audition for a pop star, but show the auditions. This simple twist has earned the creators millions and spawned imitators around the globe.

It also unearthed every desperate wannabe, prepared to humiliate themselves for the chance to get on television and the faint hope that they might get spotted and turned into a star.

Terence Surin came to audition for *Pop Idol* judges Simon Cowell, Nicki Chapman, Pete Waterman and Neil 'Dr' Fox and was denied entry to the next round. However, convinced that a singing career was his destiny, he hatched a plan.

A few days later, he turned up again for another attempt, hoping that he wouldn't be recognised. But one of the producers spotted him and he was forced into a corner. Being interviewed by co-presenter Dec (of Ant and Dec), he said that he was one of two identical twins and that he had come along to the audition after his brother got rejected the previous week.

Obviously aware that there was the potential for funny TV, he was let into the judges' room, where he was immediately recognised. But, playing along, Simon Cowell said that he was being rejected again, unless he could bring his identical twin.

Madly scrambling for excuses, Terence said that he was at work, but Cowell told him to come back at the end of the day.

Cut to later in the show. Terence had persuaded his actual brother to come down to the audition. The only thing is, he looked absolutely nothing like him. As hosts Ant and Dec talked to him, he desperately skated around the issue, persuading the siblings to perform for the judges.

As he stood in front of Cowell and co., he pleaded with them to let him sing, but, instead, they humiliated him and told him to get lost. All the while, his rather embarrassed brother was standing there silently – praying that he didn't have to sing a note! Nonetheless, for Terence, the dream still lives on . . .

IN THE DRINK

WITCHBLADE (2001)

Science-fiction fans were disappointed when the American cable channel TNT called time on this original action fantasy. After all, it had performed pretty well for two seasons, even surviving the 'Bobby Ewing Syndrome' (see *Dallas* on page 133), when the programme makers decided at the end of the first series to rewind time.

How? Well, the show revolved around tough cop Sara, played by Yancy Butler, who happened upon an ancient artefact – the Witchblade. Strapped to the hand, it enabled her to do incredible, supernatural things. After the first series, she discovered she could rewind time and did do, essentially voiding the entire show's story arc.

But the ploy succeeded, so why the cancellation? TNT executives said that it was because they wanted the show to end strongly, but, among fans and sources close to the show, debate raged about the *real* reason for the shutdown. And what was their conclusion? A boozy lead actress.

Six episodes into the second season, Butler checked herself into rehab for an alcohol problem. 'We wish her all the best,' said the producers, as the set shut down in Toronto. Meanwhile, trade reports suggested that they were trying to think of a suitable actress to replace her and continue the show.

Butler returned after a month and resumed shooting, but, despite strong ratings, the network still decided to call a halt. Inevitably, fans blamed the actress's brush with the bottle for the cancellation, although producers deny it. If only she really could rewind time . . .

CAR TROUBLE

TOUCH THE TRUCK (2001)

It was painfully obvious that an American show provocatively titled *Hands on a Hardbody* would work around the world. Well, wasn't it? While the title might allude to post-watershed material, the US original was actually a game show in which a group of contestants tried to win a big car by touching it – for as long as possible. Britain's Channel Five bought the concept, unambiguously renamed it *Touch the Truck* and branded it a 'tentpole' in their evening schedule.

Set in the Lakeside Shopping Centre in beautiful downtown Thurrock, England, the UK spin-off was hosted by perma-tanned Dale Winton. There were twenty competitors, who were allowed a ten-minute break every two hours and a fifteen-minute break every six hours.

If they were spotted letting go of the truck (well, big car) in any way, they were eliminated. It was fascinating stuff, broadcast each night over a week, as Winton mingled with the participants, chatted to 'experts' about how to win and watched highlights of the previous day.

It was considered one of the most bizarre shows ever to grace British screens, and viewing it was almost an unreal experience. This was mainly because the crowd of onlookers were utterly bored and it was also difficult to take seriously a show in which men dressed in black-and-white-striped shirts called themselves 'referees' and made sure no one took their hand off an automobile.

The farce came to an end when the truck was won by an environmentalist, who was anti-cars and planned to sell his prize to promote his ecological political beliefs.

Suffice it to say, the show wasn't recommissioned.

SETTING A PRESIDENT
LAW AND ORDER: CRIMINAL INTENT (2001–)

The 2004 presidential election took it out of a lot of people, but none more so, apparently, than the actor Vincent D'Onofrio.

D'Onofrio, who plays the slightly maverick investigative cop Robert Goren, is a staunch Democrat and rumours abounded that he was distraught at another Bush-winning outcome.

While the campaign raged, newspapers reported that posters went up on the set of the show, banning anyone from talking about politics, since there were so many arguments. The *New York Post* said that the actor would rail against anyone who was pro-Bush. Their 'spies' insinuated that the rest of the cast were getting irritated by his politicking. So you can imagine how he must have felt when Bush actually won – and it was that, so the reports said, that led to his collapsing on set.

To his credit, D'Onofrio has since laughed off the stories, saying that it was merely fatigue. But the papers nicknamed it 'Bush flu'. Then, when he fainted for a second time, it was humorously put down to the nomination of Bush crony, Condoleezza Rice, as secretary of state.

Whatever his reasons, D'Onofrio has now returned to the show and been fine ever since. Well, maybe until Bush's next big decision.

FROM BAD TO VERSE
THE BAFTAS (2002)

It was supposed to be a night of celebration. The British Academy of Film and Televisions Arts (BAFTA) awards for 2001 were being televised from the Odeon, Leicester Square, in, as they say, 'the heart of London's West End', and the cream of American and British cinematic talent were in town to pat themselves on the back.

The tabloids the following day weren't quite so celebratory. Who was the temperamental movie star grabbing the headlines? None other than Russell Crowe. The New Zealand-born thesp was up for Best Actor for his role as the brilliant but disturbed mathematician John Nash in *A Beautiful Mind*. Having been pipped, in his *Gladiator* guise, for the same award a year earlier by fourteen-year-old Jamie (*Billy Elliot*) Bell, Crowe was clearly determined to get his money's worth this time round.

So, when he won, Crowe strode purposefully to the podium and pulled a poem from his pocket – a verse penned by Patrick Kavanagh called 'Sanctity'. While there were probably tears in the audience, it was a nice opportunity for the editor (the broadcast was tape-delayed) to get back some time by trimming it for transmission later that evening on BBC1. With any other star there wouldn't have been a problem, but when the bombastic Crowe was told of the snip he went ballistic.

Come the after-show party, he pinned producer Malcolm Gerrie up against a wall and proceeded to berate him, calling him a 'f***ing piece of shit' and screaming, 'Who on Earth had the f***ing audacity to take out the Best Actor's poem?'

Gerrie, unsurprisingly, was rather taken aback by Crowe's outburst, while commentators suggested that it did irreparable harm to Crowe's Oscar bid, which was occurring a month later in Hollywood (Denzel Washington eventually took the prize ahead of Crowe).

But, to give Crowe credit, he knows when he is wrong. A few days after the incident, Crowe phoned Gerrie to apologise, admitting that he had gone overboard for what amounted to a few seconds of television time.

Ever the Englishman, Gerrie accepted Crowe's apology and told him that it was his family that had really been upset. So Crowe spent fifteen minutes talking to Gerrie's son, Oliver, about the making of *Gladiator*. Gerrie told the *Sun*, 'He said we should go out for a few pints of Guinness when he was next there. He sounded so humble and apologetic.'

Note to television producers next time Crowe wins an award: let him speak.

DEAD FAMOUS

AUTOPSY (2002)

When the last public autopsy was performed in Britain, the viewing figures were limited to a handful of onlookers. When Channel 4 broadcast an autopsy 170 years later in November 2002, it was open to anyone with access to a television.

Carried out by the behatted and slightly sinister Professor Gunther Von Hagens, the procedure drew a flood of complainants, who argued that, despite the late showing time (the autopsy itself was not shown until after midnight), this was one step too far.

Before a gallery of five hundred people – plus anyone sad enough to tune in – Von Hagens, curator of an exhibition of preserved corpses at the Atlantis Gallery, operated on a 72-year-old who had dedicated his body to art.

But, despite the complaints, the Independent Television Commission argued that there was nothing overly explicit with the show, although Scotland Yard had warned beforehand that it could be illegal.

In the end, the show – which was preceded by a debate about the issues – was relatively tame, if a little gory. And Von Hagens, while certainly showmanlike, conducted the autopsy itself with dignity.

As the body was dissected, Channel 4 claimed that it was part of its dedication to public-service broadcasting, calling it 'an important event of genuine public interest'. Whether that was true of the people who watched the show through their fingers is anyone's guess.

MY DAD THE HERO

8 SIMPLE RULES . . . (2002–)

Who knows what was happening in the offices of ABC's *8 Simple Rules . . . For Dating My Teenage Daughter* (as it was first called) when they heard the awful news about the death of star John Ritter, on 11 September 2003.

Earlier that day, the funny-man had been rushed to hospital after collapsing on the set of the family sitcom in which he played hapless father of a motley family. He died, aged 54, of an aortic dissection, an undetected problem with his heart.

After a successful first season, filming had begun on the second when the tragedy occurred, and suddenly the network was left with a mighty problem. Shocked by grief, programme makers also faced the dilemma of how to continue with a show based on Ritter – or should they consign it to history?

The season was due to begin less than two weeks later, as everyone collected their thoughts and mourned one of television's greatest talents – a man best known as the nerdy Jack Tripper in the classic flat-share sitcom *Three's Company*.

Speculation grew as to how ABC would proceed, especially as there were already three episodes of the new series in the can. Some suggested that it would be restructured around Ritter's on-screen wife, played by Katey Sagal. Rumours abounded that Henry Winkler (a.k.a. the Fonz) would be brought in as the character's brother.

Of course, the toughest decision was how to garner laughs out of such a tragic situation. *8 Simple Rules . . .* was a family sitcom. When a family member dies, it is no laughing matter.

Ultimately, ABC decided to press forward with the show, airing the three complete episodes, before going on hiatus to revamp itself. They promised that Ritter's character, Paul Hennessy, would not be recast and that the show would deal with the loss of its father in a true-to-life fashion – daring stuff for an 8 p.m. timeslot.

When it returned, the title had been shortened to *8 Simple Rules . . .* and the first post-Ritter episode was presented without a laugh track. The show addressed a family who had just lost their patriarch, while veteran James Garner joined the cast as Sagal's father and David Spade arrived to play her nephew.

It was an unprecedented and ambitious transition, but audiences liked it and it is now into its third season.

Ritter received a posthumous Emmy nomination for his role; the character Paul Hennessy was 48th in a list of *TV Guide*'s 'Fifty Greatest TV Dads of All Time' – and, according to his widow, the actress Amy Yasbeck, he would have approved of the 'show must go on' philosophy.

'John believed in this show and its message that a strong family can get through anything,' she said in a statement. 'I know John would want his friends to be able to continue doing what they love.' And the ratings helped.

MUSIC OF THE NIGHT
MONK (2002–)

Over the years there have been all kinds of TV detective – paraplegic (*Ironside*), blind (Longstreet), even mentally unstable (*Shoestring*). Played by Tony Shalhoub, Monk is obsessive-compulsive.

But, while he may be brilliant at solving crime, he isn't so good at choosing his theme music. Among the things singled out for praise in the first season was the jazzy theme tune, written by Jeff Beal.

When the show returned for the second series, fans were dismayed to discover that Beal's track had been replaced with one by veteran tunesmith Randy Newman. Outraged, the viewers staged a revolt, petitioning the show's network USA, to reinstate the old music.

All to no avail, apparently, until a suitably odd episode just into the sophomore season entitled 'Monk and the TV Star'. In it, Monk is trying to solve the murder of a television star's wife when he comes across a fan who is obsessed about the show within the show, played by Sarah Silverman.

At the end of the episode, Silverman asks Monk a favour: if he ever gets his own TV series, he has to promise that he won't change the title music. Directly addressing the controversy thanks to this postmodern twist, Monk agrees and, as the scene fades, Jeff Beal's original ditty begins to play . . .

THE PLANE TRUTH
CHARLES II: THE POWER AND THE PASSION (2003)

It was early summer and the BAFTA-winning BBC1 costume drama had just started filming in the Czech Republic, one of a number of former-communist, Eastern European countries beloved by film and TV makers from the West because of excellent facilities, good studios and relatively cheap labour.

The makers of *Charles II*, which involved the building of a large set representing the seventeenth-century Palace of Whitehall, seemed to have found the ideal place to film in an old car factory on the outskirts of Prague. The vast disused shell of a building had already been used for an American production and seemed perfect in every way.

The set was duly built and actors, including Rufus Sewell playing the king and Dame Diana Rigg as his mother, began to arrive. On the first day, all was going well until the second scene of the morning, when a light shower began outside.

Suddenly, the production team realised they had a problem – no one had noticed a tin roof that made even a few drops of rain echo like a herd of buffalo through the building. Panic ensued as take after take was ruined by sound problems. Luckily, it was summer and the rain clouds passed swiftly.

Returning to work, Dame Diana was most of the way through a moving speech about the execution of her husband Charles I when the entire crew began to notice a noise like an enraged mosquito filtering through the building. Within seconds, the 'mosquito' had turned into a veritable buzz saw and filming was completely impossible.

The rain was one thing but what was this? A quick investigation revealed the existence of a local aerodrome and dozens of daily training flights, making filming impossible in the non-soundproofed factory.

Delicate negotiations and a modest amount of money persuaded the local flying aces to restrict their activity to early mornings and late at night, so once again filming resumed. For about an hour. And then the buzz saw started up again.

Aghast, the production team now discovered that the Czech air force was on manoeuvres directly over the studio and would be for the entire three-month shooting period. The whole production looked in danger as actors staggered through their scenes only to have the whole take ruined time after time by the equivalent of an air raid.

A local aerodrome was one thing to keep quiet, but the Czech air force? Military men, after all, are not noted for their flexibility.

But the Czechs showed a refreshing preference for art over arms when the problem was rather nervously pointed out to them. To their delight, the producers were told that the air force would happily suspend its training for the time required to complete filming.

It turned out that the top brass were film buffs to a man and perfectly happy to do their training another day. After all, they commented, they weren't expecting anyone to invade the Czech Republic any time soon, so training up new pilots could wait.

All air force flights over the area were suspended for the entire duration of the shoot – but on one condition. In the event of a war, the air force might have to resume flying! Luckily, no war broke out and *Charles II* completed its filming successfully, allowing the famously randy king to seduce Nell Gwynn to the gentle accompaniment of lutes and harpsichords rather than the roar of fighter jets.

One can't help wondering if the British and American military would have been so accommodating . . .

FOOD FOR THOUGHT

BEIJING SWINGS (2003)

Never likely to shirk controversy, Channel 4 got it in spades when it decided to show this documentary, an examination into some of the extreme methods employed by modern Chinese artists.

Chief among these was performance artist Zhu Yu, who shocked viewers by eating what appeared to be a stillborn baby. Shown via still photographs, Yu was pictured washing the baby before biting into the body.

Media watchdogs were up in arms at the show, while the Chinese Embassy in London called it 'detrimental' to China. The network was accused of obvious sensationalism, with no genuine interest in art.

C4 responded by saying that it was trying to project a true image of modern China and that there were plenty of warnings about the harshness of the material. Yu, meanwhile, claimed that cannibalism wasn't illegal and that there was no religious law against it. Some suggested that, because there were only photographs featuring the act, the artist had faked it.

But the documentary's host, the art critic Waldemar Januszczak, told the reporters, 'I'm absolutely convinced it happened,' adding, 'The authorities in China are worried about this type of art, yet it does happen.'

No word yet on a second series.

OUT OF THIS WORLD

SCARE TACTICS (2003)

Over the years, many people have been duped on television by some kind of candid camera. Kara Blanc finally decided that enough was enough.

Of course, the prank played on her was slightly different from a shop assistant pretending you haven't paid for your purchase. That's because she was on a hidden-camera show on America's Sci-Fi Channel, which took the traditional jokes and gave them a horror/science-fiction spin. The first episode alone featured someone fearing his friend had been buried alive and holiday camp counsellors terrified that they were near an escaped serial killer.

Blanc got the raw end of the deal. She believed she was travelling to a Hollywood party with two actor friends, when her car stalled and they were set upon by a murderous 'alien' who appeared to kill her friends and chase her down a remote desert road. Only then did host Shannen Doherty pop out and tell her it was all a wind-up.

Understandably, Blanc was not amused and proceeded to sue the channel and the programme makers, saying that she suffered severe emotional and physical distress and had had to be hospitalised.

However, the producers said that detailed reports were carried out on potential victims to ensure they could handle the stress. It's also worth noting that the prankee's friends and family are often complicit in the stunt.

At the time of writing, there was no known resolution to the lawsuit, although a second season of *Scare Tactics* has been filmed, with Stephen Baldwin taking over as host from Doherty.

New tricks have included a carpenter accidentally releasing a swarm of killer bees, a dead killer coming back from the grave to terrorise a lawyer's daughter and a temp worker fooled into thinking he has taken part in a massive drug deal. Are you game for a laugh?

FOOTBALL CRAZY

PLAYMAKERS (2003)

This first original drama for Entertainment and Sports Programming Network (ESPN) defied critical expectations that the network wouldn't be able to pull off scripted material.

The storylines were close to home, following a fictional American football team as they progressed through a season. The subject matter was gritty – charting the highs and lows of the players, wives and coaching staff. It also dealt with drugs, homosexuality and spousal abuse.

Unfortunately, it was this content that caused its downfall. For, despite their being a critical and commercial hit, ESPN cancelled the shows less than a year later.

Why? It probably didn't help that National Football League (NFL) commissioner Paul Tagliabue described the show as 'a gross misrepresentation of our sport'. Or that ESPN holds the rights to show NFL games during the season.

It caused consternation in the media, with commentators suggesting it was sad that a sports channel had to be constantly pro-sport. After all, these things probably do happen in professional football.

Ultimately, however, if you are paying more than half a billion dollars to show live games that make up the majority of your programming, what would *you* do?

SMALL WORLD 1

THE SURREAL LIFE (2003–)

Verne Troyer became famous as Mini-Me in the *Austin Powers* films, but he became infamous after joining the fourth season of VH-1's has-been reality show.

A bit like our own *Celebrity Big Brother*, it puts a bunch of past-it stars – previous participants include Brigitte Nielsen, Vanilla Ice and *CHiPs'* Erik Estrada – in a big house, and trains cameras on them 24/7.

But the fourth series of the show properly lived up to its title, thanks to two-foot-eight actor Troyer. One episode begins with seminaked model Adrianne Curry acting as a human platter for sushi. Troyer, already fairly tipsy, rubs her breasts.

Later, he is talking to former *Brady Bunch* actor Christopher Knight and falls asleep on his arm. Knight wakes him up and Troyer starts bizarrely stroking his nose. At last, everyone goes to bed, but, because one of her roommates is snoring, rapper Da Brat gets up and goes to the sitting room.

What she sees is not pretty. Troyer is rolling around on the mini-scooter he uses to drive through the house, when, suddenly, he gets up, walks to the corner of the room and starts urinating.

Shocked, Da Brat doesn't know what to say, other than, 'Baby, that's not the bathroom.' Troyer, however, is so drunk he barely registers. Finally, after alerting surrogate house father Knight, Troyer is successfully put to bed.

The events lent tiny Troyer a whole new celebrity dimension. But, as for the man himself, he probably can't remember a thing.

HANGING OFFENCE

DAVID BLAINE: ABOVE THE BELOW (2003)

American magician David Blaine is renowned for some extraordinary stunts, including being buried alive and encasing himself in a block of ice.

But, when he came to London bent on locking himself in a seven-foot-long, three-foot-wide glass box suspended by a crane above the River Thames – with no food – cynical bystanders seemed determined to make his life as difficult as possible.

There was no shortage of publicity for the 44-day stunt with Channel 4 and Sky One both covering the event in special programmes. However, the reverence with which he was usually treated was conspicuously absent from the crowds below, who tried their best to keep the nappy-clad showman awake day and night by bombarding his box with paint bombs, eggs and golf balls.

One morning Blaine awoke to the sound of drumming. 'We were watching him at home on TV and it was really dull so we thought we would come down and liven things up,' 21-year-old Shiraz Azam told London's *Evening Standard*. 'I wanted to wake him up.'

To add to the torment, onlookers teased him by cooking food underneath him and one man was charged with trying to sabotage Blaine's lifesaving water supply.

Despite dire warnings from doctors about what the starvation must be doing to his body, Blaine stuck out his apparently genuine ordeal and walked free from his box 44 days later sobbing to cameras that, 'This has been one of the most important experiences in my life.' With gentlemanly restraint, he even told the crowds that they had been 'wonderful'.

Surely, you might think, nobody else could be mad enough to do the same thing, yet a year later a Chinese herbalist came forward with his own strange claim.

A strong believer in the art of *'pigushengong'* or 'the magic of fasting', as described in ancient Chinese medical literature, fifty-year-old Chen Jianmin fasted inside a glass box suspended 46 feet (14 metres) in the air for 49 days, outlasting the thirty-year-old American by five days.

For all the missiles hurled at Blaine during his stunt, this must have been the most hard-hitting blow of all.

SHAME OF THE NAME

CAMBRIDGE SPIES (2003)

Peter Moffat's four-part miniseries about some famous British traitors was filming one day in Regent's Park with the BBC production's trucks and equipment parked in the ring road, including the portable dressing rooms.

Instead of the names of the leading actors on the their trailers – Toby Stephens, Tom Hollander, Rupert Penry-Jones – the doors proclaimed, 'Philby', 'Burgess' and 'Maclean'.

An elderly woman passed by walking her dog. She stopped the producer and angrily said in an Eastern European accent, 'I never thought I'd live to see the day that the BBC made anything about those terrible traitors. You should be ashamed of yourselves.'

CUTTING THE CRAP
CELEBRITY DETOX CAMP (2003)

Ostensibly this was an investigative show about health, as 'celebrities' – including singer Kim Wilde, 'It Girl' Tamara Beckwith and presenter Richard Blackwood – travelled to Thailand to undergo a rigorous body detox programme.

In reality, of course, it was an exploitative and often downright bizarre and revolting assault on personal dignity. Viewers thought it had reached its pinnacle after witnessing the twice-a-day, self-administered coffee enemas, for which the participants had to stick a tube up their own backsides.

But no, on the fifth day (by which time some of the celebrities looked as though they were about to die), treatment boss Buzz told them that they had to sieve their own faeces to understand what was wrong with them and how they could make themselves better. 'If people are aware of what comes out,' said Buzz, 'they can gauge their health.'

Luckily, by this point, most people had turned off their television sets in disgust. Surely, no chance of second helpings, as it were. Wrong. Time for *Extreme Celebrity Detox Camp* (see *The Farm* on page 293).

THE DEITY TODAY
JOAN OF ARCADIA (2003)

Inspired by you-know-who, this is a light-hearted comedy-drama about an American kid (Amber Tamblyn) who suddenly discovers that the Almighty is talking to her through various people.

But in the ever-watchful Christian environment that is today's America, how do you make sure that you don't get under anyone's skin? And, what's more, how do you maintain the same deity criteria throughout the run of the show?

If you're the show's creator, Barbara Hall, you write the Ten Commandments of Joan: the 'Bible', if you will, of the show. It is as follows:

1. God cannot directly intervene.
2. Good and evil exist.
3. God can never identify one religion as being right.
4. The job of every human being is to fulfil his or her true nature.
5. Everyone is allowed to say no to God, including Joan.
6. God is not bound by time – this is a human concept.
7. God *is not a person* and does not possess a human personality.
8. God talks to everyone all the time in different ways.
9. God's plan is what is good for us, not what is good for him.
10. God's purpose for talking to Joan and to everyone is to get her (us) to recognise the interconnectedness of all things, i.e. you cannot hurt a person without hurting yourself; all of your actions have consequences; God can be found in the smallest actions; God expects us to learn and grow from all our experiences. However, the exact nature of God is a mystery and the mystery can never be solved.

Here endeth the lesson.

FALL FROM GRACE

QVC – THE SHOPPING CHANNEL (2003)

As they frequently tell us themselves, home-shopping channel presenters are the best in the business. Well, you have to be pretty good to improvise for three hours about the benefits of a wooden spoon without sending your viewers to sleep – or yourself, for that matter.

But QVC host Lisa Robertson was really put to the test while plugging a retractable ladder. This brilliant device let you climb up to fix the gutter, but then could be folded away to stop you from cluttering up the shed.

As Lisa waxed lyrical about the ladder, viewers were shown a live demonstration in another part of the studio. Here, a man grabbed a duster, pulled the ladder out of its telescopic-retraction, propped it against the wall, then climbed up and started jauntily cleaning the studio. Meanwhile, Lisa talked to viewers throughout all this riveting action and even had a chat with a caller on air, who also proclaimed the genius of the ladder.

But, as thousands of people around the country were about to pick up their phones to order one, the unthinkable happened: the demonstrator lost his balance and crashed to the floor, where he rolled about in agony.

Clearly shocked, Lisa said, 'OK, we're going to make sure he's OK.' The caller added bluntly, 'That's never happened before.'

Professional to the last, and painfully aware that this was, as they say, actuality, Lisa continued, 'He is OK. But he scared me for a moment there.'

Annoyingly for QVC, someone must have been taping the show, for the (subsequently) hilarious clip found its way onto the Internet. It's not a clip they use when trying to sell the latest PC with high-speed web connection, but you'll be pleased to know that the poor ladder demonstrator suffered only minor injuries and has since returned to work.

PRACTICAL MAGIC

THE PRIVATE LIFE OF SAMUEL PEPYS (2003)

Director Oliver Parker, best known for well-funded, star-studded recent films such as *An Ideal Husband* and *The Importance of Being Earnest*, was sent a screenplay by the BBC about the diarist Samuel Pepys, written by Guy Jenkin and with Steve

Coogan signed up as the lead. He was, he says, 'warned that it was to happen immediately and with a meagre budget'.

Parker 'read the script on Wednesday, met on Friday and started work on Monday. And then I realised just how meagre the budget was. It was a one-hour film written with some scale – not just some old codger reading his diary at a desk. There was a naval battle and the Great Fire of London – and just twelve days to shoot the lot.

'I couldn't think how we could represent these scenes without them looking hopelessly inadequate – and the single effects shot we were being offered would surely stick out like a sore thumb. I reduced the sea battle to a kind of dream moment in Pepys' mind and shot it in a drawing room.

'As for the fire, I was at a loss. Then it occurred to me to use one of the main devices in the screenplay as a way out. In the course of the action, Pepys would sometimes turn to address the camera directly.

'So, in the end, I decided to shoot Steve Coogan and Ciaran McMenamin [as Will Hewer] standing on what appeared to be a balcony with wind and smoke and fire reflected in the windows. Steve shouted at Ciaran, "The wind's changed direction. It's coming towards us. All London's on fire." Then he turned to the camera and said, "You'll just have to take my word for it." '

This, said Parker, became the production's 'mantra' as, unable to afford the various animals that also featured in the script, they would repeatedly appear just out of frame with a soundtrack stocked with barks and growls and snorts.

Given a fair wind and an altogether more substantial budget, Parker now plans to crank *Pepys* up as a big-screen project.

SMALL WORLD 2
THE LITTLEST GROOM (2004)

Some described it as a sick publicity exercise. Others – mainly the people behind it – said it was a tribute to 21st-century cosmopolitanism. Clearly opinions were extremely divided in February 2004 when Fox broadcast their American dating show for dwarfs. Glen Foster was a 23-year-old salesman who, at four foot five, still hadn't found the woman of his dreams.

Hosted by Dani Behr – a one-time presenter of *The Word*, thus no stranger to tacky TV – the two-part show was broadcast over consecutive weeks and set Glen up with twelve women of similar height. They in turn competed via one-on-one dates and group activities for his affection. The twist came halfway through the contest when three beautiful women of average height entered the contest and gave Glen some taller options.

When news of the programme broke, many dwarf advocates were up in arms, claiming Fox was using the concept to broadcast a freak show. Meanwhile the Little People of America withheld judgement, although they talked with the programme makers about trying to make sure the show wasn't offensive. They pointed out that all the participants had had a mix of relationships with both small and average-sized people.

In the event, if it was shock tactics on the part of Fox, it didn't really work, scoring mediocre ratings and fading quickly from the public's consciousness. And, for the record, the final female finalists were Mika, a little person, and Zoe, who was of average height. Glen went for the former.

SPIRIT LEVELS

I'M FAMOUS AND FRIGHTENED (2004–)

It's a very simple concept: 'I'm A Celebrity . . . Get Me Out of This Haunted House'.

LIVINGtv – well known for its paranormal programming – gave the better-known celeb reality show a twist by sticking a group of famous has-beens in a spook-filled castle and seeing what happened across nine hours of live television.

There were jumps and frights, but perhaps nothing as peculiar as the fourth series of the show in February 2005. It was the final challenge of the weekend and medium Ian Lawman took the D-list personalities into the bowels of Bolsover Castle in Derbyshire. Their goal was to contact the spirit of a young woman who was seen running around carrying a baby before throwing it into a fire.

Lawman summoned up the ghosts and was promptly possessed by the young girl. Shivering and whimpering, former pop star Toyah Willcox took it upon herself to question him/her, as the spirit explained that she was being forced to kill her baby before the castle owner found and executed her.

Stiff Ofcom regulations monitor paranormal programming and soon the director shouted to the onsite producer to bring Lawman back from his trance. However, as he emerged there was frantic calling from another contestant, actress Ruth Madoc (of *Hi-de-Hi* fame), who was begging for help. She'd spotted the all-purpose celeb Christopher Biggins standing next to her groaning and swaying.

Lawman was on hand to inform the entranced viewing public that the spirit had shifted to a weaker body and was now possessing Biggins. Genuinely afraid, the rest of the contestants – as well as some of the production staff – tried to bring Biggins back, which they suddenly did.

Questioned afterwards, Biggins admitted that he didn't remember much of the incident, only that he felt very tired. But to paranormal fans across the UK, there was convincing evidence that Biggins did actually rent-a-ghost (albeit for just a few seconds!).

BIG-GAME BOOB

JANET JACKSON AT THE SUPERBOWL (2004)

It's supposed to be the Land of the Free, but America just doesn't have a sense of humour when it comes to anyone disrupting their national pastime. The Superbowl is the biggest American football event in the sporting calendar, and as many people tune in to the network TV coverage for the megabucks half-time show as they do for the big men in helmets.

The 2004 event was no exception, with Janet Jackson and Justin Timberlake promising a dynamic duet. At the end of a flamboyant rendition of 'Rock Your Body', as the lyrics proclaimed 'gonna have you naked by the end of this song', Jackson encouraged Timberlake to rip away a leather cup covering her breast. What follows was the most expensive 'wardrobe malfunction' in history.

As Timberlake did so, he exposed Jackson's bosom to a family audience of more than 100 million. And, to top it off, her nipple was pierced with a sun-shaped metal ring. The switchboard was flooded with complaints and the nation's conservative lobby used the event as an excuse to try to clamp down on what it deemed inappropriate images on television.

The broadcaster CBS apologised and both performers said that it was unintentional (difficult to believe, considering that the patch covering the breast came off in one pull very easily). While Timberlake managed to escape much of the furore, Jackson became a national pariah, synonymous with modern tastelessness. Subsequently, the Federal Communications Commission handed out a $550,000 fine, the largest ever slapped on a television company.

Ironically, according to the Internet search engine Yahoo!, demand for pictures and/or footage of the incident topped even 11 September for volume over the 24-hour period following it. Another Internet company, Lycos, stated that it received three times as many demands for Jackson's nipple than it did for the 2000 election and four times as many as for the Iraq War after the release of footage of American POWs.

LET LOOS ON A PIG

THE FARM (2004)

Once best known for her alleged affair with David Beckham, Rebecca Loos has since become notorious for a far more beastly affair.

Appearing with other C-list celebrities on Five's reality show, she found herself donning rubber gloves and masturbating a boar to extract around a third of a litre of semen to be used for inseminating sows. Afterwards Loos told her fellow contestants, 'My arms are aching! It lasts for about ten minutes and he starts thrusting really hard and then I grip!'

Needless to say, the scene caused some consternation among grossed-out viewers, with the regulatory body, Ofcom, receiving several dozen complaints, some likening the procedure to bestiality.

A spokesman for People for the Ethical Treatment of Animals complained, 'This is just pure titillation and I'm sure Rebecca Loos was chosen for that reason.' The RSPCA, unhappy with the show generally, argued that the producers were pandering to a 'morbid and sordid fascination with farm animals'.

In their defence, Five stated,

It is just a part of normal farm life. The point of the show is to demonstrate the day-to-day workings of a farm to an audience who are not necessarily familiar with the nitty-gritty of rural life. Rebecca Loos was trained and shown exactly what to do in advance and a vet was monitoring the entire process from start to finish.

Ofcom later cleared the show's makers of any wrongdoing, stating, 'The task performed by Rebecca Loos is one that occurs regularly on UK farms. We don't believe the scene was degrading or harmful to the boar.'

Strangely enough, this was not the first time that Five had shown semen being extracted from an animal. Five's late-night show *Pub Ammo*, hosted by Christian O'Connell, also featured a pig in a compromising position and the series *99 Things To Do Before You Die* showed something definitely not on most people's lists: how to help a horse to fill a bag of semen.

As for Ms Loos, she was, at time of writing, set to 'hit a new low' (the *Sun*) in a Channel 4 show, *Extreme Celebrity Detox Camp*, in which she was allegedly required to lift weights using her private parts.

TRIUMPH OF THE SPIRIT
MEETING POINT (2004)

Reuniting loved ones on air has been a staple of television down the years, but perhaps its strangest if perhaps most poignant variation is this popular slice of southwestern African programming.

For nearly three decades, until a ceasefire in 2002, Angola was racked by civil war, latterly between the MPLA (People's Movement for the Liberation of Angola) and the UNITA (National Union for the Total Independence of Angola) rebels.

Thousands lost their lives, tens of thousands more seemed to disappear without trace. A massive country of nearly half a million square miles studded with landmines was another horrific legacy of conflict.

Observing how the women of Buenos Aires would regularly meet in a city square to draw attention to 'the disappeared' in

Argentina, a production company called Orion persuaded TV Angola to mount a weekly programme that, it hoped, might go one better.

The result is that, for more than two years, *Meeting Point*, filmed live in the capital Luanda's Independence Square, has quite literally reunited hundreds of Angolan families.

TIRED AND EMOTIONAL
SHATTERED (2004)

You can imagine the pitch meeting: 'OK, so how can we put a new, more evil spin on *Big Brother* and still pretend it's some sort of sociological experiment?'

The answer is *Shattered*. The premise was very simple: ten normal people go into a house and the last one to fall asleep wins.

As soon as the concept was announced, the medical community was up in arms, arguing that Channel 4 was playing with people's health and that 'sleep deprivation' was not a valid form of entertainment.

The channel and the programme maker, Endemol, replied that the contestants' health was of paramount importance. They employed medical staff and psychiatrists to monitor the action.

Kept in the 'lab' for a week, the participants had to undergo a series of challenges designed to test their endurance. These included having to negotiate a series of doors, some of which had handles that gave them an electric shock if they touched them. They also had to try to watch paint literally dry – for an hour.

Inevitably, the papers were up in arms, appalled that audiences might enjoy watching people suffer hallucinations and paranoia – which was, of course, exactly what the show creators were hoping for. One competitor, a 21-year-old student called Lucy, left the show midway through after talking with psychologists.

The contestants were allowed catnaps, determined by the producers, but were denied a proper night's sleep. Despite receiving only a few complaints, the programme ultimately suffered from viewer apathy.

It was won by a trainee police officer, who defeated two others in a final sleep-off and she walked away with £97,000 in prize money.

Just how scientific the whole thing was has yet to be determined.

WITH GOD ON OUR SIDE

JERRY SPRINGER – THE OPERA (2005)

'Contains very strong language, religious references and extreme images which may offend some viewers.'

Nothing that the controversial chat show has achieved during nearly fifteen years of daytime turbulence on American television can surely match the furore provoked by this musical satire broadcast by BBC2 at 10 p.m. on 8 January.

At the last count, the BBC ('Blasphemy Broadcasting Corporation', it was dubbed) had received nearly fifty thousand complaints, the regulator Ofcom more than seven thousand, and two top Corporation executives were recipients of death threats.

This unprecedented backlash was both before – Television Centre was picketed by licence-burning protesters – and following the transmission of a live recording of the award-winning stage show, written by a pair of Brits, Richard Thomas and Stewart Lee.

The scale of protest, principally fanned by Christian groups, easily dwarfed the previous record-holder, Martin Scorsese's *The Last Temptation of Christ*, when it was televised in 1995.

As if the language weren't bad enough – some 177 expletives actually sounding more like several thousand when sung gleefully by the huge chorus and multiplied by the number of singers – it was, once again, religious depictions that seemed to cause most offence. Like Jesus in a nappy admitting to being 'a bit gay'.

'HEEEEERE'S JOHNNY!'

THE TONIGHT SHOW (2005)

A single date – 23 January 2005, to be precise – for this entry admittedly contradicts the series style of this book. However, it marks the death of Johnny Carson, most famous host of America's longest-running late-evening talk show, which, though not especially strange in itself, still probably had huge swathes of that nation still shaking their heads in some disbelief.

Although Carson hadn't actually been in charge since 1992, endless repeats and his iconic status in a nation obsessed with celebrity suggested he'd never really been away.

Off air, he endured three failed marriages, multimillion-dollar alimony, the tragic death of a son and some disastrous business investments. Enough, to be sure, to keep him regularly in the gossip columns.

As the witty and laconic frontman on *The Tonight Show* for nearly thirty years – which set the style for mainstream TV chat shows around the world – he was, as the hype went, 'the last man America sees before it goes to sleep'. Filmmaker Billy Wilder once put it another way, describing Carson as 'the Valium and Nembutal of the nation'.

Much strangeness was enacted on his show down the years, but probably nothing topped the occasion of some live nuptials on the night of 17 December 1969.

This was the marriage of six-foot-one, long-haired, ukulele-playing, falsetto-voiced pop singer Tiny Tim (real name Herbert Khaury), 46, to Miss Vicki, a.k.a. Victoria May Budinger, nearly thirty years his junior.

More than 45 million people tuned in, making it the most attended wedding in television history, but it also polled the highest rating in television history for a talk show.

MARRIAGE LINES
QUESTION TIME (2005)

OK, we've done it again – but marking the specific night of 3 February 2005 also just seemed too good to miss.

After 25 years of verbal combat, rabble-rousing, heckling and often unbridled rhetoric, conducted variously by Robin Day, Peter Sissons and David Dimbleby, it finally came down to just one question.

In Derby, the panel comprising cabinet minister Margaret Beckett, Tory spokesman Andrew Lansley, Lib Dem front-bencher David Laws, former Met Police commissioner Sir John Stevens and columnist Yasmin Alibhai-Brown were readying themselves for the evening's final poser. Dimbleby called out to Alan Jordan, who replied, 'This one is not for the panel, I'm afraid. It's for the lady on my right. Sonia, would you marry me?'

As the audience and viewers at home gasped with surprise at this extraordinary turn on a show that more often than not leaves blood on the carpet, Sonia visibly reeled with shock.

'Yes, please,' came her answer, as she sealed the response with a kiss, leaving not just Mr Jordan but also the BBC mightily relieved at the end of this short but epic piece of live soap opera in the unlikeliest setting.

QUEER EYES FOR THE STRAIGHT
THE ONLY GAYS IN THE VILLAGE (2005)

Little Britain, tiny minds. Just because you're a much-repeated catchphrase from the hottest comedy show around, it doesn't necessarily guarantee smooth running in a cock-eyed 'spin-off'.

Inspired by the manic cry of delusional Welsh villager Dafydd, Sky One decided to commission six hours of reality TV in which four gay men were sent to work in a so-called 'gay-free' village in rural England.

The four 'famous' chaps – Richard Cawley, Kristian Digby, Scott Capurro and Andrew Kinlochan (no, we haven't heard of them either) – spent a month in Hartington, Derbyshire, doing various jobs including pub and farm work.

However, between commissioning and post-production, Sky One had apparently rebranded itself as a more 'upmarket' service and the powers-that-be decided this camp concept didn't fit its new image.

The result is the show has apparently been dropped from Sky's flagship channel and is likely to be tucked away in another, altogether remoter corner of the Murdoch extraterrestrial empire. Just don't mention Uranus.

SELECT BIBLIOGRAPHY

Asherman, Allan, *The Star Trek Interview Book*, Titan Books, 1988

Attenborough, David, *Life on Air*, BBC, 2002

Aylesworth, Thomas G, *Great Moments of Television*, Exeter Books, 1987

Baker, Roy Ward, *The Director's Cut*, Reynolds & Hearn, 2000

Barris, Chuck, *Confessions of a Dangerous Mind*, St Martins Press, 1984

Birt, John, *The Harder Path*, TimeWarner, 2002

Bosanquet, Reginald, with Wallace Reyburn, *Let's Get Through Wednesday – My 25 Years with ITN*, Michael Joseph, 1980

Brooks, Tim, and Earle Marsh, *The Complete Directory to Prime Time Network and Cable TV Shows 1946–Present*, Ballantine Books, 2003

Burstein, Patricia, and Susan Crimp, *Hollywood Sisters: Jackie & Joan Collins*, Robson, 1989

Carpenter, Humphrey, *Dennis Potter*, Faber, 1998

Chamberlain, Richard, *Shattered Love*, ReganBooks, 2003

Chester, Lewis, *Tooth & Claw – The Inside Story of Spitting Image*, Faber, 1986

Cornell, Paul, Martin Day and Keith Topping, *The Guinness Book of Classic British TV*, Guinness, 1993

Cushing, Peter, *An Autobiography*, Weidenfeld & Nicolson, 1986

Davidson, Jim and Alec Lom, *Close to the Edge*, Ebury, 2001

Dessau, Bruce, *Rowan Atkinson*, Orion, 1999

Donnelley, Paul, *T.V. Babylon*, Vista, 1997

Dougan, Andy, *George Clooney*, Boxtree, 1997

Dougan, Andy, *Robin Williams*, Orion, 1998

Dunn, Kate, *Do Not Adjust Your Set – The Early Days of Live Television*, John Murray, 2003

Dyke, Greg, *Inside Story*, HarperCollins, 2004

Edward, John, *Crossing Over*, Princess, 2002

Evans, Jeff, *The Penguin TV Companion*, Penguin Books, 2001

Ewbank, Tim, and Stafford Hildred, *David Jason: the biography*, Blake, 1997

Ewbank, Tim, and Stafford Hildred, *Joanna Lumley*, André Deutsch, 2000

Face to Face with John Freeman, BBC, 1989

French, John, *Robert Shaw: The Price of Success*, Nick Hern Books, 1993

Goodwin, Cliff, *Evil Spirits: The Life of Oliver Reed*, Virgin, 2000

Grade, Lew, *Still Dancing*, Collins, 1987,

Grade, Michael, *It Seemed Like a Good Idea at the Time*, Pan, 1999

Griffith, Kenneth, *The Fool's Pardon*, Little, Brown, 1994

Guest, Val, *So You Want to be in Pictures*, Reynolds & Hearn, 2001

Hayward, Anthony, *Which Side Are You On? Ken Loach and his Films*, Bloomsbury, 2004

Horrie, Chris, and Adam Nathan, *Live TV – Tellybrats and Topless Darts – The Uncut Story of Tabloid Television*, Simon & Schuster, 1999

Horrie, Chris, and Steve Clark, *Citizen Greg*, Simon & Schuster, 2000

Jackson, Laura, *Sean Bean*, Piatkus, 2000

Kelly, Richard, *Alan Clarke*, Faber, 1998

Lee, Christopher, *Tall, Dark and Gruesome*, Victor Gollancz, 1997

Lewis, Jon E, and Penny Stempel, *The Ultimate TV Guide*, Orion, 1999

Malone, Carole, *The Richard and Judy Story*, Virgin, 1996

McBride, Joseph, *Steven Spielberg*, Faber, 1997

McBride, Joseph, *Searching for John Ford*, Faber, 2003

McCabe, Bob, *Ronnie Barker: The Authorised Biography*, Chameleon, 1998

McCann, Graham, *Dad's Army: The Story of a classic television show*, Fourth Estate, 2001

McKee, Alan, *Australian Television: a genealogy of great moments*, Oxford University Press, 2001

Meddings, Derek, *21st Century Visions*, Paper Tiger, 1993

Membery, York, *Pierce Brosnan*, Virgin, 1997

Milne, Alasdair, *D.G.: The Memoirs of a British Broadcaster*, Hodder & Stoughton, 1988

Monkhouse, Bob, *Crying with Laughter*, Century, 1993

Norden, Denis, Sybil Harper and Norma Gilbert, *Coming to You Live!*, Methuen, 1985

Parker, John, *Sean Connery*, Victor Gollancz, 1993

Parker, John, *Bruce Willis*, Virgin, 1997

Paskin, Barbara, *Dudley Moore*, Sidwick & Jackson, 1997

Pfeiffer, Lee, and Dave Worrall, *The Essential Bond*, Boxtree, 1998

Pythons, The, *The Pythons*, Orion, 2003

Rafkin, Alan, *Cue the Bunny on the Rainbow*, Syracuse University Press, 1998

Reynolds, Burt, *My Life*, Hodder & Stoughton, 1994

Robb, Brian J, *Johnny Depp: A Modern Rebel*, Plexus, 1996

Robinson, Marc, *Brought To You In Living Color*, Wiley, 2002

Rodley, Chris, *Lynch on Lynch*, Faber, 1997

Roose-Evans, James, *One Foot on the Stage*, Weidenfeld & Nicolson, 1996

Rose, Simon, *The Book of Brilliant Hoaxes*, Virgin, 1995

Sanford, Christopher, *McQueen*, HarperCollins, 2001

Scott, Conroy Kevin, *Screenwriters' Masterclass*, Faber, 2005

Sheridan, Simon, *The A–Z of Classic Children's Television*, Reynolds & Hearn Ltd, 2004

Simpson, Paul (ed.), *The Rough Guide To Cult T.V.*, Rough Guides, 2002

Spada, James, *More Than a Woman: An Intimate Biography of Bette Davis*, Little, Brown, 1993

Taraborrelli, J Randy, *Cher*, Sidgwick & Jackson, 1989

Tomlinson, Ricky, *Ricky*, TimeWarner, 2003

Tynan, Kathleen, *Kenneth Tynan*, Methuen, 1988

Waldron, Robert, *Ricki! The Unauthorised Biography of Ricki Lake*, Warner, 1996

Waterman, Dennis, *ReMinder*, Hutchinson, 2000

Waterman, Ivan, *Helen Mirren*, Metro, 2003

West, Adam, *Back to the Batcave*, Titan Books, 1994

Wheaton, Roma, *Forever Young*, Warner Books, 1994

White, Patrick J, *The Complete Mission Impossible Dossier*, Boxtree, 1996

Whiteley, Richard, *Himoff!*, Orion, 2000

Wilmut, Roger & Rosengard, Peter, *Didn't You Kill My Mother-in-Law? The Story of Alternative Comedy in Britain from The Comedy Store to Saturday Live*, Methuen, 1989

Winton, Dale and Stan Nicholls, *Dale Winton: My Story*, Century, 2002

Wogan, Terry, *Is It Me?*, BBC, 2001

Zehme, Bill, *Lost in the Funhouse: The Life and Mind of Andy Kaufman*, Fourth Estate, 2000